THE Twelve Days OF Christian

CAROLINE CORVIN

First published in 2024 by Grenwyvern Publishing

Auckland, New Zealand

Cover design @ollie_creates

www.carolinecorvin.com

Dedication

To those who see themselves as ordinary:
in love's gaze, you are extraordinary

Playlist

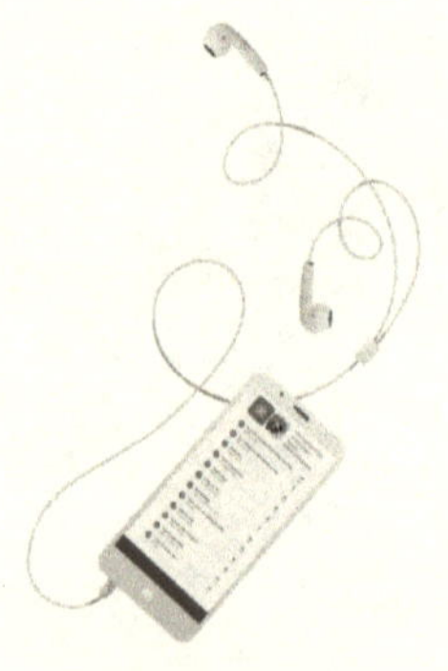

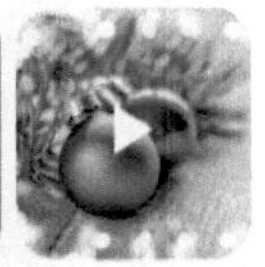

The Twelve Days of Christian Playlist

Songs to fall in love to

Rock'in Around The Christmas Tree
Brenda Lee

All I Want For Christmas Is You
Mariah Carey

Delicate
Taylor Swift

God Only Knows
The Beach Boys

Stargazing
Myles Smith

Close To You
Gracie Abrams

Santa Baby
Ariana Grande, Liz Gillies

Feels Like I'm Falling In Love
Coldplay

Something
The Beatles

Falling Like The Stars
James Arthur

Worth The Wait
Spencer Crandall

I Get To Love You
Ruelle

Chapter 1

Day One

Haley

Some days it's perfectly acceptable to still be wearing pyjamas at lunchtime and today is one of them. Especially if they're this gorgeous candy-cane coated pair that literally begged me to buy them as a Christmas gift-to-self; and especially if it's the day I've waited a whole agonising twelve months for. Finally, I can indulge in my favourite thing of the entire year: Christmas decorating.

There must be some hidden law of physics that allows time to speed up between one birthday and the next once you hit your twenties, while dragging its heels approaching other annual celebrations with painful slowness. Halloween, Christmas, and New Year's—I love them all, but this one's the biggie.

Although, it always seems to be over as quick as one blink of the fake candle lights draped on my tree. Come January 1st, once again I'm damned to eternity in a dreary wasteland—well, only eleven months, but it feels like more. Eleven months to be endured until December 1st, when I can once more set to work creating the perfect Christmas fantasy.

Today is the first Saturday in December—the traditional start of my decorating. The tree must be in place, and it is. Not just any old tree will do. There's no substitute for a live tree, and I inhale the fresh woodsy scent with deep satisfaction.

There are some tasks a girl of five foot two can't handle on her own, no matter how determined she may be. Wrangling a monster tree is one of them. However, living in London, nothing is a problem. I got off work early yesterday to meet the delivery guys who manhandled this seven-foot beauty into place. After suffering a self-inflicted headache all day—one so bad it felt like a boisterous Salvation Army brass band had taken up residence inside my skull and was playing their noisiest Christmas carols on repeat—I was grateful for the excuse. Now I admire how the fir tree stands framed by one of the tall sash windows, the delicate needles not quite brushing the white plaster ceiling. It waits patiently for adornment.

But before I can attend to this Cinderella, who will be the belle of the ball when I'm finished with her, my phone rings. Without looking, I know who it is. Britney Spears bellows out 'Stronger', my ringtone a tribute to one of the toughest people I know, my friend Samantha. She's small but fierce and she loves me in the same way.

When I pick up, her familiar "Hi hun," is submerged in the background clatter of clanging trolleys, and voices echoing off vinyl-coated walls. It might be a weekend day shift, but the A&E

sounds hectic. I can imagine her in the blue scrubs, that tumble of dark curls she battles daily piled on her head in an untidy bun, issuing directions with the air of calm authority suited to an emergency room nurse.

"Hey, I was on a break. I thought I'd check how you're doing?"

If she wasn't working, I know she'd be here. Instead, she's checking in on me. The sole guest at my Thursday night wine-fuelled pity party, and only witness to my drunken blubbing, Sam knows how fragile I am right now.

"OK," I say. "Better than yesterday. I haven't got a headache this morning." God, yesterday is one bad memory from hungover start to heart-breaking finish. "And I'm decorating the tree." I try to sound cheerful in the spirit of the season, rather than a girl still in the grip of the deep despair that led to yesterday's killer hangover.

"Great idea," she says. "Doing something nice for yourself is exactly what you need." She pauses a moment. "OK Haley—I wasn't going to bring up the 'w' word—but I think a little gloating is called for. Have you looked outside?" I turn to the window. I've been so focused on the job at hand, I've barely given outdoors a glance. It's raining. Hard. "Isn't it a perfect day for a wedding?" Sam's sarcasm is as thick as the low blanket of cloud hanging over the city. She unleashes an evil cackle.

The grey sheet of rain sends an uncharitable surge of pleasure through me. Jack Maplethorpe, my one ex-boyfriend who ever really mattered, marries my ex-friend, Paige, today. A girl who I've known since kindergarten, yet betrayed me with barely an apology.

I'll admit it: I'm the sad, pathetic creature who's tortured herself for weeks stalking their socials. I know every detail of this wedding, and today, the painful obsession is paying off. I have perfect images in my mind of what the downpour outside means: the formal gardens unusable, the horse and open carriage not an option; her white satin shoes soaked in muddy puddles. I'm not normally a vengeful person, but being cheated on is enough to send the most forgiving girl to the dark side.

"Looks like the karma train is pulling into the station."

"Exactly," she says. "The universe speaks when people do shitty things. They brought it on themselves," she adds with a satisfied sniff. I hear a flurry of raised voices in the background. "OK, gotta go," she says. "Incoming. Talk later, eh?"

Despite Sam bringing up the one subject that should make me feel like shit, I'm strangely better at having faced it. Now it's time to get back to the only important thing about today.

My fingers jab at the phone, seeking an essential ingredient, my extensive Christmas playlists. First up is the Christmas movie collection, the ultimate accompaniment for the task. There's a blissful sense of freedom as the first bars of 'Rock'in Around The Christmas Tree' ring out. I'm straight into *Home Alone*.

Today, being home alone is not a bad thing. I can flood the house with music to my heart's content. While technically I share my brother Ollie's house, he's so often away I get to revel in the delicious solitude, doing whatever I please. Today that means hard out Christmas music, the perfect soundtrack for decorating.

It's time to retrieve my treasured old friends, my collection of ornaments, from their nests of tissue where they've slept in patient hibernation since I put them safely into boxes back in January. My dogs, Tully and Mularkey, watch, fascinated, as I dance around the tree, seeking the perfect place for every decoration. I'm particular, some might say obsessively so, choosing the exact space between the strings of lights that will show each to its best advantage.

By the time we reach the end of the *Love Actually* soundtrack, I have only one last bauble to place—a spun glass sphere of pale green, with a hand-painted snowy scene of a deer and fawn under winter trees. It's a new one from Liberty. On finding the right spot, I celebrate a job well done, bopping across the room to the strains of 'All I Want For Christmas Is You', and singing with the type of abandon only possible when no one is listening.

Tully Hart raises her muzzle skyward, offering her deep alto voice in joyful harmony with mine. As we reach the chorus, Kate Mularkey joins in. We go for that final high note together, but I can't hold it. I dissolve into giggles at the sight of her earnest little face, pointed at the ceiling as she maintains a surprisingly tuneful "Woooooo."

This is the first time I've been able to have a dog. It seems everyone involved in rescue ends up with an unadoptable dog or two—or more. I'm no different. These came into the shelter as a bonded pair; neglected seniors with a long list of medical issues, and a slim chance of adoption. Especially since most people who visit looking to home a dog inevitably gravitate towards the small, cute ones, leaving behind big lumps like my girls.

Pretty much all of us who work there eventually succumb. I held out for eight months after taking up the veterinary nurse position at one of the clinics run by the Canine Haven Dog Rescue Trust. I stood firm, while needy candidates streamed in the door, each with a sad story, each a dog deserving of a loving home.

But when these two dear old ladies arrived, there was something about them that tugged a little harder at my heartstrings. I couldn't bear to see them live out their last days in the caring but not homelike conditions of our shelter kennels. Ollie doesn't care if I bring home one or ten. So here they are.

Alice, our clinic receptionist, is to blame for their odd names. Mularkey's goggles of white, where her dark hair has lost all pigment, give her the appearance of wearing spectacles. She's the spitting image of a lead character in one of Alice's all-time favourite TV shows, *Firefly Lane*. Sadly, the appealing markings result from a nasty autoimmune condition, expensive to treat, and a factor which made her a poor prospect for adoption.

Her best friend Tully's ever-present smile reveals broken and missing teeth. Adopters often pass over dogs like her, knowing the potential cost. But I don't begrudge the dental work that keeps me poor, or the pricey special food I buy so she maintains a healthy weight.

Taking on both of them is a big commitment, but no one with a beating heart could separate these two. I fear what will happen when inevitably one passes over the rainbow bridge. Maybe they'll be like some old married couples, one following the other, unable to inhabit the world alone.

I giggle to myself as our human-canine chorus ends and plunge back into decorating. There are still gaps to fill with ribbon bows. The task distracts me from not only the wedding happening today but also the dull gnawing that's taken up residence in my stomach since the events of yesterday morning at my workplace.

The announcement blindsided our team. Despite all the signs being there, none of us wanted to see them. There's a jab of physical pain in my chest every time I allow the thought to shove its way forward: soon these two scraps of canine mischief might be all I have left of the dog rescue.

Times are tough, and money is tight. Yesterday, Eloise, the President of the Trust, met with us. With the normally bright upturned creases in her cheeks absent, she explained the Trustees are considering closing our outpost clinic in Camden Town, along with the other in Lewisham. Any dogs needing veterinary care would go into the main branch.

She explained how they've been struggling to cover the leases for months. Even with the landlord's generosity in putting the rent on hold, they're in trouble. With almost a hundred thousand pounds of back rent falling due soon, they need a kind benefactor or a large windfall.

Yes, I'm well qualified, but even if I manage to get another job, it's unlikely there will be any like this one. Having worked alongside the rescue team, I can't imagine getting that sort of job satisfaction anywhere else. And as for all our community clients, who dearly love their animals but have limited resources, they'll struggle to find the reasonably priced care we offer.

My wish is for a Christmas miracle to save us all, and I haven't given up hope yet. Not while there's a guy competing on a celebrity reality show who has named the Trust as his charity—my brother's friend, Christian. I love reality shows and I plan to be glued to this one every night, cheering him on. It's not a sure thing, but possibility dangles in front of me like a shiny Christmas bauble.

An hour later, with lights, bells, baubles, bows and a dollop of tinsel weighing down every branch of the tree, I flop onto the couch. Last night's sleeplessness, as anticipation of today battled with a sickening dread of what the next month will bring, has dulled my usual decorating stamina. I need a break before dressing the room.

The two dogs abandon their carolling, ignoring the strains of 'Baby It's Cold Outside'—we've moved on to *Elf*—and join me with warm, wiggly bodies. I melt into the song and their companionable snuggles.

However, we've barely gotten comfortable when pounding on the door interrupts our blissful enjoyment of the music. My comfortable doggy huddle dissolves as the two of them race to the door, barking.

I'm not expecting anyone. Ollie's somewhere in Africa on safari, a reward to himself after his band's gruelling US tour ended three weeks ago. Sam's at work and my other bestie Rachel, the lucky cow, is taking her hot fiancé home to Scotland to meet her family.

However, there won't be any sexy guy knocking down my door. I am currently boyfriend-less by choice. I have no regrets about dispensing with the latest in a string of lacklustre men. Julian seemed quirky and interesting to begin with, but after three weeks of him juggling date nights with me and 'Elden Ring', an online game, I decided he was simply strange.

Although the real deal-breaker wasn't his obsession with gaming. He tried to hide it, but he hated the dogs. I'm a 'love me, love my dog' kind of girl and I can only imagine having a serious relationship with someone who doesn't flinch at Mularkey's doggy kisses, and can tough out Tully's eye-watering farts.

It's too early in the day for carollers. The religious door-knockers have removed me from their regular beat, after Tully lost her shit with one. I have no idea why my gentle girl did so. I can only assume he resembled someone from her sad, neglected past.

I reluctantly stumble towards the door, expecting some salesperson who I'll struggle to dispatch, given the people-pleasing nature that makes me susceptible to their wiles. However, a second round of a hammering fist on the other side tells me I'm safe from the latest satellite television sales rep. Even they wouldn't be so insistent.

I leave the chain on, wary it might be one of Ollie's fans who has tracked him to this address. It has only happened once before, thankfully; about a month after I moved in. I'd opened the door to find two young women looking at me in surprise, as if there was no way someone like me could be the lead singer of Stellar Riot's girlfriend. Claiming they were old friends, one tried to barge past me. I'm not normally a violent person, but slamming the door on her foot (a completely reflex reaction) left her howling in pain and proved effective at convincing them to leave.

Although any fan obsessed enough to find Ollie's house would surely know he's not here. The footage of him at the airport, hamming it up for the cameras, dressed in a ridiculous safari suit, was everywhere. It's no secret he's in Africa. The absence of the usual couple of paparazzi lurking outside on the pavement of this quiet Kensington street should be enough to confirm it.

I open the door a sliver. Through the crack, I can see a rumpled set of black jeans, and the sleeve of a padded jacket with a smear of mud on the elbow.

My first thought is it's Dogman Dave. He's the homeless guy who has a regular spot outside the Pret a Manger near the tube station. I pass him every day, always giving him a little cash. Or sometimes, if I'm grabbing myself a morning caffeine hit, I'll buy him a coffee (black two sugars). His dog, Tucker, is a favourite of all who pass. But the absence of Tucker's smiling face tells me this isn't Dave. The two are inseparable. If Dave was at my door, Tucker would thrust his wet black nose through it, seeking a pat.

A smell that causes me to wrinkle my nose in distaste drifts towards me and this is the second reason I'm sure this isn't Dave. He's often a little scruffy, but always clean. He takes meticulous care of himself and Tucker. No, this is not the Dogman.

My eyes widen as I crane my neck upwards to see that under the cap pulled down low, the man has a black scraggly beard, matching long hair straggling over his collar, and a heavily tattooed hand reaching for the pair of dark sunglasses that obscure his eyes.

He jerks them off and I meet an intense blue gaze. I know those eyes, although I haven't been this close to them lately. Christian Steele, my brother's best friend and bandmate, gifted guitarist and a legendary bad boy of the rock world, is staring down at me.

"Let me in Haley, fuck it," he whispers threateningly. "I need a pee." It's so long since I've seen him, I'm surprised he even remembers my name. "I've been in a car for eight hours and the moment we got within a whisper of London, the bastards wouldn't even stop to let me have a slash on the side of the road."

Even through the narrow crack in the door, I can smell beer and bourbon overlaying the rank odour of an unwashed body. I can also see he's literally dancing from one foot to the other, one hand clutching his crotch. I have no reason to doubt that unless I open this door quick-smart, a rock god is about to piss his pants on my doorstep.

I push the door shut, fumble with the chain, and once it's free, slowly open the door. But Christian shoves past me, heading straight for the bathroom. Of course, he knows where to go. I'm sure he's spent nights here before.

Just as well, because Christian has no time to stop and ask for directions. He discards a duffle bag and slings a guitar case from his shoulder. Both litter the hallway. He doesn't even pause to close the bathroom door behind him and I hear a cascade of urine being expelled at high-pressure. It tumbles into the bowl accompanied by a long, low groan of relief. He seems to pee forever.

Intrigued by this stranger, Tully and Mularkey launch themselves from where they've been observing from the couch and dive into the bathroom. Like all dogs, they want to be everywhere people are, assuming joining visitors in the toilet is perfectly acceptable. While I'm totally comfortable having an audience of two in the loo, I'm not sure if Christian will feel the same way.

I pause, weighing up whether I go after them and risk seeing him with his pants at half-mast and catch a glimpse of those famous taut butt cheeks naked. Not that I haven't seen them before. I confess I let my voyeuristic tendencies get the better of me and checked out the tasteful but very sexy shoot he did for a men's health magazine earlier this year. Rachel dumped a copy on my coffee table. I held out for a day before curiosity got the better of me. Even now, I can summon visions of that beautiful body. Not helpful right this moment.

Charging into the bathroom will most likely incur his wrath at my lack of respect for privacy, but if I don't, he might get angry with my girls. When I hear a deep throaty laugh, followed by his gravelly voice, I push out a heavy breath of relief, saved from having to decide.

"Guess a man can't even pee on his own around here."

Tully lets out a happy woof, and Mularkey echoes her. He emerges still buttoning his jeans, but leaving his belt buckle dangling. The dogs dance at his heels as if they, too, captivated by his charisma, have become canine Christian Steele groupies.

"God, I can't tell you how much I needed that," he says, dropping backwards onto my couch, sprawling there as the dogs seize the opportunity to ambush him. While they are unequivocal in their instant liking for him, I myself am still on the fence.

There *are* reasons to like Christian. The first is, of course, he's cliché rock star material—dangerously good-looking.

Second, he's my brother's bandmate and friend. In looks and personality, Christian and Ollie are like two sides of the same coin, dark and light, shadow and sunlight. Their music shows the same contrast; my brother writes the swoony lyrics and more upbeat melodies; Christian provides the counterpoint with his angsty words and melancholy chords interspersed with aggressive guitar riffs. What they print in the press tells a similar tale—implying if life were a movie, Ollie would be the romantic lead, all-round nice guy and hero of the hour; and Christian would be his evil twin.

But I know Ollie. While people inevitably gravitate to him, and he's always friendly in return, he only lets a few into his inner circle, and of those, he considers only a couple true friends; Christian is one of them. Ollie is a good judge of character, so despite Christian's thundercloud demeanour, his reputation for breaking hearts and guitars, and some ugly rumours that have swirled around him, there has to be something good underneath.

It looks like I'm about to find out now his brooding presence has invaded my house. He drapes his large, beautiful body across my couch. Tully and Mularkey, the traitors, lick at his face like he's some delicious new toy.

What the hell is he doing here? I'm bewildered, because he shouldn't be. The main reason I was prepared to give Christian Steele the benefit of the doubt that he really is a likeable and good-hearted person was him popping up on my TV screen two nights ago in the opening episode of *Wild For The Win*. It's one of those reality TV shows, where celebrities try to outplay each other. The winner claims a hundred thousand pounds for their nominated charity. Christian's choice of charity is the Canine Haven Dog Rescue Trust, my employer, and a worthy organisation, which just so happens to need money desperately right now.

I was so impressed when he revealed it with a cocky 'I'm going to win this thing' grin. I'm not so impressed now, because, right this moment, he should be in Scotland filming.

"Christian."

I try to keep my voice neutral, despite the crushing realisation if he's here in my living room, then the chances of the shelter dogs receiving this much-needed cash are now toast—along with my job. My last little Christmas candle-flame of hope sputters and dies. Snuffed out by something he's done. This man who's ignoring me.

"Christian," I bark out. The need to know why he's torn away the last shreds of possibility of a merry Christmas and a happy New Year for all of us overcomes my normal timidity. He whips his head towards me, but makes no attempt to fend off the probing dog tongues.

"What the hell are you doing here?"

CHAPTER 2

Day One

THIS IS THE THING I love about dogs: they don't give a shit. They don't care if you're the rock star getting paid the big bucks or the guy driving a delivery van around Dagenham for minimum wage.

The fact I stink from layers of grime and sweat is of no concern to them. I may as well have just leapt out of the shower, newly-washed and bearing a splash of the expensive aftershave I'm a brand ambassador for (apparently dark and brooding is considered edgy). They sniff at my bare wrists so hard they practically bruise me. Their long tongues taste me like I'm Christmas candy.

The dogs don't give my tattooed hands a second glance any more than they notice the small neat ones planted firmly on Haley Templeton's hips as she glares at me—well, as much as Haley can give a death stare, although she's doing well enough. It unnerves me to see that expression on the face of an angel.

After the fucking nightmare of the last two days of my life, I need the blind adoration and total lack of judgment these two crazy old dogs offer me in a generous yelping, licking, nose-nudging whirl of unconditional canine love. Buried beneath them, I'm safe to ignore the question she's thrown at me.

What am I doing here? It's a long story and not one I'm free to tell. Not unless I want my arse sued for an amount of money sufficient to make a dent in even my obscenely healthy bank balance, and I can't afford that to happen, not with my responsibilities.

"Tully. Mularkey."

Her voice is firm, and the dogs respond automatically. Weird names, but kind of cool. In an instant, they are sitting, bums planted on the floor, one on either side of her, eyes bright, tongues still lolling, but completely in her thrall. I can relate to that. I've only met up with Haley a few times in the last year, but I still know how easy it is to submit to her charms. I'm already falling, falling, drowning in the quiet magic she weaves simply by her presence.

Back when I first met Ollie Templeton three years ago, the pair of us battling it out with thirty others trying to make it to the final of *Star Power*, I noticed his sister straight away. With a curtain of mahogany hair, surprising gold-flecked green eyes framed with de-termined dark brows and luscious full lips begging to be kissed—es-pecially when she worries at them with her teeth, like she's doing this minute, undecided about her next move—she's always going to stand out.

Tiny but perfectly formed, her doll-like figure draws my eyes. I jerk them back towards her face. *Keep it together Christian. Don't piss her off any more than you've already done. Obvious perving will definitely do that.*

Faced with her mouth, even turned downwards in disapproval, I barely suppress the urge to leap to my feet, close the gap between us and kiss her senseless.

It's nothing new.

Haley would have been about twenty-two back when we first met, I think, but looked younger; like some sweet kid fresh out of high school, not yet tarnished by the woes of the world, all bright and shiny and hopeful. Hopeful for Ollie, and then as she saw his friendship with me grow, even a little hopeful for me, too. Her shy wishes of good luck before I went on stage, and slightly less restrained congratulations when the results kept me in for another week alongside her brother, became an addiction.

She even hugged me once or twice. I clearly remember the first time, although I tried not to make too much of it. It was a natural thing for our combined supporters to grab at Ollie and me in congratulations as we came offstage, after they'd announced who was going forward. I liked it. More than I should have. The memory of Haley's velvety cheek against the bare v of my chest, and her perky breasts crushed against me, lingers now.

Back then, I couldn't get her off my mind, try as I might. In frustration, I did what I always did and poured all my feelings into my music. You see, Haley Templeton is the sort of girl who inspires songs; for me anyway.

Ollie doesn't know it, but 'Untouchable'—the first song I wrote after the contest was over, the first thing I played trying to convince the other two guys in our fledgling band I had more to contribute than fancy guitar riffs—that song was about his sister. Although I could never tell him.

I was drawn to Haley like forbidden fruit, and I'm certain she'd taste sweet. But she's still untouchable, unless I'm prepared to risk losing my only real friend in this fucked up world of fake smiles and false banter that cover up the true intentions of everyone who wants to ride on your coattails when you're famous.

It's soothing to travel in my mind back to before all that crap. Back to when I first laid eyes on her oozing honey sweetness and quiet decency, qualities I've rarely glimpsed in the endless parade of women who have thrown themselves at me since.

Like mine, Ollie's family was there every day, waiting in the hotel lobby before we'd leave for the venue, nabbed for quick on-camera interviews like deer caught in the headlights. Later they'd follow us to the studio, sometimes allowed through to the side of the stage, and occasionally summoned forth on national television. The families are a welcome support in the pressure cooker environment of a talent show, but mostly encouraged to be there because they make good TV.

My cheer team was my slightly rough around the edges farming family: Mum, Dad, and my two older brothers, forced by my parents to be there. They still can't understand why I prefer a guitar over a tractor, or why anyone would choose to make music rather than milk cows. Ungrateful bastards.

Meanwhile Ollie's headmaster dad and head teacher mum flanked this often serious but always pretty young woman, who looked at her brother with the same loving adoration as those two creaky old dogs are giving her right this minute. Even back then, I decided it would be rather nice if Haley Templeton looked at me like that; which, at the moment, she's definitely not.

Yes, screwing around with Ollie's kid sister would not be a great idea. He's one of the few true friends I've ever had—from the first time we met backstage, two scared guys trying to put on enough bravado so the judges and the public might see potential in our music and keep us coming back week after week, and maybe make it to the end.

In a way, not making the finals was a gift. I can't imagine how it would have felt if either of us had been the last man standing. A weird mix of elation and devastation, I suppose. But while we fell short of making it to the lofty heights of finals night, we've reached far beyond that since. Commiserating over a few beers after our simultaneous elimination, Stellar Riot was born, and we never gave *Star Power* a single backward glance.

Ollie believes in me—me, the person—not only in my musical talent and my total commitment to our shared goals. I mustn't do anything to tarnish that belief. It's all I've got when things inevitably get tough. The only wobble we've ever had in our friendship of three years involved a woman, so for that reason I need to tread very carefully around this one, much as I'd love to abandon common sense.

I sit up from the jumble of dogs and summon a brave face.

"So, I'm guessing Ollie hasn't told you," I say, dragging a hand down my scruffy beard.

"Told me what?" she snaps.

"That I need to stay here for twelve days."

"No." Her frown deepens, her mouth tightening as she snatches up her phone, and begins scrolling.

It's still playing some cheesy Christmas song, a harsh assault on my hungover ears. Please God, never let them suggest the band do a Christmas single. It might be good enough for Springsteen and U2, but the thought of a Stellar Riot Christmas release nauseates me.

"Well, I definitely ran this past him. I spoke to him yesterday, around midday." I hope the earnest tone encourages her to see the truth in my eyes. "He's somewhere in Botswana. Said he'd call you straight away."

"Nope," she says. "Nothing at all."

This explains her greeting me with a slightly hostile air of surprise. I'm determined to damp that down a notch. I'm reluctant to ruin the next twelve days with accusations of lies from the start. Although, I *am* going to lie to her. I have no choice. Or at the least skirt around the truth. But hand on my heart, she's getting the truth right now.

"The connection was pretty flaky. In some really remote place, apparently. Bumping along a dirt track in a four-wheel drive. He might be out of range. And you know him, Haley. He's not exactly reliable, not when he's off on one of his trips. If Ollie said he'd call, he would have tried. I can't imagine him worrying too much if he couldn't get through."

"Guess we won't know either way." The thick suspicion in her voice is undisguisable. "OK," she sighs, "so we've established Ollie said it's fine for you to stay here."

She believes me. That's a good sign, because I'm going to need her to trust me, given what I can tell she's going to ask next.

"But that still doesn't answer the question of why you're here, not on some island off the coast of Scotland, winning enough money so Canine Haven doesn't implode by Christmas."

"You've been watching? And you assumed I'd win?"

The thought ignites a small flutter of pride. Without reservation, Haley believes—scratch that, *believed*—in me too.

"Of course you were going to win," she snorts, throwing me an incredulous look, as if anyone could doubt my ability to outplay and outlast seven other celebrities. Then she tears away my smug self-satisfaction in a heartbeat. "It's not like you had much competition," she huffs over a little laugh. "One washed up football player, two girls from a daytime soap no one's ever heard of, one of the *Real Wives Of Watford*—who I'm surprised has the brain to make it to her front door let alone all the way to Scotland and back—and three losing contestants they've pulled from various reality series?"

"Four," I say, miserably. "If you count a *Star Power* semi-finalist."

I see it clearly now Haley puts it like that. I wasn't chosen for the hard-earned success and fame I've created alongside my bandmates these past three years. The production company was scraping even deeper into the bottom of the barrel when they invited me. Channel Eight axed *Star Power* last year. It's not even a current show. Struggling to fill all the spots on *Wild For The Win*—which is no surprise; after all who in their right mind would spend ten days in Scotland, during winter, on an island so far north it's a wonder we didn't bump into Santa Claus, for no actual reward except the warm fuzzy glow of helping a charity—somehow they landed on my name.

"Yes, I suppose so," she says, with an irritated shrug. "But Christian, *you're* the only one of the whole eight with a brain in your head and an ounce of determination. I've only watched Episode 1, but it was obvious. The rest of them seem to think they're at a holiday camp for grown-ups. I can't understand why they're still there and you're here." She scrunches her eyes, shaking her head.

Here we go. Now dodging the truth begins.

"Because they dumped me. On day five."

"How can that be? It's not like it's a 'vote people off' situation. What did you do? It must have been bad for them to toss you out of there."

The accusation stings. I know she's hurting over this. My failure is personal to her. I've failed her, and all those people at Canine Haven and all the dogs like these two characters sitting here watching our conversation. If it wasn't such a tense situation, I'd crack a smile at the way their heads swivel back and forth, first to her, then to me, like it's a Wimbledon tennis final; and now the ball's in my court. I lob it back as best I can. It's not going to be easy to keep inside the lines and still make this an honest match.

"It wasn't what I did, Haley. It's what I *wouldn't* do. I know my reputation suggests I'm not exactly a guy who would take a stand on his principles, but this time I had to."

I can see doubt and mistrust in her narrowed eyes. She thinks I'm spinning her a lie. And I am—and I'm not. In her mind, my dodgy principles must seem like a flimsy excuse on which to gamble the future of the dog rescue.

"I can't tell you anything," I add, before she asks. "They slapped a ten page NDA on top of the original contract. Made me sign it before they'd let me leave. For the next twelve days, no one can know where I am. I had no choice. It was either that or the bastards really did abandon me in the wild. And then I'd have no chance to fix this."

"So," she says slowly, "what's going to happen when it airs? When it's Episode 6 and you're not there?"

I close my eyes and sigh. I'm dreading to find out what nefarious plan those fuckers will hatch to explain my departure. Scandal is good for ratings. Who the hell knows what they'll cobble together? Whatever it is, I know it will make me look bad. Nice guys who make a stand on principles don't make for good television.

"They'll have some plan. Stitch together footage. Tell the story whatever way they choose. And I'll have to live with the fallout." I grimace at the thought. It's happening again. "It's okay, I'll survive. I've made a career out of weathering shit storms from the lies other people spin."

I have a desperate need for her to know I'm not the guy the newspapers and entertainment channels say I am, and the click-bait headlines that inevitably accompany my name are untrue. I want her to understand I'm the sort of guy who has a line he won't cross. But all she's got is my word for it. I'm praying she'll take it, even if she's not totally convinced. On the strength of my friendship with her brother, I'm hoping she'll believe me.

She pinches at her forehead, eyes half-closed, and the gesture is so damn cute. Even in the middle of this uncertain conversation, her every look, every movement, enchants me. Even though she's standing there wearing an ugly Christmas jumper with a giant gingerbread man dancing across her delicious breasts. Even though her sleek dark hair is swept up in a ragged bun, with wisps falling across her face and sticking out at odd angles above her ears.

I remember the smell of her hair, so fresh and clean, when I inhaled a sneaky whiff as she offered a consoling hug on that last night of *Star Power*. Of course, the hug didn't mean anything. Not to her. Everyone was hugging everybody as Ollie and I faced the fact we weren't coming back for another night. But it meant something to me. I took my last chance to be near her, to imprint the soft warmth of her in my arms and imagine just for a moment what it would be like to have someone like her as mine.

I didn't know that night it wouldn't be the last time; that Ollie and I would put a band together, and because of it, she'd weave in and out of my life again and again over the next few years, each encounter only fanning the little ember of wanting in me. Wanting to know her more, to spend time with her; to let her get to know me. Now, just my luck, when the universe has delivered the opportunity to be with her in the most unexpected way, there's a high chance she's going to hate me.

"So, I still don't understand—why did you come *here*?" A little frown line creases between the downward slanting brows. She's still not convinced. "The middle of London isn't where I'd choose if I wanted to lie low. I would have thought Ollie's Somerset house would be the perfect place to hide out."

She really doesn't want me here. I can see that. Why would she want *me* arriving unannounced on her doorstep, a blot on her happy Christmas-soaked Saturday, asking to spoil her life for twelve days? But I need her to let me.

"Apparently not. There's some Christmas fundraiser thing going on? People paying to visit the house?"

"Oh, yeah. I forgot," she sighs. "It starts today."

"And although he swears his staff down there wouldn't breathe a word, they can't exactly help me either. That's really why he sent me here." I raise my eyes to hers, making a silent plea. "Because he knew you'd take care of the things I can't do for myself."

I hold my breath, those green eyes studying me. Either she'll accept my explanation and agree to take on this unwelcome task. Or insist I call a cab and force me to trust my luck elsewhere.

Haley gives a little nod.

A rush of air hisses between my teeth and I relax a little for the first time in two days. She's going to help me. It's not only food and a hot shower at stake here. If I have any chance to fight back against those pricks at Unscripted Productions, I need an ally who can move outside in the real world, as well as let me loose on her laptop. I might be out, but I'm not down, and I'm going to fight for what I know is right. At this moment, I need to start by simply getting Haley to let me stay.

It seems I've won the first round. She turns and pads down the passage, dainty feet encased in the most ridiculous fluffy socks. The ring of reindeer heads around the edge of each sock bobs in time to the movement, fortunately distracting my eyes away from the sight of her neat little arse in a pair of candy-cane covered pyjama bottoms.

She returns, arms loaded with a stack of fluffy white towels. Is this a hint? I know I reek.

"Guest room is made up. The first on the left. You know where the bathroom is. Don't hog it. I want a shower sometime today too," she says.

So we're sharing a bathroom? I thought she'd be upstairs. There have to be at least three bedrooms up there besides Ollie's. She notices my raised brow.

"Yeah, I moved my room down here. With two dogs, running up and down the stairs to let them out in the back garden isn't my idea of fun. Not when you've got oldies who can't hang on all night like they used to."

"Oh, yeah, right," I say. "Makes sense."

She sure is devoted to these dogs. I like that. Dogs have always been an important part of my life, from the time I was a little kid.

It's the memories of my childhood canine companion that got me to agree to this stupid reality TV show in the first place; and also what got me kicked off it.

"Thanks Haley," I mumble, standing to take the towels from her. My hands brush hers and they're so damn smooth; tiny and delicate. What I'd give for one of those hands to rest on my head as they do when offering an affectionate pat to the big pointy-eared dog. Or to run down my body, like when she slides one finger along the sleek length of the orange dog's spine. If my brain keeps on this track, I might need that shower on cold. I grab my bag and get the hell out of there before she notices the prominent lump straining at my pants.

The shower not only removes two days of filth but induces a dragging tiredness. Once dried off, I don't bother to dress, but fasten the towel around my hips and head straight for the bedroom. I fall naked but clean between crisp sheets and into a deep dreamless sleep, where not even thoughts of my delicious new roommate can intrude.

When I wake, a couple of hours later, it's to the pleasant every-day sounds of the household. Even the muffled music playing—although it's still recognisable as damn Christmas songs—is sooth-ing. Hearing Haley moving around—it sounds like she's in the kitchen—life feels normal. Realising *this* is what a normal life would be like, there's a pang of regret. Fame and money have given me a lot of things, but perhaps not the very simple ones I truly want; the things I really need.

I tug on my one set of clean clothes and wander back down to the lounge. It's like a Christmas volcano has erupted. Every sur-face is slathered with decorations: wreaths, garlands, door hangers. And then there's that tree, the most-overdressed I've ever seen. It wouldn't look out of place at Harrods. Its fresh outdoor tang blends with a sweet, spicy smell drifting from the kitchen. My stomach twists in an angry growl. I can't remember when I last ate.

The dogs, now both in matching Christmas jumpers, are curled on the sofa, sleeping. Two tails thump in greeting as I sit between them. One raises a head, while the other welcomes me with an enthusiastic bark. I breathe in their smell, slightly pungent but warmly familiar. They both wiggle their soft bodies closer so we're touching, and I revel in the contact. I've missed the easy companionship of dogs. I give each a scratch, my nails massaging their spines, and they whine with pleasure. When I stop, the noise escalates as they beg for more.

This summons Haley, who leans in the doorframe. She's still dressed for the season, but this time in a more subdued snowflake jumper, the green of the background highlighting her emerald eyes. A pair of dark jeans hug her slender form and she's replaced the silly reindeer socks with slouchy black suede boots.

My breath catches at the sight of her, and my body twitches with desire. I swallow hard, grateful for the dog now draped across my knees, its large body covering my inconvenient erection. It's shaping up to be a very long twelve days.

CHAPTER 3

Day One

A HAPPY BLAST OF Christmas songs fills the house while I'm in the kitchen. After spending all afternoon hands buried in pastry and fruit mince, it's cleanup time. With the music at maximum volume, I didn't hear Christian get up. Now, in the pause between playlists, the silence that drew me through to the lounge to attend to my phone is not silence at all. The dogs huff with joy, and he murmurs endearments to them as both hands caress their bodies. As a guitarist, he's very good with his hands, and it seems he applies this talent effectively to other purposes.

Noticing me in the doorway, he tilts his chin in recognition and offers a shy smile. This man is such a contradiction. I didn't think him capable of modesty, let alone shyness. Mularkey sprawls across him, face turned upwards in a wide, loving grin as he scratches her chest. Tully is curled under his armpit, eyes closed in a blissful doze while his fingers massage her satiny ears. Neither dog looks towards me. He's got them under his spell, and I can't say I blame them. If I had someone showering such affection on me, stroking all my most pleasurable spots, I wouldn't be seeking anyone else either.

They say dogs are an excellent judge of character and I've found that to be true. Which means I may have to go easier on Christian Steele. If Ollie, Tully, and Mularkey are in Team Christian, then I might have to join them. Even so, my mind protests the thought; I'm not ready to go there yet.

"I thought I'd order in pizza. Want some?" I offer. It's definitely dinner o'clock, but I'm too exhausted to cook. All the decorating and then my little baking spree—whipping up some Christmas mince pies to take into work on Monday—has left me with no energy to be creative in the kitchen.

"Thanks, that would be great," he says. "I've barely eaten for two days."

I can believe it. He looks tired and gaunt, with hollows under his eyes and a sallow undertone to his olive skin.

"Only the liquid stuff, eh?" I remember the alcoholic haze wafting around him earlier.

He gives a rueful smile. It tips up at one corner, suggesting the possibility of a dimple waiting to pop under that damn beard.

"Haley, I swear the last forty-eight hours would have driven any-one to drink—even you. But yeah, some proper food would be good, thanks."

I grab my phone and place an order. While we wait, I opt for some mindless television, a house renovation programme on the

Living Channel. Anything to spare me from catching up on the second episode of *Wild For The Win* I missed last night. Now I know Christian isn't there working hard for the rescue, I've lost all interest. It would only turn up my simmering anger with him to boiling point. Why he's here and not there, I don't want to ask. Knowing Christian's reputation, he's done something awful. The details would only stir me up more.

My phone chimes with a text confirming the arrival of my delivery. A few seconds later, there's a knock on the door. Before I can stand to answer it, Christian wades from between the sleeping dogs, rousing them with surprised looks while holding a finger to his lips. He dives down the hallway and doesn't reappear from his room until I close the front door with a firm thud.

He's taking this hiding out thing seriously, and to be fair, it was probably wise. That pizza delivery girl would sure have something to tell her friends if she'd glimpsed Christian Steele lounging on my couch.

He wolfs down more than his half share. Luckily, I'm not a big eater. Carefully wiping his hands clean, he returns to thumbing listlessly through Ollie's copy of *The Lord of The Rings*. After running the boxes out to the recycling bin and emptying my baking utensils from the dishwasher, I return to the TV, finding a rerun of *The Great British Bake Off*. I startle when a few minutes later the Tolkein hits the coffee table with a thwack.

"Why don't we watch a Christmas movie?" he suggests.

Is he a mind reader? How the hell did he know I was going to start my Christmas movie binge tonight? With no other plans—friends all busy, no boyfriend—I'd intended to make my own happy Saturday night, blotting out all thoughts of Jack and Paige with a nice Christmas rom-com. Until he turned up.

"So, how did you know by coming to stay here, you've signed up for the compulsory Christmas movie marathon?"

"What else would be happening in a room that looks like this?" he deadpans, rolling his eyes as he surveys the room, that even I have to admit is literally heaving with decoration. However, I also detect a faint spark in his eyes, the first trace of actual enthusiasm I've noticed for anything except the pizza. Maybe Christian has a secret weakness for sappy Christmas viewing?

"OK, so what shall we watch?"

"How about *Love Actually*? That's a good one." His teasing mouth twitches at the corners. Somehow, he's zeroed in on my absolute favourite. I don't argue. A quick stab at the remote, and I settle in to enjoy the familiar much-loved montage of stories unfolding on the screen.

We reach the part where we meet the two unlikely film body doubles, who are having a normal conversation while simulating a sex scene, and Christian snorts loudly.

"What the fuck?" He mutters under his breath, before dissolving into loud rumbles of laughter. OK, it is a funny scene, but it's not that funny unless you're seeing it for the first time—and the lights go on in my head. I hit pause, and he turns to me, still chuckling to himself, and his eyes meet mine, sparkling with amusement.

"You've never even watched this movie before." I can't help the accusing tone.

"No. But it's great."

"Then why did you suggest it?" I frown.

"While you were in the kitchen, I was flicking through and saw your saved list. Figured me being here shouldn't disrupt your Saturday night plans."

I'm not sure whether to be pleased with his consideration or annoyed he's assumed I'd have no plans for the weekend other than watching Christmas movies alone. I brush away the thought and press play once more.

I wouldn't admit it to Christian, but it's actually fun observing someone enjoy the movie for the first time. Out of the corner of my eye, I see him smile at sleazy Billy Mack's snarkiness. He chokes with laughter at hapless Colin's mission to find love in the USA. Watching Christian's unfolding discovery of something special to me is kind of endearing and despite my resolve to hold on to my anger, I find my stance on his actions wavering a tad.

As the final credits roll, I'm sure he even gets a little misty-eyed at the beautiful scenes of people reuniting with friends and family at the airport. Who would have picked Christian as a man who'd go all mushy over a chick-flick?

"That was really good," he says, and I do believe he means it. "But you can't tell anyone I said that, right?" He points a cautionary finger at me. "Not even Ollie. Not good for my image." He wipes at one eye. "Damn it, I should have taken these contacts out hours ago."

I try not to smile at the lie—I'm positive he's not wearing contacts—and instead hit him with the most important question of all.

"OK, there's a compulsory end of viewing test for all *Love Actually* virgins."

One brow flies up to his forehead, and he flashes me his lopsided smile, the same one that sends the fan girls swooning. Of course, *I'm* not susceptible to its heat.

"Really?" His smile morphs into a grin that shows off perfectly white teeth.

"Yes, really. The good news is there's only one question and no wrong answers. So, Christian, you need to take a stand here." I fix him with my most serious quizmaster stare. "Which story did you like best?"

He answers without hesitation. "The guy who's in love with his friend's wife."

God, that's my favourite too. Strange Christian and I have this in common.

"Why?" I ask, unable to mask my surprise at his unexpected choice.

"Because it's not easy to have feelings for someone who's off limits to you." His voice drops to just above a whisper. I have a sense there's something personal in this, but curious as I am, I've no right to pry. "Brave of him to admit it. Even though he knows it's hopeless."

The grin has dissolved into a sad smile and there's an odd expression in his eyes. He looks away from my gaze, as if fearful I'll read something there he doesn't want to share. Fair enough. He's my brother's best friend, but we barely know each other. He's under no obligation to spill his secrets to me.

He turns back to me. "And yours?"

"Same," I admit. He doesn't demand a reason for my choice, but I have a strange compulsion to offer one. "I've always admired how she handles his feelings in that scene. I mean, he's so fragile. And she gets that." His nod encourages me to go on, the words somehow tumbling forth, pushing past my usual reserve with people I don't know well. "It's a special thing to be gifted another person's admission of love, to have someone be vulnerable and face the risk of rejection. Especially when it's from someone unexpected." I don't know why I'm saying this to Christian Steele, but I can't help myself. "I hope if it happened to me, I could accept that sort of declaration with the same graciousness, no matter who it came from."

"I hope so too," he says, his voice low.

Something hangs in the air. It's as if I'm observing him through a gauzy curtain that blurs the space between us. It ripples in an invisible breeze, flickering light and shadows softening the contours of his face. Then the moment is gone. Christian breaks our gaze and leaps to his feet.

"God, I'm still absolutely exhausted," he announces with a sprawling, almost theatrical yawn. "I guess I'll leave you to enjoy *The Holiday* in peace. Number two on your list, if I remember correctly?"

I can't help but mirror the teasing grin he tosses over his shoulder. Tully's sad eyes follow his progress across the lounge, disappointed her couch buddy should abandon us so early. Mularkey tracks him to the doorway, gazing at him hopefully. I follow. It's time the girls went out, anyway.

"No girl," he says gently, fondling her pointy ears in a way that causes her to melt into the floor. "Maybe you can sleep with me another night, if the boss lady says you can."

It melts my heart a little too. Christian has many critics, me included after today's bombshell, but I struggle to hold it against him as I see his affinity for animals. No wonder he chose the rescue as his charity. As if he senses my softening, he pauses at his bedroom door.

"Goodnight, Haley," he says. "Thanks for everything."

"You're welcome." I was brought up to meet politeness with grace.

He's about to close the door when he hesitates, turning back to me.

"Look, I know you're pissed at me about the show." He's far more perceptive than I'd ever have given him credit for. I thought I'd hidden it well. "I promise I'll tell you everything sometime. I just can't right now. OK?"

"OK. Goodnight Christian."

I sit up a little longer afterwards, wondering what the hell really went on up in Scotland while flip-flopping between a parade of pathetic television programmes. I'm too tired to start another movie, no matter how tempting the thought. It's been a long day and, finding no reason to delay further, I summon the dogs for a final quick potty stop and bed.

I slip into a pair of cheerful red tartan pyjamas and tuck up under my heavy blankets, ready to fall into cosy oblivion. However, my brain hasn't got the memo. The intriguing presence of Christian Steele in the second bedroom off the hall, with only a shared bathroom separating us, and the weighty baggage he brought with him, stir questions and emotions.

He's so damn likeable once he drops that frowny face. A closet romantic too, if his thoughts on my favourite movie scene ever are anything to go by. I wonder what lies beneath his words—maybe he too loved someone he couldn't have?

Thoughts of Christian clatter through my head, jangling metal like one of those chatter rings I loved as a kid. They're a frenetic chorus in my brain, keeping sleep frustratingly beyond reach.

As the minutes drag on, I attempt to damp down the chaotic whir, reaching for the familiar thoughts of my dogs that usually occupy the space between being awake and asleep.

However, focusing on the dogs doesn't bring peace, but rather allows very real and more worrying sounds to intrude.

Day One

Haley

WHEN YOU HAVE AN elderly fur kid, your ears become as attuned to the sounds of them as those of new parents with a young baby. In the night, lying in my king-size bed, with Tully and Mularkey taking up more than their share of it, I always sleep lightly, subconsciously monitoring their presence. Most of the time it's companionable snuffling, as they snuggle into their hollows in the covers. Although more frequently these days, those softer sounds morph into raucous snoring. I've learned to zone it out for the sake of waking up a functioning human being the next morning.

Doggie dreams sometimes intrude on my own too, as they scrabble with wonky legs that no longer work well in real life. Hearing them relive long gone frolics and the thrill of the chase always brings a smile. I love that they still have this pleasure available to them, even if it's only while asleep.

Tonight the dog noises don't trigger comfort. Half an hour after she dragged herself up beside me, I'm concerned about Tully. She's gone from the odd quiet whimper to actively in distress. She's panting—even though it's not warm—and drooling. A couple of times she's retched but nothing's come up. Normally I'd be pleased the dog didn't actually puke on my bed, but not tonight. I sit up and trail my hands carefully across her stomach. It feels distended. When I flip on the bedside lamp, I read an expression of pain in her dark eyes.

Deep-chested dogs like Tully are more prone to bloat, and it's a killer. If it's what I think it is—and I'm fairly certain, having seen quite a few dogs present like this at the clinics I've worked in—she could be dead by morning. I need to get Tully to a vet and I need to do it now.

But no cabbie will take me and two dogs; I can't leave Mularkey here alone. The only option is Ollie's car, his pride and joy: a Porsche 911. A GT2 RS to be as precise in naming it as he is.

I always maintain fame and money haven't affected my brother, and that's ninety-nine percent true. The other one percent is the outrageous German sports car parked in the garage. At least beyond the aggressive exterior, it harbours a rear seat of sorts. Designed for stuffing in a few parcels or a gym bag, it will be tight, but I think the girls will fit.

However, there are two large problems with this plan. One, I don't usually drive. And two, even if I dared to try, how would I manage in this situation? With me, an unlicensed novice, white-knuckled and trembling in fear, plus two dogs, one whimpering in pain, the other restless with concern at her friend's distress; it would be an accident waiting to happen. Or, at best, attract a confrontation with an irate police officer and a stiff fine. Neither outcome would see Tully to a vet in time.

I have no choice. It's Christian or nothing. I tiptoe to his door, aware it's almost midnight, giving it a tentative tap with the back of my hand.

"Christian."

There's no answer. I knock again, with a little more force. Repeat his name. Still silence. Another whimper from my room decides for me. I'm going in, invited or not. The risk of not getting help for Tully is a thousand times more terrifying than the prospect of Christian Steele's displeasure.

He's lying with the sheets tossed back. He hasn't bothered to pull the heavy blackout drapes, and streetlight filters through the filmy curtains, picking out his shape in a surreal half-light. I'm transfixed.

It's as if we're in some wintery faery forest, painted in greys and gilded with silver. I've stumbled across the elven king, slumbering in a tumbled nest of pale ferns (in reality an expensive set of Garnet Hill sheets). My gaze follows the curves of his naked upper body, pale and beautiful in contrast to the deepest indigo etched on it in a glorious riot of patterns and plants. I've seen his tattoos before, of course, but always at a distance; from the side of the stage, or front row VIP seats. Generally, it's only his forearms and hands exposed, and the v of his neck. And ogling him in the magazine, I'd focused on the whole man, the very attractive body, not the extra decoration.

As I edge closer, almost reluctant to wake him when he looks so peaceful, I see higher up, on his biceps and beyond, animals peep through the foliage. A wolf stares back at me from one shoulder, a lifelike gleam in its eyes. There's a fox and a badger. A squirrel and a tiny field mouse. It's as if Christian invited the same artist who created my precious Liberty Christmas bauble to use his skin for a canvas, and it's enchanting.

There's an unexpected gentleness in the subject matter. It's the innocent feel of *The Wind In The Willows*. Even the wolf has a benign expression, not the snarling beast one might expect on an angry young musician. He really is a contradiction. Farm boy turned rock star. Formidable tattoos with secret softness.

I'm hoping there's a similar softness inside of him now, as I reach over, laying one palm against his shoulder. It's cool and smooth and I shiver a little at the contact.

"Christian." I shake him gently and he startles awake.

"What the fuck?" Then, as recognition strikes, he relaxes. "Shit, Haley. Sorry, you gave me a fright."

"Yeah, I'm not the best sight to wake up to."

He gives me a strange look, before reassembling his features. "What's up?"

"It's Tully. Christian—" My voice breaks. "I'm so scared. She's sick. Really sick. She needs the vet. I think it's bloat."

"Bad in cows. Worse in dogs, right?" Of course, growing up on a dairy farm in Cheshire, he has a practical knowledge of animals.

"Often fatal." I choke on the words. I'm hoping we can get her there before her stomach flips. Gastric torsion. Then the odds of saving her drop away to a frighteningly small number. "Can you drive us?"

"Of course." He springs from the bed, totally unashamed of his nakedness. I look away. He might not be embarrassed, but I am definitely uncomfortable with his lack of inhibition.

"Oops, sorry." He snatches at the sheet on seeing my discomfort. I'm heading for the door, anyway.

"Ollie's got a car here?" He calls after me over the rustle of clothing.

"Yeah, the Porsche."

"Yes," he hisses. "All right." He sounds pleased at the prospect. "Well, we won't need a police escort to get us there in a hurry. That baby can go."

Diving back into my own room, I swap pyjamas for jeans and a sweater. As I'm tugging on my boots, there's a soft tap on the door. I usher Christian in, his lips a taut line of concern. His dark brows knot at the sight of the dog sprawled on the bed, too distressed to even acknowledge his presence.

"There's no way I can carry Tully. I'm afraid you need to be both paramedic and driver here, Christian."

"Hey there, girl. Not feeling so good?" He sits on the bed next to her, murmuring into the folds of her neck. "It's okay, sweetheart. We're going to get you some help."

His voice soothes her. Her panting stops a moment, and she swallows down a whimper. She's a big dog, but he scoops her up like a baby. She looks up at him, and while there's still pain in her eyes, there's also trust, and I relax a little, feeling in his capable arms things are not quite so bad as they were.

I clip a lead on Mularkey, and we head to the garage. One click of the fob triggers a discreet beep, and I open the passenger door, tip the front seat forward, and she clambers up into the almost non-existent rear seat. I whip around the car, reaching past the driver's seat to bundle a blanket into the leather cocoon on the other side. Christian gently lowers Tully into the woolly nest I've made. She gazes up at us with uncertain eyes, and he stretches a kind hand to her head while Mularkey takes up a sentinel pose, ears pricked, eyes alert, totally focused on her friend.

Christian springs into the driver's seat and takes the wheel with confidence, like he's driven this car before. The engine bursts into life with a throaty rumble. He expertly backs out into our quiet street, and the roar of an angry beast fills the night air as he floors it.

"Christian!" I squeal, hands braced on the dashboard. He ignores my protest as we speed through the empty streets of sleeping central London.

"We're not going to lose her, Haley," he says, eyes fixed straight ahead. "Not on my watch."

I press back into the seat, his words reassuring, as we screech to a halt at a red light. Not on his watch. I'm terrified, but at least I don't have to do this alone.

Despite a suspicious stare from the two occupants of a stationary police car, we make it to the nearest after-hours emergency clinic without incident. Surprising, as I'd have thought any cop worth his salt would have pulled over someone who looks like Christian, with cap pulled low and wearing dark glasses even though it's the middle of the night, driving an expensive car. Perhaps they'd just started on their mid-shift burger order. Whatever, I'm grateful for their lack of motivation.

We're in luck as we arrive at the clinic, too. This late on a weekend night, there's only a small team on duty, but they inspire confidence. The receptionist looks to be in her fifties and fires the sort of questions at me that suggest competence. The kindly vet who appears has a sprinkling of frost on his tight, springy dark hair, and I breathe relief. He will have dealt with this before. The nurse hovering at his shoulder reminds me of my mother, oozing a reassuring efficiency.

They leap into action the moment they see Tully cradled in Christian's strong arms. He's not so different to his farmer brothers in this respect, lifting my big girl effortlessly with broad forearms and muscled shoulders. He lowers her gently onto the trolley and they whisk her off into an examining room. I have this sense she's in safe hands tonight. I slump onto a waiting room seat, Christian on one side, and a subdued Mularkey on the other. She knows her doggie sister is sick.

The receptionist approaches us with a hesitant expression. She clears her throat. I know the drill. They'll want money up front.

"Ahmm," she says, glancing at Christian, but choosing to address me. In those clothes, he doesn't look like somebody who could afford the bill. "We need a credit card, I'm afraid. Of course, we'll do the best we can for your girl, but this type of intensive medicine can be costly. So we ask for a payment method on admission."

She seems a little embarrassed broaching the ugly subject of money at a time like this, but I get it. In this profession, no matter how much we're committed to saving animals, the cold hard fact is medical treatment costs. I swallow down my nerves as I wrack my brains, trying to recall how much room I've got on my card. Sure, I live rent free, but choosing to work in the charitable sector means my vet nurse's wages are low. Living in London is crazy expensive. I'm still paying off my massive student loan, plus debt I racked up through my stupid pride after Jack and I broke up; and the girls' day-to-day care isn't cheap.

Before I can fumble in my little cross-body bag, Christian is on his feet. He produces a wallet from the back pocket of his jeans and I haven't time to protest before he's waved a card at the machine.

"I got this, Haley," he says. "It's the least I can do for the girls who've welcomed me into their home."

I hold my breath. Not only is Christian fronting up to pay my bill, he's flashing around a credit card with his famous name on it in shiny gold letters. The receptionist is fortunately of a vintage that the name on the card means nothing to her. He risked his secret, but it's safe.

"Thank you," I say as he eases back on the bench seat beside me. The tears spill over, the whirling inside overtaking me. Fear and worry mingle with profound gratitude at his kindness. He lifts an arm and hovers it uncertainly above my shoulder for a heartbeat, but then wraps it around me, anyway. I welcome his warmth as we settle in to wait. I suppose I doze a little against him, but I'm sure I see every jerky hand movement of the waiting-room clock.

Three hours later, we're ordered to head home to bed. The veterinary surgeon pronounces Tully's emergency surgery a tentative success. He's managed to relieve the build-up of gas in the dog's stomach. Fortunately, the organ hadn't twisted, and he's carried out a preventative gastropexy, anchoring the stomach in place should this happen again—which it well might. Dogs who've had bloat once are likely to have it reoccur, so I'll always need to be vigilant. That's if my darling girl makes it through the next few hours. There's still the risk of toxic shock, and they'll monitor her closely, so they can act quickly if her vitals take a downward dip. We, meanwhile, must wait it out at home, even though I know I'm unlikely to comply with the kind vet's instruction to get some sleep.

I'm conscious I'm racking up a bill in the thousands for Tully's intensive care. Christian insists he's going to cover it, but it's awkward taking charity from someone I hardly know. Perhaps this is his way of making it up to me for the *Wild For The Win* debacle. I'll pay him back, but it's going to take a while.

Back at the house, he guides me inside as if I'm a faulty robot, unable to propel myself forward. I crash onto the low couch. Mularkey slides up beside me and circles, once, twice, three times, as is her habit. I sit, eyes closed, tears leaking down my face again. I feel so helpless. Knowing as much as I do is worse than being blissfully oblivious; I understand how this could end.

After banging around in the kitchen, accompanied by the chug and hiss of the coffee machine, Christian comes to set two mugs on the table. He's found my special pumpkin spice coffee capsules, and the sweet smell drifts up. Normally, it would spark immediate comfort, but not when it's five am after some of the worst hours of my life.

He slides in beside me and draws me into him. He rests his lips against my hair and whispers in the same soothing tones as when he whispered goodbye to darling Tully, before we left her lying sedated in a jumble of tubes. It's a tender, comforting gesture. I'm grateful for his presence, steadying me; lulled by his warm body wrapped across me, protection against bad things. Unlike when he arrived, he smells good, a fresh whiff of shampoo and shower gel, tangy with a woody note.

"Hey," he murmurs. "It's going to be okay. It has to be."

I angle my face towards him, reaching for further reassurance in his eyes. Their normally fierce blue is soft and they glisten with emotion. He brushes it away with a rough swipe of his hand. I want to believe him, and so I do. For the first time, I realise all my resolve to be angry with him has melted away and although it's purely selfish, I'm thankful Christian's here and not in far off Scotland.

CHAPTER 5

Day Two

THIS IS BAD, AND so fucking good all at the same time. I'm glad Ollie can't see this; his little sister melted into my arms, but I can't help how much I'm enjoying it.

She's seen straight through all my bullshit and bravado. These damn dogs of hers have opened me up, showing a part of me I've kept well-hidden. Self-preservation will drive you to do things that once seemed totally out of character.

As a kid lost in a world of music, books and hell, even poetry—and daring to have a 'pretty boy' face (according to my brothers)—growing up in a small rural backwater was a nightmare. Teasing and bullying followed me around. Even my own brothers joined in; sometimes they led it; taunting me, calling me gay, a potent insult in a small town where homophobia still lies not far below the surface.

So I put up a tough guy front, and it's served me well. I survived the last of school, escaped to London, worked in crap jobs, and then forged a multi-million pound career doing the thing I love—all behind this protective mask.

Those pricks who made my life miserable should take a look at me now. I got the last laugh, because although I've done my best to roughen up my face, with this scruffy beard my mother hates, it seems girls still like it fine. And this one seems to not only like my face, but has seen the person beneath the beard, tattoos and long hair and—unlike my family—hasn't found me wanting.

"I don't know how I can ever thank you enough," she murmurs into my chest.

"Just seeing that dog make it through was all the thanks I need, Haley."

Within minutes, her breathing slows, and sleep claims her from me. I could lay here forever, feeling the rise and fall of her chest against mine, but after ten minutes I admit to myself her needs must come ahead of my selfishness; and she needs bed.

I loop one arm under her knees and, taking care not to wake her, raise her gently from the couch. After years on the farm hefting calves and hay bales, lifting Haley's featherlight form is effortless.

With the dog supervising at my heels, I head for her bedroom. I manage to sidle up to the wall and angle one hand to flick on a light switch without disturbing the sleeping woman in my arms. Soft light floods the space. Her space. I didn't have time to take it in amidst the frantic panic of a few hours earlier. I steal a moment now;

pause to breathe in the smell. It's like her, the fragrance of tropical flowers.

Everything is neat but with a feminine touch. The small sofa looks inviting, the cushions arranged in a tasteful row. A stuffed bookshelf tells me she's a reader like Ollie—and like me; but I note the arrangement, with colourful spines facing out, in a carefully organised rainbow.

The bed is the only off note in this orderly room, a cue to the mayhem of earlier. Bedcovers lie askew, white sheets in a tangle. The floral spread hangs to one side, its edge brushing the floor.

I loosen an arm and stoop low, dragging a pillow back into place. Lowering her onto the pristine sheet, the sight of her fucking grabs me. She's perfection; even with her hair disheveled, cheeks blotchy from her earlier tears, and little creases in them where she's lain, sleeping against my shirt.

Although reluctant to leave her, I have no excuse to stay, so I drag myself away to bed, and between exhaustion and satisfaction, sleep finds me quickly.

"It's OK, Christian," Haley says as I reach to open the car door. "You won't need to come into the clinic. Would you believe she's up on her feet?" There's a mixture of weariness and elation in her voice.

Like me, she's exhausted. We met at the breakfast table way too early, both mumbling about our inability to sleep. As she gloomily munched toast, I reminded her, with guarded optimism, no news was good news. When the call came, seeing the glow of hope return to her face, like the first wash of a spotlight across a dark stage, I couldn't contain my happiness for her—and for that damn dog that's already gotten hold of my heart. I wrapped her tight in a spontaneous hug of celebration. She didn't object. It felt so fucking good.

It's great news I don't have to leave the car, not only for the dog. We were fortunate last night. The entire vet team fell outside the demographic for stupid reality shows and rock music. The woman at reception didn't show the slightest flicker of recognition at the name on the credit card. It's just as well, as these few days before the damning Episode 5 airs are crucial. Anyone suspects I'm not on that show before Wednesday night and the arsehole production company's lawyers are going to grind me into nothing.

So I'm happy not to take a risk with the day staff, letting Haley go inside alone to collect Tully, while Mularkey and I sit in the car park out front, trying to look inconspicuous. That's kind of difficult when it's Sunday afternoon and this bright yellow super car is the only one here. Anyone passing by is definitely going to take a second glance at the guy in cap and dark glasses inside it on a wet winter London day.

Not to mention the large wolf-like dog perched in the tiny backseat. I breathe the unavoidable smell of damp canine, one that triggers an avalanche of childhood memories; most good, a few sad, and I embrace the nostalgia of those days. With Mularkey silhouetted against the rear window, it looks like Batman is keeping watch over my shoulder. Somehow she suspects what I know—her best friend is going to appear from those sliding doors any moment now.

I'm grateful Haley takes my need to lie low seriously. It's heartening she's accepted my word that all this shit is important, trusting me even though I've given her so few details. Maybe she doesn't see me as such an arsehole after helping her with saving the dog. Where dogs are concerned, I'd have done something, anyway. I couldn't stand by and let an animal suffer. But when it's for *her* dog, fuck it, I'd have walked right in there myself without this subterfuge if that's what it took. I'd do anything for Haley Templeton, risk anything.

Behind me, Mularkey tenses and then disintegrates into a whole-body wag. She pokes her head alongside mine, leaning through the tiny open window, while with muzzle raised, she sings the song of her people into the chill air, welcoming her buddy. It echoes off the brick-walled buildings and a woman and kids walking by laugh and point. So much for lying low.

Haley and Tully walk slowly towards us, a pair of matching grins as wide as the sky and my mouth curves upwards in response. I feel like punching the air in celebration. We did it; victory over the evil bloat that tried to snatch this beautiful dog away and break Haley's heart. There's not a trace of the previous night's trauma on Tully's smiling face.

"Dogs are bloody amazing, aren't they?" I say, as she hauls herself into the back seat on her own, moving with surprising ease despite the stitches which lie hidden along her stomach, a large shaved strip on her side the only hint of their presence. If it was a human, they'd be in hospital for a week after going through something like that.

"For sure," Haley nods. "This one in particular. She's staunch. Even the vet can't believe how well she's come through. Although they would have kept her until tomorrow except for her having her own personal nurse on call."

Haley ruffles the back of Tully's neck, below where it peeks out of the large plastic cone.

"Tully won't love her nurse when she realises you're not going to take that off."

"No, the cone of shame stays till Friday," Haley laughs.

"My boy, Jet, had to have one once. He went around ramming everything with it—doorframes, walls, posts, even our legs. Then sat there sulking and giving me the stink eye." There's a twinge of pain at the memory of how he ended up in that state, but Haley pulls me back from it with a question.

"Your dog, Jet—what was he?"

"Border collie. Failed cattle dog. Scared of cows."

"Kind of a deal-breaker on a dairy farm, I suppose?"

"Yeah, he wasn't ours to begin with. Belonged to the farmer next door. Said he was going to put a bullet in him."

I still recall those chilling words. An idyllic summer afternoon playing with the neighbours' kids turned into a nightmare, but it was one I could do something about. Nestled high in a tree hut, I'd overheard the death sentence pronounced and tumbled down in a heap at the man's feet. I begged for that dog like I've never begged for anything before or since.

Then I had to do it over again when I took him home to face my father's sour summing up of the situation: the dog could stay, but there was no room for freeloaders on our property. Every cent of his food and care had to be paid for by extra work on the farm. It was worth every minute of those hated chores. The farm work took me away from the books and music that were my only love until Jet, but I willingly put more of them aside so he might have what he needed. And everything I gave to him, he gave it back in double with years of companionship to a lonely boy, the cuckoo in the nest of a traditional farming family.

"Oh my god, that's terrible." Her eyes are wide, mouth aghast. Like most kids raised in the city, Haley has no idea of the cold hard facts of rural life.

"Yeah, not an uncommon attitude," I say. "Can't save them all, but I saved him."

I still feel a surge of pride. Even as a scruffy eleven-year-old, I stood up for what was right; and now that sense of justice has got me in deep shit once again.

I sigh internally. Today I'm going to have to face it. No lounging around at Haley's, pretending it hasn't happened. Exactly what I'm going to do about it, I have no idea, especially as the one person who could possibly help me, my only ally on *Wild For The Win*, is stuck inside the prison camp up there in Scotland while I'm doing time in solitary down here in London.

Anyway, that will have to wait. It's time to get these three gorgeous girls home. With Tully installed in the rear seat, Mularkey perched beside her, tongue dangling loose and relaxed, and Haley beaming at the pair of them in the rear-view mirror, I fire up the car.

It's hard to drive this car conservatively when everything about it taunts me to plant my foot and set free the beast rumbling behind us. Stopped at a red light, I can't help but give the engine a blip.

"God, I love this car," I murmur.

"If you love it so much, why don't you just buy one?" Haley asks. "I mean, I can understand you not wanting the whole house in the country thing, like Ollie. Rural life's no novelty to you, I suppose. But a car..."

So here it is. My chance to tell her why I'm not rolling in cash. Why I can't afford to be sued by those pricks at the production company. Why I can't simply throw a hundred grand of my own at the dog charity and be done with it.

I'm not comfortable casting myself in the role of hero. However, languishing here as a villain in Haley Templeton's eyes is torture. The temptation is great. I take a deep breath and consider how I can explain this without revealing all the details. To do so might make me come across as a saint, and I'm definitely not that.

"Yeah, well, I do have a place in the country. Overspent on that, so no fancy cars for me."

"You do? Where? Why didn't you go there?"

Yeah, Haley might appreciate my help last night, but she's still keen to get rid of me. Damn it, I'm so fucking stupid to hope otherwise. My brain remains sluggish from lack of sleep and I'm not thinking. Her questions are completely logical, and it looks like there's no choice but to answer them. Damned if I do and damned if I don't. So I do.

"I can't go there. Because it's actually the family farm. Mum, Dad, my two brothers, their wives and kids—I guess you could say it's a bit crowded down there in Cheshire. No room for me."

"You bought your family's farm?" Her confused frown suggests more questions are on their way, so resisting the urge to drown them out with the roar of the powerful engine, I pull away from the green light driving like a nana, and begin.

"Yeah, it kind of became necessary."

I hesitate again. Apart from Ollie, who I asked to say nothing, Haley is the first person I've told this to. I should resent my father and brothers begrudging gratitude towards me for saving them from losing a hundred years of family tradition and their livelihood. I shouldn't care about exposing their ineptitude, but somehow, I'm reluctant to paint them as the useless bastards they are.

I'm not sure where this loyalty comes from. They haven't been exactly my biggest supporters over the years, but they did play the game back on that first opportunity, reluctantly but consistently showing up on set at *Star Power*. So I owe them something.

"Dad made a few bad decisions." Like twenty years' worth. "Production was tracking downwards, and he didn't seem to be able to turn it around." Because he's a stubborn old git who buries his head in the sand. "And my brothers tried a few suggestions, but nothing worked out." Spent thousands on a consultant and then thought they knew better and didn't take his expensive advice. "So, it was heading for a mortgagee sale. Before the bank could act, I bought it. Well, paid them enough to keep it in the family. And took on the ongoing payments to keep it there."

She's so quiet I can almost hear the cogs turning in her head over the purr of the engine idling as we pause at another set of lights. Haley is as smart as she is pretty; a thinker like her brother and I glance across to see ripples of thoughts glide across her face as she's processing what I've told her.

"Wow," she says. One word; and nothing more, as we weave through the build-up of Sunday afternoon tourist traffic along the last stretch of Bayswater Road.

CHAPTER 6

Day Two

THE MOMENT HALEY UNLOCKS the front door, the smell of the Christmas tree punches me in the nose. The normally pleasant fragrance of the forest is tainted for me now. What happened in those woods in the wilds of Scotland last week is going to haunt me—unless I do something about it.

The dogs bound back into the house, fizzing with joy at being home. They grab a large armchair each, and I flop back into what seems to have already become my seat on the couch with a huff of relief. Two days out of the hellhole and I've already broken the rules twice, as far as I know undetected. I hope the bastards haven't got me under surveillance. I wouldn't put it past them.

Without asking, Haley has correctly worked out I need coffee and one of those damn hard to resist Christmas mince pies. She returns from the kitchen with both, taking a seat on the couch that emphasises the gaping space between us. Fair enough.

By the hard light of day, with the dog out of danger, Haley is spelling out in no uncertain terms that last night's closeness was simply her need for comfort at a tough time. Much as I tried my best not to revel in it at the time, I can't help but be thankful for three hours spent on a hard bench in the clinic and my arse going numb. For a while, the world shifted. With her tucked in under my arm, it seemed a more hopeful place.

And I can still conjure up that moment in the early hours, sitting in this exact spot; the fragrance of exotic flowers lingering on her body, the soft satin sheen of her hair when I dared to brush my lips against it, our eyes meeting with shared intensity, our need to reassure each other that things would be OK.

If those two snippets of time are all I'm ever going to have of Haley, I'll live with it. It's better than the nothing I had before. But if there's one thing I've learned in the past day, I'm not happy with that situation. I want more. The flip side of this disaster means now I have eleven more days of opportunity to try and get it; as long as I take things quietly.

"Tell me," she says, with an inquiring tilt of her head. "About the farm." She bites at her lip, as if unsure the question is appropriate. "That's if you want to. If you don't, that's OK. But I'm curious."

I push past my awkwardness at talking about this. I won't say no to her.

"Well, it's an ongoing commitment, really. Getting the bank off their back was only the half of it. Like Ollie, I've invested in a vehicle." Laughter spills spontaneously from me at the ridiculousness of it, even though it should really make me angry. "Except mine's a big green tractor. Do you wanna see?"

I pick up my phone and locate a picture of Dad seated in the cab of the enormous John Deere on the day it was delivered. He wears the grin of a delighted kid with a new toy. My brothers stand alongside its knobbled tyres as tall as they are, dour faces frowning into the camera.

"Holy shit," she says. "Are you sure you couldn't have found something bigger?"

"Well, I did need to keep some money aside for a bit of bling."

I show her the pictures of shiny new stainless steel vats installed in the dairy.

"Impressive."

"Necessary," I reply.

"And it's going OK?"

"Yeah, great," I say, with more confidence than I feel. Me having to bail them out should have shamed the three of them to do better this time. I think Dad really is trying, but I worry my brothers' still might sabotage it—subconsciously perhaps—in response to the resentment they try to hide but still lurks near the surface. What guy wouldn't feel pissed about their useless little brother riding into town like a white knight to save the day?

"They're really lucky you could help. Lucky they've got a son who would go that far for them."

I say nothing. I can take praise for my music all day, lapping it up, but this simple compliment makes me draw inwards in discomfort. It's a natural impulse for me to reach for my guitar as a diversion. I strum a little of the first thing that comes unbidden to my fingers, losing myself in the rippling chords of 'Untouchable'.

The words play in my head, but I won't sing them, not here. That would be dangerous with the woman they're about sitting right next to me. Oh, I can do it on stage in front of thousands, no problem—and I always do, since Ollie knows this song is special to me, but not why. Although we've both got the voice to hold lead vocals, he's the natural showman, so I'm happy to defer to him—except for on this one.

"Beautiful guitar," she says.

"It is," I say. It's a Gibson acoustic, with sweet Sitka spruce on top. I love its sound, as warm and full-bodied as the mahogany that wraps around the back and sides.

"Guess you're not going to break that one?"

"Nope," I say. "Not unless the day comes when I need to put it out of its misery, like my old Fender." She frowns at me, brain whirring so hard I'm sure if I leaned in close I'd hear it. "The one I famously destroyed on stage? I guess that's what you were referring to?"

"But—"

"It was already broken, Haley. Some roadie dropped a fucking great speaker box on it. The boys thought it would be hilarious if I did the angry musician thing and smashed it on stage. So I did. At least I got something out of it. God knows I was seriously pissed about the situation. I loved that guitar."

"But it looked so real, like you hated the thing."

"Guess I did a good job then, huh?"

"And the papers. They quoted you on it. Claimed you said you and Teddy had a fight backstage, and you were still mad about it."

"Yeah, well, lots of things get printed that were never really said. Come on, you've met Teddy. Who would fight with Teddy?" Our drummer is as cuddly and inoffensive as his nickname. "Smoke and mirrors, Haley. Surely you know that? They don't want to hear I'm a nice guy. Makes much better headlines when they have shit to throw."

"Like with Kendra and Ollie," she says with a resigned sigh.

Poor Ollie. He's almost as mild-mannered as Teddy, a nice guy they can never seem to make anything stick to. But they showed no mercy when he started dating Kendra Cole. She's exactly the kind of girl they love to hate: the lead singer and only girl in her own band; she is too talented and too opinionated. Perfect fodder for their crap. In the end, that's what killed any chance they had of making a relationship work.

"Yep. And like me and Waverley." I'm not going to miss the opportunity to set Haley straight on this one. "I know you'll have heard *that* story."

She stares down at her hands, a flush rising all the way to the apples of her cheeks. If this means she believes I did even a fraction of the things they implied in that relationship, I'm definitely going to fill her in.

Heat rises in my own face but it's not embarrassment, it's a red hot flare of anger. To my shame, a tiny bit of it is directed at her, that she could believe that crap. Mostly it's my fury at those bastards who printed it—gossip magazines and tabloid papers greedy at the expense of people's lives. The frustration of how they steamrolled over our futile attempts to tell the truth is a lead weight in my stomach.

"God, Haley. Not you too. Surely, even though you don't know me very well, you know Ollie. And you know Ollie would never be friends with someone who would be abusive to their girlfriend? Right?"

I try to channel calm in my words, but inside I'm seething. Even now, more than a year on, the lies spun about me come back to slap me down. She nods, the colour on her face blooming right to the tips of those cute ears that hold back her swinging hair.

"If you don't believe me, you can ask her." I pull out my phone and scroll to a number. Waverley and I may not have been a long-term thing, but we will always be friends and I know she's got my back on this one. She hated every minute of that shit as much as me.

Haley scrunches her eyes and shakes her head, but I don't pull back, thrusting the phone at her.

"I'm so sorry, Christian."

Her voice is tiny. I'm a bastard doing this, and I drop the phone, as I'm flooded with immediate regret at my impulsive gesture.

"No, no, it's me who should be sorry." What the hell was I thinking? "It's just some days I feel like there's not a soul who cares about what really happened."

"I care," she says, with a small sniff that's like a knife twisting in my gut. "Tell me," she whispers. "I want to know."

And so I take a deep breath and let it all pour out. How I dated Waverley for a while back in high school, and then on one visit home, when I was sorting out the farm, we hooked up again for a bit. How she was never destined to be the love of my life, or me hers. And how, after agreeing we'd quietly go our separate ways, the media decided that was way too tame. And how the tiny insinuations I got rough with her—never enough that I could sue them, but always enough to cast shade—had devastated her as much as me.

When I'm finished, we sit in silence as I search Haley's face, desperate for a sign she accepts it's the truth. But there's the whine of a dog, and Haley's up on her feet. As she pads down the hallway to let Mularkey out to pee, she glances back at me. I feel like there's still a flicker of doubt in those velvet eyes, but I can see her inner struggle—she wants to believe me. And I'm going to prove she should.

CHAPTER 7

Day Two

Haley

I can't believe he's done it. The opening music for *Wild For The Win* taunts my ears as I follow the dogs back into the lounge.

"What's this?" I ask, even though I know exactly what it is. And even though I have every right to question Christian taking control of my television without asking, the words come out tiny; timid.

I'm still unbalanced from our conversation about Waverley. In my heart I knew it was the truth, but five minutes ago that little part of me that wanted to find fault with Christian not only seized control of my brain, it gleefully painted it all over my face as well.

I mean it's not like I dislike the guy—I don't know him well enough to have strong feelings either way—but even if I didn't like him, that's no reason to accept the lies I know dog his every step as they do Ollie's. And after all he's done for me in the past twenty-four hours, I owe him. So I'm going to cut him some slack, repay him some for my uncontrolled reaction, and let go of my annoyance at his TV takeover.

"Thought it might be best to just rip the band aid off," he says. "For both of us."

I sit myself at the opposite end of the couch. Hugging my favourite reindeer cushion to my chest, the joyful tinkling of the decorative sleigh bells is at odds with my dread as the opening images roll across the screen. Mouth set in a tense line, I fight back a retort.

"Look Haley, it's happened. I'm here, not there. There's no prize money coming the way of the rescue. We're both upset about it. But we can't change the past. Best we both face the situation, eh?"

"OK," I say, too weary to argue.

"Besides," he adds, "consider it an intel gathering exercise. If I'm going to fight them, and I fully intend to, I need to study every second of the crap they push out into the world. Maybe you can help me there?" There's a small pleading note in the question, and he tosses me a hopeful look.

"Sure." I'm not at all sure there's anything I can do to help extract him from this mess he's got into, but I nod obligingly. With his talk of contracts, and NDAs, and legal teams, I'm inclined to think it's a lost cause. Going into battle with a large media company with deep pockets is as useless as trying to bottle the wind. Pushing the boundaries with people like that is never going to end well.

But I've done enough damage for one day by not believing in him. I saw the flash of anger and hurt my doubt provoked in his eyes and shame still smoulders inside me. Right now, I'll shut up and offer some moral support by watching what I suspect will be a train wreck.

Instead, the hour-long Episode 2 of *Wild For The Win* fans that small ember of shame inside me into a brightly burning realisation. I've judged this guy unfairly. Faced with Christian's dumping from the show, I'd painted a dark picture of what happened in Scotland. And it's wrong.

For the first two days at least, he was the model contestant, his actions cutting a bright optimistic swathe through the gloomy spectre of seven other pissed-off and, quite frankly, pathetic contestants. This is a show about surviving in the wild. What the hell did they think they were signing up for—a week in Ibiza?

I watch him step up when the rest of them have no ideas but to wander around the tumbledown farmhouse, whingeing about their plight. I see his patience, herding them into teams, assigning tasks, taking on the trickier ones himself, even picking up a hammer so they all have a weathertight place to sleep the first night. I note his skill in the grimy kitchen, coaxing an old coal range into life and enlisting the best of the rest to help him cook a meal.

He correctly predicted the wife from Watford, Loreena Bunt, might have talents beyond artfully applying lashings of make-up, and enlisted her as head chef. I cringe at her fawning over him, her collagen pout and fake lashes punctuating a face that is no stranger to the Botox needle. It's also a face that must be known to everyone in the country, her smart mouth and argumentative antics drawing viewers to the *Real Wives* show like it's crack cocaine.

But there's no sign of her belligerence here. Maybe it's because she fancies her chances with Christian—she certainly looks at him like he's the main course, even though she must be almost twenty years his senior—but whatever the reason, she complies with his suggestions, proudly delivering dinner to the table with a saucy wink at the camera.

My initial assertion was correct: Christian was marked as the winner from the start. I take no pleasure in being right. It only makes me more sad. He was a lifeline for the dog rescue, the money a sure thing that slipped from his grasp.

Both the studio host, the so slick he's slimy Bernard Bennett, and on location host Lisa Mayberry, already rate him the frontrunner. Bernard's studio audience agrees. Episode 2 features the first end-of-episode poll. Eighty-seven percent of them furiously click their voting buttons in Christian's favour.

Christian says nothing as the closing credits roll; just puffs out a deep, resigned exhale. It must be hard watching the grudging respect of the other contestants, the adoration of the audience, the confidence of the show hosts, while knowing it all came to nothing. He senses my attention and turns to me, expectant. I look into the challenge of those stormy blue eyes and ask the obvious question.

"What happened, Christian? For you to go from that—to this?"

"Well, it started with me refusing to do a challenge."

I nod. I understand how the show works. After each episode, the audience votes for the contestant they think did the best on the challenge, and the points accumulate, although no one really knows until the final night who the winner will be. Clever editing keeps the viewer on the edge of their seat right until the end. However, there was no disguising the lack of support for anyone but Christian tonight. Surely, a missed challenge in Episode 5 wouldn't kill his chances, and opting out of a challenge would have only cost him points, not complete eviction.

"But there's more?"

"Yeah." He drags his hand down his beard, looking thoughtful, as if mulling over how much to reveal. "And then...I may have threatened the producer..." He grins. A little triumphant laugh escapes. "That got their attention. Bastards deserved it for the stuff they wanted us to do. For what the rest of them felt pressured into doing. I simply let them know my intentions to give a few interviews afterwards. Tell people my reasons for not doing the challenge. I can't change the things that happened this time, but I can make damn sure they don't happen again."

"What things?"

"I can't tell you."

"You don't trust me?"

"It's not that. I do trust you. I know you won't go around blabbing. But if it comes to court, Haley, you'd have no option but to tell them what you know. Or lie for me."

From his bitter laugh, I know he thinks that's ridiculous. What is more ridiculous is I'm already considering the possibility I might. Me, the good girl, the rule follower, the one who never steps out of line. Would I do it? Lie to help Christian? I think I really might and the prospect doesn't scare me.

"But I can still help, right?" Something has shifted between us over the last hour, as I've watched him show me the honest, well-intentioned man he is. There's another uncomfortable stab of shame as I acknowledge I was more ready to accept evidence of his basic goodness from watching a stupid TV show than I was from all he's done for me and Tully. I want to make it up to him. "Maybe not perjury..."

His deep laugh is music to my ears. "No, not that. Not yet," he chuckles. "You're off work tomorrow, right?"

"Yeah, on personal nursing duties for Tully. Not that I think I'll be too busy with those, looking at her now." Hearing her name, Tully grins across at us, her lips peeled back, showing all her wonky teeth. There's no sign of the seriously ill dog of last night.

I rang in earlier to let my boss know, so she could pull in one of the part-timers to cover. It's a godsend when you work in a place willing to accommodate the responsibilities of being a dog parent.

"What do you need me to do?"

"Go over to my apartment. It's not far, just over in Chelsea. I need my laptop. I have all the documents on it—contracts, the original NDA—pages of boring shit that I signed without reading. Megan was furious."

I can imagine. I've met the band's business manager, the ferocious Megan Lamont, and I've heard from Ollie how risk averse she is on their behalf—comments like 'I can't even take a piss without running it past Megan' spring to mind—which is great because I imagine they pay her a large sum to do exactly that. She will be the first to say 'I told you so' when she finds out about this disaster.

"Ouch," I wince. "That wouldn't have been pretty."

"No. I'm dreading her finding out about this." The sick look on his face matches what appears to be genuine fear in his eyes. "Anyway, I need that laptop. Start at the beginning and see if there are any loopholes in those contracts."

"Sure, I can do that. You're good for dog nurse duties?"

"Absolutely," he says, smiling across at Tully perched like a queen on her throne and Mularkey on the chair next door, her attentive lady-in-waiting, alert and attempting to anticipate her needs. "What better way to spend a couple of hours than hanging out with you, eh?"

The soft expression on Christian's face, as he watches my smiling girls wag their tails furiously under his gaze, melts my heart. His genuine love for the pair of them is written there, and it's not a look I've seen from any other guy I've introduced them to so far. Another reason I need to back off from the frosty way I've treated him. And also why tingling, butterfly-like sensations twirl inside of me.

"Looks like they're pretty happy about that suggestion."

He turns to me and stretches a hand across the gap I've placed between us. He rests it over mine, offering a gentle squeeze. Warmth floods through me, up my arm, and settles somewhere in my middle, flowing like honey around the fluttering there.

"Thanks Haley. I owe you."

"I think we're more than even Christian. Thank you," I say, smiling at Tully, who is trying to dislodge the evil cone by butting her head on the arm of her chair.

THE NEXT MORNING'S EARLY rain has disappeared and the clouds are bright silver, backlit by the sun, as I emerge from the dim underground station and stroll along the tree-lined street towards the waterfront. Christian may be cash-strapped now, but it seems, like Ollie, he made a smart investment when those early royalty cheques rolled in. Apartments in this neighbourhood don't come cheap. Ordinary people like me might sometimes live in posh places like this, but we'll never own one.

According to the map app on my phone, this is the building. I check the address in Christian's text, and yes, this is it. It felt weird giving him my number so he could send the details. How many girls would kill to have Christian Steele ask for their phone number? And, now the initial tension between us has eased, I feel an odd warmth at the sight of his name on the screen.

I tilt my head back, sweeping my eyes up the brick walls of the historic building. Perched on the very top is a modern cocoon of glass and steel. That's where I'm headed.

I'm searching for the apartment number on the panel, repeating the door code in my head—1208, 1208—when my phone howls. Luckily, there's no one close enough to hear and flash me one of the strange looks it always provokes. Recording sweet Mularkey's 'woo-woo' for my text alert was a gift from my more tech savvy sibling. Ollie's creative thinking lets me take her wherever I go.

Christian again. I tap the screen, and it bursts to life with a picture. It's a selfie; Christian, with perhaps the first real smile I've seen on his face in three days. He's flanked by two grinning dogs. It's as if the girls have taken all his worries and gulped them down, like the creature in a creepy old book of Scottish folktales Ollie had as a kid, a beast who will swallow your nightmares away.

The dogs' soothing presence has worked a miracle on this sad, brooding man, lighting him up in a way I've only ever seen when he's on stage. Or like when he picked up that guitar last night and strummed away, humming to himself with a sweet smile. Dogs will do that to you.

My own heart is lighter for seeing it. For, troublesome as Christian is, he's kind of growing on me. I see glimpses of the person whose friendship my brother treasures.

I look over my shoulder before punching in the code for the outer door that will let me into the foyer beyond. There's no one near, except a man across the road, leaning on the stone wall of the river embankment. He's wearing a scruffy looking leather bomber jacket, like he's escaped from one of Dad's favourite 80s TV cop shows. Is it my paranoia, or is that guy actually watching me? He meets my gaze casually and then looks away, as if it's nothing. It *is* nothing. I'm just on edge. All this talk of hiding out and sneaking around is getting to me.

I tap in the four numbers, a green light twinkles, and I'm in.

The gleaming copper doors of the elevator part with a hush and then whisper closed behind me. It glides smoothly to the top floor, opening to reveal a gleaming post-box-red floor to ceiling door. It's the entrance to the one apartment on this level, Christian's penthouse. I knock on the door out of polite habit, then, feeling stupid, pull the key from my pocket.

The door is heavy enough to protect a bank vault. I use one shoulder to pull it open, then, with both hands grasping the oversized chrome handle, close it behind me. When I turn back to the interior, I'm confronted by a vast space with soaring white walls. I crane my neck to see a pale timber ceiling hovering somewhere far above me. The side facing the river is all glass and I have the feeling I'm floating over the sluggish waters of the Thames.

To my right is a kitchen that looks like it's big enough to hold a party in. The wide concrete worktop is almost big enough to hold a party *on*. Ten people could dance up there and not topple off. There's not an appliance in sight. Everything is hidden behind banks of sleek white cabinetry.

The place is immaculate. Living with my brother, I suppose I'd expected untidiness: dirty dishes in the sink, pages of lyrics and music littering the huge dining table, and discarded clothes strewn on the wide leather sofas behind me.

In fact, everything about this expansive minimalist space is not what I'd imagined as Christian's choice. Not with his ruffled image, like he's just rolled in from an all-night drinking session in a club. There's certainly no hint of his farm boy past.

The only thing that prevents this room from looking like an advertisement for Marie Kondo is the shelves of books. They fill an entire wall, and I sigh in envy at the rows of spines: smooth leather with tiny-gold lettering, and shiny paperbacks with bold capitals. There's even one of those sliding ladders like in old libraries, but this one has an industrial look.

I could stand there all day and gaze in awe, but Christian suggested I get in and out quickly. I'm not sure that's solely to do with all this secrecy. Perhaps he doesn't want me poking through his things. Silly really. It's not like I'm some Christian-obsessed fan who's going to steal his underwear or enjoy a little self-pleasuring seated on his pillow. But I can't help myself. I want to see and know him more by checking out the place he calls home.

Behind the first door is a music room. Guitars, a piano, a drum kit even. There's a strange zig-zag instrument—perhaps a bizarre type of violin—and a saxophone, both on stands. Is there no instrument this guy can't play?

The second room houses a small office. I spot the laptop, and as instructed, grab it, along with cables, a fancy separate keyboard and a mouse. There's a case in the third drawer of the desk, exactly where he said it would be, and I zip everything neatly inside.

I should leave now. I have what I need. But I can't. My curiosity takes over.

Next door is a marbled bathroom all soft whites and greys with the largest shower I've ever seen. As I step through into the loo, more lights flicker on and the toilet lid raises itself. I sit on the seat feeling instant warmth even through my jeans and marvel at the view through the floor-to-ceiling window, sweeping across the river below.

Two more bedrooms come off the hallway and at the far end, I step through into the final room. It has to be his. Although the aesthetic is the same, all white cavernous space, and pale Scandi style furniture, Christian's imprint is here.

On the nightstand beside the bed, there's a small framed montage of photographs. In one, a black and white border collie swims in a stream, mouth wide, barking. In a second, the same dog is clasped in the arms of a boy with untidy dark hair, both of them laughing into the camera. The final photograph shows the dog poised on the top of a hill, eyes bright in anticipation as if waiting for the humans to catch up. And I see Christian's dog, Jet, was a tripod, posing comfortably on only three legs.

Facing the river, there's a complete wall of glass. On the opposite one, a bright abstract watercolour dominates, again not at all what I'd expect, and this choice tells me a little more about Christian. Above the bed, there's something else, in a pale timber frame. I sit on the sage green bed cover, peering at what's captured inside: a ragged page torn out of one of those spiral bound notebooks. It's filled with scrawled words in black ballpoint that, in places, have broken free from the confines of the blue lines. There's strident crossing out here and there, with emphatic new words written above, the pressure of the nib visible in the dented paper. And at the top, underlined with a slash of black, one word: 'Untouchable'.

I know this song was the band's first hit and I know only Christian sings it. I suppose you never forget your first. He's made sure of that.

The intimacy of his inner self revealed by these framed lyrics makes me feel I've overstepped the line here, gone into places he doesn't let people see without invitation. I smooth the ripple in the bedcover, eliminating all evidence of my intrusion and leave.

I step out into the watery sun, pulling the door closed behind me with a click and the whirr of a locking mechanism. And come face to face with Mr Bomber Jacket.

"Is he up there?" he asks, with a lift of his square chin, casting his narrowed eyes at the penthouse.

"Who?" I ask, as the hairs on my wrists rise, and it's not from the cold.

"Mr Steele. I saw you up there." He jerks his head towards the glass wall of the rooftop apartment, the spot where I stood admiring the view only minutes ago. "Is he there?"

I hesitate, unsure which is the right answer. If I say no, then he'll ask if I know where Christian is. If I say yes, he might leave me alone. I go for the truth.

"No," I blurt, scrambling for a way to avoid more questions. "Look, I'm just the cleaner," I splutter out. Under pressure, it's the best I can come up with. "I don't know where he is. I just clean and leave."

"Pretty fast clean there, luv," he says, lips curling in a crooked smirk.

My brain frantically searches for an explanation. "I forgot something. Had to come back." I tap the laptop bag slung over my shoulder.

"Didn't know cleaning had got so hi tech."

"I'm a student. Doing cleaning to pay my way," I say, sliding the bag so it's now clutched against my chest, arms crossed protectively around it. I wouldn't put it past him to make a lunge for it. "Left my laptop behind yesterday."

I don't know why I'm still standing here, answering his questions, and spinning him a story. I guess it's the authority in his voice. He not only dresses like an old time copper, he talks like one. I'm hoping, even if he's not a cop, if I offer him a legitimate-sounding story, he'll leave me alone. His disbelieving shrug, as he turns his back on me and strolls off towards the river, sends a surge of annoyance.

"Not that it's any of your business," I call after him, but if he heard it, he ignores me.

Trying to look more confident than I feel, I head in the opposite direction along the embankment. I want to look back to see if he's following, but I don't. Worried he might be, I take a convoluted path back to the tube station. This guy is looking for Christian and there's no way I'm letting him use me to find him.

I deliberately let the most direct train home pull away from the platform without me. Instead, I catch another, and another, jumping across different train lines, always keeping a discreet eye on my fellow passengers. However, I don't see the man again. I think I'm safe. It's surprising how sneaking around like this comes so naturally. Maybe I could have an alternative career at MI5.

I hear it the moment I walk through the door of my house. There's yelling and the dogs are yelping excitedly at the door to Christian's room. They race towards me, barking, and sliding to a halt with a clatter of claws on the wooden floor. But before I've had a chance to greet them, they're off again. They sit at the closed bedroom door like they've trapped one of those pesky squirrels in the tree out back, tails thumping and letting out little yips.

What the hell is going on? Is Christian playing some game with them? Then there's a bellow from behind the door that tells me this is no game.

"Get. The. Fuck. Off. Me." There's a thump and an audible 'oof'. "Fuck! That hurts. For chrissakes," he yells, "you don't have to do that. Don't you know who I am?"

CHAPTER 9

Day Three

Christian

I AM PINNED TO the bedroom floor, my cheek pressed flat against the hard surface, unable to raise my head, because a small hand is exerting incredible pressure on it. One of my arms is bent painfully up my back.

And a tiny woman, even more slight than Haley, is sitting on top of me. Growling. That's the only word for the guttural noise coming from her throat. It's audible even above the yelping dogs who are going nuts out in the hallway.

The door flies open and the dogs spill in, leaping over me in delight as if this woman has laid me out on the floor purely for their entertainment. Out of one eye, I look up to see Haley standing there, hands on hips.

"Sam," she barks, wide eyes fixed on the crazy woman. "It's OK. I know him. He's staying here."

The woman's grip on my arm loosens a little and I groan at the release of the pain.

"Really?" she says. "You didn't say?"

"No," Haley sighs. "I didn't. Look, it's a long story, but—"

"But it's one that can wait till this mad cow gets off me," I say.

The cow in question shoves my arm upwards again, and I wince.

"Sam." Haley's patient voice is like a mother trying to calm a toddler tantrum. It's easy for her to be patient; she's not the one who's being assaulted. "This is Christian. You know, *Christian Steele*. From the band." I hear a small huff of annoyance from above as Haley pleads with this wild creature who's hurting me to do as she asks. "Please, let him up and I will explain."

The woman mutters to herself, as if reluctant to free me, but does as requested. She releases my arm and clambers to her feet. Even though she's small, it's a relief to get her weight off my back. I crane my head upwards and glare at her. She meets my eyes with an unapologetic glower.

I roll over and sit up, drawing my knees towards my chest and resting my forehead between them for a bit. I'm still dazed from when my head whacked the floor as I went down. Not to mention the shock of being wrestled to the ground by some five-foot-nothing girl in navy scrubs. There's a damn big dent to my ego bigger than the one in my head.

"Sam," Haley says, in that same smooth tone, "how about you go make some coffee? And maybe take the dogs?"

Tully and Mularkey are still dancing around us, the only ones enjoying this damn situation.

"Come on girls," Sam calls and they follow her out the door. Haley closes it behind them. Now it's safe, I rise to my feet and stagger to the bed.

"What the fuck, Haley? Who *is* that?"

"Shh, Christian," she hushes. "Look, it's a long story."

"OK, I'm listening," I grumble.

She sits beside me and continues in that toddler-soothing voice.

"Well, that's Samantha. My friend. She's a nurse."

"Better get her back in here, then, to fix the damage she's done." I rub at my shoulder, where jabbing pain like I've touched a mains-powered electric fence still shoots all the way up from my elbow. "Why the hell did she grab me like that? And why doesn't she know who I am?"

I'm not vain about my fame, and sure, guitarists don't get their face splattered around like lead singers, but surely most people of a certain age in this country would recognise me.

"Look, Sam's not really into popular music. Apart from knowing it's Ollies band, she hasn't a clue about Stellar Riot. And she's one of those rare people who has no interest in social media."

"Well, can't fault her for that," I say. I've never hidden my loathing for all that shit. "But really, to just launch in and attack me..."

Haley sighs impatiently and carries on in a low voice.

"About three years ago, late one night when she was coming off shift, Sam was attacked in the hospital car park. It was awful. She was lucky—some people came along and the guy took off. Cops got him later. She wasn't badly hurt, but it still really messed her up."

"Shit, that's terrible."

OK, maybe I'm feeling a tiny bit sorry for this girl, Sam—even if my head still throbs, and the tendons in my arm are so stretched I doubt I could even hold my guitar.

"And as part of moving on from that, she took up martial arts—Krav Maga. She's been doing it for a while."

"Well, she's really good at it. Black belt, I suppose?"

I rub at my temple where I can feel a lump. My fingers graze over my brow. Can you break your eyebrow? There's bone there and sharp pain.

"They don't have belts."

"Well, if they did, hers would definitely be black. She's a fucking master."

"Thanks," a shy voice says, as the door swings wide.

The tiny nurse stands in the doorway. She's clutching something wrapped in a cloth. Her face wears a benign expression that's hard to reconcile with the ferocity I've seen she's capable of.

"Let's get some ice on that."

No one would believe this is the banshee who, with one flick of the slender arm now presenting what looks like a bag of frozen peas tied up in a tea towel, had me down and begging for mercy. Her voice is efficient but kind. Even so, I draw back, wary, but she's not deterred, and presses the freezing parcel against my head.

"Hold it there with your good arm."

She guides my left hand upwards and I cup the makeshift ice pack tight. It's painful yet immediately brings some relief to the throbbing. Then, with a delicacy I'd not have expected, Sam unbuttons my shirt and slides my right arm free. I see her eyes flicker over my tattoos as her fingers probe gently.

"Does that hurt?"

"A little." Under her touch, my muscles relax and my tendons no longer scream at me so loudly.

"Haley, do you have anything we can rub into this? You know, a muscle cream, sports liniment or something?"

"I doubt it." Haley laughs. "We're not exactly the sporty types around here. But I'll check the bathroom. You never know."

I'm not hopeful. My friend Ollie is a notorious slug when it comes to deliberate exercise. Lean and wiry, he's one of those people who looks like he's super fit, when actually his morning workout is simply getting upright. When you see him on stage, where he brings a huge energy, you'd swear he'd be the sort of guy who runs a marathon before breakfast. Not him—that's me. Growing up on the farm, I crave early rising and time in the outdoors. Pounding the streets each morning keeps me sane. The lack of this outlet is yet another reason I'm struggling after being a caged animal for days.

Haley returns a minute later with a plastic tube.

"Well, guess Ollie had this from when he was training for that charity run."

I remember it well. The lazy bastard moaned for weeks in the lead up. Even though it was only a pathetic little 10k, he'd had to run each day to avoid total embarrassment, hated every moment and didn't hesitate to let us all know.

Sam grabs the tube and squirts a large blob of the gel onto her hand. It smells like a locker room, searing my nose hairs. With well-practised strokes, she works it into my arm. It's both fiery hot and icy cold at the same time. I close my eyes, succumbing to the soothing pressure of small fingers. By the time she's done, it feels much better. Not good, but better.

"OK, I'll finish those coffees," she says, manoeuvring my shirt back up over my shoulder.

She scurries from the room. I suspect with the job completed, she's dropped out of nurse mode and shame at the damage she's wrought on an innocent man is rearing its head. As it should.

I look down at my shirt still hanging loose, my chest and stomach exposed, and try to fumble at the buttons with my good arm. Seeing I'm losing the battle, Haley steps in front of me.

"Here," she says, a tentative hand reaching for the flapping shirt front, her eyes not meeting mine. I'm sitting on the bed, legs spread wide, and she's standing between them. My cock twitches, sensing her nearness. God, I'd love to pull her in close and crush her tight against me.

I tense under the brush of a dainty finger tracing my collarbone as she tugs the two pieces of fabric, fastening the top button. She's taking it slowly. I'm sure it's because she's trying to avoid touching my skin as much as possible. But it's merely having the effect of pro-longing the process, and I'm not complaining. It's like the delicious intimacy of slow undressing in reverse and I tingle all over.

The shirt is spread wider the lower she gets, and I shudder a little at the delicate fingertips which graze the skin at my waist as she draws the two sides together. Her eyes are on the job and feeling her focus on my body sends a surge of heat through me.

The final button doesn't want to go, and the sensation of her hands working at it just above my navel has the hairs on my body standing to attention, not to mention what's beneath. There's nothing I can do to cover the fact she's totally turning me on. I should be worried about this, but whether it's the smack to the head, or the haze of pain in my arm, I'm beyond caring.

If Haley notices my hard-on, she gives no indication. Maybe shyness prevents her gaze from roving that low. I can't meet her eyes to check.

"There, all done," she says. There's a bloom of colour in her face as she steps back, as if she's as acutely aware of the arc of energy between us. Mine is blatant attraction. And hers?

I feel the absence of her from my space with a jolt of loss. I already miss her closeness, the caress of her hands, even though it wasn't a touch of affection—or was it? It felt good to have her attend to my needs.

My other need is making its presence felt, uncomfortable in my jeans. I rise to my feet with the shirt buttoned, but hanging all loose. I'd love nothing better than to ask her to tuck it in for me. I imagine that little hand forcing itself into the waistband, the curve of it thrusting over my arse, or pushing down over my hip bones at the front. But the length of the shirt conveniently covers the even larger bulge in my pants produced by these thoughts.

No matter anyway, she's already heading for the door.

"Let's get that coffee," she says.

The dogs, who've been sitting observing us with curiosity, bound out ahead of her, as if the invitation is for them.

CHAPTER 10

Day Three

I spot my laptop bag dumped on the hallway floor. Discarded in her haste to see the circus going on in the bedroom, Haley hasn't mentioned the success of her mission. I scoop it up with my working arm and head for the dining room. It's a challenge to haul it onto the table, unzip the case and flip the laptop open. Operating with one arm is already sending my frustration levels through the roof. I glare in annoyance at Sam's back.

Stationed at the coffee machine in the kitchen opposite, she's deep in hushed conversation with Haley standing next to her. I hear my name a couple of times, and I assume Haley is filling her in on the saga of me being here. I hope Sam's as good at keeping her mouth shut as she is at slamming people to the ground.

I try to focus on getting this computer running. The sooner I can find those documents, the sooner I can begin on a plan. I hit the power button. It's dead. I scan the room and spot a power outlet next to a sideboard behind me. I'm crouched down, fumbling to plug in the power cable, when I hear my name once more. This time I pay attention.

"Very easy on the eye," Sam says, voice still low.

"Yeah, well, no surprise you're only noticing now when you're no longer trying to beat the shit out of him."

"Just because he's gorgeous doesn't mean he's harmless. Bad guys still come in pretty packaging."

"Not this one. The inside matches the wrapping."

"You like him."

The teasing whisper sends a little thrill of anticipation. Haley's delay in answering kills me. I dare to sneak a look as I slide back into a chair. She's turned to lean against the counter, facing me, but head still tilted towards Sam. Her face is alight, and she's nodding at her friend, her mouth turned up in a small grin.

"I knew it," Sam hisses.

"Let's say he grows on you."

"Oh god, a man with a body like that—now that I know he's harmless of course—I'd let him grow all over me. And me on him. Climb him like ivy."

"Sam. Shhh. He'll hear you."

I stare extra hard at my laptop screen, forcing a frown of concentration, but inside I'm bursting. Three years. Three whole fucking years. That, and this ridiculous situation with the TV series, is what it's taken for Haley Templeton to notice me as more than her brother's friend. But that thought brings forward the looming presence of Ollie and his inevitable disapproval, tarnishing the moment. I push him away, weighing the possibility of stealing another glance at Haley.

I'm dying to see what she thinks of Sam's suggestion. God knows if she let me tangle myself around those slender limbs, fit the smooth curves of her body against mine, I'd hold on so tight I'd never let her go; except perhaps until her brother found out.

Although, to look her way is risky. I don't think I'd see Haley with an expression of disgust at the thought, but I'm still unsure. And if she sees me watching her while she thinks those sorts of thoughts—her knowing that I know—it could be too much, too soon, and blow it.

There's a soft giggle, and her words are low and husky. Sam responds with a dirty little laugh and I feel their eyes swivel towards me.

I keep mine fixed on the screen and put on a mask of intense concentration, while inside I'm silently cheering. I can't decipher what was said, but Haley's tone suggests there's hope where previously I had none. My fingers fly across the keys, the only outlet for this surge of optimism, as possibility dances before me. This day suddenly got a whole lot better.

There's a thump of a coffee mug on the table, black and strong exactly how I like it. I look up into those eyes, pupils wide, the colour of the dark liquid in the cup. Rimmed with green and delicate flecks of gold, Haley's gaze is hypnotic. She slides into the chair opposite me and I see the trace of something in her face, as if the residue of her awareness of me as more than an annoying burden still lingers.

"Thank you," I say, as I grasp the solid mug. "Not just for this, but for getting the computer."

"It's not a problem," she says, then takes a sip of her coffee, licking a slight wisp of pumpkin-spiced foam from those peachy lips. God, I'd love to lean in and taste it for myself. "Whatever you need, I'm your girl."

I swallow hard. There are a lot of things I need, and to be able to call Haley 'my girl', well, that would be like winning a Grammy. I'm sure there's elation written all over my face, no matter how much I try to hold it back. But I'm saved by a distraction. Sam arrives, coffee in hand and a plate in the other.

"Here." She shoves the plate towards me. "A peace offering." Three curved squares of pastry dusted with icing sugar sit there.

"Beignets," Haley says. "Have you tried them?"

I nod, thinking of a trip to New Orleans, and two hungover guys, me and Ollie, in the French Quarter seeking food, any food to ease a queasy stomach after a big night on Bourbon Street. In the absence of our usual antidote, a greasy British fry up, a couple of these had done the job.

"Best in London," Sam says. "And fortunately for you, sold in boxes of three. Haley and I usually split the last one."

"Generous of you, then." I reach for one. "Probably me who should be buying to celebrate Haley's successful mission."

"About that," Haley says. "There was a man."

I stop chewing and mumble between flakes of pastry.

"A man? At the apartment?"

"Outside," she says. "I'm sure he was watching when I arrived. Over by the river. Then when I came out the door onto the street, he was right there."

My first thought is he's press, but it seems unlikely, with film of me in Scotland still rolling across the TV screen every night.

"What did he look like? Did he have a camera?"

She shakes her head. "I'm fairly sure he wasn't a journo. He just didn't have that sort of look about him. Older guy, jeans and a leather jacket."

I almost wish he had been a photographer, not some random guy staking out my place. My neighbourhood is pretty safe, but dodgy stuff can happen anywhere. There's a sick whirl in my stomach.

"And did he say anything? Do anything?"

"Yeah, he asked if you were up there. I told him no. Said I was the cleaner, come back to get something I'd left behind. He didn't believe me."

I'm freaking out. I have no idea who this guy is, but he wants me. What if he'd hurt her? The thought I may have put her in harm's way wrecks me.

"He didn't touch you, though? Follow you?"

She breaks into a little grin.

"No, I made sure he couldn't. You'd have been proud of me. Took the long way home. He's no match for me."

"God, Haley, I'm really sorry," I say. "If I'd have thought..."

"Don't be silly," she interrupts. "I was a bit rattled at first. It felt weird, this sneaking around. Once I was on the train, I realised it's OK. He wasn't interested in me. Only you."

"But he might have thought you'd lead him to me."

"Yeah, well, that may be true. But I made sure that didn't happen." Her face dimples in a smug smile. "You should have seen me duck and dive in and out of streets and trains. I didn't know I could be so sneaky." She studies my face, the fact I'm not convinced written there for her to see. "Christian, it's OK. I wasn't in any danger."

I'm not sure I believe that, but smart girl she is, she avoided the possibility of him tracking her.

"If you need Haley to do anything else, I'll go with her," Sam volunteers enthusiastically. "She's safe with me."

"Yeah, I absolutely believe that," I say. I can't help but crack a smile at this crazy woman's offer, even though my head still throbs and I'm not sure she hasn't fucked up my right arm permanently; although she assured me it will be fine in a day or so. "But I think I've got all I need here."

Inside, the bright blue folders in orderly rows on the screen are copies of the documents I signed. My last hope is there's some tiny loophole I can wriggle through. Some obscure clause that allows me to spill all on what's happened. However, the production company is large and experienced in this game, and so my hope is like a tiny fish gasping for air in the polluted ocean of shit suffocating me.

"God, I've got to go," the ninja nurse says, looking at her watch while stuffing almost the whole of a beignet in her mouth. She gulps a mouthful of the coffee and gathers a tote bag from the floor. It's huge and I'm glad she dropped it on her way to investigate my bedroom, otherwise I'd have probably worn a blow from that to my skull as well.

"Might catch you tomorrow, Hales," she says. "My first day off in a week."

"I'll be back at work," Haley says. "That's if Christian will watch Tully for me." She glances over at me under those thick lashes. "Work will give me as many days as I need, but with the current situation, I'd rather not risk it. You know, if they have to decide who keeps their job and who doesn't..."

Guilt nips at me, knowing I threw away the chance to keep the job she loves safe.

"You got it," I say. "Anything for my girl Tully."

I rub the head of the grinning dog. They're both camped at the table, no doubt hoping for beignet crumbs. *Anything for my girl Haley.* That's what I'd like to say, but it's too soon to even think of going there.

After Sam leaves, the house descends into a scene of peaceful domestic bliss. Haley folds onto the couch in the room next door with a book. How she can read with a giant flashing snowman in a Christmas hat on the table beside her is beyond me. I adore this girl, so I suppose I'll have to get used to her obsession with the season of the year I hate.

For me, it just brings back unpleasant memories; my family, all trapped in the house together, with Mum tiptoeing around Dad's grumpy mood. Him resentful at her insistence he not work on the farm for this one day of the year; and my brothers quietly siding with him, while happily stuffing their faces with the food she'd spent days preparing. Perhaps, in this time here with Haley, I might see another side of Christmas. Maybe, for her, I could even learn to like it a little.

Mularkey snores comfortably at Haley's feet. Perched on the armchair, Tully swivels her head framed in its huge cone, like Queen Elizabeth the First surveying courtiers gathered in her chambers. Eventually, accepting neither of us will free her from the confines of the plastic ruff at her neck, she collapses with a resigned canine sigh and is soon snoring, too.

I settle back in the dining room, burying my brain in numbing legal jargon, searching for something, anything, as a way out of my dilemma, staring at the screen until my eyes hurt. Two hours flick by before I give up. I'm not an unintelligent guy, but I need help.

I stand and stretch my body tall and wide, then lean through the lounge room door. Haley raises her head with a smile. It's a small smile, but my brain, desperate for any sign that her feelings towards me have possibilities, magnifies it so it's like I'm basking in the heat of a high wattage spotlight.

"Don't happen to know any lawyers, do you?" I ask. The record company could produce one in an instant, but I want to keep a clear line between them and this disaster.

"I do, actually," she says. "My friend Rachel is an absolutely kick-butt corporate lawyer."

"You have some pretty impressive friends there."

"Yeah," she says, a little wistfully. "I'm the slouch of the group, no doubt about that."

"Don't say that. You're no slouch. Just because you don't go around literally or metaphorically kicking arse, doesn't mean what you do isn't important."

"It's OK," she says. "To tell it like it is. I'm perfectly fine with it. Growing up with Ollie the musical wunderkind as your brother, you learn to accept being ordinary."

I'm speechless. The words I'd like to say—that she's not ordinary, that there is some indefinable quality about Haley that makes her the most extraordinary girl I've ever met—stick in my throat.

I'm torn. I'd love nothing more than to dispel this lie she's told herself by holding up a mirror to show her how I see her. But if I do, I risk her glimpsing what lies beyond that; realising how obsessed I am with her. How I've always been obsessed, ever since seeing her unassuming goodness, her gentleness, her kindness; and that might frighten her off.

I'm saved from the decision.

"She's on her way back from Scotland today. I'll call her after dinner," Haley says, heading for the kitchen. "Do you like lasagne?"

CHAPTER 11

Day Three

CHRISTIAN'S FACE IS EXPRESSIONLESS as the third episode of *Wild for the Win* blares into life on the TV screen. That's no surprise—he's seen all of this before. Although from what I've heard, the edited versions of these so-called 'reality' shows bear little resemblance to the reality of those living them.

I hadn't realised how annoying the theme tune is. It's deliberate, of course; they want to etch it into your brain, triggering an automatic response every time the endless trailers air, stimulating anticipation of what's to come in each new episode.

Tonight, dinner finished in plenty of time, we're tuning in to see how the eight contestants are paired. It's a thing on this show; in the first six episodes, the celebrities are forced to work with someone they're actually competing against, adding a layer of tension as they strive to achieve common goals, while keeping their eye on an individual win at the end. There have been some explosive pairings over the years.

"And tonight…" Host Bernard Bennett gazes skyward, with a dramatic pause. "Tonight we get to see fate play its hand, watch how the dice roll, observe lady luck cast her favour, check how the cards fall…"

"Bloody hell," I snort. "How many different ways can he say it?"

"As many as he likes, but it doesn't change a thing. There's no luck involved, believe me," Christian says. "They know well in advance who they'll put together. They make very sure there will be maximum fireworks. Well, usually." A small satisfied smile twitches around his mouth.

Lisa Mayberry fixes her co-host with a glare and interrupts his meandering.

"So, Bernard, how about we get started?" she gushes through pouty, pink collagen lips. "And first up, come on over, Christian Steele."

Sitting in a chair opposite him, I shuffle in my seat, self-conscious at the pressure of his gaze upon me. He's watching me, watching him.

I see Christian make his way on camera, taking a seat on a rumpty sofa in the lounge of the farmhouse. His rock star swagger is there, but his face is all angular tension. I don't blame him. Anyone would be nervous knowing they are about to be forced into spending several days in the company of someone they probably hated on sight.

"Well, well," Lisa croons. "I bet there are some ladies out back right now who'll be hoping their name comes up." She places an arm around his shoulders. "Especially with those overnighters. Cosied up in a tent with Christian. What do we think of that, people?" She gives a wink as the studio audience back in London laughs and applauds. "I'm sure Christian has made a little list of prospects…"

"You think so?" Christian replies, the sarcasm lost on the vapid presenter. I'm pleased he's giving them a hard time.

Lisa is either too dedicated to the script or too stupid to notice, and carries on, oblivious.

"Well, let's check *my* list, because that's the only one that matters."

An irritating burst of her childish, wide-eyed laughter topples out. She pauses theatrically, looking down at her clipboard. She licks at her lips, tilts her head towards Christian with a flirty smile as if *she's* vying for the place on his team, and takes a deep dramatic breath.

"There's a spot here on the couch with your name on it—*Loreena Bunt.*"

"Holy shit," I say. I can't suppress the shock of what I've just seen from spilling onto my face and coating my words.

It's not only the announcement that floors me. Christian on the screen smiles, a mirror of the man next to me whose face is lit up with a triumphant grin.

"And there," he says, "is where they made their first mistake."

Loreena explodes onto the stage in a froth of pink, the fake fur jacket, so inappropriate for the setting, but perfectly matching the thick coat of iridescent lipstick smothering her wide mouth. She bounces onto the couch with delighted shrieks, grasping Christian's head, and planting an exuberant kiss on his cheek.

"Oh my god, Christian. Loreena Bunt?"

"There you go again, Haley." His voice is quiet. "Believing every-thing you see on TV."

Chastened, I lean back, reassembling my features and herding my words. I pick up the snow globe on the side table and twirl it in my hands, my thoughts as chaotic as the flurry of tiny flakes inside.

"It's just so—unexpected."

Christian chuckles, a fond smile softening his face.

"Everything about Loreena is unexpected. I swear, if you met her, you'd like her. She's smart and funny—and sure, there's a touch of that OTT screen Loreena there—but she's not the crazy bitch they want her to be. She's a very good actor, and it's made her a lot of money."

"OK," I say. "So you and her didn't..."

I stutter into silence, embarrassed the thoughts in my head have spilled out of my mouth. To my horror, I realise there's even a twinge of jealousy at the prospect Christian and Loreena might have hooked up. Where the hell did that come from? I push it away fast.

He laughs. "Fuck no. God, even if she'd suggested it, I'd have run a mile."

"Not your type?" I tease, trying to cover my stumble.

"Well, there is the fact she's almost old enough to be my mother, even though she's in good shape. And you're right, there's way too much make-up and cosmetic surgery there for my tastes. I prefer women who don't buy into all that shit."

I feel his eyes roving over my untidy hair, and brush it back, conscious of my face naked of anything except a sweep of BB cream this morning and probably now long gone. I see his approval. I'm not imagining it. When Christian looks at me, he likes what he sees. It could merely be I don't trigger his aversion to women who need to hide behind a mask. Or it might be a sign of something else. And if it is something else—that he finds me attractive—I'm not at all sure how I feel about that.

A dangerous thrill shivers through me, suggesting parts of me like that idea very much, while my cautious brain screams at me to stop it. This guy is not right for me for so many reasons. Hell, I've only just got to the stage of accepting he's not the arsehole the media portrays. But underneath, my body is waking up to the animal attraction that draws women to Christian even though they don't know him. My mind tells me if they did get to know him, like I've been doing these past few days, it would only add to their desire. I struggle back to the safety of the topic at hand.

"Yeah, but..." I feel a strange need to defend Loreena. "It's easier when you're young. While I don't think I'd go there, I can see why some women feel they need a bit of extra help as they get older. Every woman wants to feel attractive."

"I suppose so," he concedes. He nods at the screen where an animated Loreena, an arm draped across his shoulders, burbles at the camera. "And in Loreena's case, while it definitely doesn't do it for me, it works for the person that matters most. Apparently, her husband, Tommy, adores her."

He's right. I cast my mind back to the *Real Wives of Watford* series, remembering the occasional appearance of the husbands. There was no disguising the jealousy from the other wives at Loreena's blissful marriage. Tommy Bunt, a rough around the edges rather cocky little man, as well as self-made multi-millionaire from an automotive parts business, made no secret of the fact he loved his wife. I nod in agreement, but say nothing, not sure whether I want to advertise my obsession with *Real Wives* given Christian's current feelings towards reality TV.

We sit through the rest of the reveals which take up most of the episode. There's a short challenge tonight. A bit like on *Masterchef,* they're given a mystery box of bizarre ingredients from which they have to create dinner.

Loreena takes charge and I'm impressed by her ability to organise and innovate. She boils up two gnarly turnips, and mashes them furiously, while directing Christian. He dices the onion, wiping away tears, fries it with the canned sardines and tosses in some chopped herbs. Mixed altogether, shaped into fishcakes, and browned in the pan, they don't look too bad. Even Lisa Mayberry braves a tentative nibble and declares them edible. Christian and Loreena win, of course.

"You've been holding out on me, Steele," I say. "You never told me you can cook. I'm putting you on dinner duty from now on."

"Happy to," he says. "Especially as you'll be back at work tomorrow." He tickles Tully's head. Showing no trace of the dog who has recently survived emergency surgery, she raced Mularkey to the couch earlier, claiming the spot next to Christian. "I can look after this one. You'll be a good girl, won't you Tully?" She answers with a rhythmic thud of her heavy tail and a long high-pitched fart like a train whistle.

"Awww, fuck Tully." Christian grimaces as a foul odour wafts up, fanned by her tail, so even from my seat in the armchair, I catch a whiff. "That's a ripper." He chokes theatrically. "Glad you're not sleeping in my bed tonight, baby."

"Sorry," I say, heat rising in my cheeks. Damn dog has no manners. "Put her down on the floor if you want."

"Hell, no." He affectionately scratches her neck around the edge of the cone. "I've missed having a dog. Even though they do come with farts. Tully stays."

We turn back to the final minutes of the show, and the crucial voting phase. Whatever the crowd might feel about Loreena, at the end of the episode, the votes are overwhelmingly in their favour. Whether it's the halo effect of teaming up with Christian, or the fact the audience sees what he does—and now he's pointed it out, I too realise Loreena isn't so bad—most buttons click for 'Team Christeena'. Trust Bernard Bennett to coin a nauseating couple's name for them.

Loreena is certainly a better partner for him than the other three airhead women in the group; and it's not only because they're young and pretty, or because I may just happen to feel a sense of relief that it's not them sharing a tent with Christian over the next two nights on the show. Loreena is smart, and as I know Christian has no chance of winning, I hope she does.

"If it's OK with you," Christian says, stretching as a yawn steals across his face, "I might take a book and go to bed. I'm knackered. God, I must be getting old. Once, a couple of all-nighters wouldn't have even made me break stride."

I laugh. "It's nothing to do with age. We've both had a pretty shitty few days. Stress is exhausting. I think I might do the same. Work tomorrow, so I'll need to be up early."

He stands and the dogs slither off the couch and twine themselves around his legs so he can hardly move, upturned faces questioning.

"Hey, since you need to get up early and I don't, why don't I take these two into my room tonight?" he says, as Mularkey mouths his tattooed wrist playfully. It looks like she's trying to gulp down the tiny swallow that flutters across the tanned skin where he's peeled back his shirtsleeve.

"They'll have you up at least once to go potty."

"Not a problem."

"And they snore. Loudly."

"Then they'll have competition. I do too," he says, with an embarrassed grin. "Scar tissue from a broken nose as a kid." He slides a finger along the centre of it, and I follow it, seeing the slight bump. "I was shit at cricket. Didn't even see the ball that smacked me right between the eyes. The guy bowling thought it was hilarious until the blood started pouring out."

I can't help but giggle at the thought of Christian snoring. What would all those fangirls think if they knew? None of them would ever imagine having hooked up with this man, with his sexy bed hair and come-play-with-me eyes—two features I'd never paid attention to until he was here in my house—he might roll over and start snoring.

"You're not laughing at my misfortune, are you Haley?" he teases.

"No, just shut the door so I don't hear you all competing. It'll be like a very bad orchestra. However, that too has its problems. You run the risk of dying in the night, asphyxiated by a Tully fart." A grin splits his face. "Please don't tell me you'll out-fart her as well." The grin broadens.

That's definitely not something the fangirls would think of. But yes, even rock gods burp and fart like normal people. I know they do. Living with my brother, he's just as gross as any guy when you get him home.

"I don't think anyone can out-fart Tully," he says. Hearing her name twice, she butts at his leg with the cone. "OK, ladies. Time for a pit stop." They seem to know what he's saying and bound off down the hallway to the back door that leads out to the garden.

He goes to follow them, then hesitates. He turns those blue eyes on me; no longer hawk-like, they are more like a soothing summer sea.

"Haley, I can't thank you enough for what you did today. And every day since I arrived."

"You're welcome," I say, with a flush of pleasure. It hits me that even if I didn't owe Christian for everything he's done for me with Tully, I'd happily help him. He's a good guy and I like him. Just like he and my brother, two opposites, somehow Christian and I fit alongside each other well; we've become friends.

Two nights later, I sit at the dining table, wondering what the world would say if they could see this domestic scene. I'm reading through my notes for the exam I'm taking on Friday. While I'll never be a vet like I dreamed of back in high school, I'm determined to become the best, most qualified damn vet nurse I can be. Passing this Dermatology Certificate might also help secure me another job if I lose this one. Christian is busy clearing the table. He reaches for my plate.

"Done?"

"Yeah, it was good, Christian. Where'd you learn to cook like that?"

While I was at work yesterday, Christian ordered in a mountain of groceries and had them delivered to the doorstep. And, for the second night in a row, I've arrived home to the smell of dinner filling the house, and a meal that puts even my reasonable culinary skills to shame.

"Mum insisted," he says. "She held out hope the next generation of women married to Steele men might fare better than she did. Dad is old school. Expects food to appear magically in front of him."

"So your brothers cook?"

"Nah, not anymore. I'm not sure their wives even know they can. Perhaps I should enlighten them sometime. It's tempting." He gives an evil smirk, as he whisks away my plate, so empty there's not even a trace of the delicious salsa he'd made to go with the vegetable bake.

We've fallen into a strange normalcy these past two days. I go to work. Christian stays home with the dogs. At the clinic, Alice teases me about my overly attentive focus on my phone. Texts arrive regularly throughout the day, mostly photographs of the dogs—and Christian—being adorable. Occasionally, it's him venting at the mess he's in, or lamenting the futility of his quest for a way out of it.

He's spent the days trawling through his laptop but finding no solutions. Today he admitted defeat—for now. Rachel has promised she'll beg off work early tomorrow and call in. I haven't told her exactly what I need her to do, not that she'd blab. I've only said it's legal stuff, and it's messy. Until tonight's show, where the world will know that Christian Steele is no longer in the wilds of Scotland, it's safer to say as little as possible. Beyond that, Rachel is our best hope.

Tonight I arrived home to the smell of dinner cooking, and Christian sprawled on the couch reading. I'm used to book-loving men. Like me, Ollie was raised by two teachers who know the value of the written word, and he's a voracious reader. But I didn't expect it of Christian. I kind of thought that wall of books in his apartment was simply part of the aesthetic. I got the impression that in his family, practical skills, especially outdoor ones, were everything. Somehow, just like he bucked the family expectations and forged a career in music, he also found books.

Today, he found my books.

"Hope you don't mind, but I borrowed one from your room," he confessed. "I've read most of what Ollie's got out here."

He waved my beautiful gilt-edged copy of *Wuthering Heights* at me, and it did something really weird to my stomach. There's something sexy about seeing a man immersed in the pages of my favourite classic. Am I imagining him as Heathcliffe to my Cathy? A week ago, I'd have thought he'd have the perfect brooding man vibe, but now I know he's way more stable than Heathcliffe, and a lot better person. Still, there's a little thrill that he's into love stories, even ill-fated ones like theirs.

The dishwasher hums to life, as Christian gives the counter top a final wipe down, neatly hangs the tea towel and then turns to me with a gloomy expression.

"Time to face the music."

He glances down at his fancy watch, the one I teased him about the other day, given watches like that cost about the same as a family car. Of course, he got it for free, some brand he's representing. I'm not sure what tonight's events will mean for all of that. Will his income from those endorsements go the way of the money for Canine Haven, evaporating alongside Christian's decision to make a stand? I hope whatever he stood his ground for, it's worth it.

I follow him to the lounge, feeling like I've been summoned to the town square and forced to watch an execution.

Last night, on Episode 4, he and Loreena slayed the challenge. 'Team Christeena' was the only pair to have a decent little camp set up in the forest, right down to a neat fire pit for cooking. Apparently, their correctly pitched tent was the only one that didn't leak. And, according to Christian, the only one with a blanket rigged up inside, so the two of them had a little privacy. Not that the show hosts would have revealed that, given their love of nauseating innuendo about everyone 'sleeping' together. Just like they made a thing about everyone squatting behind the bushes, when apparently off camera there was a line of Portaloos. As Christian continues to advise, don't believe everything you see on TV.

With the dogs each claiming an end of the couch, I head for the vacant armchair, but Christian grabs my hand.

"Sit with me."

There's a quiet plea in his voice and I don't need to be asked twice. He needs me to be there for him through this. I snuggle into the tiny space beside him, nudging Mularkey over a little, and point the remote.

The TV fires into life, and as the opening music for *Wild For The Win* blares at us, Christian's body is hard and rigid against mine. Tonight, there's no sign of the relaxed guy who sat through the previous three episodes with me; who even laughed and joked a little.

Jaw clenched, brow furrowed, he leans forward towards the screen. With fists balled on his knees, the knuckles are white. I place a hand over his, circling my thumb, but it's as if he's in his own world right now, and it isn't a happy one.

I can't go there with him; no way I can understand what it's like. All I can offer is quiet support and belief in what he tells me; what the footage rolling across the screen doesn't show.

CHAPTER 12

Day Five

IT'S NOT WHAT THEY show of the Episode 5 debacle that provokes a surge of blinding white heat in me. Although it should.

They make a big deal of the part where I have the director's shirt front twisted in my fist, with the other clenched like I want to hit him. I thought I showed amazing restraint, because I *did* want to hit the prick. But I didn't—because I'm not the thug they've made me appear here.

And I can still feel the humiliating pressure of that security guy's hand on my head as he pushed me down into the back seat of the car. Like a cop forcing a criminal under arrest into a squad car. I watch myself shrug the bastard off, pissed they're making me look like the bad guy; as if I wasn't going willingly. By that stage, I was more than happy to leave, even if it meant walking to the coast and swimming back to the mainland.

But no, it's what they don't show that unleashes a hot rush of fury, causing my nostrils to flare, turning my knuckles white from tension and my mouth thick with disbelief. And, because of what they've relegated to behind the scenes, the viewing public will be as confused as Haley. She turns to me, eyes doubled in size, mouth dropped open, as on screen the car speeds down the metal driveway, whisking me away from the nightmare that was *Wild For the Win*.

Then, in unison, our eyes turn back to watch the aftermath, as the stream of misinformation flows from the sickening pair of morons fronting this whole disaster.

"Well Bernard, it seems some people just aren't cut out for this show," Lisa Mayberry croons with a rueful smile and a toss of her blonde mane. Bitch. She's only sickly sweet when the cameras are rolling.

Back in the studio, Bernard tuts and shakes his head, before stepping into the audience and asking for comments. They aren't complimentary, but at least I take some consolation when most people express disappointment. Many admit, up until that point, they really liked me; they wanted me to win.

They still would, if only they knew what triggered this whole thing. They'd realise it wasn't just some aggressive male provoked into finally revealing his true colours by a simple request. They'd know those bastards asked me, and everyone else there, to do something horrific. And Loreena and I were the ones who stood alone against it.

I snatch at the remote, stabbing my finger on the button. I don't need to see any more of this crap.

"What happened, Christian?"

Haley's voice is gentle, her brows narrowed in a concerned frown as she angles her body towards me. She's not stupid, and now she knows me better, she can see there's more to this.

"Tell me what happened. Your secret's safe with me. I won't tell. Even under oath." Her mouth tugs up at one corner, and I'm flooded with tenderness for this sweet girl.

She doesn't need to offer me a guarantee. She's trusted me with her most precious possessions, her dogs, and I can trust her with the truth. I drag in a breath and begin.

"So, you saw them announce the challenge? The 'hunter gatherer'?"

"Yeah, so you were meant to find your food—catch fish or something? Find some edible plants?"

"That's right. They provide fishing rods, even some bait. And a book on plants—which ones will kill you, those which will give you a guts ache, and those that are safe. But there was something else in that kit you didn't see. I know they have footage showing it. The cameras were rolling all the time, but they've cut it. At least my tantrum might have had some effect."

The amount they edited out was huge, including every glimpse of the item that sent me over the edge.

"What?" She inclines her head, a deepening frown. Maybe she expects it's a hunting bow; perhaps a gun. Both kill swiftly. Either would have been preferable to the cruel invention lurking in that box. I tell her.

"A snare. A loop of wire. When an animal steps into it, the wire closes around it. Traps it there. Until someone turns up to finish it off by whatever method they choose."

"Ugh," she shudders, her nose crinkling, making her faint freckles dance. "That's awful. I know I shouldn't be so squeamish about the thought of killing animals for food, not when I enjoy a good steak, but I can't imagine having to do it myself. A bit hypocritical, really."

"No," I reassure. "You're no different from most people who grow up in the city. When you're from a farm, you're closer to the reality of how meat gets from the field to the table. So I can live with the killing, as long as it's done humanely. But there's no such thing as a humane snare."

"Are they even legal, then?" she asks. "Shouldn't they ban them?"

"They are banned in some places, or at least strictly regulated. Not in Scotland. The rules there are more lenient than anywhere else. For now, anyway." I've never felt the need to be a crusader, however, this time, it's personal. "But I intend to do something about that."

"So that's what got you kicked out?"

"Yep. When I found it, I just saw red. Especially when I heard some of the other teams actually planning to try it out. If they could imagine the terror an animal must feel caught like that. If they could see the damage it can do..."

My voice cracks. It was years ago, but still a tidal wave of emotions rises up, crushing me with memories as vivid as if they were yesterday.

"And you have." She's looking at me with those big green eyes, mossy and soft with empathy.

"Yeah, my dog. Jet. He went missing one day. Dad kept saying not to worry, dogs roam, he'd come back. But he didn't. After three days, I went out searching for him. Found him miles away, in the forest bordering the farm. And when I found him..."

"That's how he lost his leg."

With a bob of my head, I confirm it. Although, I don't recall telling Haley that Jet only had three legs, but I must have. I sure enjoyed talking about him with her the other day. It's something we share; this deep love of dogs that's impossible to explain to someone who doesn't have it.

"He'd tried to get out. Mangled his leg beyond saving. He was dehydrated. Hungry. And the look in his eyes, like he'd given up, lost all hope. It took a while for him to even register it was me and I could help him."

My eyes well up, and I blink furiously. Haley's small hand reaches up to cup my cheek. Delicate fingers smooth away the tear that has spilled over. Slender arms lace behind my neck and she nuzzles into my shoulder. It's still sore from the attack of the ninja nurse, but I don't flinch. One hand smooths my hair, offering soothing strokes.

She raises her head from my shoulder, leaning in to press her forehead against mine. I breathe in the smell of her, like cinnamon and honey. With eyes closed, I'm revelling in her nearness. If I wanted to kiss her now—and it takes every ounce of self-control not to—it would be so easy. But I dare not.

"You did. You saved him," she whispers.

"Yeah, me and a local vet who refused to put him down."

My voice is hoarse at the memory of how, even though I found Jet, I still came so close to losing him. Even though I'd managed to carry him home, stumbling through the forest, my arms aching with the weight. Even though I convinced Dad not to put a bullet in him around the back of the barn. I fought for Jet. Like I'm going to fight to ban this barbaric invention, for him and for all those other animals.

"That's what Dad said she should do. I've never forgotten that vet. She totally ignored him. She looked at me and said, 'This is *your* dog. What do *you* want, Christian?' Even though Dad was right there. God, he was pissed off with her. Insisted I pay the bill. He never knew she waived most of it."

Haley slides back, releasing me from her embrace, but I'll carry the warmth with me for a while.

"We're going to fight them, Christian. For Jet." There's fire in her eyes.

"We are," I say, my heart leaping at that little word 'we'.

Me and Haley. In this together. And maybe from this, something more could grow. The possibility ignites a flutter of hope in my chest.

"Right now, I think *we* need a drink," she announces. "Name your poison."

She's right. A little numbing solution would be welcome. Might help me sleep, given the anger that pulses inside me every time I think of the way those arseholes at *Wild For The Win* have stitched me up.

"I'm sure Ollie's got a decent whisky stashed somewhere. How about that?" I suggest.

My friend, exposed to the good things in life, now considers himself a bit of a connoisseur. Haley's already rummaging in an antique drinks cabinet, and who knows what expensive plonk she's going to find.

"Good idea," she says. "Payback for the radio silence, too. I haven't even had a single text for days. Serves him right for ignoring us if we drink his whisky."

"To be fair, Ollie did warn me he'd be off grid most of this trip."

"Me too." There's a sly grin on her face. "More fun if we pretend he didn't and we're drinking his whisky as punishment."

While this should rank up there as one of the worst nights of my life—since millions of people have now seen me portrayed as an aggressive arsehole on national television—it doesn't.

With a clink of glasses, we toast to fighting the bastards at *Wild For The Win* and settle back onto the couch. A good whisky in my hand, a beautiful girl leaning into me, the two of us flanked by dogs—it's a perfect picture. I grab the remote and within minutes, the opening scenes of *Home Alone* are rolling across the screen. Haley grins up at me.

"Great choice. Thank you," she says.

Now it's a perfect picture.

By the time the movie ends, we're both sleepy, lulled by the fire and the whisky. Reluctantly, I stand, immediately feeling regret at the loss of her warm body against me. I extend a hand and help her to her feet.

With the other, I grab at my phone and ram it into the back pocket of my jeans. It's on silent and that's how it's going to stay after the steady stream of texts and calls lighting it up for the past three hours. I didn't bother to read any, or even check who they're from. I know who will have been hunting me, and I know what they're going to say: you fucked up Christian. Big time. Tell me something I don't know. Better still, tell someone who cares.

"Don't worry about this." I survey the rubble of empty glasses, a half-eaten packet of crisps, and the pieces of stray popcorn littering the couch.

Haley insisted we have an interval in the movie so she could make a bowl of popcorn, salty and dripping with a decadent helping of butter. We scoffed it down in handfuls, but as always, some escaped. Strangely, after leaping to vacuum it up, the dogs screwed up their noses and left it littering the rug. Fussy little shits.

"You're sure?" she says, brows slanting in a small frown.

"Of course, and I'll take the dogs to my room again, too. You have work tomorrow."

"Yep, and that's why I shouldn't have had three whiskies," she says, swaying a little.

I slip an arm around her waist and guide her down the hallway to her bedroom door, as the dogs make a beeline for the back door to the garden and sit there waiting expectantly for a toilet stop.

"You'll be fine," I say, smiling at her beautiful upturned face, the faint glow of the alcohol painting her cheeks a delicious shade of pink.

"So will you," she says, stepping in and folding herself against me.

My arms come up to wrap her tight. It feels so damn good, and I stand there drinking in the comforting press of her small weight. It's not lust that grips me—though god knows if we stand here like this much longer, my eager cock will decide to make its presence felt—but a deep need for this person, for everything she is and everything she could be.

Something has shifted between us tonight. And it's not only the whisky. It happened before that. Somehow, these things Haley and I are going through together have brought us closer. We may be different in so many ways, but in the ways that really matter, we're the same.

I sigh, wishing we hadn't drunk that whisky. Because if we hadn't, I would risk taking this further. But I'm not prepared to, not while there's any doubt she'd be going into it fully aware. I'm not a guy who takes advantage of a girl, especially one whose guard is down after a few drinks. Especially not this girl. Ollie would have my balls.

And her guard is down. I know it when she rises up on tiptoes, murmurs, "Thanks for everything, Christian," and places a feather-light kiss on my mouth.

I can't help but respond, my lips finding a home against hers, then I pull back gently. We'll go there again sometime. But not tonight.

"Thank *you*. For everything," I say. "Goodnight, Haley."

She peels away from me with a sweet smile and disappears to where I can't follow—not yet.

I stand there in the hallway, stunned, watching the door close behind her, running my hand through my hair, still processing the events of the evening. Until the whimper of a dog draws my attention to the job at hand. I open the back door and Tully and Mularkey make a dive for the grass. I'm not worried that these two are probably going to be at me to go out half a dozen times before dawn. I doubt I'll be sleeping much, anyway.

CHAPTER 13

Day Six

Christian

RUBBING AT MY ACHING eyes, I stare at the glare of my laptop. I inhale, sucking in a deep breath and huff out a resigned sigh, having found nothing in this one last sweep through all the contracts before Haley's lawyer friend takes a look over them. I'm pinning all my hopes on Rachel MacDonald.

The moment the show was over last night and my phone blew up with texts and calls, I knew I needed someone else to help. But I can't face Megan Lamont and all the other suits at the record company, or Vivi, our social media manager—not even Ewan, our laid back band manager. Every one of them will say the same thing: I've been stupid and only have myself to blame for this mess.

And while they'll be quick to point the finger at me, I know when it comes to finding a way out of it, Megan will roar in like the captain of the cavalry and take control. She'll have solutions, but they're unlikely to be ones I can live with. It suits their purposes just fine to paint me as the bad boy of the band. This time I'm not having it. That's why I've blocked the lot of them. I'm keeping them out of it. I'm going to fix this my way.

There's a twist of a key in the lock, the front door swings open and the dogs are gone, like racehorses out of the gates.

I'm both expectant and nervous about Haley's arrival home from work. We've talked lots today. I hope I didn't get her in trouble with my endless texting, but even with the two dogs shadowing my every move, it's lonely.

There's been no mention of that kiss. Is it embarrassment? Or she doesn't remember? Or is it, as I desperately want to believe, she's OK with it because she's taken another step towards the thing I hardly dare hope for—seeing me as more than just her brother's friend? Something inside me balls up into a knot of nerves and anticipation at the thought of that conversation. It squeezes tighter, as I'm reminded that down track there'd be a conversation with Ollie to face, too.

A Scottish-accented voice calls out from the foyer.

"Hales? Are you here?"

There are clattering claws against the wood, the jubilant steps of the dogs' exuberant welcome dance echoing from the hallway.

"Hello there." I hear giggles interspersed with murmured endearments and kissy noises. The sound of prancing paws subsides, replaced by a slither of upturned bodies, the dogs presenting tummies for scratching. The happy rhythmic thudding of tails vibrates through the house.

Rachel is here. It seems all Haley's friends have keys and come and go as they please. Hopefully, this one isn't going to attack me.

I wander out, pausing to lean on the doorframe. A blonde-haired woman dressed in a business suit sits on the floor, wrestling the two wiggling dogs. Sensing my presence, she looks up, and her strong eyebrows converge.

"Ahhh," she says, ice-blue eyes boring into me. "Christian Steele." This one knows who I am—and from the small scowl tugging down her pretty scarlet bowed mouth, that may not be a good thing. "So, I would be correct in assuming Haley's problem has something to do with you?" Her tone suggests she's less than impressed with the disruption I've caused to Haley's happy existence.

"Right first time." I cross my arms over my chest. "Guess you've been watching the TV."

"Yes," she says, lips pursed in disapproval. "Well, that's a right shit show."

"You could say that."

She rises to her feet, a tall woman, made even more so by a pair of towering heels that allow her to look me right in the eye.

"Lucky for you, I'm pretty good at getting people out of the shit. Make me a coffee and let's get started."

I like her direct manner. Certainly, from the way she's dressed and the confident tone, there's a small beacon of hope; I might get out of this mess after all. She's older, too, mid-thirties, so I presume there's actual legal experience there, not simply bravado. She's very different from Haley. As I show her to a seat at my laptop, I'm glad of their unlikely friendship, apparently grown out of a few girls going for drinks after a Pilates class.

By the time Haley arrives ten minutes later, Rachel is deep in legalese, peering through a set of studious glasses with a small divot between her brows.

"Hey there," Haley says, "Seems you two have met. Sorry I got held up. A surgery went overtime."

"Yes, we've met." Rachel casts me a judgmental glance. I can see she's only doing this for Haley. It's probably fair enough she's dubious about me. Anyone would be after seeing the crap on TV last night. Not to mention the shadow of those other lies about Waverley and me that seem like they'll never go away.

"How's it going?" Haley stands at her shoulder. "Anything jump out?"

"Not yet," Rachel says, but her intense gaze, and the determined set of her jaw, tell me she's going to do her best. The challenge has piqued her interest, even if meeting it means getting a scumbag like me off the hook.

"How about I start dinner?" I suggest.

I've prepped for the three of us. Hopefully Rachel likes steak. I retrieve the chunky slab of best fillet from the fridge, finding a spot on the worktop so it can come up to room temperature. Tucking it safely out of reach of marauding dogs, I begin to assemble the ingredients for a simple but impressive red wine jus. I ordered in a heap of vegetables, in case she's not a carnivore like me and Haley. Plying her with good food might ease her distaste for the task at hand.

"I'll help," Haley offers. "Leave Rachel to work her magic, eh?"

I'm not sure Rachel is the answer to my prayers. Only one page into the contract, she muttered about it looking watertight. Still, I'd rather take my chances with her than Megan and her mates, who'll only try to bully me into doing what's best for others, even if it's not good for me.

But working in the kitchen alongside Haley takes the edge off my gloomy mood. Even if Rachel fails to save me, having her here has delivered an opportunity to do something so ordinary, but at the same time, special: cook dinner alongside Haley. What I'd give to be doing this every night when we're not on the road. To have Haley arrive home, share a glass of wine together, talk about nothing and everything while we make dinner.

I'm not giving up on that possibility. The thought of that kiss still dances seductively in my head, but I'm scared to raise it with Haley. Best to leave that to her; to choose when—or if.

Ollie's kitchen is spacious and well-equipped, with wide work-tops and sleek cabinetry, two sets of gas hobs and two ovens. While there's room for both of us to work in here without ever colliding, we gravitate to the centre, drawn to each other. The task provides an excuse to flirt with the tantalising nearness of her, and it feels as if she wants it too. The relaxed brush of her body past mine, as we dance back and forth, peeling and chopping, measuring and stirring, mesmerises me. I tingle all over as she leans past me to pull open a drawer, her fingers grazing my hip.

I offer her a taste of the jus, and the sight of her dainty tongue lapping at the spoon has me regretting it immediately. I force my brain to retrieve useless information. I recite the monarchs of England since 1066, the names and dates of Henry the Eighth's wives, the names of Shakespeare's tragedies and then move onto the comedies—anything to damp down all the messages my body is sending; anything to drive away the taunting images of Haley; the ones that invade my dreams and now seem to have braved my waking hours. I fail, but at least the apron I tied on covers the physical evidence of my arousal.

She gives me shit the whole time, bantering with me as if she doesn't believe I can really cook, even though two pretty damn good meals the previous two nights prove otherwise. It's playful and flirty, and I lap it up like a cat with a bowl of fresh cream.

"Better hold the steak. These are still hard." Haley leans into the oven, stabbing viciously at the tray of roast vegetables with a knife. The sight of that sweetly curved arse pointing in the air captures my gaze, and I jerk my eyes away just in time as she slams the oven door and turns to face me. "I told you twenty minutes wouldn't be enough."

"Are you always so right about everything?" I say.

She rolls her eyes. "Always. Especially in the kitchen." She pokes my chest with a pointy little finger, trying to look bossy.

I adopt a hurt expression. "You don't like my cooking, then?" I pout.

"Lose the puppy dog eyes, Christian," she says, attempting to suppress a giggle, and failing when I respond by exaggerating my down-turned mouth. God, it's like the music of angels to my ears, the sound of her unbridled happiness. What I'd give to hear that every day of my life.

"Send that puppy dog in here." Rachel's voice has an edge of excitement to it.

I pull the pan off the gas element and try to walk casually. Haley isn't so restrained, dumping the knife in the sink and running to

Rachel's side. I join her, staring down at the lines of black print that hold me prisoner.

"Right," Rachel says, a smug smile lighting her face. "I think I've found a loophole. Yes, you might have to take a risk, be prepared to defend it in court, but it might not come to that."

My heart races, the blood roaring with possibility.

"So, you want to spill some dirt on these guys?" she asks.

I nod. "People deserve to know what really happened."

"OK. But *you're* not allowed to talk about why you were asked to leave—"

"Chose to leave," I spit.

"Settle down, Christian," she commands. "I'm not the enemy here."

I swallow. "Sorry."

"OK," she says, pointing at the document on the screen. "First, you were right, you can't leave this house. Not until the day of the live show, next Thursday. That's still a whole week away. Anyone catches you breaking that condition and they'll sue your arse."

Hayley's panicked eyes meet mine across Rachel's head. I smile reassuringly and give a little shake of my head. I don't want her to feel bad about what she asked of me. I have no regrets about risking those two trips to the vets. I'd do it again without hesitation if I had to; for her, for Tully, no matter what.

Rachel scrolls down some more. "And it's very clear, in this clause—you can't talk about why they asked you to—why you *chose* to leave. They've got that sewn up tight." She trails a finger down the contract, pausing to reread each numbered clause.

"But," she bites at her lip, her chin resting on one hand, "there doesn't seem to be anything in here that prevents you talking about other contestants. Or them talking about you. I'm at a loss as to why they've left it out. It could be an oversight, which is kind of surprising given the money these guys would spend on contracts—"

Haley interrupts. "I bet it's not." There's a small satisfied grin on her face. Rachel and I sport twin questioning frowns. We obviously have something in common—unlike Haley, neither of us are regular consumers of reality TV.

"What causes the most fireworks on these shows?" Haley looks between us as if we should know this like she does, but seeing our blank stares helps us out. "The gossip. Contestants dissing each other. All those secret asides where they're encouraged to let loose with what they really think. On shows like this, they *want* people to talk about each other, stir up trouble. They don't want to rule out their best source of conflict. The magazines are full of it, long after the season ends."

My brain whirrs, the cogs spinning wildly now. There is another person who knows exactly what went down. One who could talk about what I did and not be sued for doing so.

"Loreena," I say. "She knows everything."

But, still stuck on the inside, she can no more talk to the press than I can. And even if I could sneak out of here, there's no way I can reach Loreena. It would take a paramilitary operation to get back undetected. My practical skills don't extend to parachuting in behind enemy lines, or stealthy landings on the wild beaches of a remote island. My brief flash of hope is gone as quickly as it came, followed by a new realisation. I sigh.

"Even if I could get a message to her, there's no way they'd let her reveal my secret on air. They can cut anything they want."

And yes, I could wait for it all to be over. However, that's not an option I want to live with—the world thinking I'm a creep for weeks until the whole story is allowed to come out.

"But it's a start, right?" Haley's voice is bright. She's practically bouncing with excitement. I can't bear to crush her optimism.

"It is." I force a smile. "We'll work something out. Thanks Rachel."

"Anything for Haley," she says, making it perfectly clear she's helping me under duress. "Now, how about a glass of wine while you finish dinner?"

I should be more hopeful, sharing some of Haley's positivity, but while I take care of the rest of the dinner, and the two girls relax and chat, I slowly sink back into my despondent mood. Since last night, the world knows I'm not on that island. It's even more crucial I lie low. Reporters will be hunting me now. Their questions alone would provoke the wrath of the production company lawyers, whether I choose to answer or not.

I lean on the worktop, head in my hands. Not knowing there's a lifeline was bad, but knowing there is one dangling out of my reach—somehow it's worse. And beyond that, there's a quiet dread, a dark shadow lurking at my shoulder. I have this strange premonition, a twisting in my gut; the bastards at *Wild For The Win* aren't done with me yet.

Day Six

Haley

ALONGSIDE ME, CHRISTIAN'S BODY is coiled as tight as the trigger on one of the damn snares he hates so much. As the theme song for *Wild For The Win* blasts from the TV, the opening credits for Episode 6 rolling across the screen, his mouth thins in a terse line. The moment he sees me looking, it moulds into a curve, but the smile doesn't reach his eyes. I pat his knee, and he reaches across and squeezes my hand. We're partners in this now, him and me.

"You should relax a little," I say. "Surely the worst is over."

We faced the footage of his eviction together last night, and now he's away from those jerks they can't hurt him anymore.

"I suppose so," he says. "I'm worried all of it was for nothing. What if, behind the scenes, the cruelty still went ahead?"

"I doubt it," Rachel says. "They wouldn't take the risk. Once one person called them out, raised doubts, they wouldn't have risked another."

"Yeah, I suppose you're right," he sighs, his shoulders dropping, a little less on edge from her reassurance.

Christian trusts Rachel, even though it's obvious she's not a fan of his. Her help wasn't the silver bullet we'd hoped for, but it *is* something. Loreena Bunt is the key even though for now she's out of our reach. Over dinner, Christian praised Rachel to the point where she told him to shut up. But I know my friend has a big ego—she's quietly pleased she found a way forward, and secretly loved his every grateful word.

"I still feel bad about Loreena." He frowns as she appears on the screen, poking at a small fire with a stick, and giving the steaming billy can sitting on a frame above it a stir. "I totally fucked up her chances."

"Maybe not. I think Loreena can take care of herself." Rachel has a distinct hint of admiration in her voice.

"Yeah, I suppose she can, can't she?" He chuckles a little at the thought. This time, a genuine, undiluted smile lights Christian's face.

I smile too, realising my less-than-charitable opinion of Loreena—and now I'll admit it, the unexpected stab of jealousy I felt back on the night when they partnered up—has evaporated. Seeing her through Christian's eyes is part of the lesson he's taught me about myself. In the past, I've been as bad as the rest of them out there; quick to judge, forming opinions based on flimsy superficial evidence, believing the crap the media spins. But I'm determined to not be that person anymore. I want to be a better person, for myself; and for him.

"She's an inspiration," Rachel says, as they continue to focus on Loreena. She's gamely shoring up the tent, even though the rain pours down. One of the other contestants gives her some shit, and she flips him a middle finger. "I love the way she doesn't care what anyone thinks."

We sit and watch in silence. There are fireworks between some of the other pairs. It seems it's not all warm and cosy inside those tents. The pressure is showing as they bicker and snipe. Hunger is taking its toll as some turn their noses up at their wild food concoctions. I can't say I blame them. They look disgusting.

One of the guys—who I'm sure I last saw as a naked contestant on one of those horrible dating programmes—steps behind a large tree and the cameras follow. He's certainly bundled up in plenty of clothes now, with a faint dusting of snow on the ground. He slides his hand deep into a jacket pocket, producing a silver flask. Toasting the viewers with a secretive "Slainté", he slugs back the illicit alcohol.

"Ooh, whisky," I say, remembering its pleasant warmth sliding down my throat last night. It was surprisingly good, at least to me, a whisky rookie. "Anyone want one?" I offer.

"Nah, I'm driving," Rachel says. "Plus, after four days in Scotland with my family, I think I need a break from whisky."

"Better not," Christian says. "Ollie's already going to be pissed about us drinking half a bottle last night."

He's right. It's probably not the best idea, but not because I'm worried about Ollie. I hold the whisky directly responsible for latching my mouth onto Christian's last night. I thought he enjoyed it as much as I did, but he hasn't said a word today. What that means I don't know—for me or him.

My feelings for Christian flicker like the fairy lights on my fabulous tree standing over there in front of the window. They're like bright eyes blinking at me as they rotate through all their different programs. Sometimes they pulse slowly, a steady, comforting rhythm, almost hypnotic. It's a mantra, telling me it's fine to feel this way; this is how it's meant to be. Other times they flash rapidly, like an excited beating heart. And then they launch into a wild random sequence, both delightful and unnerving. That's what they're doing now, the perfect accompaniment to the swirling inside of me that's growing every day he's here.

I'm jolted back from gazing lovingly at the tree, as beside me Christian lurches forward, a sudden intense fixation on the TV. His eyes are torn wide, hands pressed to his mouth.

"Fuck, no," he says, his tone lethal.

In front of us there's Loreena, crying, suitcase in hand. Other contestants crowd around her. One guy wraps an arm across her shoulder, rubbing at her back with a soothing hand. The mics seem to have failed. Their words are erratic, a faint burble. What the hell is happening?

A burly guy in a security uniform approaches, putting a large paw on Loreena's arm. She flicks him off; her plump lips contorted in a scowl, her brows fighting against the Botox, plunging downwards in an angry frown. He steps back, startled, as she pushes past him, and dives into the waiting car.

She tries to drag the suitcase after her, but it's too big and sticks in the doorway. She gives it a violent shove, and it lurches back. Loreena leaps out of the car after it and screams at the driver to open the boot. He gets out and tries to help her wrangle the case, but she's not having any of it. She hisses at him like an enraged wildcat, poking at his chest with one of her pointed red nails, a threatening scarlet talon. He raises both hands as if to placate her, backing away, and sliding back into the driver's seat. Finally, she wrestles the case into the boot, slams it with a deafening crash, and stumbles into the rear seat of the car. The security guy thrusts the door shut, and it races away.

It's déjà vu. Just like Christian, Loreena Bunt is no longer on *Wild For The Win*.

Christian grabs the remote, turning up the volume so there's no possibility of missing the conversation between the contestants, hanging on their words. All of us are trying to make sense of what we've just seen.

"You can't blame her," says Kelly, a scrawny blonde who never even made it to the altar in the last season of *Love By Arrangement*. "After being alone in that tent with him, of course she'd want to leave."

"Surely you've read about him in the papers? He's a shit," says Tiffany Rose, the soap star, her character recently killed off in a fiery car crash. No doubt she needs all the screen time she can get and isn't missing her chance here.

Tiffany's co-star, who goes by the unlikely name of Chardonnay, is equally damning. "Honestly, what woman puts up with a guy like him?"

And so it goes on. Bit by bit, person by person, the producers fabricate an elaborate lie. With snippets of comments taken out of context, then stitched back together again, they've created a monster worthy of Dr Frankenstein.

Although it's not said directly—because suing for slander is still a possibility—anyone watching will come to the same inevitable conclusion: Loreena wasn't asked to leave; she chose to. And Loreena chose to leave, not out of solidarity with Christian, but because she's upset by something Christian did *to her*.

"Can they do that?" I croak, my horror at what's happened here rendering me almost speechless.

"They can, and they have," Rachel says quietly.

Beside me, Christian is a man frozen in time, anguish carved on his face, unable to take his eyes off the screen, unable to turn away from the vile insinuations that continue to swirl back and forth.

Finally, they cut to ads, offering a chance for him to break free. When he moves, it's an explosion. He slams his hand on the remote so hard it skews off the table, flying through the air and landing with a clatter. He's a storm cloud tumbling down the hallway. His bedroom door crashes shut, the house quaking as the sound reverberates off the walls.

"Do you think he really..."

"No!" I blurt, leaping to Christian's defence.

Rachel's brows fly upwards. "You seem awfully sure about that."

"I am. He's not like that Rache."

"You know, as my mum always says, where there's smoke there's fire."

"That's the thing here, Rachel. There never was any smoke. All that stuff about him and his girlfriend? A heap of crap. Just like they did to Ollie."

She has the decency to look a little ashamed, as she should be. She might be engaged to another guy, but like all my friends, Rachel has a soft spot for Ollie. Everyone hated what they did to him as much as I did.

"Fuckers," Rachel spits. How she manages to control that potty mouth in a courtroom I'll never know. "He's screwed."

"Why would they do that?" I can't understand what they hoped to gain from this.

"An insurance policy perhaps? In case he was brave enough to out them, take his chances—if they discredit him, who will the public believe?"

"Yeah, but was it necessary? To go that far?"

"No," she says, looking thoughtful. "But it did make for some pretty memorable TV. No one's going to forget that in a while. If the programme's been struggling, hooking viewers in with a big controversy will make sure they get another season."

"At the expense of people who don't deserve it. Messing with their lives."

"You see why I don't usually watch this stuff, don't you?"

She's gentle in her chiding, but I'm still ashamed. Viewers like me feed this voracious machine that chews people up and spits them out simply to make money and boost ratings. A blushing warmth creeps up my face.

"Hey, it's OK," she says. "Don't feel bad. This one was supposed to do some good, wasn't it? I was watching too."

She grabs at my arm, offering a solid squeeze.

"Yeah," I say. "Looks like they had us all fooled."

"I was even on Team Christeena," she laughs. "Anything for the dogs."

That's another thing we have in common. Rachel's a champion for dogs too, under that severe suit and stern lawyer demeanour.

She's been an angel, taking on pro bono work for the Trust. That's why, despite her grumbles, she happily gave her time to help out Christian tonight. She knows his heart's with the animals, too.

"How's it going down there at the clinic?" she asks, her voice a little wary.

"A bit grim," I say. "We're all trying to keep positive, but it's hard knowing we might be out of a job soon."

"Something will come through, I know it will," she says.

"Just not *Wild For The Win.*"

"No, we might have to find our Christmas miracle somewhere else. This house looks like one great big summoning spell for it," she teases, standing to gather her coat and briefcase.

"It had better start working its magic soon. The clock's ticking." I survey my beautiful decorations, savouring the small surge of happiness they bring, even in the middle of all this mess.

"It will happen," she says. "All those rich people love to make themselves look good by splashing a bit of Christmas spirit around." She quirks a brow. "What about Ollie? He's always happy to throw money around. Would he come through for you?"

My breath comes out, a sharp exhale. Her eyes bore into me, and I shrink a little under her scrutiny, before deciding this is the one person who might understand my selfishness at not wanting my brother to help.

"Yeah, he would. But I don't want to ask him." I swallow, fearful of putting it into words. I wander over to the Christmas tree, rearranging an ornament that's slipped, adjusting the arc of a strand of tinsel, moving a light that's tucked behind a branch. Delaying.

"You know I think I only got the interview for this job because Mum knows one of the trustees, right?"

She nods, and her eyes soften. It might not be true, but it's the thing that tarnished my delight when I phoned my parents to tell them I'd been offered the position—my mother pointedly mentioning how only a week earlier she'd seen the woman at some school fundraiser. When I voiced it to Rachel, of course she shot the idea down, trying to bolster my confidence. But I can't let go of the sickening possibility. I blunder on.

"So, if Ollie was to give them the hundred grand, it would kind of feel like he's buying me a job."

"I get it." She steps in, pulling me into a stiff hug, and I fight back tears, not wanting to dampen the front of her smart jacket. "Honey, if there's another way, we'll find it."

She strokes my hair with awkward fingers. Warm fuzzies don't come naturally to Rachel, so I know she's worried about me. I step back, and she gives a small relieved huff, self-consciously smoothing down her skirt.

"Call me if you need anything else. Promise?" I nod. "And don't worry. I'm not giving up on your miracle, OK?"

As I shut the door, I'm hoping Rachel is right. But our clinic isn't the only thing deserving of a Christmas miracle. There's a man locked in the room opposite mine who deserves saving, too.

CHAPTER 15

Day Six

I'M UNLOADING THE DISHWASHER while the dogs are out pottering in the garden. Over the clatter of sorting cutlery into a drawer, I don't hear his footsteps. Christian's at my shoulder before I realise and I startle at his voice.

"Thank you," he says. "That was a really nice thing to do."

I turn and he's right there, his blue eyes soft and smiley, his lips so damn close; and then they're on my cheek, a light brush, but it sends my senses spiralling. It's only a kiss. Simply him thanking me. But I'm like a meteor; bursting into flame the moment I'm in his atmosphere, a blaze of fire across the night.

When he steps back, I see he's clutching the frame with the pictures of Jet I placed on the bedside table. I knew he'd love it.

"I thought it might be a good thing to have with you. A reminder of why this is important." Now he's seen it, I'll have to confess. "I'm sorry—I snooped in your bedroom at the apartment."

"Hope it was tidy," he says.

"Immaculate. Impressively so. I think you need to move in here and retrain Ollie."

The flippant suggestion of him moving in brings a warm rush of possibility. I've become used to Christian here. No—I *like* Christian here. Is that because despite all my claims—that I love the independence, cherish the freedom to do whatever I want—I'm lonely in this house? Or is it something else? Now our lives have been twined together like this, I'm finding it hard to imagine anything less. That word 'less'… I didn't pluck it out of the air by accident. My life *was* something less prior to him showing up at my door. I have to admit it—Christian has made my life more.

"How did you even get it past me?" He's staring down at the photographs, his mouth soft and tender, blue eyes like a clear sky, not the raging storm of earlier.

"While Rachel was interrogating you."

He grins. "Yeah, I wouldn't want to be a witness under her cross-examination. Your friends," he laughs. "They're something else. No wonder I didn't notice you sneak this into the house on Monday. The ninja nurse had me pinned to the floor."

"No, I only brought it over tonight. That's why I was late. Little white lie."

His eyes jerk up to meet mine. "Tonight? You went back to the apartment tonight?"

"Yes," I admit. "Sorry, I used your code again."

"Haley," he says, his eyes wide with concern. "You shouldn't have done that."

"I know, I overstepped. I shouldn't have gone there without asking. But this idea only came to me last night. After you told me about the snare. And I couldn't stop thinking about these photographs."

"No, no," he says, shaking his head. "I mean, you shouldn't have gone there on your own. And after dark. What the hell were you thinking? It's not safe."

"Oh, come on Christian," I scoff. "It's Chelsea. The streets are lit up like daylight and there's probably a hundred security cameras trained on every pavement."

"Don't brush it off like that," he scolds. "After last night, there might have been press there. They could have cornered you. And that guy the other day. What if he'd come up to you again?"

"I'd have told him the same thing as I did then. I'm your cleaner. In fact, if he was still watching, me going back makes it all the more believable."

"Haley, promise me you won't do anything like that again?"

I know there's only concern in his request, but an irrational need to argue grips me.

"No, I won't promise," I say. "Christian, you're not my mother or my father. I'm a grown woman, not Ollie's baby sister. I'm not a kid to be bossed around."

"I'm not trying to boss you, Haley. I just don't think you should—"

"Stop." I hold up a hand. "Stop right there." He rears back at the gesture, and the assertive tone I've found.

While I appreciate Christian's genuine concern for my wellbeing, it's dredged up a past I'm still desperately trying to overcome. Because my parents didn't have much time for us, Ollie and I fell into our own roles. Me, the younger child, a little girl, always needing shelter, protection, kept safe within the rules; while, as the eldest, Ollie blazed through life big and bold, with his devil-may-care attitude, confident and unrestrained.

He only did it because he cared, but Ollie suffocated me. With him always checking up on me—where I went, who I was with—and laying down limits, I lived my earlier life like a caged bird, cherished but confined. It's left me a timid adult, quick to worry about potential problems, always on alert for threats, wary of stepping outside the boundaries. This past couple of years, I really feel like I've pushed beyond that, especially this last one. First left alone in the apartment—and fully responsible for the rent I couldn't afford after Jack abandoned me—and then living here, most of the time only me and the dogs, I've felt more powerful than ever. And I won't let anyone diminish that. This might be Ollie's house, but in it I'm living life on my own terms.

"Christian, I may not be a fighter like Sam, or have Rachel's ability to use words as a weapon, but I'm not stupid. I don't take stupid risks."

"I don't think you're stupid, Haley. You're smart. A thinker."

"Then trust me to think for myself," I whisper. I'm battling between my need to stand up for myself and the underlying gnawing nervousness as I think of the text I fired off to Rachel twenty minutes ago. There's a high chance Christian's not going to be a fan of the tentative plan I'm hatching.

"OK," he says, thickly. "You know that's not going to be easy, right?" He looks at me from underneath those dark lashes, too lush and pretty for a man. I nod. "I don't want something bad to happen to you on my account. God knows there's enough people who've suffered already because of me."

"But more who are better off for having you around."

His hand comes up to trace my jaw. I shudder as fingers trail along my neck, follow the curve of my ear, tuck back a rogue strand of hair. He leans in and presses his lips to my forehead.

"Goodnight Haley," he murmurs. "And thank you."

He breaks away and I follow his progress down the hallway, in his t-shirt and baggy sweats, the photo frame clutched to his chest. The sight of him reminds me of a small child, one who needs *my* protection. It only hardens my resolve to follow through with the decision I made earlier.

I pick up my phone and look at the texts. No going back now.

HALEY: Rache, I need your help. Can you get us Loreena Bunt's address?

I said us, but I meant me. I know she has access to investigators who do lots of this sort of thing. Like all celebrities, Loreena probably doesn't advertise where she lives. But I know from Ollie's experience that type of information can be found, if you know where to look.

I stare at her reply.

RACHEL: Absolutely. On it already. Loreena is definitely your best bet. But don't let Christian go there. Us on Saturday?

HALEY: Sounds a plan. We need that address.

My answer is deliberately vague. If Rachel knew my real plan, she'd try to talk me out of it. I call the dogs in, dancing wet feet tracking prints up the hallway in an exuberant celebration of their unexpected extra time out in the yard. I was meant to sit my exam tomorrow—but I'm not. I should take Tully to get her stitches out—but I won't. There's less than a week before the show is over. I'm hoping it's enough time to do what's needed, whatever that might be. For that reason, I must start tomorrow.

Christian

"HEY, DO YOU THINK you could help me out here?"

Haley's voice drifts up from where she sits cross-legged on the lounge floor. She's in another set of those crazy pyjamas. The girl seems to have a different pair for every day of the week. These are possibly the least offensive I've seen.

On her bottom half, the pants cling tight to her legs, following every curve, even the riotous tartan pattern unable to mask the shapeliness of what lies beneath. The top is a simple white sweater with a huge red tartan heart and the words 'Santa Baby' in gold. Yep, I'd sign up to be Santa if she'd come and sit on my lap.

Tully sprawls beside her, legs dropped wide like a harlot, exposing her soft beige tummy and saggy teats. Haley says she was used for breeding, maybe to produce guard dogs, or worse fighting dogs. It's hard to imagine anything produced by this amiable boofhead could have an ounce of aggression.

The hated cone lies discarded on the floor. Free of it, no wonder Tully's mouth hangs open in a broad smile, huge pink tongue unfurled.

"I need help to hold her. She's so damn wiggly."

"You'd be wiggly too, if you'd just got rid of a plastic neck wrap you'd been forced to wear for a week."

I slide to the floor, facing Haley across the furry bundle of writhing joy. She reaches a hand to the coffee table where a small curved scissors sits on a cloth. There's a long set of tweezers and some small foil packets of antiseptic wipes.

"Figured I'd do the job myself." She slides the blunt tip of the scissors under one plastic knot of suture thread. "It's healed really well. I don't think a vet's going to have any concerns. No point paying someone to do what I can do myself."

Trapping her lip between her teeth, she leans in closer and carefully lifts the thread away from the skin of the crinkled seam. With a click, the stitch is cut. She swaps to the tweezers and pulls the thread clear.

"Nice work, Dr Templeton," I say as she settles to work on the next stitch.

"Nice assist, Nurse Steele. One down, nineteen to go. Just keep the patient steady," she says, a grin pulling her mouth wide.

I tickle at Tully's bristled neck, and she relaxes under my touch. Haley's hands are so careful I hardly need to distract the dog. I'm sure she doesn't feel a thing.

Remembering that same gentle touch, those soft fingers trailing over my stomach the other day, when she helped me dress after Sam checked my arm, I crave to feel it again. But I swallow hard, focus my mind on the task, and try to damp down the surge of desire at the closeness, the smell of her. *Her.* Not only the green apple of her shampoo, or the delicate floral perfume she wears—but her own sweet scent that hints of warm secret places. I inhale slow and deep, enjoying the time afforded by the unhurried movements of those dainty hands. It's precious moments like this I never expected to have, without Ollie's presence always there between us. I savour it knowing there's a deadline looming, where I'll be gone and he'll be back.

"Not going into work?" I watch as she tackles the next stitch, her pink tongue caught between her teeth, eyes narrowed in focus.

"It's my exam today. One o'clock. They've given me the morning off as well for study."

"Ever thought of doing the full vet training?" I say. "You'd be good at it."

She says nothing at first. Have I upset her? Then she sighs.

"I have. But it's not easy."

"Bullshit," I protest. "You got your A-levels, right?" I'm sure her parents would have insisted. There's no way two teachers would let their kid drop out of school early. "And to get your vet nursing qualification is no small thing. What did it take? Two or three years?"

"Three. I did it part-time—nights and weekends—while I worked at a clinic."

"Which proves you've also got some determination there. Hell, I couldn't stick with something that long."

She silently plucks at another stitch. Her face is all concentration, but there's a whirl of trouble in her eyes.

"Look, it's not that I couldn't do it. I'm good at the practical stuff."

"I can see that." Her hands are steady, her touch gentle but confident.

"The study doesn't bother me. With Mum and Dad on my case right through school, I learned how to do that."

"Then what's stopping you? Is it the time? Like it would be five years, wouldn't it?"

"Probably four. My vet nurse diploma would credit across for some. Four or five years, it's all the same. It's not happening." Her sigh is deeper, sad and resigned. When she meets my eyes, there's a defeated expression there. "Do you know what it costs?"

It's obvious now. I'm such an idiot. I may not be rolling in cash right this minute, but there's a steady inward stream of pounds into my bank account. I can't wildly throw money at big items, like a flash car, but I can sleep at night free of any financial worries. Unlike many people. Unlike Haley. I shake my head, feeling an awkward flush at my insensitive probing.

"Around nine thousand pounds a year," she says. "And I'd have to give up work. I did the vet nursing diploma on the job. But you can't do a degree like that. Sure, I might be able to squeeze in a few hours' work each week, but that's not going to get me through." She blinks at me, dark lashes fluttering, pink rising on her cheeks. "Christian, this past year has been hard. I had a few changes in my living arrangements that put financial pressure on me."

I suspect I know who caused those problems. I'm fairly sure she lived with that creep I met down at Ollie's country house one time.

My face is a blank, masking the hatred for the prick that flares from this knowledge.

"Staying here in London, trying to be independent, having too much pride to be a twenty-something moving back in with her parents—well, it wasn't the smartest move."

She shuffles uncomfortably under my sympathetic gaze.

"I had debts up to my eyeballs. It's only moving in here that's allowed me to claw my way back. I've almost finished paying off my student loan. I can't put myself back in that position again. Not now, when I'm finally almost free of it."

"I get it," I say. "But that's a shame." I can't help but tell her what I see, an intelligent woman who could be so much more if she just had a chance, and would be brave enough to take it. "You would make an amazing vet. You remind me of the woman who saved Jet. Good hands and a big heart. That's what really counts, right?"

She nods, turning her attention back to the job, but I see her hands shake a little now.

Yes, I regret saying anything because I've upset her. But I despair at how circumstances hold this capable woman back, denying her what I have, what her brother has; the chance to wake up every day and do the thing you love. For Haley, being a vet nurse, must be like it would be for me if I was a sound tech, watching the music happen but not allowed to make it. There must be a way out for her.

"Your parents wouldn't..."

"No way I'd ask that of them." She tries to shut me down.

"Didn't they put Ollie through?"

I'm still not prepared to let this go. I love Ollie like a brother, but it's become all the more clear over the time I've spent here that Haley stands in his shadow. I don't think they meant to do it. The

Templetons are good people, but while helping their famous golden boy reach his dreams, they've neglected their other child, someone just as talented, and just as deserving of their pride.

"Ollie was eighteen when he went to the Academy. I'm twenty-five. I'm not their responsibility." There's a fierce independence in this woman, and while I admire it, I'm disappointed there's not some way for her to honour that spirit while still chasing her dream.

The flash of her eyes and the terse tone tell me this conversation should end now. There's no good will come of it. But I can't leave it alone; it seems so wrong. There has to be some way. As if she reads my mind, she fixes me with a determined look.

"Just let it go, Christian. I have. Now, can you please hold Tully still?"

The dog's head has been swivelling between us, following the conversation, as if watching a game of ping-pong.

"Not much more to go, girl." I stroke her velvety ears. "Good girl."

That's what Haley is, too. A good girl. Never rocking the boat. Never demanding anything. Supporting everyone else. Taking care of them. But who's taking care of her? I want it to be me. So I shut my mouth and let her think that's the end of it. But it's not.

Over this last week, so much has changed. I arrived here on Saturday as someone Haley knew, but didn't, really. Some of what she knew was great: Ollie and I are good friends, I love my music, I'm committed to the band. And then there were the things she thought she knew, like everybody else; all those lies and the shade cast on me simply because it makes a better story.

Spending these days together, we've become friends, confidantes. There's trust between us. I've let myself share stuff with her I'd never offer even a glimpse of to anyone else and she's received it with a wide open heart and a generous spirit. I've always avoided making myself vulnerable. A glowering expression and a prickly attitude is an effective set of armour against the world. Here with Haley, I don't feel any need to put it on. What it would be to wake up every morning like this and for a few hours each day, just be me.

It's not purely selfish. Haley has let me in too, and I'm starting to wonder if there are things I know about her she doesn't normally share, either. I suspect her friends don't know about this dream of being a vet she's put aside as out of her reach. I bet Ollie doesn't realise she won't accept help from her parents like he did.

If Ollie had any idea of Haley's secret ambition and what stands in the way of her achieving it, he'd write the cheque. But letting him in on that information won't help. Haley's obviously not one for charity and I can see even living in this house of his doesn't always sit comfortably. She'd knock him back. Hell, I know I could do the same, but she wouldn't take money from me either. There's stubbornness under that agreeable facade.

Silently watching her work, the capable movements of her hands, the quiet murmurings of reassurance to the dog, is a beautiful thing. I might not have the solution to all of this yet, but I'm not letting go of the possibilities—for Haley to do the thing she was born to do, and for me. I should be grateful to have her in my life as a friend; but I'm a greedy bastard where she's concerned. I want more.

"There, all done," she says as she drops the last thread onto the cloth on the table. She brushes over the zig-zag line with a wipe and then ruffles the dog's neck with a playful hand.

Tully springs to her feet and begins a celebration wrestle with Mularkey, who's been supervising with interest. They roar off up the hallway and I hear twin thuds as they land on my bed. Playful growls and small yelps drift our way, and Haley and I smile at each other like indulgent parents enjoying their offspring.

"I know. I should have shut the door," I say. My bed will be a whirlpool of sheets and covers, with pillows tossed around, and I don't care in the slightest.

A loud howl echoes from the kitchen. When a text comes in on Haley's phone with that damn bizarre ringtone, you'd swear Mularkey was right there beside you. She leaps to her feet and heads to grab it from the counter.

I follow, seeking a jolt of caffeine to kick start my day. Helping with Tully offered a brief reprieve from my troubles. I tossed and turned all night and through the quiet morning hours, barely sleeping, my mind full of anger and frustration. I lay in the dark, fighting the desire to get up and destroy something. The sum of those hundreds of minutes spent turning it over in my head is the crushing realisation: if I thought I was fucked before—now I'm really fucked.

There's no escape from what's about to happen. The ugly rumours about me and Waverley I thought might finally no longer dog my every step are certain to come hurtling back. And hard on their heels, a new rumour—that I did something shady to Loreena Bunt—and there's nothing I can do about it.

Haley's frowning down at her phone.

"Everything OK?"

"Yeah," she says absently, while her fingers tap away.

"Coffee?" I offer.

"Sure." She's still in another world.

"Haley," I say, fearful of the answer but desperate to know. "Are we good? Still? You and me, after last night." I rush on. "I'm sorry for bashing your remote around like that and all the door slamming. I wasn't the best version of myself. And I felt like a right prick when I cooled down and found the pictures of Jet. That you'd do that for me...I don't deserve it."

"Christian," she looks at me, eyes soft. "I know you didn't do anything bad to Loreena. You haven't got it in you to hurt people like that."

That's what I really needed to hear, but was too frightened to ask, and she knew that. It's dizzying yet scary to be so seen by someone. To have a person sense the very things that are ripping you apart inside, and to know instinctively how to put you back together. I'm humbled by her belief in me. She rests a hand on my forearm, tracing the lines of ink, delicate fingers making the hairs stand on end.

"And I know it doesn't seem like it right this minute. I know it's eating you up, Christian." I shiver as she leans into me, eyes wide and intense. "But we *will* find a way out. I know we will. Especially with Rachel on the case."

"She's a bit of a ball-buster, your friend."

"She is." Hayley's face broadens with a grin. "And right now she's got the balls of a few people at *Wild For The Win* in her sights. They should be very afraid."

Reading has always been a refuge for me. So I'm pleased to be deep in an imaginary world this morning, a fantasy book—no, a romantasy she called it—that Haley threw at me yesterday. I'm hoping if I give my brain a rest from the relentless search for some solution, it may actually come up with one.

In this chapter, the main character—a High Fae Lord, who has a disturbing physical resemblance to me as well as possessing a similar bad reputation—is slowly revealing his obsession for a human woman. I look up from the page when, on quiet footsteps, the woman I'm definitely obsessed with appears in the doorway.

She's wearing a slim, soft grey skirt that ends just above her dimpled knees, grey tights and black knee-high boots that make her legs look twice their length. There's no ugly Christmas jumper today. Instead, it's a luxurious pink sweater, fluffy and soft, like fairground candy-floss. The playful colour only serves to highlight the delicate pink of her cheeks.

The only nod to the season are her earrings, tiny silver snowflakes glittering under the curtain of her silky brown hair. It's hanging long and loose, and the memory of what it feels like, what it smells like, swamps me with an overwhelming need to touch it.

She's put on a bit of makeup, only a little. I love that she doesn't slather herself in it like so many girls. She doesn't need it. But the flick of eyeliner and the way she's emphasised her curved brows and dense black lashes magnify those eyes. I marvel at the way they surprise, the exact shade of green unpredictable. Right now they're bright emerald, sparkling. Perhaps it's nerves as she prepares to face her exam; or maybe anticipation because she knows she's going to nail it.

There's a sweep of pink lipstick that draws my gaze to her soft mouth, lips glistening, inviting. I remember the warmth of them against mine. It may have been impulsive on her part, the glow of the alcohol making her bold, but I'm hopeful it won't be the last time I get to feel the press of her mouth. Surely she can see how fucking beautiful she is, reflected in my eyes.

"Pretty nice outfit for an exam. And makeup too. You look great. Extra points for presentation?" I tease.

She colours a little.

"Just something to give me a bit of confidence," she says.

Her voice is anything but. It quavers with uncertainty. She breathes in and I see the small shudder as she huffs it out, as if she's preparing to step in the ring for a fight.

"You've got this Haley. You'll smash it."

I know she will. She's been in her bedroom studying her notes for the last four hours. There can't be a thing about dog and cat dermatology she doesn't know by now.

"What time will you be home? I'll cook."

Not only is cooking something I love doing for Haley, it's another way I can soothe my frustration at this whole fucking mess. There's something so simple and normal about working in a kitchen that helps to push away the world outside and all its crap.

"Not sure," she says, her voice trailing off as she fumbles in the drawer of the hall table for her keys.

"Hey, that's OK, just whenever. I'll make it something quick. Maybe a pad thai?"

I shouldn't have asked her to commit to a time. Who do I think I am, imposing a commitment on her? She might want to go for a drink afterwards. Let off some steam with her vet nurse friends. I wonder if they're all female? I resent the thought some big-hearted, animal-loving dude might charm her. I shouldn't. I have no right to Haley's affections, but damned if I can help it.

She nods. "Sounds good."

"And let's crack another bottle of Ollie's wine. To celebrate you finishing up your course."

"Yeah. Let's do that." There's hesitancy. Her chin dips, she sweeps her hair behind one ear, and doesn't meet my eyes. The confidence of earlier, when she spoke of her studies, seems to have deserted her.

"Go well," I say. "Remember, you've got this, babe."

I swallow back the word the moment it's out. Babe. God, there's no way I should let these little terms of endearment pop out. I'll scare her off. But she doesn't seem to notice.

"Thanks, Christian. You'd make a great cheerleader," she smiles, edging on her coat and pocketing the keys with a rattle.

Once she's gone, I settle back onto the sofa and dive back into the book. The dark pointy-eared dude is about to make a move on the girl, having prised her off some other limp-dick fairy guy who seems to think he still has a right to her. Maybe the bad boy will get the girl after all. It might be a sign.

My attention flits towards a sound. The garage door opening. She must need something in there, but my brain doesn't linger on exactly what. I'm too invested in my fictional doppelgänger's success right now.

Until a distinctive rumble vibrates through the house. There's a surge of the engine, a few stutters, and then a motor roars.

She's taking the fucking Porsche.

I leap to my feet, fling open the front door and almost arse over on the icy steps. The skin on my bare feet screams from the pain as an intense chill shoots through them, and every nerve burns. My toes recoil from the stinging sensation and I spring back to the safety of the doorway.

I'm helpless to prevent this disaster. In fact, I unwittingly aided it when I neatly backed the car into the garage on Sunday. The Porsche surges out into the thankfully empty street. Haley doesn't drive, but she is. And there's nothing I can do to stop her.

Day Seven

Haley

Now I KNOW WHY my brother and Christian call this car a beast. It certainly has a mind of its own, like a barely restrained wild thing. But I have no choice except to master it.

Sitting in the driver's seat, feeling the pulsing of the engine, is like perching in a saddle atop an antsy pony that's been chomping spring grass. There's this sense that one little nudge and it will bolt.

I ease the car into the street, thankful I don't have to reverse it out of the narrow garage. Backing a car isn't something I've done too often, and the last thing I want is to graze the paintwork on my brother's pride and joy. If I'm careful, he'll never find out I've driven it. Christian's not going to rat on me. Not after what I'm about to do.

It's been at least a year since I've been behind the wheel. I don't drive, but I can drive. Ollie encouraged me to do lessons, but I didn't go the next step and sit my licence. Right now, I regret making what felt like a sensible decision. I couldn't see the point when I didn't have a car. Not only do I not need one—London's public transport system is second to none—but it's a luxury I can't afford. Parked up most of the time, sucking pounds I don't have for insurance and on-road costs, it wouldn't be a smart move.

Once out of the driveway, I pause, knowing I should punch the address into the car's navigation. I glance up and see Christian standing in the doorway, face rigid in shock, waving at me and yelling. This guy cares for me, so I know it only comes from a place of concern. I don't like being the source of the distress on his face. But there's no choice but to put him through this short-term pain. I'm doing this for him. Because, damn it all, this squooshy feeling inside of me, when I think of Christian Steele—the one that's crept up on me on stealthy feet—tells me I care about him too.

I don't hesitate. Slamming my foot on the accelerator—grateful it's automatic and I don't have to worry about my poor gear-changing skills—I'm off down the street, the raucous scream of the engine advertising my escape.

A few blocks away, while I'm still on the quiet leafy streets of Kensington, I find a spot to pull over. I pick up my phone, ignoring the two texts from Christian. My mind is made up and I fear reading them will only undermine my resolve to do what I must. Another arrives, and as the dog howl echoes through the car, I switch the phone to silent. Driving will take all my concentration and I don't need that distraction.

Thinking about Christian in any way is a distraction. I've caught myself daydreaming at work. Chuckling about things he's said—like "Do we really need that nativity scene in the kitchen? I feel like Baby Jesus is judging me every time I'm in the fridge reaching for a beer." Smiling to myself about things he's done—such as when I came home on Wednesday to find a five-foot inflatable Frosty the Snowman standing in a corner of the downstairs toilet, who now watches me every time I sit down to pee. I had no idea you could order and have such things delivered to the doorstep in literally an hour until Christian moved in.

For someone who is so adamant he's not a fan of Christmas, Christian is more than just tolerating my obsession, but leaning into it for me. Much as I claim otherwise, his constant teasing about my OTT Christmas aesthetic is a flow of warmth and fun between us, and the thought it won't be there when he goes next week gives me an unexpected pang of loss even now when it hasn't yet happened. I told myself I liked being alone; I was happy having the freedom of a house to myself, with no one to tell me what to do.

But Christian's not no one, he's someone. Like all those fangirls out there, I may have fallen for him. Unlike them, my feelings are not built on an image, but a knowing of the man behind the rock star strutting around the stage. His vulnerability, the side of him they will never see, stirs a tenderness in me. He's done it again, distracted me, and I go back to my task.

Rachel's earlier text has what I need—the address for Loreena and Tommy Bunt. She sent it through, along with the suggestion we go there tomorrow. Sitting at my desk, leafing through notes on eczema and mange, while having that information in my possession, it monopolised my brain, eating away at my common sense. The crazy idea I had last night became a certainty. I have to go today, alone.

Every day goes by is another day where the lies about Christian and Loreena swirl across the internet, and I'm not sure we can prevent that; not with last night's episode now unleashed into the world.

But Christian is trapped in that house, powerless to do anything about it. He got another email from the bastards this morning reminding him of his contractual obligations to remain where he is until after the final episode when the winner is revealed airs on TV, and to speak to no one before the live in-studio post-mortem the following day.

However, I'm not bound by that. I can at least try to find some way to help him. And that starts with Loreena. She's likely also a prisoner under house arrest, but even the toughest jails have visiting hours, and I'm off to demand my time with her.

The images of the village of Sarratt that pop up when I enter the address into my maps app are far removed from what I expected. Only a few miles from the town of Watford, yet it's a world away. There's idyllic countryside, with a stone church, meandering canals, rolling green farmland, thatched cottages and manor houses. I suspect it's more manor house where I'll find the Bunts.

Before I resume driving, I fire off an email to my course tutor. With fingers crossed, I hope they'll allow me to take the exam with the next class intake. Or if I'm really lucky, they might grant me a pass based on my coursework, which would be the best outcome, given that string of straight A's for my assignments and practicals. My low-key obsession with getting perfect grades might pay off.

Guilt at the lie grips me as I type the words, but there's no option. I've never taken a day off in my life when I wasn't actually sick; never forged a note from my mum. Yes, I'm a goody two-shoes. My lack of practice at deception triggers a nauseating fear I'll be so bad at lying I'll be found out.

Another reason not to crash the car. It would be fairly difficult to sustain the untruth I'm home in bed with a blinding migraine if I end up in hospital after a traffic accident. I also have this irrational feeling about using the migraine as an excuse, as if next time I have a real one—thankfully that's not so often these days—no one will believe me. The girl who cried wolf. With a tentative tap, the message is gone. There's no going back now.

I take a deep breath and edge out into the street, steeling myself for what lies beyond the next intersection. In moments, I will be on Notting Hill Gate in the thick of lunchtime traffic and soon on the A40. When I was learning to drive, I hated the motorway; wanted to cling to the city streets with one or two lanes and sluggish traffic, but today there's no realistic alternative. I hand over my trust to the soothing voice of the navigation, set my mouth in a determined line and drive.

As I merge into the slow lane coming onto the motorway, I grip the wheel so hard my fingers hurt. I'm aware of the curious looks from other drivers. It's probably not every day they see a bright yellow Porsche hugging the left-hand lane, sedately keeping below the speed limit. It's not only my nervousness from lack of experience; if I'm pulled over by the traffic police, there's more than a speeding ticket coming my way.

I follow the instructions carefully—A40, M40, M25, A404—each one just as daunting. Finally, the exit leads to an actual road, not another motorway. I breathe a sigh of relief, taking a hand off the wheel one at a time to flex my aching fingers. I roll each shoulder backwards and forwards in turn, trying to ease the tense, painful knots.

Now I no longer need to focus my attention so tightly on the traffic, thoughts of what lies ahead of me creep in. What if I've driven the thirty miles out here and they won't see me? Loreena might have decided to go to ground and let it run its course. Knowing her, she may plan to give them a giant middle finger by carrying on as if nothing has happened. But I saw her on that TV screen. Her tear-streaked face and the huddle of contestants trying to comfort her suggest that whatever happened got underneath that hard-arse devil may care attitude she presents to the world.

And last night's episode, the way it portrayed her as some sort of victim to Christian's villain? If it's one thing Loreena Bunt isn't, it's a victim. I'm counting on her being as blindingly angry as Christian, the difference being she might be able to do something about it, with my help and Rachel's smarts.

The road narrows until it's little more than a lane buried between high hedgerows that look like they'd be home to all the creatures that adorn my favourite Christmas baubles—and Christian's body. The navigation announces the destination is on my left and I swing into the wide entrance to a driveway.

Ahead of me, flanked by two high stone walls, a set of wrought-iron gates with a row of pointy Fleur de Lys along the upper edge bars my way. I imagine it's an effective deterrent. No one would want to climb over such an evil-looking barrier. With a tap of a button, the electric window whirs downward and I push the intercom. I look up to see a small camera directed my way. Someone is watching me and it's creepy knowing some invisible person scrutinises my face.

"State your name and business, please." The voice through the speaker has an unfriendly metallic tone to it.

"Haley Templeton," I say. "I'm Christian Steele's girlfriend."

Driving here, I felt a growing panic. What if having come all this way, the Bunts refuse to let me in? I needed something compelling. I figured this lie might do the trick. I've told so many lies today I'm already going to hell, so why not another?

I don't think Christian would mind. The way he looks at me sometimes, I think he might even like it. If I admit it, I might like it too. But if there's a chance for this unexpected friendship between us to blossom into something more, it has to wait. Right now, the best thing I can do for Christian is carry on with this mission.

The intercom falls silent, the faint hiss of static the only reply. Perhaps the person speaking had to think about it a moment. Or ask someone else for permission to let me through. Eventually, the gates glide open.

There's no sign of a house at first; only a winding driveway between massive oak trees, bare of leaves. Branches like stark fingers reach for each other, meeting above my head, while others point at the gloomy grey sky. I inch forward, the car gliding over the fine gravel surface; the mosaic of tiny pebbles crunching under the tyres.

Over a small rise, the house comes into view. Walls of honeyed stone rise three storeys, two broad wings either side of a turreted central tower. Not quite Downton Abbey, it's impressive all the same. By comparison, Ollie's beautiful country home down in Somerset seems modest.

The trees give way to gardens, manicured lawns and shrubs trimmed into precise geometric shapes—balls and pyramids, elaborate spirals and cones.

I pull up under the pillars of a portico and step out onto huge stone pavers. Beyond the imposing columns, water cascades in layers down a tiered fountain. A frowning Neptune sits on a rocky island at its centre, one arm held aloft, clutching his trident, the other cradling a pitcher. Water pours from it, spilling into the lower level where horses with curled manes like the crests of waves leap from the depths as if trying to escape. It's stunning, but the friendly bubbling water is not enough to drown out the pounding of my heart or soothe the knot in my stomach.

I walk up the steps to the door, my boot heels echoing in the cavernous entry way. In the centre of the door is a gigantic Christmas wreath. Red and green velvet ribbons ensnare stems of sleek green holly and bundles of cedar. Gilded pine cones and seed pods sprayed silver glint in its depths. The tiny bird figurines nestled amongst the greenery are so realistic I expect them to take flight at my approach. A huge deep red velvet bow drapes artfully from the base. I trace my fingers across the greenery and the fragrance of the woods, overlaid with a hint of cinnamon, fills my nose, a sweet soothing smell.

The beauty of the wreath gives the imposing wooden door a benign feeling, as if the house welcomes me. I'd love to spend more time examining the intricate work, but that's not why I'm here.

I reach for the huge brass knocker, then freeze, hand poised in mid-air as the door swings open. It's not a stiff butler in a starched suit that greets me, but a man in a leather bomber jacket. A man I recognise. It's the guy who accosted me outside Christian's apartment. I take a step back, my instinct to flee triggered.

"Hello, luv," he says with a smirk. "Here to do the cleaning, are we?"

His smarmy face makes my hackles rise, like Mularkey in the park one day, when an aggressive dog zeroed in on us, intent on starting a brawl. In the same way as she did then, rather than run, I choose to stand my ground and prepare for a fight.

This guy will not be the reason I fail to see Loreena Bunt. Seeing me draw myself straighter and narrow my eyes only provokes greater amusement in his. I peer around his bulky form at the sound of approaching footsteps from somewhere inside the vast entry hall beyond.

The man who appears from the left wears a crooked smile on his face, bracketed by deep lines. His tanned skin looks oddly out of place on this mid-winter day, as if he's just jetted in from the south of Spain. Wiry bristles of steely grey hair, cut flat like an exotic form of scrubbing brush, sit above darker brows. His eyes sparkle, an unusually intense shade of blue that reminds me of Christian.

He's not a big man, but he walks with the confidence of one. Even though he's dressed casually—jeans, a sweater with a Burberry logo and a pair of chunky Nike trainers that make his feet look huge—he projects the air of the boss as much as if he wore a suit and tie.

"Get your big ugly mug out of here, Raymond, you tosser," he says, in an accent straight out of *EastEnders*. He elbows the big man aside. "You're scaring the girl."

"Hello, luv." He extends a broad hand with thick stumpy fingers. "Tommy Bunt."

I respond without thinking, offering my own. He clasps it firmly, but with care not to crush my fingers against the row of heavy gold rings adorning his every finger. Diamonds sparkle off some, their flashy rays at odds with the very down-to-earth ordinariness of this man.

"Nice to meet you, Tommy." My voice comes out small, betraying my bravado is only surface deep. "I'm Haley."

"Christian's girlfriend, eh?" he says. "I wasn't expecting you. But I'm damn glad you're here."

"So am I." A raspy voice sounds from somewhere above. I look up to the top of the grand central staircase, with its gleaming bannisters and deep burgundy carpet. Loreena Bunt stands in the centre, barely recognisable.

Normally dressed like some exotic bird, in flamboyant clothes and extravagant colour, today she's wearing skinny black jeans and a plain cream roll-neck sweater. Her famously big hair isn't teased into its usual golden halo. It hangs long and loose, as if she's a refugee from a surfer movie. Naked of makeup, her face is still attractive, but she looks more like the forty-something woman she is. The bruised hollows beneath her eyes suggest sleepless nights. Like Christian, the aftermath of *Wild From The Win* weighs heavily upon her.

"So am I," she repeats softly, advancing towards me down the stairs, her smile warm, her face open and welcoming. She stands tall, taking elegant steps, like a debutante descending into a ballroom. Those jerks might have tried to beat Loreena down, but they haven't succeeded.

CHAPTER 18

Day Seven

LOREENA PUSHES OPEN THE heavy wood-panelled doors of a lounge room and waves me inside with a smile. Here is still more evidence of this woman's dual life. Rather than the tacky over the top furnishings one might expect from someone who appears in public in neon orange fur, the decor is subdued and tasteful. Neither fusty and old-fashioned or jarringly modern, it offers a warm welcome.

A fire crackles in the hearth, below a wide mantle lush with garlands of greenery. A log crackles, spitting out smoky bursts of tangy pine-sap.

There's a Christmas tree in the corner, decked out in an elegant minimalist style. I step towards the regular pyramid-shaped tree, breathing in its sweet aroma, and confirm it is indeed a Fraser Fir.

Not native to the UK, it's the classic American Christmas tree, imported—and therefore expensive.

Delicate silver filigree baubles nestle amongst the foliage, light bouncing off others with tiny birds captured inside glass spheres. I smile at the irony of Loreena's tastefully restrained Christmas decorating compared to my own exuberant style. Christian would probably suggest I take note. Although from his theatrical eye rolls as he stumbles across festive pieces in new spots, and the constant good-natured teasing, I suspect he doesn't mind indulging me in my need to lavish Christmas cheer on every space in the house. He might be right on one count—perhaps the toilet cistern doesn't really require decoration, but I'm not going to admit that to Mr Grinch.

I'd love to spend time admiring the tree more closely, but Loreena is settling herself into a wingback armchair. It's modern and com-fortable-looking but still completely at home in this room, with its traditional floral-printed wallpaper in soft tones of duck-egg blue. I sink into the deep-seated sofa opposite, rubbing my hand across the lush blue velvet, before arranging myself in a comfortable valley in the mountain of cushions.

Loreena sits, elbows on knees, her chin propped on clasped hands and gazes at me as if I'm some rare species of animal invading her lounge. Her eyes are wistful as she speaks.

"How is he? How's he doing?" Her first thoughts are of Christ-ian.

"As well as can be expected. He's looking a lot better than when I found him on my doorstep last Saturday."

"And after watching...Episode 5...and then last night?"

"Not so good. Upset. Angry. Pissed off. Frustrated."

I see the glisten of emotion in the corner of her eye.

"I'm so glad he's got you," she says, her voice low. "If it wasn't for Tommy, I'd have broken out of here and gone to their offices, and then...well, I did look up how long you get for murder."

She shakes her head and lowers it into her hands, fingers covering her eyes, and a muffled sound, almost a sob, escapes. After a moment, she drags her hands down her face with a weary sigh and braves my gaze again.

"The crap those bastards implied...that maybe there was something going on between us, and that Christian roughed me up a bit—you have to know that is so far from the truth, right?"

I nod and swallow hard. There's a ball of anger and sorrow swelling in my throat.

"I know." I choke out the words.

"Tommy and I have been together a long time. We were so young. Two teenagers with nothing but each other and a determination to get something better for ourselves. And we have."

There's a small upturn in her mouth as she scans the room, a modest pride as she notes the material evidence of their success. There's obviously a lot of money to be made in auto parts.

"And we've been happy, for the most part. But we couldn't have kids. Tommy would have loved a son. A boy to take to the footy. For me, if we had—I'd have wanted him to be like Christian."

"Tommy might not have got his football fan then," I smile. Christian doesn't neglect his body, and it certainly shows. He had a set of weights delivered on Tuesday. But while he might be dedicated to his own fitness, Christian doesn't seem to nudge the TV onto sports channels or show any interest in that direction.

"He'd still have been satisfied, I think." There's a fond look in Loreena's eyes, a motherly expression in the curve of her mouth, a softness in her voice.

Those people out there who think she and Christian are a thing, a juicy reverse age-gap hookup, him the prey for a conniving cougar, couldn't have it more wrong. Christian's protectiveness towards this woman, and hers for him, is more than an unlikely sudden friendship, but much deeper, each providing something the other lacks. He's told me a bit about his father and brothers, but hardly a mention of his mother. I know why Loreena was drawn to Christian. I wonder why he might seek that type of bond with a virtual stranger? He's shared so much with me, I suppose he'll tell me if and when he's ready.

It's been a new experience, being Christian's confidante, his safe place. Usually I'm the one being encouraged to unburden my problems to my protective friends. Now it seems Loreena is happy for me to be her confidante, too. It inspires a strange feeling; this incredibly strong woman looks to me for strength.

"Figured you might like a cuppa, luv." The fluted silver tray, with a floral teapot and delicate bone china cups, looks bizarre in Tommy's meaty hands. He's got the build of a scrappy prizefighter; not someone you'd imagine as a footman waiting on ladies in the drawing room of a stately home.

Loreena surveys the plate of brownie so heavy with chocolate it's almost black. "Tommy's been baking. My favourite, but I'll share."

A throaty cackle spills from him, and the crinkles bracketing those brilliant blue eyes deepen in amusement.

"I'll leave you to it," he says. "Don't need me sticking my beak in."

"Thanks, love." Loreena places a gentle hand over his. The long scarlet-tipped nails are the only recognisable sign of TV Loreena. As Tommy leaves, closing the door with a definitive clunk, the real Loreena in front of me lifts the pot and pours tea as daintily as the countess who probably lived here before her. She offers me the cup, and a piece of the rich dark brownie on a fancy side plate. I clutch my grateful fingers around the warm rose-patterned china and wait.

"I can see why he's smitten with you," she twinkles at me.

Confusion whirls in my brain. And then the wisps of denial clear, like mist slipping away, chased off by the revealing light of the sun. I've tried to hide from it, but it's pointless. The way he looks at me. Touches me. I know this to be true, and it brings a flutter of something strange yet magical deep inside me. A little feeling I haven't felt for a long time.

"How do you...?" My words falter.

Her smile is conspiratorial, brimming with delight at the secret, and revealing the faintest hint of wrinkles around her big blue eyes. They're more beautiful for it, more defined. She should let the Botox go.

"Darling, when you're confined to a tiny tent in the long dark of a winter night in bloody Scotland, you've got a lot of time to talk."

"He talked about me?"

"He did. A real heart to heart. He's scared, though. Burned by what's happened in the past."

I nod, remembering what they did to him and Waverley, as if the world can't bear the thought of Christian being happy, in love. Although he and Waverley weren't in love—fond of each other, friends, but not love. What might they do therefore to someone he does love?

Is he in love with me? That possibility scares me, too. After the disaster of Jack, my bruised heart realised he hadn't loved me. It's wary of that word.

"He's worried what might happen if he lets it out. I'm so glad he at least found a way to tell you what he's feeling. If that's the one good thing to have come out of all this shitty stuff, then it was worth it. Love will find a way, as they say."

Her mouth tips up in a smile, and she leans forward, squeezing my hand. I'm not going to let on that Christian hasn't said a word. Although I think without words, he may have said a lot, except I wasn't listening. A kaleidoscope of memories tumbles through my mind, tiny fragments of time we've spent together reflected in the new light of Loreena's revelation. I turn them over, watching the old patterns of Christian's and my past reshaping themselves into colourful new ones. My chest tightens, as if my ribs are trying to contain the expanding bubble of awareness inside that threatens to burst, altering my entire world.

"He's chosen well who to give his to. The fact you're here tells me that. And, look at you." She tenderly tucks back a strand of hair, and I almost want to close my eyes in bliss, like one of my dogs accepting a fond pat. I'm not sure what I expected of Loreena, or to feel towards her, but it certainly wasn't this warmth. Somehow, Christian saw this in her.

"Lovely," she murmurs. "He said you were."

CHAPTER 19

Day Seven

Haley

I SIT, STILL REELING from the knowledge. Somehow, across the years, in all those small encounters, Christian has built up feelings for me while I was oblivious. Did I just not see? Or did he hide them well? I scroll back through those times, replaying them in exquisite slow motion through a new lens, bringing them into sharper focus.

In the early days, behind the scenes of the *Star Power* show, there were almost daily hugs of congratulations and consolation. Did my innocent embraces and brief kisses brushed on his stubbly cheek offer him the hope of something more?

There was one night later on, when the band was really taking off. We were all together at an awards ceremony, Ollie the only one of the four guys whose family turned up in support. During the dinner before, Christian sat opposite me, and we talked across the table. All of us there hummed with anticipation, the air tingling with electricity. But it seems perhaps something else lay behind the intensity in Christian's blue eyes, and his singular focus on me.

At the after party we all danced, a riotous celebration of their first big win. In the final slow dance, as the evening wound to a close, I laughed with Teddy, he so painfully shy back then, stepping all over my feet, and Christian teasingly nudged him aside, claiming he needed to save me from being crippled by his bandmate's clumsiness. There are nuances to the memory of those minutes—his breath on my neck, a firm hand splayed on my lower back, a small contented sigh, and a shy kiss on the cheek as he thanked me for dancing with him—all rushing back in bright colours. In the glow of alcohol and with the lingering buzz of the band's success pulsing in my veins, I'd thought nothing of it. But it wasn't nothing. Not for him.

There was the record launch when Ollie insisted I come along. They imitated a U2 publicity stunt, playing unannounced on the roof of a city building. When the crowd got out of hand, and security started looking skyward, the guys abandoned their instruments to the crew. We raced down the stairs of a back fire escape, tumbling into their manager, Ewan's tiny Citroën, an unlikely getaway car, like a group of naughty kids, laughing and squealing. Teddy in the front seat beside Ewan, Garrett trying to make himself small in the centre of the back seat, Ollie falling in one rear door and pulling Kendra in after him and Christian doing the same on the other side, dragging me onto his knee. I can still feel the heat of his body beneath mine, the strong arm looped across my waist bracing me so I wasn't flung all over the place by Ewan's stunt driving.

And then last year at Ollie's country house, that awful bank holiday weekend when we were all there—me with Jack. Jack and I argued, our relationship in its death throes. He sniped at me endlessly, over tiny ridiculous things, in what I now know was his pathetic attempt to make me the one to call time on it. Desperate to create an excuse for me to walk away before I found out what he and Paige were up to behind my back. I can still picture Christian's look of disgust, the tense set of his jaw, him brushing past me in the hallway, in a whisper asking if I was OK. I wasn't, but I'd lied, ashamed.

Over three years, we've spoken, touched, hugged, offered chaste kisses of greeting, yet all I saw was a rather distant but pleasant, polite guy; my brother's friend. But Christian has seen more, and wanted more. This is another reason he chose me as his sanctuary. I swallow hard. A whirlwind of emotions swirls like I'm in a snow globe, plucked into the air by a giant hand and given a vigorous shake. I buy myself time, deflecting Loreena's curiosity with a question.

"And he stopped them using the snares?" Christian feared with him gone, they'd go ahead anyway, even though Rachel believed otherwise.

"Yes, that too. Tell him it worked. They collected them all in. Issued everyone with a 'bonus gift' of some supermarket chicken and told us all to stick to fishing."

"So, how come they kicked you out?" I ask.

She laughs. "No darling, they didn't kick me out. I demanded to go. There was no way I'd stay and be a player in that charade so they could profit from it. I was so damn happy to leave."

"But you were crying. You looked so sad."

"Oh, that wasn't about the leaving," she scoffs. "Well, it kind of was. There were a few of the other contestants, the men, who were decent human beings. Not the sharpest tools on the shelf, but I can forgive stupid. I got a bit emotional, hearing they were sorry to see me go. Wasn't expecting *that*. And, then, seeing the car there, the security staff—like a replay of the day before when Christian left. It hit home how awful they were to him—and me. The same shit happening again. With one important difference—those bastards don't see me as a threat. Which gives me an advantage."

"How come you two teamed up so well?" I'm curious. Christian hasn't really explained why he sat there with such a smug smile when they announced Loreena would be his official partner. "Opposites attract?"

The moment the words are out, I cringe a little, thinking I've offered this woman a back-handed insult. However, she takes no offence and laughs, that throaty rasp the nation knows spilling out.

"No," she chuckles, "and it wasn't me going all cougar on him either. Although it was fun pretending." Her eyes spark with wicked glee at the memory.

I smile. "You did a good job convincing a few million people otherwise." She's a brilliant actor. Anyone watching that show would fully believe her goal was to sink those red claws into Christian's young body.

Now, seeing her and Tommy together—her love for the stocky rough around the edges guy with his incongruous Cockney accent and designer leisure wear is on full display here in their home; and his adoration and tender concern for the surprisingly serene and kind woman in front of me is indisputable—I have no doubt Loreena had no need or desire to ensnare Christian.

"Oh, of course I was drawn to him," she says. "And him to me. But not like that. You see, while we might appear very different,

Christian and I are the same. We recognised that in each other. The world sees both of us in a certain way. They want to label us, judge us, and find us wanting, so they can feel justified in saying hurtful things about us. They get to say things they'd never say to our faces, and no one calls them out on it. I'm no psychologist, but I think most people need an outlet for all the nastiness inside them. Society expects us to hide it. Be nice, polite, respectful. But with celebrities, particularly ones who are portrayed as behaving badly—well, they're fair game."

I nod and shuffle a little in the seat, feeling the warmth of shame rising in my cheeks. Loreena is exactly right. I know, because I've been one of those people. Judged her, judged Christian, and all the others paraded across our screens and in the newspapers. From Loreena's sympathetic gaze, I suspect she understands the reason for my discomfort. Shouldn't I be the one offering sympathy here?

"I'm sorry," I stumble over the words. "I..."

She extends a hand across mine. "It's fine," she says. "And I'll be the first to admit I bring some of it on myself." There's that hint of wicked fun in the upturn of her mouth. "But he doesn't. It's not fair." Her smile falls, a wistful shadow dimming her eyes, like a cloud marring the blue of a summer sky. "Anyway," she says briskly, gathering herself a little straighter in her chair, summoning a brighter tone. "Let me tell you how we ended up here."

Loreena explains how things rolled out on the show. I know most of it, but it's safer to pretend ignorance. If I have to live the lie, swear Christian told me nothing, she'll be a useful witness, who can back me in the claim that everything I know about *Wild For The Win* came from her.

She howls with delight at the producers unwittingly throwing her and Christian together. But there's a fleeting sadness in her eyes as she suggests what everyone knows—from the beginning, it was obvious one of them would have won the prize. Her charity, a women's refuge, is one she's supported for a long time and she'll donate to them, anyway. There's no doubt, judging by this house, Tommy and Loreena are seriously wealthy. Through their ability to give generously, the refuge won't be short of money over the holiday season. Sadly, Christmas isn't a time of peace and harmony for everyone, rather one where family violence escalates, so it's much needed. Although, it's because of Loreena's connection to the refuge that the implication in last night's episode, that Christian hurt her enrages her even more.

"That they'd fabricate a story about something like that...it's so wrong." She shakes her head with a frustrated huff, blue eyes blazing. "You see, if I say nothing, Christian has to live with everyone thinking he's a bad man, not the gentle, caring guy we know. But, if I come out and claim it's not true...well, some people are going to say *I* lied—accusing him and then backing off for fear of being caught out in the lie. It feeds the myth that women make false accusations." There's an angry set to her mouth, her face flushed with indignation. "You know I've spent a lot of time at the refuge. I've sat with these women, heard their stories. So many are too frightened to speak up; often they're scared no one will believe them. Things like the kind of stunt those bastards pulled on nationwide TV perpetuate that fear."

She pauses a moment, one arm folded across her chest, propping her chin on the other, and her mouth lifts in a smile. "I'm ashamed to admit, when I watched the episode last night, it made me want to dish out a bit of violence of my own," she says with a coy dip of her head. "But Tommy told me to settle down. And he's right—there are better ways. Money is their god, and that's where we're going to hit them. Right where it will hurt them most."

"We?" I ask. "You and Tommy."

"No." She spreads her palms wide. "What can I do? I'm stuck here. *You* and Tommy."

I nod. I'd thought if I was to help Christian, I'd be fighting this on my own. Now it seems I'll have an ally. That's a relief, especially as it's a man who looks like he's the veteran of a few fights. Tommy Bunt certainly didn't achieve all he has by being timid.

"My lawyer friend came by last night and took a look at the agreement Christian signed. She thinks it only prevents *him* from blowing the whistle on them. That they can't touch him legally if the information about what he did comes from someone else. Like you."

She smirks, nodding. "Tommy's going to be pissed. He paid his lawyer a large amount of money to come to the same conclusion. It seems, in the hurry to bundle us off out of there, they didn't cover all their bases."

As if he's heard his name, Tommy arrives with a fresh pot of tea and a plate heaped with neat triangular sandwiches. He settles into an armchair, a twin of the one Loreena's in. They're an unlikely king and queen, side by side on their thrones.

"Right," he says, keen blue eyes darting between us. "Whatcha thinking, ladies?"

Two hours go by, and as I stand to leave, there's a wrench as if I'm parting from old friends. I want to spend more time with these two; and it seems I will be with Tommy at least, as we fire off texts to lawyers, mine to Rachel, and his to a man named Jeremy. The plan is for the four of us to meet to plot strategy tomorrow.

Raymond, who oddly doubles as a makeshift butler as well as Tommy's spy, greets me at the front door with my coat in hand. I button it tight, ready to face the bleak outside, where the day has disappeared, and the late afternoon sky hangs heavy with cloud. Loreena waits, Tommy the shorter of the pair hovering behind her. As I sling my bag over my shoulder, she steps in, embracing me in a hug so hard I can barely breathe; my face crushed against her ample breasts, her hands clasped around my head. I breathe in the heavy spice of her perfume, a sultry oriental fragrance, so like the sexy bedroom-eyed Loreena she presents to the world, it might have been crafted for her. Standing back, she gives me a smug smile.

"Did he tell you about the song?" One immaculate brow arches, and I can see she's fizzing like a fresh glass of champagne.

"The song?"

"Untouchable. Is that right? His favourite."

I nod. "Yeah, he wrote that one."

She leans in and whispers it against my ear, a secret just for me.

"He wrote it for you, darling."

"No," I say, pulling back with a frown, shaking my head in disbelief. "He wrote that three years ago. I mean, I hardly knew him."

"Oh, but he knew you, Haley," she says.

'Untouchable'. The song *only* Christian sings. The lyrics framed on his bedroom wall. For me. About me. I don't argue with the truth now it's in front of me. The pieces of the puzzle of Christian Steele's feelings for me have fallen into place this afternoon, while my own lay scattered haphazardly; my mind in disarray, challenging me to make sense of this picture. It's complicated, even before I begin to consider the weight of the fact he's my brother's best friend.

As I coax the engine to life, with its decadent purr rumbling through the portico, Tommy and Loreena stand side by side on the front steps. They offer cheery waves as if they're seeing me off after a tea party, not a secret meeting of the resistance. Things could still get ugly, but after our conversation, my anxiety has subsided. Hope we could actually win this war surges in me, knowing Tommy and Loreena are in our corner. In *our* corner. Christian's and mine. It's strange how easily the 'he' has become 'we'. And this half of the 'we' has put him through unnecessary worry today.

Guilt drives me to pull over just before I get to the road and I send a response to his earlier frantic texts. I try to sound casual, like nothing much has happened, hoping he'll forgive my recklessness when I later confess what I've already done for him, and what I'm about to do.

Day Seven

Christian

THE CHIRP OF HALEY'S text is the best sound I've heard all day. I plunge towards the coffee table where my phone has sat, silent, brooding like me. With every hour that's passed, my worry has escalated. I'm like an anxious parent who's let their kid take out the family car for the first time.

Part of me feels guilt at my fear. Haley's a capable woman, not a silly teen, and doubting her ability seems disloyal to her and to the belief I have in her. But my feelings for this woman, and how important she is to me, ride roughshod over that.

My eyes race across the message.

UNTOUCHABLE GIRL: Be there around 5. Hope the girls are behaving.

I glance at the sideboard where Haley's treasured Christmas clock, a gift from her parents, ticks off the minutes. The little alpine town in miniature glows warmly in the deepening dusk. Lights have flickered on in the tiny cottages, and the realistic-looking flame of an old-fashioned gas street lamp has sprung to life. It's been agony listening and watching the jaunty nutcracker figure—a more Christmassy alternative to a cuckoo—stride out every quarter hour, marking her absence with the blare of his cornet. The hands show ten past the hour. Four more outings for the little soldier and she'll be here.

Forty minutes later, I hear the grumble of the automatic door. *This* is the best sound I've heard today. I leave the dogs where they are, frolicking in the back yard, their happy place despite the cold. With their knitted Christmas jumpers, neither seems to notice the wintery chill. I feel this need to meet Haley at the door by myself. Just me, without their welcome dance to distract us.

I hover in the hallway, as the thunk of a car door and the beep of a remote echo from the garage, then pace a little, trying to walk off the jangling emotions clashing in my brain. My chest is tight with relief—she's home, and that's the main thing—but I also harbour a simmering irrational anger at the risk she took. It's not the possibility of the fine a cop would have slapped on her—a few hundred pounds wouldn't be great, but it's not the end of the world. I'd pay it for her in a heartbeat.

Nor is it the prospect of a pissed off Ollie if she'd damaged the car. He'd be as forgiving as I am where Haley's concerned. These siblings have a closeness I've not experienced. He adores her and she can do no wrong in his eyes.

It's my protectiveness towards her that has caused worry and anger to battle it out in my head all day, preventing me from concentrating on anything. I abandoned the book even though I wanted to reassure myself the villain in the story still might actually get the girl. I should have read through all the contract paperwork again, but my brain was zinging in all directions—and anyway, what more could I find that Rachel couldn't?

For five hours I've languished here, my gut tied in knots, sick with fear of her being harmed, conjuring up dire scenarios. I visualised some idiot pulling out in front of her, cutting her off, and her, lacking experience, unable to brake in time and avoid a collision. Or someone running a red—they do it all the time—ploughing into her, the airbags blooming around her like oversized flower petals. Even in a slow speed crash, people can get badly hurt—some die. The cocoon of the Porsche's leather sports seats, tested on a racetrack, should protect her, but in a freak accident they might not.

Now I know I can relegate all of these worries to fiction, the product of my overactive imagination. I should relax, but I'm still coiled tight. Hearing the click of small booted heels, I can't help myself; I fling the door wide.

Haley stands on the top step, hand poised in mid-air. Her pale face and the little furrow of tension between her brows trigger my concern. Wary wide green eyes meet mine, but her kissable rosebud mouth curves upwards in a small smile; there's no hint of anything amiss. Worry has no place here anymore. She's here, and she's safe. My little wavering flame of anger sputters and dies, too. How could I ever be properly angry at Haley?

Relief takes over and on impulse, I scoop her into my arms, wrap her so tight, reassuring myself she's whole and undamaged. No, I shouldn't be doing this, but I am. And fuck it, I'm not damn sorry. I tense a little, pausing to put out tentative feelers of sensation, checking she's OK with this, not repelled by the gesture.

She's tired. I can feel the weariness and perhaps relief as well. Her exam is over; she drove that beast of a car without incident; she's home. Maybe this is why she doesn't flinch. It's been a hell of a week for her, too. That she'd accept comfort in a friendly hug isn't unexpected after everything that's happened. But this is not a friendly hug to me. I don't want to accept a future where this is as good as it gets. I'm not sure how to get to that future, so for now I savour the present, the warmth and softness of her damping down my own anxieties, helping me forget *why* I'm here, and focus on just *being* here in this moment.

The scent of green apples and flowers tantalises my nose as I rest my head on her shoulder. Outside, the chill of a dark winter evening has settled on the world, but I close my eyes and inhale the fragrance of spring in my arms.

"I'm sorry," she murmurs. Her warm breath penetrates the flannel of my shirt, like a kiss against my collarbone. "For ignoring you when I left. For ignoring your texts."

"It's OK," I say. "I shouldn't have pestered you like that. Not while you were in your exam."

I feel the slightest stiffening of the compliant body in my arms. She lifts her head, tilting it up at me, and I see the wariness return to her gaze.

"About that." Her throat pulses as she swallows. "I didn't go."

"You didn't go?" I draw back, my brows flying upwards. There's a tick in my jaw as I try to restrain my shock.

"There was someone I needed to see."

"Someone you needed to see?"

Why the fuck am I parroting everything she says back at her as a question? She's caught me off guard. I can't imagine what was so important Haley would blow off her exam, not when I know how much this whole vet stuff means to her.

"Look," she says, pulling away and shrugging off her coat. It's a casual action, like there's nothing out of the ordinary, but why the hell do I feel something bad is coming my way? "Go sit in the lounge and I'll bring you a coffee," she directs, as she hangs up her things. "I've got a lot to tell you."

"It's me who should be making you coffee," I protest. "After all, I've just been lounging around here all day."

"Just lounging?" One dark brow tips upward.

"OK, lounging, worrying, and text bombing you because of it."

"Yeah, I think twenty texts could be classed as bombing." Her lips purse, and both brows dip, as if she's about to growl at me like the parent of a naughty toddler. But, just as I can't be mad at her, Haley seems to have difficulty scowling at me, and she relents, her mouth lifting in an amused smile. "It's fine. You were probably right to be concerned, but I assure you the car is as perfect as when I left." That's good to know, but I'm more concerned that she's as perfect as when she stepped out that door. "Just don't tell Ollie, OK," she adds, tapping her nose with a finger and tossing me a conspiratorial grin.

"No way," I say. "He'd be pissed I didn't fling myself in front of the car to stop you."

"An odd hood ornament?"

"Odd?" I adopt a hurt expression.

"Cute," she offers. "Especially when you're giving me those damn puppy dog eyes." Her voice has the faintest touch of breathiness. She's flirting with me. If she's flirting, I'm flirting right back.

"Like this?" I exaggerate them more.

She tilts her head to the side, sweet dimples bracketing her lips as they curve into an amused smile at my expression.

"Works every time." My mouth slants up in a sly grin. "Learned from Mularkey and Tully."

"Yeah, where are they?" she frowns.

"Oh, shit. I need to let them in." I turn to head down the hallway. "Locked them out. They've been in and out about ten times this afternoon. Camped around that big tree in the corner, scratching at the bottom. They seem to think there's something up there. A squirrel maybe?"

"*Squirrels*," she laughs. "Three of them. Smart ones. They come into the yard when they're bored and mess with the dogs for enter-tainment. I worry they'll get it wrong one day and become lunch, but they never seem to slip up. Drives the dogs crazy."

"Them and me too," I sigh, thinking of the afternoon spent tracking up and down the hallway in response to pleading paws scraping my knee and urgent whines. "Anyway, I figured you wouldn't want their muddy feet leaping over you. I'll go get them."

I leave Haley in the kitchen. Grabbing up the now mud-smeared old towel I found in the laundry from where I left it on the hall floor, I head for the back door. The moment I open it, the dogs come barrelling towards me, tongues lolling happily, although casting re-luctant glances back towards the tree.

I deal with their muddy paws one dog at a time. I dab at Tully's first, the easier to clean with her shorter, more club-like feet. Once done, I open the door a crack, letting her through and then close it immediately to stop Mularkey plunging after her with her filthy brown paws. It's like drafting cattle, something I know how to do well, and the second dog eyes me, frustrated.

"Look, you, if you want to be first, you need to stop doing this to yourself."

I gently lift each of her wide paws, wiping at the webbed feet with hooked claws, perfect for gripping snow like her sled dog ancestors. Also perfect for gathering mud. She sighs and stands more patiently than she'd prefer and lets me clean them. Once finished, I open the door and Mularkey blasts through the narrow gap like a rocket, a blaze of red in her jumper with its pattern of dancing Santas. It's freezing out here; maybe snow tonight. I shiver a little and seek the warmth of the house.

Passing Haley's room, there's the creak of the door and she appears, hair a little wispy and dishevelled. She's changed out of her day clothes and donned pyjamas. They seem to be her favourite thing to wear. I swear she'd go to work in them if she could. Damn it, if I was her boss, I'd let her.

There's something about the intoxicating mixture of child-like innocence and very adult allure that turns me on when I see Haley in pyjamas. Maybe it's the way the tops reveal the slight movement of bare unbound breasts beneath, freed of a bra. I'd love nothing better than to slip my hand inside, work my way over the soft skin of her stomach, cup each one, and reverently pay homage to the peaks of those nipples that even the wildly-patterned fabric—a riot of puppies in Christmas hats—can't obscure.

The plain red pyjama bottoms hug her neat curves, leaving no doubt there's all woman underneath, begging my hands to cup that beautiful arse, press her body against my blossoming erection and grind myself against it. Fuck, I've had a near permanent hard-on since I walked in the door of this house.

I pause to let her go ahead of me. It's not only the gentleman in me. This way I can watch the sway of her hips as she pads along the wooden floorboards, footsteps muffled by bright red slippers with reindeer faces on the toes. And she can't see the hunger in my gaze, the look of a man desperate and starving, with the thing to sate his need there in front of him, but still beyond the reach of his hand.

Two mugs of coffee wait on the kitchen counter; mine strong and dark, hers milky-sweet and spicy. Even our drink choices scream to the world how opposite we are. Cup in hand, Haley heads to the lounge, choosing a place on the sofa I've claimed as my own, which I interpret as permission to sit beside her.

I sip at the coffee, warming my cold hands on the mug, the burning bitter liquid a welcome hit of caffeine to wake me up for this conversation. I have no idea what Haley has to say, but I have a suspicion I'm not going to like it.

"I didn't go to my exam today, because there was something more important I had to do." I grit my teeth, wanting to tell her showing the world her ability is incredibly important; and surely any qualification is another step towards her becoming what she should be—a fully-fledged vet, not the nurse assisting at their side. As if reading my thoughts, she adds, "And that's fine. My tutor confirmed they'll give me a grade based on my coursework because I was sick on the day of the exam." She looks up at me from under dark lashes, lips pressed together, a little pink of shame colouring her cheeks. "Yeah, I lied," she admits. "But sometimes lying is necessary."

"So, where did you go?" I probe gently.

"Sarratt. It's near Watford."

I feel like I've heard that name before, but I'm too shocked by the fact she drove the Porsche all that way. On the motorways as well, for god sakes. I shudder as images of her journey spring to mind. In the low yellow sports car, buried in traffic; impatient cars whizzing by and brutish trucks thundering past almost grazing smaller vehicles.

"Haley—" I chide.

"Don't start," she says, holding up a hand. Her eyes close in frustration, and she bites at her lip. "Please."

The rebuke freezes in my throat. My words on this subject are unwanted and unnecessary. If I'm going to have any future with Haley, I need to squash down my overwhelming need to protect her. Let her see I have faith in her to make decisions and to take action without the shadow of all my worry and what ifs. It's not going to be easy, but I take the first step and swallow down the words my instincts are screaming at me to say.

"Sure," I nod. "Sorry."

"I went to see Loreena. And Tommy," she adds with the ghost of a smile. My mouth falls open, a whirl of questions circling in my stunned brain. Only one reaches my mouth.

"How is she?"

Haley's mouth tips up at the corners. "That's the first thing she asked about you."

Of course she would. Loreena and I formed a strange bond there in that godforsaken place on that fucking useless show, the only good thing to come out of the whole sorry saga. Except for holing up here with Haley for twelve days.

"And?" My last sight of Loreena was on the TV screen last night, upset and angry, but in reality, that was days ago. I'm hoping time with her beloved Tommy has taken the edge off all those emotions, just as being here with Haley has damped down my rage, leaving me with a simmering need for justice, or better still, vengeance.

"She's doing OK. Tired. Down but not out."

"I'm pleased to hear it. You know she's pretty special to me." I'm not afraid to own it. Loreena deserves my loyalty. She's certainly shown it to me.

"Yeah," Haley says, her voice gentle, green eyes on mine, serious but soft. "I can see why now. She's a special person."

My heart leaps at her words. Somehow, Haley recognising this, that her feelings for another person—beyond Ollie—should mirror mine, gives me hope we're not so different after all. Underneath, the people we care for and the things we value are the same. Hope maybe our lives could intertwine, we could become a 'we', flares inside me. I nod, swallowing down the surge of emotion, yet feeling a little reckless.

"So, what did my two favourite women talk about for a whole afternoon?"

A smile twitches at the corners of her mouth. There's an unreadable expression in her eyes. I'm getting dangerously close to spilling all. Every tiny detail of my unrequited adoration of her. Tossing it out there and waiting to see what happens. But I'm still scared, because to do that risks her tossing it back at me, unwanted.

"You, of course. Isn't that what you wanted to hear?" she teases.

"Of course," I say. "You know that old Carly Simon song, 'You're So Vain'? That's me."

"I don't," she frowns. "But it sounds perfect. Your theme song, maybe?" A grin splits her face. The banter has taken the edge off my tension, and perhaps hers too.

"Yeah, I'll own it."

"Well vain or not, Loreena has been worried about you. More so after last night."

Bile rises in my throat as I do the numbers. How many people tune into *Wild For The Win*? How many of them believed the poisonous picture of me woven through out-takes and innuendo? What was a battle to expose the show's endorsement of a barbaric practice has now become personal.

"So, has Tommy got his heavies out looking for me? Sent them to rough me up—or worse?" I know Loreena's husband is protective of her. He sounds the sort of guy who might well act against someone he thought had wronged her.

"No, Tommy's always going to believe Loreena. He knows exactly what did and didn't happen in Scotland. It's OK." I relax at her re-assurance. At least the most important people know the truth. "But they did have someone looking for you. That guy lurking around your apartment the other day—would you believe he opened the door at their house? I nearly fainted."

"Shit, so he *was* staking out the apartment." I immediately tense again at the mention of the mystery man.

"It's fine, Christian. Loreena asked him to. She was hoping to get word to you. Let you know Tommy's been working on the legal side." I'm relieved at Haley's assurance there was nothing sinister in his presence. It's been worrying me for days.

We talk for an hour, the only interruptions me feeding lumps of wood to keep the fire crackling and Haley topping up coffee. I'm reassured Loreena is fine. She's not the tough bitch the world would choose to see, but she does have a strong core, the heart of a fighter, and she's drawing on it now. Meanwhile, Tommy has thrown weight and money at legal opinions and things are moving.

Tomorrow morning, Haley and Rachel will meet with Tommy and the Bunt's lawyer. They'll plot strategy and then set up a meeting with the production company. Knowing I'll be sitting here, powerless, unable to be part of it, frustrates me. But I need to keep my eye on the prize and hand over my future to others. And when one of those others is Haley Templeton, there's a strange sense of calm.

"Thank you," I say, rising to toss more wood on the hungry fire. The moment I'm on my feet, I'm also aware of the gnawing in my gut. "I'm starving." I barely ate today, stressing about Haley. But, now I know she's safe, my neglected stomach screams for attention. "How about you? There's leftover veggie bake from Wednesday night. I can heat some up," I offer. If I was any sort of friend, I would have got my arse into the kitchen earlier and made something decent for her to come home to. Although that bake was pretty good. Serving it up for a second night isn't a bad alternative.

"I'm fine," she says. "The Bunts fed me continuously from the time I arrived. Tommy's a good cook."

I nod. "Yeah, I hear that. Loreena swears she'd have married him for his cooking alone."

"I'd marry a man for the brownie he served up. Damn, it was good," she sighs, eyes dreamy at the memory. I'm thinking it might be time to expand my own repertoire to baked goods. "But you go ahead."

Without hesitation, I head for the kitchen, grab the dish from the refrigerator, and sling it into the microwave. Haley follows, perching at the countertop on a high stool. Two minutes and it's done. I don't bother to plate it, simply place the hot dish on a trivet and dig straight in. I'm shovelling greedy forkfuls into my mouth when Haley slides open the cutlery drawer and grabs her own fork. She aims enthusiastic jabs at one side of the dish.

"Hey," I say, fending off her fork with a thrust of my own. She giggles and parries. "I thought you weren't hungry."

"I wasn't, but it smells so good. Please, just this little corner here," she begs.

"OK," I say, feigning a frown, as I carve a boundary line into the eggy yellow surface. "That and no more."

She chips away within her own territory, smiles, and scoops a piece into her mouth. I watch it slide between her lips and she smacks them together with a lazy "Mmm."

It's so fucking sensual. God, I can't help but stiffen as I think of parting those lips with my tongue, tasting her. Sharing a house with Haley is both bliss and the most exquisite torture. I dive back into the safety of conversation, asking her about the book she gave me. Even that doesn't completely dim down my arousal as, with a sly grin, she asks what chapter I'm at. I'm forced to reveal, yes, I have indeed got to the steamy stuff.

She helps me with the dishes, filling me in on more of the details of Rachel's plan. The two of them meet with Tommy and his lawyer at ten am. After that, they'll reach out to the production company and try to scare them into a meeting over the weekend. By the time Monday comes around, if all goes well, we'll have some sort of agreement.

"Thank you," I sigh, heading for the lounge, after dinner coffees in my hands, while she follows, balancing a little stack of Christmas cookies on a plate. "I'm sorry you got dragged into this whole mess."

"It's OK." She tips her head. "It's not as if I haven't got a vested interest in this. I mean, the whole snare issue is important. But there's still a chance the dog rescue might get something out of it. And Loreena's charity, as well. Even if it's only publicity. Animals get caught up in family violence too." She frowns. "Did you know lots of women won't leave an abusive situation because they fear leaving their pets behind?"

I shake my head. I didn't know, but I believe it. I'm not the only one who would take a risk to save my animals. But that's next level, risking your body, your life even, to protect your pets from harm.

"That's terrible. What a choice to have to make."

"Loreena and I have some ideas about that. Ways we could support women to get away and take their animals with them. When all this is over, we'll talk some more."

"You two covered a lot of ground."

"Yeah," she says, eyes falling away from mine as her small hand twists at the fabric of her top, twining and untwining the stretchy band at her waist. "We did."

"It's no surprise," I say, softly. "Same big hearts."

She grabs at the snow globe on the table, and leans forward, elbows on knees, rolling it in her hands like one of those stress balls. A flurry of white fills the glass. In the silence, from her lips drawn tight, and her eyes fixated on the dancing flames in the hearth, I sense there's a storm inside her too. I wait, and eventually her words come.

"There's something else we talked about."

Day Seven

LIKE A COUNTRY SUNRISE, a slow blush of pink rises on Haley's skin. I want so badly to press my lips to one of those cheeks, and drink in the warmth.

"I may just have told them…I was your girlfriend—so the security would let me in—and Loreena was…kind of pleased. Well, maybe very pleased."

"Oh…" I stutter out.

"Because there were some things you'd shared with her," she says. Her green eyes lift and meet mine, pupils large and dark with something indefinable.

I know *exactly* what she's talking about. Bloody Loreena. If she was in the room right now, I wouldn't know whether to swear at her or hug her. I couldn't feel more exposed than if I'd walked on stage naked at Glastonbury. Having my secret revealed, there's a pit filled with dark clouds of roiling fear in my stomach, unsure of how the object of my adoration feels about it. I'm not reading shock—maybe she's had time to get over that in the hours since Loreena chose to spill all—and it's heartening. I don't see distaste written in the soft bow of her lips.

Haley and I have become friends these past days, and I don't want to damage that. To lose what we've built in small steady steps would devastate me. But I can't spend the rest of my life stuck in the friend zone with her, either. I've wasted too much time on the outer; been too cautious about what Ollie might have to say if he suspected I was even a little bit attracted to his sister. Now, in his absence, I've become bold. Having tasted what it might be like to have her in my life has made me a greedy bastard. I want more with Haley, and I want it now.

"What things?" I venture, the crack in my voice showing I know full well what she means, although I'm unsure of the extent of Loreena's tell-all.

I shared a lot with her in the quiet darkness. When you don't have to face someone, it's easier to open up. And when it's Loreena, in whom it seems I've found my unlikely twin—not to mention one of the most perceptive people I've ever encountered—it was hard not to let my defences fall.

And now Haley knows.

"Christian." Haley reaches across and wraps a dainty hand around mine, stroking my calloused fingers with a soft swirl of her thumb. It's soothing and wildly erotic at the same time, electricity arcing through my body at the sound of my name, gentle on her lips. "I never knew."

I huff out a nervous laugh. "I thought I was so damn obvious. Every time I saw you, I couldn't help myself. It was like that Beatles song. 'Something'. From the beginning, Haley, there was something about you. And I was so scared of what you'd think. I mean..."

"You shouldn't have been. It's OK."

I have to go there. I'm shit-scared of the answer, but I must ask. I swallow. Hard. Once. Twice. The lump of tension in my throat is a tight, painful knot, strangling the words, but I shove past it.

"And what did you think? When she told you?"

I see a similar nervous swallow ripple down her pale-skinned neck, right where I'd love to place my mouth and kiss my way downwards. I shudder, thinking of what lies at the end of that trail, below the v of her top.

Her words aren't what I expect. She meets my question with a question of her own that tells me just how far Loreena went.

"Will you play it for me?"

"She told you..."

The secret of my heart has always been laid bare for everyone to see in the lyrics of a song, but no one's ever known it. I've always brushed off people's questions about 'Untouchable', letting them think it was based on remembered angst from those overemotional teenage years, when your feelings are dialled up to the max, raw and painful. Other times, in interviews, I've implied it's about some nebulous fictional woman who I've yet to meet and fall for. Fans like that theory, some hoping it might be them; others swayed by the romantic notion of the unknown soulmate waiting for me out there somewhere. I've hidden the truth for three years—and then I told Loreena.

My crazy new friend has dropped me right in it. I can't blame her. After all, everyone loves a love story. From the moment I confessed my pining for my best friend's sister, Loreena nagged me. Told me I had to do something about it. Life's too short. What's the worst that could happen?

And now the worst that could happen might not have actually happened. I don't see rejection on Haley's face. There's curiosity. Interest. Maybe a quiet invitation to explore these feelings, as she asks me again.

"Please, Christian. Don't be shy. Play it for me. You wrote it for me. I've read the words. Heard you sing it."

"Not like this."

"Shouldn't it be like this?"

My breath snags in my throat. I can't answer. Dragging myself up onto shaky legs, I stagger towards my guitar case. At the movement, two dog heads lift and swivel towards me. Tully gives an expectant thump of her tail. Mularkey's eyes meet mine and she offers a hopeful woo. It's not my song they want.

"I'll let them out," Haley says.

They follow her down the hallway. It's a relief, the tension broken, buying me time to summon courage.

Opening the case, I lovingly pull out my guitar. To the outside world, I can be gruff, sometimes serious, other times brash, but always awkward with my true feelings. Music, and this instrument in particular, allows my emotions to come out to play in a way that's been safe for me. Now, despite its presence, I'm way out in the danger zone, and perhaps about to be shot out of the air, crashing and burning, my heart a twisted wreck on the ground.

Or maybe, because it's Haley, she'll let me down gently. That might be worse; a slow, painful death. Yes, perhaps I'd rather she put me out of my misery quickly, like the vets she helps, granting an animal speedy peace where there is no hope.

I pull across a footstool and settle onto it, cradling the guitar in my lap. I take a moment to tune it, my fingers twisting the smooth keys, coaxing each string to the perfect pitch while my own nerves jangle off-key. With the strings aligned, one hand strums in rippling strokes, the rhythmic movement damping down the anxiety gripping me. My fingers work across the frets, the familiar chords soothing, the necessary precision welcome when everything else around me is chaos. I'm as prepared as I can be, as calm as is possible hearing her footsteps approach.

Haley curls back onto the sofa, legs tucked beneath her. Her mouth tips in an encouraging smile. Anticipation sparkles in her eyes, and I lower my gaze to the guitar, as if in concentration, but in reality trying to hide my jitters.

I've never felt so nervous to play; not even taking the stage for the first time on *Star Power*; not even when the band played our first big venue, finally looking out on not hundreds, but thousands. I'm about to give the most important performance of my life. To an audience of one.

I close my eyes, allowing the music I wrote to drift towards her, a unique arrangement of chords only existing in this form for her. Then I grasp onto the melody, releasing my words into the air, sung like they've never been sung before, to the person who inspired them.

At first my voice is ragged, struggling through a verse. But approaching the chorus, I feel a soft and unspoken reassurance projected back at me. As my voice grows in confidence, my eyes flit open, only to meet her gaze, green eyes anchoring mine. And that is where they stay, how we stay, in total stillness, except for my hands on the instrument and the invisible waves of the music, rippling through the air between us.

I can't name this feeling I have for Haley—infatuation, obsession, adoration—maybe it's love. I don't know her well enough to be sure of that yet. But I want to. If she'll give me a chance. I haven't ever loved a woman, not in the way the songs, or poems, or books tell it. But from the moment I met her, something screamed at me; this might be the one. A person who love could grow with.

In this song, I pour out all of my hopes, my longing, and my frustration, because back then she seemed out of my reach. Not only because of the Ollie thing. I suppose I've put her on a pedestal, and never felt I'd be worthy of her. Now here she is, right in front of me, hearing my words.

As the last strum vibrates beneath my fingers and the sound wavers, I drop my head. I'm such a coward, afraid to face her with the memory of my song hanging so close in the air. My fragile hope held tight inside my vulnerable heart is like one of those spun glass baubles dangling from her over-dressed Christmas tree. She could crush it with a look, a word. I hold my breath, waiting.

Her voice comes low and husky.

"I'm not, you know," she says. "Untouchable."

I put down my guitar and reach for her.

Untouchable

You command the room like a silent storm, a surging wave capturing my soul
Your emerald gaze a searing flame, where all reason slips away
And then I'm locked out, pressed against the glass
Watching you shine while I'm stuck in the dark, unseen

Untouchable, you're my beautiful collision
A dream that haunts my every waking moment
Untouchable, forever just beyond my reach
Crushing me beneath the weight of my own shattered hopes

Your ruby razor smile slices through the noise, a sweetly curved blade held to my heart
Your pretty words a siren call drowning out my doubts and fears
And I'm just static, white noise, invisible
Choking on words that die before they leave my lips

Untouchable, you're my beautiful collision
A dream that haunts my every waking moment
Untouchable, forever just beyond my reach
Crushing me beneath the weight of my own shattered hopes

Beneath this scarred exterior, I'm hiding
Walls built from the pain of broken expectations
If you could look past my ragged edges
See the vulnerability, touch my insecurities, maybe I'd step out of the
shadows

Untouchable, you're my beautiful collision
A dream that haunts my every waking moment
Untouchable, forever just beyond my reach
Crushing me beneath the weight of my own shattered hopes

Songwriter: Christian Steele

CHAPTER 22

Day Seven

WITH MY INVITATION CLEAR, Christian is on his feet, towering over me. His eyes are unnaturally bright, the blue almost incandescent, like the dangling Christmas stars in my bedroom window. But more beautiful for the raw emotion glowing in them, the wanting, his longing for me held in check now allowed free.

Christian's large hand seeks mine, and I reach for it like a lifeline. I grasp his long fingers, feeling the calloused tips wind around mine, skin hardened from the pressure of fingers on strings, yet so soft as they caress my hand, like the way he strums the guitar, a reverent touch that elicits something of beauty from the ordinary. There's a gentle questioning in their tentative movement. He's still unsure, but I'm not.

I'm ready to explore this thing with him. Maybe it's what I've needed since my relationship with Jack crumbled. While Christian is learning, as Jack did, I don't need his protection; I'm stronger than I appear; he also understands what Jack—and my so-called friend Paige—never did. Even the strongest people can have a vulnerable heart. I trust Christian not to hurt mine like they did. This is someone who really cares for me, even if my feelings for him are still hazy. And that is why I need to remember there are two vulnerable hearts involved here.

I stumble to my feet and crash into him, our bodies fitting together like two pieces of a puzzle. I loop my arms across his shoulders, tilting my head upwards. He searches my face, looking for something in my expression, and when he finds it, drops his head to press his forehead gently against mine, eyes shut, a little of the tension ebbing from his body.

I let my eyes fall closed, drinking in the warm reassurance of his bulk, and the smell of him, his musky maleness with a subdued woody undertone, the same fragrance that lingers in the bathroom long after he's gone.

The one I realise I'll miss when the twelve days are up, and he really is gone.

We stand together in silence; the only sounds our soft breathing and the crackle of the fire. Even the dogs sleep, oblivious, happily snoozing, undisturbed by this development.

His arms settle around my waist, pleasantly heavy, our heartbeats thudding like the insistent rhythm of a bass guitar underlining the sweet melody of desire surging between us.

When his eyes open with a flicker of those thick lashes too pretty for a boy—there is truth in his brothers' old taunt—he pulls back a little, studying me. There's still a question there, and I answer with a smile. He responds with a teasing brush of his nose against mine, his eyes so close I can barely focus, but I see the silver flecks and the pupils huge and dark, feel his own face lift, the smile reaching his eyes too, as they soften.

He drops his mouth, lips brushing mine oh so gently, restrained and tender. One kiss, two; more.

His fingertips sneak beneath the neck of my pyjama top, gliding along my collarbone, and then skimming up my neck. He pauses, his finger finding a tantalising spot behind my ear. The touch is exquisitely sensitive, and my breath hitches as he circles it, making my nerves hum and sending shivers through me. I sigh against him with pleasure and he responds with a more demanding kiss, capturing my mouth.

Christian threads a hand through my hair, tangling his fingers in its length. The subtle pressure urges my lips back to his, and I yield to it, desperate for more. At the same time, his other hand drifts low, fingers skimming across my back, caressing the base of my spine, cupping my bum, and I melt into him.

He tastes so damn good, sweet and spicy, like the cookies, and just as delicious. His tongue parts my lips and I give way to it, allowing him in, as he devours my mouth.

He walks me backwards, and my knees buckle against the edge of the couch. He breaks my fall, catching me in his arms and lowering me onto the soft leather. And then he's above me, a knee nudging between my thighs and I allow him in close. My body aches for more than the delicate kisses he showers on my neck. I want to offer him the rest of me, to take me as boldly as he possesses my mouth.

"Haley," he whispers, his breath hot against my neck, when I clasp that firm butt under my hand, making it mine.

He's hard, the erection straining against his jeans, the heat between us burning me up. I grasp him tighter to me, rolling my hips against him, shameless in my need. My rational brain is offline, and animal desire has me in its grip. I want him. Badly.

My hand fumbles between us, fingers snaking under the waistband of his jeans, gliding across the muscles of his stomach, following the groove of his hips, tracing the line of hairs that leads downwards.

I'm licking at his collarbone, where two buttons of his shirt are undone—I don't even remember undoing them, but the access to his beautiful body swamps me with desire—when, with a groan, he slides off me.

Christian props himself up on one elbow, long body stretched along the back of the couch, an amused smile blooming on his face. He trails a finger along my nose, hovering on my lips, where ragged breaths huff out.

"Not tonight." The husky whisper is mesmerising, the tone capturing me, blurring the words he's saying. "Much as I'd like to. We shouldn't go there tonight."

Realisation dawns, sending me tumbling down off my lust-crazed high. I colour a little, hot embarrassment creeping up my neck and spilling onto my cheeks. I look away, dropping my chin, burying my face behind my hand. What must he think of me? I bet this wasn't the sweet little Haley he was expecting.

"And I thought it was me with all that pent up need." He chuckles as his finger brushes a delicate tease at one of my nipples, which still proudly advertises my arousal.

He reaches across, cupping my chin, turning my head in his direction, forcing me to meet his eyes. Mine dart back and forth, uncomfortable under his scrutiny. But his expression is kind, and I let out the breath I was holding.

He's so beautiful like this. The hard angular line of his bearded jaw softened by his lips, plump and bruised from our frantic kisses. His blue eyes that can flash with ice now gaze upon me, soft as faded denim. His dark hair sticks up, dishevelled from my fingers threading through it, and I can't help it. They find their way back, sinking into the lush thickness, as I coax his mouth against mine.

"You know I want you," he murmurs into the kiss, his voice low and raspy. "But not only like that." A swallow ripples down his throat. "And I hoped you might want me for more than that, too."

I draw back with a gentle nod. I get what he's saying. Christian is an object of lust. Women desire him; fantasise about him. But they don't know him. I admire the way he's set this standard for himself. He's decided he deserves better than an unthinking hookup based on raw physical attraction, or someone taking the opportunity to grab a celebrity trophy. Even though he knows that's not what drives me into his arms, still he's asking for more before we cross the line.

"I do want you for more than that," I whisper. "I'm sorry. I think so much has happened this last week, and then today—I got a bit carried away. Overwhelmed."

I haven't had sex with a man since Jack. Haven't even wanted to for almost a year. I've fobbed them off, choosing the safety of satiating my own needs behind my bedroom door, alone in the dark with only my pretty mauve vibrator for company. But tonight, my desperate body said yes. Perhaps it knows what my heart doesn't:

going down this road with Christian is not going to leave me cruelly dumped. He's a better man than that.

"Haley, don't apologise. It's OK," he says, brushing a strand of tangled hair away from my face. "But I figure we should take it slow. After all, I've learned to be very patient where you're concerned." His mouth tips up at the corners. "There's no need to hurry. We've got all the time in the world to see where this goes."

I want to say we haven't. That by the time he leaves this house next week, I need to know where this is going. If it's even going anywhere at all.

There will certainly be speculation; most likely criticism, and not only from strangers who think Christian's fame gives them the right to an opinion. People close to us, especially Ollie, will be shocked by this sudden pairing. It could be a rough ride, and not one I'm sure I want to take unless I know it's worth surviving for the sake of this relationship. But I stay silent, not wanting to give voice to the pressure I feel from the deadline hanging over us.

Instead, I place one last delicate kiss on his mouth and snuggle into him. Taking it slow never felt so good as his body, hard muscle yet tender softness, wrapped tight against me, his grip protective.

Yes, I often push back against those who only want to care for me, fearful they'll stifle the person I'm working hard to become. But somehow, with Christian, it feels more equal, as we both find refuge in each other's arms.

I'm like a puppy, soothed by the ticking of a clock in its basket, as I relax into the rhythm of his breathing and the steady beat of his heart. My own matches it, slowed from the wild thumping of minutes ago. We lay face to face on the wide couch, me with my cheek tucked into his shoulder. His broad arm drapes around my waist and, bit by bit, I dissolve into sleep; no fear of falling, no fear of anything.

I'm so deep in, I don't even hear the tapping of dog feet in the middle of the night. I stir a little as Christian unwinds himself from me. There's the nudge of a wet nose on my hand and I attempt to sit up, but he holds me back, whispering against my ear.

"I'll go."

He clambers over me, pulling the patchwork quilt back up to my chin. A treasured gift from my Gran, with its hand-stitched blocks of Christmas stars in red, green and gold, it's also super warm. I snuggle beneath it. The fire is now a faint glowing heap of embers, but the central heating on its thermostat has kicked up a notch, and the gentle hum of hot air fills the room. Still, it feels good to huddle under the blanket now Christian's warm body is no longer pressed against mine.

I listen to their footsteps; his muffled by socks, soft and even; the dogs' a noisy random staccato. The back door rattles open and a trickle of cold air drifts up the passageway.

"Hurry up, girls. It's fucking freezing," I hear him hiss before pulling the door closed with a thud. The thought of him out there, watching over them, like he watches over me, even when it's the middle of a winter night, tugs at my heart. This man.

My mouth tips up in a smile at how easy this feels. Christian, for all his chaotic current situation and his patchy past, blends into my life with an unexpected ease. But I'm still wary.

I lie in the half-dark, moonlight slanting through the bay window, bouncing off the gleaming tinsel on the tree. Will I be like that tree—at the moment, a bright shiny thing, glittering and alluring—yet underneath, come January, when you strip it all off, just something ordinary with nothing special to offer? Something to discard until next year's new one comes along?

Christian has been obsessed with the idea of me for a long time. Conjured up an image of me in his mind, based on a few sparse encounters where our lives have brushed up against each other's, woven with second-hand knowledge of me from my brother. He's fantasised about this. But I'm no fantasy princess, just an ordinary girl. How can I even hope for the reality of me and what this is, this ordinary life, to measure up to his imagination?

Still, maybe I can indulge in his adoration for a while, even if it doesn't last. As long as I prepare for the possibility of it being a short flash of something, bolstering me through what has been a tough time. God knows, it's certainly taken my mind off the Jack and Paige show. Tucked in this cocoon, Christian and I can explore in safety. If it dissolves into nothing at the end of these twelve days, no one will know except us.

We won't have to deal with Ollie going all overprotective. He suggested taking a hit out on Jack when he found out about the wedding, and I'm not sure he was joking. Ollie's unlikely to be quite so extreme when it's Christian, but it's still safer if he doesn't know until we're certain. I'm not going to be the one who unnecessarily drives a wedge between my brother and his best friend.

Sam and Rachel both know Christian's here. It's probably better if they continue to think he's simply a surprise house guest, a roommate who's become a friend. While they are both more trusting of my judgement, neither are likely to consider a sudden impulsive hookup wise, especially when my emotions are extra fragile around the wedding. I'm not in the mood for even a gentle suggestion that this is a bad idea.

We are sheltered from prying media or lurking paparazzi desperate to thrust our tentative relationship into the spotlight or revel in its demise. There's no way I'm ready for that sort of exposure, and I wonder if I ever will be. There are huge consequences in joining my life to Christian's. But I don't have to deal with those at the moment.

Even if Christian is destined to become a fond memory to look back on as we go our separate ways, I can enjoy this while it lasts. And, if, although perhaps unlikely, it should become more, then it will be better than what I hoped for.

The returning dogs crash towards me, each offering a quick lick as I extend a hand. They climb back onto the armchairs, and are settled into furry balls, noses tucked between paws by the time Christian arrives. I hear the swish of him rubbing his hands together and huffing breaths on them.

"Snowing yet?" I ask.

"A few flakes," he says. "It's like ice out there. See."

He lays his mouth on mine, his lips chilly.

"Get back under the blankets," I mumble against them. "I'll warm you up."

"You're too good to me." He climbs over me carefully, lying alongside me, nuzzling against my ear, his breath tickling my hair. "You're too good for me," he whispers.

I spin to face him. "Don't say that."

"It's what I've always felt. Why I never..."

"Shhh." I lift my head, pressing a kiss to his lips, silencing his doubt.

Day Eight

I'm dragged into the new day, as on most days, by the sound of dog feet scrabbling on the floor, tap dancers warming up for their routine. I fight against facing it for a moment, allowing myself a little longer to luxuriate in our cosy nest. Christian is twined around me, his soft snores comforting, the safety of his arm thrown across me, his large hand gently cupping one breast, a reminder of this new territory we've crossed into. There's no regret. I could get used to waking up like this. Even if it is on the couch in the lounge.

I reach carefully to lift his arm off me, trying not to disturb him. The sliver of grey half-light spilling in from the edge of the bay window, finding its way around the bulk of the Christmas tree, tells me it's morning. Saturday morning. My still sleep-fogged brain registers other sounds. The rattle of a key in a lock, the click of the door opening.

The dog dance becomes a flurry, an Irish jig, excited feet flying. By the time Rachel steps into the lounge, they've gone full-on River-dance, while I'm struggling to swing my legs onto the floor, still heavy from sleep. She flicks on the light, and my eyes scrunch against the painful glare. So much for keeping this secret.

"What the fuck?" she says. I've never worked out how Rachel keeps a filter on her foul mouth in a courtroom. You'd swear she picked up her vocabulary from graffitied bathroom walls. She scans the scene, me in pyjamas, barely upright, a sleepy Christian rousing behind me. "Still, I'm not surprised." Her mouth tilts up in a sly grin.

"What do you mean?"

"That's what happens when you let the wolf into the house."

"Actually, I find that comparison rather flattering," his voice drawls from behind me, amusement dancing in his words.

"He just wants to eat you all up," she announces. "And it looks like he has."

His breath is warm at my nape. He smiles against my skin. "No, but I'd like to."

I can't help but grin at the words just for me, but I squash it back, composing my face in what I hope is an innocent expression.

"No, Rachel, it's not what you think."

I make my hands into fists, rubbing at my eyes, then stretch my arms, trying to iron out the kinks. Damn, I'm stiff. The couch is wide, but not exactly designed for sleeping on. Especially not con-fined against a large, although rather comfortable, body for an entire night.

"Look. Pyjamas," I say, pointing at myself. "Clothes." I jerk a thumb towards Christian, whose chin rests on my shoulder.

I wince a little at the thought—if it wasn't for him being such a gentleman, if he'd taken advantage of my little flash of lust—there may well have *not* been clothes.

"That doesn't mean much," Rachel says, weighing my evidence and finding it unconvincing. It's as if she knows a few hours earlier her friend teetered on the edge of doing something very rash. "But hell, why not?" She stands, hands on hips, ignoring the dogs who've settled at her feet. "About time you had some fun. It's also about time you got your lazy arses out of bed. We've got work to do. Besides, I don't see why you should get to linger in your little love nest when I've had to drag myself out of mine. Pierre is not happy."

Beyond her friends, Pierre is the only person whose opinion truly matters to Rachel. Which is good, since she's agreed to marry him. As he's arrived back on a late flight from New York last night, where he's been busy doing the mysterious but very important work hedge-fund managers do, I can imagine he's unhappy with her working a Saturday morning. Probably very unhappy if she's confessed it's working for free.

"Tell him I'll shout him a drink," I offer.

"Buy you both dinner?" Christian adds.

She ignores us. "Get in the shower, Haley. And, you—" She stabs a finger Christian's way. "Make yourself useful and make me a coffee. I brought breakfast."

She tosses a box onto the coffee table. I recognise the bold lettering on the lid: Bread Ahead, my favourite doughnut place next to the tube station. If anyone wanted to kidnap me, all they'd have to do is wave one of those boxes out the door of the van, and I'd jump right in.

"Maple bacon?" I breathe.

"Of course." She knows me so well.

"Wasn't sure what he'd eat, so I threw in a few other flavours."

"More maple bacon?" Christian asks, hopefully.

"You don't even get to fight me for that one," I inform him. "It's mine. I don't share maple bacon doughnuts."

"Not even just a little bite?" He's giving me those damn puppy eyes.

"Maybe just a little bite." I press a playful kiss to his lips and drag myself onto my feet.

I catch Rachel's eye, and she gives me a grin, half-approval, half-disgust. Even though she claims it's not unexpected, I can see her finding us together like this is a surprise.

"Not another word," I warn.

I'll be a prisoner in the car with her on the way to the meeting. Plenty of time for her to interrogate me then, with no chance of my escape, unless I jump from a moving vehicle.

In the shower, I turn the water up as hot as I can bear. Standing under the flow, I slather on my new body wash, its delicious citrus scent with a subtle underlying dash of cinnamon drifting in the steamy air. It makes me think of Christian's kisses, the taste of the spicy cookies I baked for him sweet on his lips. But there's no time to linger. Rachel doesn't tolerate lateness, and I owe her not to be, when she's giving up her Saturday for us. I push those thoughts aside, squeeze out a blob of cleanser and massage the foam onto my face. It's still sensitive, grazed from bearded kisses in the dark.

Twenty minutes and I'm unrecognisable from the dreamy, mussed up girl who woke up with Christian wrapped around her, flushed with the heat of his body; hair tangled from his twining fingers; lips swollen from his molten kisses. I need to be a different sort of girl for him today. Hair scraped up into a ponytail, make-up done, and dressed in navy pants, with a crisp white blouse underneath a smart jacket of muted navy and beige plaid, I feel almost business like. Not the sharp-edged lines of one of Rachel's designer suits, or her expensive Jimmy Choo heels, that scream she's a capable and well-paid lawyer; but smart enough to suggest I'm someone who might be able to afford a lawyer like her.

The voices from the kitchen sound reasonably civil. Maybe they've declared a truce. That would be good, given she's one of my best friends and he's the man I've spent the night with. The man I've let peek through a crack in that wall around my fragile heart. Although I dare not let myself consider whether this is anything more than my need for comfort meeting his unrequited longing.

But now my two best friends have both met Christian, I'd like to think they see some of what I see in him, the person he really is, behind the man the world sees. I'm not sure why, but I want them to like the idea of us together, even if it is only some temporary thing.

Hearing my name in the conversation, I pause outside, leaning against the wall.

"I promise you, if you hurt her..." Rachel's voice is lethal. "I'll kill you. I might be a corporate lawyer, but believe me, I have good friends in criminal law who would see me walk free."

"I won't." His words are as adamant as Rachel's threat. "There is no way. I'd never hurt Haley."

"You better not. Not when she's only just clawed her way back after that fuck-up broke her heart. If he ever shows his face anywhere near me, I swear—"

"What?" he asks. "Who?" This time, Christian's voice is threatening. "Who hurt her?" he demands. There's a pause, Rachel's hesitation hanging between them. Christian doesn't need her answer. "Oh, Jack. Of course," he sneers.

"Yes," she confirms. "None other than Jack fucking Maplethorpe."

"I met the bastard down at Ollie's country house one time." Now it's Christian's words that threaten murder. "The way he treated her. Fuck, I wanted to smack him. But I figured it wasn't my place. After all, she's Ollie's sister. But you know Ollie. Did nothing. Doesn't like to make waves."

"Yes, well, that douche-bag Jack happened to be shagging one of Haley's friends behind her back. Paige Walker, the sneaky little bitch. She still has the audacity to claim she's Haley's friend after seducing her boyfriend." Rachel lets out an angry huff. "Would you believe they even sent Haley an invitation to their wedding?"

"What the fuck?" Christian growls.

"Of course, Haley had the sense not to go. They got married last Saturday. Pissed down with rain all day, I hear." There's an ugly satisfaction in her voice. "It's only a fraction of the shit those two deserve to rain down on them. They seem to think because they ended up married, it exonerates the pair of them from what they did to her."

"She hasn't said a word," he says. "Ollie neither. Wish I'd known. Not that there's much I can do."

"Not really anything any of us can do." Rachel lets out an exasperated sigh. "Apart from keeping her busy—and off socials. I don't think she's seen it, thank god, but they've been posting all over. Makes me want to puke seeing their smarmy faces. If I knew how to hack their fucking accounts, I would. Tear it all down."

I slide my phone from the pocket of my pants. Why? I have no idea. I promised myself I wouldn't. Not after it triggered my bender last Thursday. Told myself I was done. No more stalking Jack and Paige on socials. No more torturing myself.

But it's too late. I stare at the little square on my phone, its sunset colours drawing my finger. With one tap, Instagram floods the screen. I search for Paige's account and the universe punishes me for my weakness.

They're in Venice. The secret honeymoon location Paige has been gushing about for weeks, now revealed in sickly sweet post after post. I can't be happy for their happiness—posing on a bridge, cuddled up in a gondola, clasped together outside the towering church in San Marco square—especially not when it's Venice. Jack's walked those cobbled streets before, done all those romantic things before—with me. When I recognise they're seated in the same little restaurant tucked beneath the Rialto Bridge, where he and I had dinner one night, it's too much.

My hand drops, my arm useless, as I'm confronted with the reality of what they did to me. I crumple against the wall, paralysed by tears. I stuff a fist against my mouth, uncaring of the damage to my carefully applied lipstick, as I stifle a sob.

They've been married a whole week. And, for a week now, I've pushed back the pain. Christian's arrival, Tully getting sick, my uncertain work situation, the drama of the show; these things have consumed my days, a convenient distraction. I've been proud of myself, not allowing Jack and Paige to enter my thoughts, at first for a few hours, but slowly longer, not thinking about them for days. Until overhearing Rachel giving Christian the sordid details; and now this, seeing their new happy life laid out for the world to see, brings it all tumbling back, sadness crushing my heart, while a cold rage floods my veins.

I don't love Jack. I did, but I definitely don't anymore. I don't want him back. Paige is welcome to him. But the damage he did lingers. The parade of men I've worked my way through since has done nothing to repair it.

"Shit." Christian's voice is a low hiss.

I hear footsteps, and he appears in the hallway. His angry eyes sweep across my face, taking in my tears, narrowing at the sight of the phone in my hand. It's not anger at me, but for me. And, in the tender brush of his hand, the arms that wrap around me, the whisper of my name, his breath on my hair, there's a seed of hope. I can move on from Jack; and this man wants to be the one to help me.

He places a finger under my chin, tilts my head up, and brushes his large thumb across my tears. Then, lowering his head, his gentle lips settle on mine in a delicate kiss. As I give over my mouth to his he responds, one hand at my neck, pressing me closer, deepening the kiss. Warm reassurance floods my chest, pulling me back up from despair.

In Christian's arms, I decide I'm going to give this a chance. For the next few days, inside our protected little bubble, we can explore without the eyes of the world upon us. It's selfish, I know. Because I might not have much to lose, but he does. If I lead him along and then slam the door on this, I'm ending the possibility of something he's wanted for a long time. It's not me that could get hurt the most here. It's him.

"You going to be OK?" He pulls back, scanning my face.

I nod; brave a smile. "Yeah, I am. I will be."

When his eyes meet mine, they're troubled, as if an unspoken question lurks there, one he's afraid to ask. And then I understand. He deserves to know the answer.

"I don't love him, Christian," I reassure. "He can't hurt me that way anymore. But I am hurt. And angry. That he could just insert her into places we went and do things we did that I thought were special to us. It just makes me feel so replaceable."

He cups a large hand behind my head, pressing his forehead to mine. "He's an idiot," he whispers. "He doesn't know what he gave away."

There's a click of heels and an exaggerated sigh.

"Really? Wasn't a whole night snogging on the couch enough?"

We jerk apart. Rachel leans a head around the corner. She's joking in her usual flippant way, although there's still a faint undercurrent of concern. But despite the theatrical eye roll, her lips curve up in quiet approval. Knowing my friend backs my decision reassures me. I need that. After the mess of my one serious relationship, I doubt my ability to be a good judge of men. Rachel is brutal in her criticism. If she's eased up on Christian enough to smile at his arms wrapped around me, he's passed her initial assessment, at least.

He releases me gently, and we head for the kitchen. I gulp down the waiting coffee. The caffeine works its magic, and I immediately feel better. As if with coffee, food and Christian, I can put all the bad stuff behind me and face the day.

"Come on. Get your things." Rachel bustles around, wiping icing sugar from her fingers with a dainty swipe of a napkin. She slides on her black suit jacket, which immediately renders her even more formidable, and scoops up her hefty briefcase. "And grab your doughnut before the wolfman eats it," she orders. She gives Christian a smirk, and he returns it with a lopsided grin. They've definitely made a truce. Perhaps even an alliance. "We've got work to do," she says, scooping the keys to her Mercedes from the counter.

Christian reaches for my one hand that's not currently grasped around a doughnut and squeezes it. "Thank you," he says, searching my eyes.

As if seeing permission there, he leans in and kisses me again. After relishing the attention of his mouth more than even my first hurried mouthful of doughnut, I pull away, reluctant to leave, but knowing it's necessary as we head into battle for him.

CHAPTER 24

Day Eight

WITH A WHOOP OF triumph, I find the one last doughnut waiting in the box has a small curve of bacon on top, smiling back at me. I pounce on it, sinking my teeth into the crispy outer, the sweet yet salty flavour, and the subtle smokiness of the doughy inside filling my mouth. I close my eyes in bliss and chew, slowly savouring the new experience. Haley and I have so much in common, and one bite is enough to tell me I now share her addiction to maple bacon doughnuts. It's another little thing, more evidence of how easily she and I fit. And it's the sum of all these ordinary little things that somehow matters a lot.

We got off to a rocky start when I appeared on her doorstep a week ago. Seeing the surprise in her eyes morph into dismay as her quick brain put together all the pieces, knowing I'd let her and the rescue down, cut me deep. But I've worked my arse off to try and make it up to her; and I'm glad I did, because everything I've done since prepared her to accept the secrets Loreena shared.

Although, it's more than my obvious commitment to put this whole disaster right that led Haley into my arms last night. Much as she says she never knew, I think some subconscious part of her did. It's like my heart whispered to hers in secret, offering itself to her, a hidden promise to be kept when the time came. And yesterday Loreena's words reminded Haley's heart, and it came calling, asking me to keep that promise. I shake my head, a smile sliding across my doughnut-filled face, when I think of what I'm going to say when I can finally talk to Loreena. Give her a hard time for spilling my secrets.

Beyond breakfast, the hours drag. I wish I could be like the dogs, curl into a ball and blissfully sleep away the day, but I'm too wired about the outcome of the meeting for that. I can't face reading, even though the book—this romantasy thing—is really good. Although, I'll never reveal how much I'm enjoying it to anyone but Haley.

She's told me girls are attracted to a guy who reads those sorts of books. The last thing I need is news of my latest reading preferences to get out. It would be like wearing a billboard around my neck, advertising another reason for crazed female fans to make me the object of their attention. I wonder about the subtext in Haley's comment. When she says girls, does that include her? When she says 'a guy', does she mean this guy? And what exactly is attractive about a guy reading romance, anyway?

Perhaps there's some shared intimacy in knowing he's reading the sex scenes—far more graphic than anyone would suspect beneath the plain cover—the book equivalent of watching a sensual movie together. Or maybe it's the unexpected masterclass in romance offered by the men in these books. Currently, I'm getting one courtesy of a fairy lord. The anticipation that a mere mortal man like me might find inspiration in his romantic gestures could definitely be a turn-on.

But I'm not in the mood for the pointy-eared guy's lessons today. Instead of diving back into the fictional world, where his ethereal city sparkles with starlight, I set to work on restoring Haley's own magical fairy lights. The ones in the dining room sputtered and failed partway through dinner last night. Seeing the disappointment in her eyes, I promised I'd fix them.

It takes half an hour just to unwind the endless strings she's woven through a wooden lattice that covers the entire dining-room window. I search You-Tube—which seems to have a tutorial for everything—and find it's a matter of methodically working through them to find the single bad bulb. Only there must be a couple of hundred bulbs, and the laws of the universe say it will most likely be the very last one. What else have I got to do?

I sit at the table, untangling the bird's nest of wires and begin. It's tedious, but somehow the repetitive actions are soothing. Twist the bulb out. Click the power switch. Do the other lights go? No. Put the bulb back. Move to the next. Repeat. The mundane task allows my brain to meander towards more pleasant thoughts.

Last night still feels surreal. A couple of times, I woke up sure I was still dreaming. But no, I checked and there was a very real woman tucked into a small s-shape beside me on the couch, allowing me to spoon her, my body moulded to hers. Lying there, simply listening to the soft rise and fall of her breath under the protection of my arm, was so much better than anything I could have imagined. Her murmur of thanks when I pulled the covers tighter, capturing the two of us in a cosy nest as we eased back into sleep, was another of those ordinary little moments that, when pieced together, become extraordinary. All of these things happened.

The kisses happened too. Again, my brain could have never conjured up the taste of her, deliciously sweet, or imagined what it would be like to experience her raw hunger for my mouth. And that's not all she was hungry for. Her less than subtle invitation was a bit of a shock. I suppose while I've often let my mind wander to what lies beneath Haley's colourful wardrobe—more often since I've been confined in her house this week—I hadn't even dared to give it permission to expect she would want me like that in return.

Don't get me wrong—I *like* that she wants me. That in itself is an indication she's different. I'm so over the girls who flaunt themselves in front of celebrities, offering themselves up on a plate. I don't want *them* to want me. Like fast food, it might be cheap and readily available, but afterwards, you're always left unsatisfied. Or one of those all you can eat buffets, where you stuff yourself beyond full just because you can, and then regret it later.

I want someone who wants all of me. Not only the rockstar image the record company and their PR machine grinds out into the world. To do that, the person needs to know all of me. The unexpected silver lining to this crazy situation is Haley has a chance to really get to know me. As long as I don't fall back into my 'man of few words' persona. I know I adopt it to protect myself, but I don't need protection from her. It's time to take a risk. It's big.

Getting her to take a risk with me may be bigger. After that prick, Jack, hurt her so badly, why would she trust any guy? I'm not any guy, not him, but she needs me to convince her of that. God, just thinking of the bastard makes me want to punch him.

I'm a little disturbed by this latent aggression surfacing in me. I've always been a runner, not a fighter. Probably just as well, given the bullying when I was a kid. If I'd risen to the invitation every time someone hassled me and wanted to settle it with fists, I'd have been in brawls almost daily. With my size—tall even then and muscular from all the farm work—I may well have come out on top in some. Although in the village school, that would only have made me more of a target, and added visits to the headmaster's office and parents summoned to school to the list of reasons for my father's dissatisfaction with his youngest son.

So why now? Maybe this is the first time I've felt passionate enough about something with the whole snare issue; and about someone—Haley—to consider laying my body on the line, as well as my heart. It's strange to have this hatred for Jack surging through me.

On impulse, I scoop up my phone. Instagram is on there somewhere. I know I've got an account. Not that I've ever posted. Our social media manager, Vivi, takes responsibility for presenting me and the rest of the band online, with carefully curated shots designed to appear unscripted. She insists on me taking a look every so often, and I comply, giving nodding approval at the version of me there, even though I couldn't care less.

This is the first time I've ever opened the app without Vivi's prompting. I have to wait for it to reload, the small arrow and circling icon giving me a moment to wonder if this is wise. I do it anyway.

There's a little magnifying glass in the top corner and I type in his name. Why am I not surprised when I see his ridiculous handle: @jackthelondonlegend. If there was any doubt this dude's a douchebag, after seeing that, there's none. My eyes flick to the profile details below, which only confirm it.

How Haley could even hook up with this guy, let alone fall for him, is completely at odds with the woman I know. She deserves so much better, but perhaps she's only realised that now. The fact he still has the power to hurt her breaks my heart. Scrolling down his pictures, I still want to punch him.

The most recent shots are in Venice. There are a few touristy ones, ornate buildings and canals. In most, he's with his arm wrapped around a woman. Paige, I presume. In every one, she's grinning like the cat that got the cream. More like the booby prize, if he ends up treating her the way he treated Haley. She's pretty enough, straight blonde hair to her shoulders, big blue eyes, wide and innocent, like a Disney cartoon character. But she's not innocent. She's as guilty as her arsehole of a husband.

I jump across to her profile and the recent pictures are almost a mirror of his: a wedding and a honeymoon. More of the wedding on here, some wedding prep ones. Maybe a hen night—god, could she have been callous enough to invite Haley? I don't see her there and feel pleased. Even if she did get an invite, Haley had enough self-respect not to front up.

Rachel and Samantha aren't there either. While I don't think I've won either of them over yet, their absence in these photographs is evidence of why they're hesitant to give me their approval. They're good friends, who have stuck by Haley in a really shitty time of her life, and they don't want me to be the source of any more problems.

However, what guts me most when I think of Haley, and causes a seething heat to rise inside me, isn't the cute honeymoon shots, all romantic. They just make me want to puke. It's not the wedding pictures—with satisfaction I note lots of umbrellas in those; even the weather gods didn't approve of what they did. The thing that makes me regret even looking, causes my fingers to tense like claws around the phone and triggers a roar of hatred in my ears is what I see when I jump across to his profile and scroll back further.

There are photographs, so many of them, from the time before they shafted Haley. When he was *with* Haley. Even a couple taken in Venice, of all places. This guy has no class, taking his wife on a honeymoon to a city where, not that long ago, he'd spent romantic days with Haley. Pictures of Jack and Haley, laughing, happy, together—in love maybe, although the thought sickens me. Because it had to have been one-sided. Haley probably did love the bastard. But he didn't love her back, despite the expression on his face, or the pretty words he most likely whispered in her ear. If he'd loved her, he wouldn't have done this.

And when I flick across to the woman's feed, there they are—pictures of her and Haley, too, the best of friends, at a bar, on the beach, and then one the most sickening of all: the three of them. Was he fucking this Paige then? Screwing around behind Haley's back while posing there as if she's the only woman for him. Most likely. And, if it wasn't for the fact I can't easily replace it right now, I'd hurl this phone across the room.

Why would you not remove those photographs? I shake my head in disbelief. It's as if they want the whole world to see the then and the now, and show how Paige has snared the prize, edging out her friend to win this man—who's such a great catch. Yeah, right? Those two deserve each other.

I toss my phone onto the coffee table in disgust. And then change my mind.

I know it's childish, but I can't help myself. I grab it up, and go to the picture Jack's posted of himself leaning against the railing of a water taxi, the dark green canal sparkling behind him. It's only a one word comment, but it brings me immense satisfaction as I hit the blue arrow: *Wanker.* My mouth twists in a smirk as I see it recorded in black and white, indelible, my name against it for him to read.

While I'm standing there, admiring my work, the phone vibrates in my hand, lighting up with a text. My first instinct is to ignore it, like I've ignored all the others. But when it's Ollie's name there, I swallow down my guilt at the memory of last night and tap the screen.

It's dated yesterday, around eleven pm. Right around the time I was falling asleep, wrapped around his sister, like he somehow knew. Where the message has been for all the hours since I have no idea; drifting around in the ether like some digital messenger pigeon until just now, finally homing in on its target.

OLLIE: Just checking in to say I'm alive. Hope my sister is looking after you. No point texting back. Coverage still shit. Got a signal here but tour guide says it won't last. This place is amazing. Not sure I'm ever coming back. Fancy taking over lead vocals?

I close the message quickly, dropping the phone like it's burning hot. While I do want my friend to come back, right now it might be a very good thing if Ollie stayed away a bit longer.

CHAPTER 25

Day Eight

I DON'T HEAR FROM Haley at all. No phone call, not even a text. Once the fairy lights are back in place, I head for the kitchen and begin on dinner. I figure she'll appreciate something warming. She seems to like Italian, so I grab my phone and pull up a recipe for meatballs I've made before. The smell of tomato and herbs simmering on the cooktop fills the house.

I throw more wood on the fire, pick up my guitar case, and settle with my instrument. My fingers automatically begin to play around with the little tune that's been in the back of my head lately. For the first time today, something besides Haley occupies my mind. Losing myself in music is always a place to find certain pleasure when the rest of the world seems so unsure, like now.

It's not until around four when I hear her stomping her boots on the mat at the front steps and I know she's home. The dogs and I arrive at the door, flinging it open in welcome. Her cheeks are pink, her dark hair dusted with a few white flakes. Framed against the backdrop of the grey world outside, where snow swirls in delicate feather-soft flurries, her deep green coat intensifying the colour of her eyes, I take a mental snapshot. I want to remember her like this. Just in case things don't go to plan. In case this moment is as rare as the snow settling on the ground behind her. Snow in London in December isn't unusual, but snow with the absence of rain and sleet that usually rob us of this perfect Christmas picture is almost unheard of. It's like even the weather knows there's something special happening here between us.

I step back and usher her past the dogs with their tapping feet and lashing tails. She strips off a pair of woollen gloves, unbuttons the coat and shrugs it from her shoulders into my waiting hands. I hang it on a peg on the big old-fashioned coat stand and then turn back to her. I spread my arms wide in invitation, unsure whether last night's closeness and this morning's comforting hug entitle me to have her step inside them now.

She relaxes into my embrace like an exhausted marionette, as if she's danced one too many times across the stage, and is relieved when the puppet master releases the strings, allowing her to collapse in a heap. I'd like to slump against her with relief at her choice. She crossed a line with me last night, and thank god she hasn't leapt back over it in regret. But I'm careful. If I pressed myself against her as I'd like to, she'd be confronted with the instant hard-on stiffening in my jeans.

"How did it go?" I try to sound nonchalant, as if not so much depended on the outcome of this day.

"Pretty good, I think." The tickle of her words across my neck makes me shiver. She steps back, taking my hand. "Pour me a wine, and I'll tell you about it."

I let her lead me to the kitchen, where she settles on a stool. While I open another bottle of the merlot, she scrabbles for dog treats in a big jar on the counter. The dogs circling at her feet snatch them from her hands, disappearing to the lounge to gnaw on their antler chews.

"Is that what happens to Santa's reindeer when they retire?" I raise a brow, my mouth sliding into a teasing grin. "Dogs chewing on bits of old Rudolph in there, are they?"

She snort-laughs. "I know you're from a dairy farm, but surely a country boy like you should know a little about deer farming."

"They're a by-product of the venison industry, right? When they kill them for meat, they process the antler too?"

"No," she shakes her head, her eyes incredulous. "No deer were harmed in the making of these dog chews. They shed their antlers every year."

"Oh," I say, stupidly. "I knew that." It's true. I did know that, but in Haley's presence, my brain is scrambled. Her rippling laughter is like the tinkling of the bells on those crazy Christmas socks she loves to wear. I'd be happy to play dumb any time to provoke that sound.

Those first few days here, there was a sadness in Haley. I thought it was me. My fuck up with the show. My disastrous failure of the dog rescue. And, yes, some of it may well have been those things. Although I'm thinking it was more this fucking Jack and Paige who made her that way. She's doing well tonight, holding it together after seeing those terrible photos, and then the stress of all this legal stuff today. I'm going to work damn hard to make sure she stays that way.

Her giggle trails away and her eyes are serious now, a dark mossy green, as she sips at the wine. I take a nervous slug of my own and wait.

"Well," she says, a slow swallow travelling down that pale neck. The one my lips dotted kisses on last night. The one I felt a shiver of need ripple through under my touch. I drag my eyes away from it and focus on Haley's face.

"Rachel and Jeremy—that's Tommy's lawyer—insisted they meet with the production company lawyers on their own this afternoon. Tommy and I hung out in a coffee shop. I think it was a good move. Tommy's like a stroppy little Jack Russell dying to get his teeth into the rats in the barn. I don't think it would have gone well with him there."

"But...did it go well?"

"Apparently, they pretty much just listened. Didn't reject our argument out of hand. Said they need time to consider our 'request'." Her fingers make air quotes around the word. "Suggested it's more like blackmail. I suppose from their point of view it is. Rachel told them either they put out a press release and film an explanation of what really went down in Scotland to go out with Monday night's new episode, or Loreena contacts the media."

I smile, imagining the delight on Rachel's face delivering that ultimatum.

"They'll get back to us tomorrow. Jeremy was all smiles and talking it up to Tommy; like it's going to be just fine. Although Rachel said to me on the way home, we shouldn't get our hopes up. She doesn't trust them. Says it almost went *too* well."

"She thinks they're stringing us along?"

"Possibly. Not much we can do but wait it out. The ball's in their court now."

"OK." I'm not happy about that. But it was unrealistic of me to expect an instant solution to this mess. Those lawyers were always going to make it difficult, even if we win in the end. I reach for her hand and give it a squeeze.

"Thank you. For everything."

She slides off the stool and comes around the counter to stand behind me where I'm stirring the sauce.

"You're welcome." Her firm breasts nudge against my back as she leans around to press a kiss on my cheek.

I suck in a breath, overwhelmed by the nearness of her, and lapping up this casual ease which has sprung up between us. I'm not sure how we've come this far in one day, but I'm not going to question it. Simply accept it, gratefully.

"I'm going to get changed. Into something more comfortable." She pulls away and I feel the loss immediately.

"Christmas pyjamas?" I tease.

"Of course," she says, tossing me a grin as she heads out of the room, like the Pied Piper with the two dogs trailing behind her. I'd happily abandon dinner prep and join the parade. I'd love nothing better than to help her strip off that stuffy shirt and pants, but after I put the brakes on last night, I have to live with the repercussions. Haley's room is off limits for now. Removing Haley's clothes is also off limits for now.

I down the glass of wine and pour another large one, hoping it will dull the aching need and my apprehension over the uncertain outcome of Rachel's work today while I wait for Haley's return.

CHAPTER 26

Day Eight

ON THIS WINTERY SATURDAY night, the pretty snowflakes of earlier give way to a chilly rain. It's miserable out there. But inside, it feels like we're on safari in Africa with Ollie.

The fire roars in the hearth, a smoky, crackling inferno. I've discovered Christian is a veritable pyromaniac. He wields the poker like a wizard's staff, a feverish gleam in his eyes, constantly stoking the flames, encouraging them into a violent dance.

I watch in silence, quietly concerned. I hope Ollie had the chimney swept at the end of last winter, otherwise we might be in trouble.

Relief courses through me when, after lobbing one last chunk of wood on top, he brushes crumbs of bark off his hands and steps back, admiring his work.

"There," he says. "Shouldn't need much more attention now."

He settles onto the couch with a satisfied smile, sprawling down the length of it.

I move from the armchair nearest the hearth, where I've been covertly keeping an eye on his fire-making, while pretending to read.

I picked up a new Christmas rom-com in a little bookstore next to the coffee shop today. It's nice and light, allowing me to supervise Christian, my phone ready to dial 999 if necessary, without losing the thread of the story.

As I approach, his grey sweatpants-covered legs spread wide for me and he pulls me down to tuck in between them.

I lean back against his broad chest, resting my head against the woolly jumper I tossed at him earlier to ward off the chill while he resurrected the fire. It's a Christmas jumper I bought for Ollie last year.

Christian tried to fob it off, saying it was too small, but I knew it had enough stretch. He looks so damned adorable in it, his very masculine bearded face and solid build, contrasting with the whimsical ice-skating penguin plastered across his chest. But his frustrated frown and the small huff of displeasure every time he tugs it down tell me he's not impressed.

Maybe he thought his mission to rev up the fire to maximum heat would provide an excuse to remove it. Not that I'd object. I love Christian in only his t-shirt, those patterns of leaves and vines twining across his hands and circling his forearms, then disappearing to where the secret animals lie hidden.

"Wanna watch *Wild For The Win*?" I ask. "We missed Friday night."

I don't really want to watch it, but I still make the offer. After all, Christian has lived it. If he wants to see what happens in these last episodes, I'm not going to deny him.

"Fuck, no." His answer is immediate. "I vote we give it a break. Until Wednesday. The final. I want to see who wins—even though the fact I have any interest in knowing kind of disturbs me."

"Want to bet on who?" I offer, knowing it's a wager I'll most likely lose.

"Gavin Markham," he says without hesitation.

"The football player?" He didn't seem like a contender to me.

"Yeah. You've watched *Ted Lasso*, right?"

"He's a Roy Kent," I reply, catching his meaning.

"Exactly. Gavin's had a rough time. He's not a bad bloke. Was a good player. Just like Roy, injury dogged him till he had to throw it in. He's doing some coaching now. I admire the guy. Firstly, the grit to play on for a couple of years, even when his body let him down. And secondly, the humility to get back in there to the game he loves, even if it's not on the field."

"Definitely a Roy Kent. Well, if that's the case, I'm not taking a bet against him. Let's both hope he makes it through on Wednesday. And that his charity is something decent."

"Support for underprivileged kids to get into football."

"I can live with that."

Christian reaches a long arm to grab the remote. "And I bet you can live with this," he says, switching onto the movie channel where *The Holiday* is queued ready to go.

I suspect Christian enjoys my Christmas movie selections as much as I do. I snuggle into him, trying to ignore the part of him that hardens between us, nudging my spine and triggering a flood of heat between my legs.

"Cameron Diaz or Kate Winslett?" I quiz him as the closing credits roll.

I'm still basking against the warm width of his chest. Apart from getting up once for a pee and to restock the big bowl of snacks we've been munching on—I broke out the Christmas candy—I haven't moved. Now I've eaten too much to move. In fact, it's a wonder I'm not throwing up after scoffing all those sweets. Will we even be able to sleep tonight with that huge hit of sugar zinging through our veins?

Both of us pounced on the foil-wrapped 'coins' first. Every British kid shares memories of peeling off the stiff gold wrapper and biting into the hard chocolate disc beneath. The chocolate is never the best, not the smooth mouth-filling sweetness you'd expect, but nostalgia coats it with a layer of deliciousness.

I also have no willpower to resist the little chocolate-covered snowmen. The contrasting textures, a cloud of spongy white marshmallow, with a layer of chocolate so thin it crackles under my teeth, are irresistible. Christian hasn't fought me for them. He spent the whole movie feeding an addiction to the Trebor candy-canes.

"Cameron," he sighs, his peppermint breath against my ear. It's tempting to spin around and press my mouth to his, taste his minty lips, and the faint lingering hint of chocolate. "Those big damn eyes, just like yours." Christian leans down and plants a kiss on my nose. "How about you—Jack Black or Jude Law?" he asks.

"Definitely Jude," I say, smiling up at him with dreamy eyes. I'm not usually a big Jude Law fan, but in this movie, no girl could help but fall a little in love with him. "It's the single dad thing. There's something attractive about a guy who's a good dad."

"Yeah," he huffs, a pensive divot dividing his brow, and his jaw drawing tight. My words now seem insensitive when I recall his revelation of the fraught relationship between him and his own father, but it's too late to take them back. "I didn't have that. Not like you," he says. "You and Ollie are lucky. To have your dad—and your mum—get it right."

I give a small derisive snort and tip my head away from him. Christian's view of my parents is no different to anyone else's. The need to correct him is automatic.

"Mum and Dad are far from perfect," I blurt. "Really, Sam's mum and dad should take the credit for raising us, not them. We practically lived at their house."

My parents weren't *bad* parents. Just absent ones. Career focused, sometimes I felt they cared more about other people's kids than their own. Both are so proud of the difference they've made in the schools they've led. But I still wonder what it might have been like to come home to our own house after school, instead of to Sam's.

Her mother, Wendy, cared for Ollie and me from the time we were both small, while Mum and Dad worked their way up to higher positions and more prestigious schools. Once we were school-aged, it was Wendy who dropped us there each morning, picked us up at the end of the day, took Ollie to all his music classes, got us to swimming lessons, even signed the trip permission notes.

It's why Sam is like a sister to us. It's at her house I fell under the spell of dogs, with the family's ever present floppy-eared spaniels. It's there I learned about rescue when Wendy opened up their home to foster pups. Where I learned to bake cookies and cakes, and decorate Christmas trees.

But it's also why I was the pathetic kid, trying to get my parents' attention the only way I knew how, desperate to please, never wanting to put a foot wrong. In many ways, I'm still that kid.

"Really?" Christian is naturally curious. It's understandable given the glowing impression Mum and Dad made on everyone behind the scenes of *Star Power*. It's only in recent years, now they've clawed their way to the top of the heap, that they have more time for us, like when Ollie was on the show. Or at big moments in his music career since. They came to my graduation. It's kind of sad—here they are, available now when we're grown adults, yet they weren't when we needed them most. I love my parents. They love me. However, I don't seek to imitate them.

"Really," I sigh. "From the time I was a few months old, Sam's mum cared for me while Mum went back to work. Ollie was the same. At least it was a family situation, a good one. We were happy there."

"So the ninja nurse is practically your sister. Now I get why she slammed me so damn hard."

I nod up at him, biting at my lip. We're on difficult ground here, but now I've started, I can't stop.

"Sam and her parents will always stand up for me. Not like my own." The bitter words tumble out. I can't forgive them for the Jack situation. "They've done some pretty shitty things lately, to be honest."

I don't plan to belittle my parents, but today, with the hurt of Jack so close to the surface and Christian's piercing gaze upon me, I give in. Outside their stuffy schools, no longer wearing their serious head teacher faces, they're a likeable pair. And they like people too. Which is part of the problem. Even now, Mum and Dad still see the good in Jack. It's as if having scooped him into our family like a second son, they can't bear to let him go. I bet they sent a wedding present, thinking it's the polite thing to do.

Christian's questioning expression, curiosity and confusion mingling in his eyes, and the knowledge he cares, invites my confession.

"Mum and Dad loved Jack. They're disappointed we broke up. There's always this unspoken accusation—" I gulp a breath, like I'm bobbing in rough water, about to go under. "Like I did something to cause it—" I struggle to the surface and grab another half breath-half sob. "And it pisses me off."

Christian narrows his eyes. "It should. That was *not* your fault, Haley." It comes out as a low growl. With a few words, I've knocked my parents off their lofty pedestal in his eyes, at least.

"I know." I choke back the emotion. "I know."

It's easy to say, hard to believe, even though I know in my heart Jack's cheating wasn't my fault. Although my parents' attitude towards him might be. They don't know all the details; it was just too damn humiliating. Only Ollie knows the truth of it, and I convinced him to say nothing; that it would only hurt me more. Sometimes his need to protect me is helpful.

"God, I'm tired." I change the subject, lean my head back against his shoulder, stretching into a yawn. I'm not sure if it's my theatrics, or Christian's perceptiveness; he can see I'm not up for any more of this conversation. Either way, it works.

"Bedtime?" he says, drawing his legs from around me. "I'll put the girls out."

The quiet way Christian has insinuated his way into my life as an equal partner still baffles me. I'm not used to someone stepping up to take on a share of all the small, mundane tasks. During the sixteen months I was with Jack, and especially the nine we lived together, he never thought to lift a finger with domestic stuff.

He considered himself generous; and money-wise he was, recognising the huge disparity in our incomes by adjusting my share of the rent in proportion. Perhaps he considered all the cooking and cleaning, shopping and taking out the trash, my contribution to the shortfall. If that was the case, I suppose it was fair enough, but we never talked about it. We didn't have an agreement, simply his assumption. That should have been a red flag.

I wait at my bedroom door until the dogs arrive back with a draught of frigid air and a rattle of claws. Christian locks the back door and pauses in the hallway, my room to the right, his to the left. A fork in the road. Which path will we take?

We stand, his stormy eyes searching mine as if seeking my answer to the unspoken question hanging between us. Last night, although it was on a couch, I had the best night's sleep in ages. I want Christian to join me in my room, in my bed. Going slow doesn't mean we can't sleep together. Just sleep, like last night; clothing and a commitment to not messing up this thing, standing chastely between us and the lust that still fizzes invisibly beneath the surface.

Again, it's the small things I crave. Not that I can deny the rush of heat between my legs at the possibility of rampant sex with Christian. But it's the warm comfort of his presence, soothing away all those crappy images of Jack and Paige that haunted my day, that I seek first. I stretch out a hand, and he takes it. I don't want to let it go, or let him go. Heading to my room alone, I know in the dark, the hurt will stalk me. I don't want to sleep alone tonight. So I take a chance.

"Will you...sleep with me—just sleep?" I venture. "After today...those pictures." As if the photographs are there hanging in the hallway, taunting me, I close my eyes.

"Of course," he says, squeezing my hand and tugging me close. "As long as you promise not to jump me while I'm asleep."

His low chuckle is seductive, and I look up into blue eyes, sparking with mischief. Like jumping on him is exactly what he'd like me to do.

And I'm sure I'd like to as well. Before Loreena's big reveal, I spent almost a week with Christian, oblivious to him as more than my brother's friend, and possibly my friend, too. But I won't deny that during that week, there were plenty of times when his attractive body so close to me did what it would do to any girl with eyes and a beating heart. Now, knowing Christian has these feelings for me has torn away all caution. My mind and my heart want to trust what he says, and my body sees that as permission to open the floodgates, sending jolts of electricity through my core at the thought of taking this thing further physically.

Heat rises in my face, and my laugh comes out shaky. My over-eagerness last night is still coming back to bite me.

"Would you feel safer with a pillow wall?" I tease, trying to cover my awkwardness at the memory. My eyes dip low, darting away from his gaze.

"Don't be silly," he says, his hand tipping my chin up. "Haley, I was only joking. Do you really think I'd pass up the opportunity to spend the night in your bed?" He dots a kiss on my lips and pulls me into a hug. It feels like home, his arms wrapping me like this, so safe. "That's if there's room for us as well as them?"

Behind me, the dogs have barged open my door and settled themselves onto one side of the bed.

"I can deal with that." I turn and head into my bedroom, tugging him along behind me. I stand beside the already messed up bed, where the dogs have twirled the covers into nests.

"Off!" I point a finger at their cosy baskets on the floor in one corner. They avoid my eyes, so I repeat the command. "Off."

"I feel bad," Christian says as they grumble to their feet and slither off the bed.

"Don't. Those dog baskets cost a fortune."

"I presume I can get rid of this?" He grips the Christmas jumper, bunching fabric in each hand, poised to remove it.

"Sure," I grin back at him. "I think you've done your time."

He lifts it up over his head with a brisk tug. I'm not prepared for what happens as a result. The smile falls from my face. As the jumper pulls up, the t-shirt underneath moves with it and I'm treated to the sight of bare stomach, taut muscles, and a dusting of dark hair trailing downwards to disappear beneath the waistband of those hip-hugging sweatpants. I should look away, but I'm paralysed.

My breath hitches. What I can see of Christian is beautiful, all lean and hard. But it's what I can't see that causes warmth to flood my body, radiating out from the centre. My imagination fills in the details, as I picture my hand following that happy trail of dark hairs downwards, before deviating off to trace the groove of those hips, the skin I know to be so soft.

I attempt to compose my face into what I hope is a passable version of normal, just in time. He tosses the jumper onto the stool by the dresser and the t-shirt settles. But my torture isn't over.

He points at the t-shirt. "How about this? I run hot." A swallow works down my throat and he must see my eyes widen. "Sorry," he says with a bemused expression. "I really do. Especially if there's two in the bed."

"Fine by me," I squeak out. His smile broadens at my obvious discomfort. I should look away. I have to look away. But I don't.

I'm treated to a repeat performance, the fabric sliding up, the bare skin—oh my god, the bare skin—and then his arms emerge. Now I have a valid reason to stare. This is the first time I've fully seen Christian's tattooed upper arms and shoulders in the light. They're even more incredible than I remember.

He notices the direction of my gaze.

"Can I—" I stutter, my hand rising of its own accord, begging to not only look, but touch. There's something about the artwork on his skin that draws me in, inviting exploration with more than my eyes.

"Sure," he says, as casually as if it's the sort of request he gets every day. He steps towards me and takes hold of my fingers. Placing them on his biceps, right where the wolf peers out between the trees, my eyes lock onto the creature's, its gaze mesmerising. I think of Rachel's words this morning. Now the wolf isn't just in the house. He's in my bedroom. I invited him in. And I'm not sorry.

"How come you never show them?" I ask. "Except in that magazine shoot—" I realise my mistake immediately, and heat flares on my cheeks. I'm suddenly overly conscious of my hand on his body, a body I've seen an awful lot of, if only in pictures. Then I remember

I've also seen way too much of it in the flesh, and the memory of him on that first night flashes—Christian in the half-dark, without a stitch of clothing. In the drama with Tully, I'd pushed it aside, but now it comes back in a searing rush. I swallow audibly.

Christian's brows fly up, and his mouth slants in that way-too-sexy crooked grin. "I didn't know your reading extended to men's health magazines." His voice is low and teasing.

"It doesn't. I don't." The words of explanation tumble out in a splutter. "Pierre does—Rachel's boyfriend. She brought it over."

He laughs, a deep rumble. "So, Miss Buttoned-up Rachel has a secret love of ogling pictures of half-clothed men."

He chuckles to himself and I relax, allowing my hand to wander, tracing the indigo lines of plants and trees, running a thumb over the head of the badger, almost feeling the soft fur although it's merely etched in ink.

"The reason I never show them," he says, as I explore the other arm, the fox and the deer peering from their woodland hideaway. "Is because in my world, it feels like nothing is secret. There's nothing you can hide. They want every damn piece of you; and I decided I wouldn't give it all."

"But the magazine..."

"Yeah, it pissed me off. Our publicist, who set it up, told me it would be all dim light and moody tasteful shots. And when it didn't quite come out that way—" He pauses and his mouth tips up a little. "She assured me people would be looking at my arse, not my arms. She seems to have been right."

"I wasn't," I lie.

"Really?" he laughs. "I don't know whether to be pleased or disappointed."

My face blazes and I tip my head down, concentrating on the tiny mouse hidden beneath a bramble bush. He pulls me into him, and I lay my face across his bare chest. Inhaling the scent of his skin, beautiful musky maleness overlaid with spice and wood smoke, I know I'll never be able to smell the tang of a fire again without thinking of him.

"Come on, let's get to bed before those dogs stage another takeover bid," he murmurs against my hair.

I head to the bathroom, and he follows, the two of us companionably going through our bedtime routine at the twin basins, side by side like a couple who've been doing this every night for a long time.

Back in my room, I sit on the bed, stripping off my socks. The little bells are cute, but not helpful for peaceful sleep.

Meanwhile, Christian loses his sweatpants, allowing them to pool on the floor in a grey puddle. At my eye level, I'm confronted with black boxer briefs clinging to wide thighs. My gaze drops below them, noting the dark-haired muscular legs sculpted from the running he says he loves.

I drag my eyes away, slide between my crisp sheets and scoot across to the other side of the bed, where I like to sleep. Christian slips in beside me, his weight tipping me a little towards him as I adjust my pillow.

"Sorry, I didn't ask which side you wanted."

"Any side is fine with me." He tucks one arm beneath me, offering his shoulder for my head. His other arm loops across, settling on my waist. We lay there, our breath in sync, peaceful.

"Ahh, do you sleep with the light on?" he asks after a moment. "Because I suppose I could, if you do..." He's grinning across at me.

I roll my eyes and leap out to get the light. It's like the whole world is upended by his presence; even the simplest of routines disrupted. His rumbling laughter is a beacon of sound, guiding me back through the darkness. I navigate around the bed and wriggle across to him. Lying on his shoulder once more, I know sleep will come easily tonight, secure inside the safe harbour of his arms.

CHAPTER 27

Day Nine

I WAKE IN HALEY'S bed regretting I didn't insist on a pillow wall. The pressure of my enormous morning wood against boxer briefs—even this stretchy pair of Calvins—is almost painful. She's sleeping on her side, facing away from me. My arm is across her, just below those beautiful tits; under my hand, her breaths rise and fall in a contented rhythm. Right now, the exquisite curve of her bum against my dick is not helping. She wanted me to sleep here, and there's no way I'd have turned down the offer. But I'm not sure she'd thought it through.

Sleeping with me means waking up not only with me—but my friend down there who has taken no such vow to go slow. Normally I'd just take matters in hand, slink off to the shower and find quick relief. Do I move and risk her waking, to find that pressed to her back? Or do I stay here absolutely still and try to think of something very unsexy to distract myself in the hope eager 'Mr Ready and Willing' gets the message to stand down? I don't get the chance to decide.

Haley stirs and turns sleepily towards me, her mouth tipping up in a lazy, "Good morning." She presses a small kiss to my chest, before snuggling across so her body and mine are close. I swivel my hips back a bit, trying to make space for this annoying prick that's determined to make his presence felt. If she's noticed, she says nothing, sparing me the embarrassment.

"Good morning. Sleep well?"

"Like a baby." She gives a little yawn. "The dogs too. Didn't wake us up even once. That's unusual."

"Oh they did," I say. "I let them out around two. There was a pretty nasty smell circulating from their direction. Figured it might be best to kick them out for a pit stop."

"Really?" she says. "Wow, I didn't notice."

"Well, I'm pleased I didn't wake you. Although I'm a little hurt, you didn't notice I'd gone."

She elbows me playfully. "How about I cook you breakfast? Make it up to you."

"Sounds great." She slides out of bed and I'm saved. "OK if I grab the shower first?" I might need a cold one.

"Sure." Her muffled voice struggles upwards from the depths of one of those oversized Oodie things. When her head emerges, it's like she's wearing a tent, although the heavy bright red fabric with Christmas trees dotted all over is unlike any tent I've ever seen. She looks ridiculous, but totally adorable. "Come on, dogs." They leap to their feet.

The trio disappears and I make a dash for the shower, where I can deal with my unruly body parts in private, and arrive in the kitchen a little more composed.

Although she claims baking is more her specialty, and cooking meals not so much, the breakfast is delicious. Waffles dripping with syrup are an American innovation I fell in love with on our last tour there. It's kind of perfect to be sitting here in this kitchen, eating them with her.

After cleaning up, Haley announces she's baking gingerbread cookies. Some volunteers for the dog rescue have a stall at the market selling Christmas crafts and baked goods. She wants to do her part in the fundraising. A twinge of guilt grabs at me as I think of how much difference I might have made for them if things had been different. How many bake stalls will it take to make a hundred grand?

"You should help me." She flicks the oven on to heat and turns back to the recipe book open on its stand. "Take your mind off things."

We both know what things loom over us today. Anything to stop me from dwelling on all the possible outcomes of yesterday's meeting is a good idea.

"Sure, as long as you tell me what to do."

I'm the opposite of her in the culinary department. I can rustle up a decent meal, but—surprisingly, given how much I love to eat them—cakes and cookies are not my thing.

Before I know it, I'm wearing an apron and a frown, calculating the most efficient placement of the star-shaped cutter to get the maximum number of cookies from the slab of dough she's rolled out. Wrestling with the task partly occupies my mind, but it's the conversation with Haley that chews up most of it.

Two days ago, Loreena shared my secret. Since then, so much has happened, and Haley and I haven't really talked about it. To find out I've had feelings for her for three years, and hidden them so well she's never noticed, has to be unnerving. It's no surprise; she's got questions. This morning, Haley's trapped me here in the kitchen, and she's determined to get some answers.

"So, you're telling me it started the first time you saw me? That's bonkers."

I nod. "It sounds crazy, but yeah, it did."

It never seemed crazy to me. There was always something so right about wanting Haley. The logical part of my brain never argued back on that, although it reminded me every day that wanting her and having her were worlds apart.

"What was I wearing?"

"Jeans and a floaty green top, almost the colour of your eyes. You walked in there to the studio lot, so beautiful, but humble, like you didn't know it. I wanted to come over there and talk to you, but I was too shy. Couldn't believe my luck when I found out you were Ollie's sister, the one guy I'd made a connection with."

It was an early spring day when Haley drifted into the studio, trailing her parents. My life changed in an instant, like one of those years where the seasons don't slide slowly from one into the next, but, in an abrupt overnight change, winter has gone and spring has taken control of the world again. Haley appeared dressed in green, like the first flush of new leaves on a tree that's languished with bare branches for months.

"I loved that top."

"It looked so good on you, believe me. Then it got cold, and Ollie gave you his hoodie, which was ten sizes too big and you were embarrassed because they interviewed you in it. It was the first family interview, and you insisted on sitting huddled right in the middle so it wouldn't be so noticeable."

No one might have noticed the oversized clothing, but they couldn't help but notice her. Haley was the odd one out in her family, flanked by her parents and Ollie, all tall, and she small. And her, the only one with hair of dark chocolate, the studio lights reflecting burnished copper in its depths. Her mother's hair no doubt once looked the same, but now dyed a natural-looking shade of blonde, is more like the men in the family, only a glimpse of dark roots betraying her true colour. I hope Haley never follows her mother's lead. I loved waking up to find the dark strands splayed across the pillow next to me; loved burying my face in their depths.

"Oh, my god. You remember that? Even I hadn't remembered that until you said. How can you possibly?"

I shrug. "I dunno. I just remember."

"Did you write it down?" she asks through a laugh. "Do you have a little Haley Templeton file?"

"Don't need one." I tap my head. "It's all in here. You remember things that are important. You're important to me."

She drops her chin shyly and deflects with another question. "OK, so after *Star Power*, when was the next time we met?"

We carry on like this; her quizzing me like she's Bradley Walsh on *The Chase*, me answering with ease. She won't trip me up; not when this is my expert subject. Our every encounter of the past three years is permanently imprinted in my brain. I've been like a dragon with its hoard, from time to time picking out a precious stone of memory and considering it for a while before placing it back carefully, soothed by the knowledge of its existence. Doing it now, with her, is even better. I want her to understand this isn't some infatuation based only on a physical attraction. I want her to know that while our time together before this last week has been short in terms of minutes or hours, it's been enough for me to see things about her as a person that tell me she could be the one for me.

I've noticed Haley has a different ringtone for each of her friends. 'Stronger' by Britney Spears is Samantha. Not that I think the girl needs to develop any further in that direction. She's already a lethal machine. When Rachel calls, it's the suitably Scottish band the Proclaimers, belting out a promise to walk five hundred miles, which I'm sure Rachel, with her determination, is perfectly capable of. I wonder what mine is—that's if Haley's decided I've earned one. I hope so.

Around noon, while we are concentrating hard on finishing up one last batch of cookies, we both startle when Rachel's song bursts from the phone laying on the kitchen worktop. The strident music is harsh, drowning out the modern acoustic versions of traditional Christmas carols we've been listening to—the playlist Haley picked out to provide a chill Sunday morning vibe, while not straying from her happy little seasonal music bubble.

Haley quickly wipes her hands on her Mrs Santa apron, leaving dusty streaks of flour. As she reaches for the phone, I pause, placing the star-shaped cookie cutter to one side and wait. I watch Haley's face, anxious to read the news in her expression. The clipped tone of Rachel's voice echoes down the line. It's not good. Haley's down-turned mouth as her eyes meet mine tells me everything. The call is short.

"I'm sorry Christian," she says. "Rachel says they've called our bluff. Haven't budged at all. All that talk yesterday, total waste of time. She thinks they never intended to do anything different. That their lawyers were stringing us along, toying with us for the fun of it—and to collect more fees from their client. They've pointed out very clearly, if Loreena or you, or anyone, says a word publicly, they're going to take you down. She doesn't think there's any more we can do."

"Fuck." It's the only word that seems appropriate. "Fucking bastards." I slam my fist on the counter, causing a small cloud of flour to billow in the air as a red haze of frustration and anger rises in my vision. I immediately feel bad. Poor Haley has put up with a lot of me crashing around the place like a thunderclap this last week. "Sorry."

"Don't be. They *are* bastards. And you have every right to be angry. We all do."

"I don't know what else we can do."

"Me neither. Maybe ride it out to the live show and see what happens?"

"Yeah."

I can't go back to the cookie making. Anger surges through my body. Frustration is a painful writhing rope constricting my brain. Other times when I've felt like this, I've had an outlet for it. My natural reaction to stress is to flee. To put on my running shoes and pound the streets. That's not an option.

Or maybe it is. It's raining outside. Hard. We're only a few blocks from the Royal Parks. How many tourists are going to be wandering the pathways today?

"I'm going for a run." I take a decisive step away from the counter.

"But—"

"I'll find something in Ollie's room."

"But what if you're seen? Recognised?"

"I'm beyond caring."

She nods, giving me a sympathetic look, before grabbing a tray and going back to arranging cookies.

After a forty-minute run, incognito in rain jacket with cap pulled low, followed by a hot shower and dry clothes, I slump on the couch feeling better. Relaxed even. My anger has given way to acceptance. I should have expected this outcome, but I let that small seed of hope grow into a wild possibility the bad guys might not win. My rational brain has now taken a machete to it, chopped that unruly and unrealistic idea off at the roots.

I'm right back where I started. Nothing to do but ride out this rogue wave and hope I don't drown. And pray it doesn't take Haley down with me—that's if we have a future beyond these four walls. With every passing day, the tantalising prospect grows. It's ironic this nightmare should provide the fuel for my dreams to come true, and Loreena the spark to ignite it.

"Christian, come and have some lunch." Haley's still busy in the kitchen, amid the happy clatter of pots and pans and the smell of spice hanging heavy in the air.

I don't feel like food; I barely need it after all those waffles. I head to the kitchen anyway, recognising Haley's need to care for me helps keep her mind off her troubles too. There's something soothing about cooking. Perhaps it's the need to pay attention, freeing your brain from dwelling on other things.

She places a huge bowl of soup in front of me. Bright orange pumpkin with a swirl of cream. A faint smell of nutmeg drifts towards me in a small waft of steam.

"Looks like I've got competition. And here I was thinking the *Masterchef* title was all mine."

"It's only soup. Nothing fancy." She takes a seat at the counter next to me, plunging a spoon into her own bowl.

"But very good soup." I take a large slurp, and it tastes even better than it smells.

"Comfort food. Figured we both could use some." A resigned sigh slips out.

"What's wrong?" I ask, leaving my spoon poised mid-air.

"Oh, nothing. It's just..."

"Haley, tell me," I urge. While I was out there pounding the pavement, something else happened to take the shiny edge off my girl.

"It's nothing, really. Sam rang. We were planning to go to Kew Gardens tonight. To see the Christmas lights. But she's had to cancel. They're super shorthanded at her work. Sick staff. So she's picked up an extra shift tonight."

"That's a shame." I can imagine Haley's childlike delight in all things Christmas finding its peak in the outdoor lighting displays.

"It is, especially now the rain's easing off. Meant to clear by mid-afternoon."

"Yeah, it would choose to disappear now, after I got completely drenched."

"I'm sorry I didn't mention it. The gardens." She drops her eyes to the bowl. "I felt kind of guilty. Going out and leaving you home alone."

"It's OK. It's not your fault I'm under house arrest." As I'm saying it, that same recklessness that sent me running round the park in broad daylight nudges forward an idea. "It'll be dark, right?"

"Yes, and no. There's so many lights in some parts it may as well be daytime."

"I think we should go. You and me. That's as long as Sam won't be upset about you going without her."

"No, it's not really her thing. She only agreed because she didn't want me out after dark on my own."

"Not without your own highly trained bodyguard?"

"No," she laughs.

"OK, well, I'm no expert in—what is it?"

"Krav Maga."

"Right. That. But I'm big enough to be a suitable deterrent for anyone lurking in the gardens with nefarious motives."

"The place will be packed. How will you stop anyone recognising you?"

"It's going to be cold. By the time I layer up, I'll look like every other person there."

I take a casual tone, although I know this is risky. But in my new world, what Haley wants, Haley gets. And, much as I tease her relentlessly about her obsession, there's such joy in her when she's immersed in her Christmas stuff. It's strangely contagious. Of course, taking her to see the lights is not a totally unselfish suggestion on my part. I want to make some special moments with her. Just in case this time next year, I'm stuck with living on the memories. In case I'm just a memory to her, too; I want it to be a good one.

"What about the dogs?" I ask. "Can we take them? Would they be up for it?" I'm told the two oldies don't venture much beyond the backyard. A little outing might be good for them too.

Haley rests a thoughtful finger on her chin. "I was going to leave them here. To keep you company. But we could..."

"Leave it with me. I'll sort out a rideshare that will take all of us. This will be fun."

My smile is confident, but underneath, I know—this is *super* risky. If it goes wrong, it won't only be bad for me. It will be tough for her, too. She's witnessed fans mobbing the band, seen their reaction to her brother. However, it's completely different when you're no longer an observer, rather the centre of their attention. At least here in the UK, most are a little more respectful than in some countries, usually happy to settle for a selfie. If I'm unmasked, there's a chance the fans will be gentle. It's the rabid paparazzi who are more concerning. I can hold my own with the bastards, but I'm not sure I could control myself if they come for her, too.

Seeing her bright eyes as she sips at her soup, I'm not going to back out now. Although I have to do everything I can to prevent this from turning into another Christian disaster.

CHAPTER 28

Day Nine

"God it's so beautiful it could be Velaris." My words are a fog in the icy air.

"The City of Starlight." Christian's voice is muffled behind the scarf he's wound high to cover his mouth.

"See, I knew you'd like those books," I tease. I love that he loved them.

It's nine pm, as the staff member at the entry to Kew Gardens scans the tickets on my phone. The last timed entry slot has the advantage of fewer people. On a Sunday night, many of those with kids will have hurried them off home to bed before school tomorrow. So while it's busy, it's not too overwhelming for the dogs. As we rarely venture further than the little park one block over from the house, this is a big outing for them. But they seem happy to be here—excited even—linked to us with harnesses and leads. They step along jauntily, looking so sweet in their Christmas jackets. I've got Mularkey, while Tully is with Christian. She's developed a major crush on him. I totally get it.

Fewer people hopefully also mean less opportunity for someone to brush up against us and recognise the man who has me tucked in tight to his side. So far, so good.

And I'm enjoying the warmth of his body pressed to mine, because at this later time, it's also way colder. We might get proper snow again tonight. Twice in a week at this time of year is unheard of. But we came prepared. We're dressed like twin Michelin men, bulky jackets, hats, scarves, gloves. Christian's *Wild For The Win* wardrobe has come in handy. Suited for winter in Scotland, it's more than adequate here, as well as ensuring hardly any of him is visible.

However, I'm not sure about the addition of his sunglasses. I know his very recognisable, piercing blue eyes framed by long lashes, and the dark slanting brows could still give him away. So covering them is a good idea. Although a guy in dark glasses on a winter night isn't exactly inconspicuous. Strangely, no one seems to give him a second glance, so I shrug off my doubts and allow myself to fall into fairyland.

My arm linked with his, we weave our way along the paths. Somehow, tonight the decorations seem even more magical than previous years. Have the designers outdone themselves? Or is it the man beside me, his presence illuminating my life, like the bursts of light transforming the gardens, picking out the beauty that was already there in new ways?

Overhead, towering trees with wintery branches stripped naked of their leafy summer beauty, are clothed in winding strands of lights. They shimmer like galaxies against the black velvet night.

Waterfalls of light cascade over intricate archways, beckoning us to explore what lies beyond. We find tunnels of shrubbery swathed in kaleidoscopes of colour that shift and blend. Emerging from them, we stand in outdoor rooms where intricate patterns of golden light adorn walls of waxy green leaves.

Outside, shimmering fairy lights guide us along new pathways, leading us deeper into an enchanted realm. Gigantic sculptures tower over us, rainbows of pulsing light flowing across their features.

We speak little. There's not really any way to describe this experience. It's one of those things to be lived. When each new delightful surprise appears, we simply turn to each other, without saying anything, and I know we're thinking the same thing: this is amazing. The trail might only be one mile long, but by the time we reach the end, it feels like we've been on a magical journey of a thousand.

And along the way, there's been this luminous glowing ball growing inside me. It pulses, its light and warmth slowly expanding with each thud of my heart, with each step I take in time with his, in every squeeze of his hand and the way his arm tightens across my shoulder, pulling me in close as we pause to gaze in awe at each new marvel, under the spell of this place. I recognise what blooms within, even though I haven't felt its nearness for so long. Happiness. Christmas makes me happy. But this year there's something else. Someone else. Christian makes me happy.

We emerge into an open space, where stalls are set up around the edge, and bright music spills forward.

"You want some?" Christian tips his chin towards a food vendor. People are queuing for hot roast chestnuts. The sweet nutty scent, with hints of caramel, fills the air around the cart. There's a subtle smoky undertone, and the rattle of brittle shells as the vendor stirs with deft movements. My stomach growls, our quick dinner of mac and cheese long forgotten.

"Oh yes. Chestnuts are a must. And there's mulled wine, over there." Another stall opposite is doing a brisk trade, the spicy smell from steaming paper cups wafting towards us. I can't resist. "Let's go for both. I'll get the wine."

When Mularkey and I return, the cups of wine warming my hands even through my gloves, we find a small girl eyeing Christian and Tully. Her blonde brows beneath a striped beanie are knotted in a frown as she looks him up and down suspiciously. She purses her rosebud lips, and the words spill out.

"Are you blind?"

Christian and I exchange puzzled glances over her head. And then I get it.

"Dark glasses, dog in harness." I slide the whispered words out of the corner of my mouth while biting back laughter at the thought of Tully being a guide dog. She'd be better than Mularkey; with her short attention span, it would get wild if she was in charge. But I wouldn't want my safety to depend on Tully, either. That obsessive need of hers to follow any interesting smell would most likely have you grass skiing before ending up buried in a hedge.

A grin splits Christian's face, and he stoops down to the child. Raising his glasses, revealing twinkling blue eyes, he offers a wink. "No. But it's a pretty good disguise, isn't it?"

She gives him a solemn nod, satisfied. "Can I pat your dog?"

"Sure." She reaches for Tully's head, undeterred by the dog's wide toothy grin.

A woman, bag of chestnuts in hand, comes to stand alongside the little girl, and carefully checks over this stranger talking to her mini-me. Christian smiles up at her and it's then I see her mouth fall open.

"You're…"

He immediately swings into action. With the dark glasses shoved back on his face, Christian is on his feet. "Sorry sweetie. Gotta go."

And he's off, heading for the gate, Tully sensing the urgency towing him through the crowd. No one would take him for a blind person with the speed he navigates the streams of people leaving the gardens.

"Wasn't that Christian Steele?" The bewildered woman stares at his disappearing back.

"No. Just my brother." I shake my head, trying to assemble my face to match the lie. I'm becoming surprisingly good at lying. "He gets that all the time. The likeness is uncanny, isn't it?"

"Oh." Confusion still whirls across her face, but as she takes the child's hand, it seems she's accepted my words.

"Nice meeting you," I say, attempting a relaxed, cheerful tone. "But we really do have to go. Our ride will be waiting." Mularkey and I sprint down the path, trying to catch him up without spilling the wine, leaving woman and child staring after us.

"Shit, that was close." He's breathing heavily when I finally make it to his side.

I'm puffing too, after zigzagging in and out of the trails of people like a pro footballer on attack.

"Sure was. I told you the glasses were a bad idea."

I shove a cup of wine at him, and he takes it gratefully. We amble to the end of the queue for taxis and stand politely. A few sips of the hot wine, the sweetness and spice a pleasant contrast to the slight tang of underlying tannin, and my pulse has almost returned to normal.

I glance back towards the gardens, and there she is. The same woman, daughter in hand, walking our way. It doesn't appear intentional, like she's following us. However, the last thing we need is to be trapped in this line, unable to escape her scrutiny and more questions.

I elbow Christian. "Don't make it obvious," I hiss against his ear. "But look, she's just over there." She stands to our right by the gate, scanning up and down, as if trying to spot someone. I don't think it's us she's hoping to find, but I'd rather be safe than sorry. "We should go."

How we might escape, I don't know. We're still five from the front of the taxi line, and to jump ahead, breaking the very British rules around queuing, would draw unwanted attention.

"Fuck." Christian's low growl, as he gives a quick tip of his head to the left, immediately sets my teeth on edge. "Photographer."

The man is conspicuous by the huge camera over one shoulder. He pauses by the entranceway and swings it upwards to one eye, steadying the unwieldy length of the lens with a practised hand. His hefty gear marks him out as a professional. No one else would bother with anything besides a phone.

An ominous whirr cuts the air as he shoots in rapid-fire, taking picture after picture of people leaving the gardens. They'll be great photos, the stream of smiling faces, all still under the spell of the enchanted world inside. It's unlikely he'll turn his attention to the line at the taxi stand—unless someone points out there's a celebrity lurking in between the rest.

Christian's not going to take that chance. He grabs at my cup and before I can protest I'm not finished, stuffs it and his own into a nearby bin. He grabs my hand and tugs me and the dogs to the front of the queue.

We fall into the next cab as it edges forward. Ignoring the indignant cries from some of those waiting in line, we organise ourselves and the dogs in the generous back seat. Others in the queue make the same assumption as the child. Allowing for Christian's 'disability', they admonish the ones complaining about us. I slam the door on the fuss.

Luckily, the driver doesn't object to canine passengers. Maybe he, too, is reluctant to test the possibility that Christian really is blind. This time, the dark glasses might have saved us. We ride in silence for the whole twenty minutes, but my blood hums with a mix of fear and exhilaration from the close call. Christian maintains the charade, only ripping off the sunglasses as we sprint up the steps, still high on the danger, and stumble into the house.

"That could have ended really badly, couldn't it?" I say. We stand in the entrance hall, the reality of the risk Christian took so I could have this night beginning to sink in.

"Ahh, the things I do for you, Haley Templeton."

He shakes his head and tries to look severe, but fails.

"Including impersonating the blind," I quip.

We both dissolve into relieved laughter. The dogs wag happily as if they're laughing too, nudging at our knees. We pull off our gloves, tucking them into coat pockets and, taking charge of one dog each, set to work unbuckling their harnesses and leads. Once free, they dance away from us down the hallway and I hear them land with dual thumps on my bed.

"Well, at least they had a good night." He coils the two leads into a tidy circle and scoops up the harnesses.

"Admit it Christian," I tease. "You're actually starting to like Christmas. In fact, I think you enjoyed every minute of this evening. Including the thrill of the chase."

"The thrill of *avoiding* the chase," he corrects, his back to me as he kneels to stash the dogs' stuff on the bottom shelf of the hall table. When he stands, his eyes meet mine, dark and unfathomable. "Yeah, it was a bit of a thrill," he admits. "But not as thrilling as being here with you." Anticipation seems to battle with apprehension in that blue velvet gaze. The husk in his voice ignites every nerve in my body. And I'm a goner.

Christian strips off his hat, his dark wayward hair all tousled underneath, his eyes not once leaving mine, as he unwinds his scarf slowly. I'm not sure how he manages to make taking off bulky winter clothing look sexy, but he does. The moment his face is fully revealed, my eyes are drawn to his mouth. As if aware of my obsession with his lips, they slide into a slanted, panty-melting smile. My god, I think he's discarded going slow along with his hat and scarf. I'm ready to do the same.

Last night we shared a bed while tiptoeing around the possibility of going further. I may have slept in his arms, and woke with his obvious desire prodding at my back, but somehow he kept our touch chaste and controlled. While every part of me was begging him to forget who I am, forget who he is, to ignore what I've been through this past year, to not wrap me up in cotton wool and simply take me and make my body hum, still I held back the words. I usually don't ask for what I want. Now I'm about to.

"Christian…" I barely recognise my voice. "How about we forget going slow?"

He doesn't speak, but any trace of uncertainty in his eyes is gone, replaced by blatant longing. His hand reaches for my scarf, carefully unravelling it just like I'm unravelling under his touch, his fingers deliciously cool on the bare skin beneath. Tugging off my hat, he lets it drop to the floor. He smooths my hair, so gentle, and my breath catches. His hand shifts to tuck back some loose strands behind one ear.

I shiver as his fingers graze my neck, dropping my head to one side, leaning into his touch with a sigh. He catches my chin in his hand and guides my face to his, while one thumb drifts up to trace my mouth. I close my eyes and part my lips. My tongue licks at them, and he lets out a low moan. He presses his lips to mine, and we both shudder out a groan.

His kiss is slow and deliberate, savouring me like the first bite of a maple bacon donut. It's tender, yet demanding of more. His tongue thrusts between my lips, tasting me while I delight in the sweet spiciness of his mouth. One of my hands threads through his hair, the other pressed to his neck, cupping his head to me hungrily.

There may be layers of clothing between us, but I'm as turned on as if we were skin to skin. I claw uselessly at the zipper on his coat as his hands fumble with the buttons on mine. Giggles overtake me and he shakes out a laugh as we both realise how ridiculous this is, trying to get all hot and heavy while still bundled up for the outdoors. I'm bubbling with laughter against his chest, his throaty chuckle warm on my neck, when he murmurs against my ear.

"My room, two minutes?"

I lean back to meet his gaze. He arches one dark brow, and I nod.

"Sounds a plan."

Moments later, sitting on my bed, coat tossed aside and unlacing my boots, I'm wondering exactly what the plan is. God, how much do I take off? Only the bulky stuff? More? Casually stroll in there half naked? Somehow it doesn't feel right baring too much. I'm under no illusion as to the end point here, but I don't want to look over eager, the sad dumped girl desperate for a man.

Instead, I opt to leave most of my clothes on, a present for him to unwrap. I know underneath my slouchy sweater and jeans, there's pretty red lingerie waiting for him to discover. I've been reaching for my nicest sets these last few days, perhaps subconsciously preparing for this possibility.

Part of me wonders what the hell I'm doing. Is my selfish need to feel wanted taking charge? I worry I'm taking advantage of his feelings for me. But then I can't deny it: I have feelings for Christian too. They've snuck up on me, day by day, moment by moment. I can't ignore them any longer.

I hear him clear his throat. He leans against the doorframe, trying to look casual, but I see the nervous dart of his eyes. My eyes rove over the t-shirt, bulky chest muscles straining at it, and I swallow with anticipation of getting my hands on him. I remember how I woke up this morning. I know what it feels like to rest my head against the bare skin beneath that shirt, to press my lips lightly against it while holding back the urge to taste my way down the length of him. An urge I no longer need to fight.

His jeans hang low on narrow hips, and I cringe, remembering my clumsy attempts to remove them, overwhelmed by that first surge of desire the other night.

"Changed your mind?" His normally confident voice wavers a little. "It's OK if you have…"

I shake my head, and he steps forward and reaches for me, relief flooding his face. Pulling me onto my feet, he cages me inside those broad inked arms. He presses his forehead to mine, our eyes locked, his with pupils huge and darkly smouldering.

His mouth seeks mine, and I offer it willingly. His kiss burns. Large hands rove down my spine, leaving trails of electricity in their wake. He cups my bum, pressing my hips into him, and I sigh and grind myself against the hard press of his groin.

A questioning whine interrupts the moment. We turn our heads in unison to see two pairs of dog eyes fixed on us, curious.

"Maybe not in front of the children?" His low raspy laughter rumbles against my chest, and we stumble from the room, shutting my door firmly behind us.

CHAPTER 29

Day Nine

As IF TO LOCK out the world completely, Christian closes his door. It's just the two of us in this secret bubble. The room is dim, only a single lamp on the bedside table, casting a golden glow. We stand facing each other, hesitant, like we're unsure what comes next now we're here.

Perhaps deciding one of us needs to do something, he rips off his t-shirt. My breath catches at the sight of him. I can't imagine ever tiring of looking at Christian, the lightly burnished skin with its patterns of deepest indigo, the dark untidy hair that invites fingers to thread through it, the shadowy scruff of his beard framing a sensuous mouth which right this minute tips up at one corner, in a shy smile, as if nervous under my scrutiny. I don't think he realises how beautiful he is. That lack of awareness just makes him all the more attractive.

"Haley," he says, a whisper, a husk, drawing me to him. My hand brushes the chiselled line of his hip, moving up over the taut muscles of his stomach, drifting across the curve of his chest, fingers gliding over the dusting of sleek dark hair there, before moving up to curl over the angles of his shoulder. My pulse quickens at the warm, reassuring, solid feel of him.

He fingers my jumper; its wide neck hangs loose, revealing my collarbone. He eyes it thoughtfully, before dotting a decisive kiss on my bare skin. Then, placing his hands firmly on my shoulders, he spins me away from him, so we're both facing the large, freestanding mirror.

I look so small, almost fragile, against his large body, his arms clasped protectively around me, his dark head nestled against mine. But in the strength of his hands and the determined look in his eyes, I sense he's not planning to be gentle with me. The thought sends a white hot thrill of anticipation through my body. I want him so badly.

His breath is hot against my ear as he murmurs my name again. His arms drop to my waist, and he slides one hand under the edge of my top. His fingers snake upwards, lifting the top with it, coming to rest below my breast, cupping it with a deep exhale. He pauses to tweak one nipple, barely confined by the whisper-fine lacey web of my bra. Then he sweeps the top upwards and off, dropping it on the floor before returning his large hands to fan across my stomach, pulling me into him.

"You are so fucking beautiful, Haley." His voice is gravel, his erection straining at his jeans, his body pressed hard against my bum, as he rubs himself against me with a groan.

His fingers move to the waistband of my jeans, and without breaking our gaze in the mirror, he flicks the button undone and tugs down the zipper. I escape from his arms a moment and shimmy them off, revealing the flimsiest of lace panties. As I kick my jeans away, he pulls me back into his orbit, his hands travelling across my hips, tracing the skin of my thighs. Goosebumps explode all over my body.

He sinks back to sit on the side of the bed, drawing me down with him. Leaning back against his chest, I'm nestled between his thighs. He snuggles his chin against my collarbone, his breath skimming my bare skin, and our eyes meet in the tall mirror opposite.

"You OK?"

His words come out a whisper as his hand slides from waist to hip to the delicate skin of my thigh. I shiver at the teasing dance of his fingers as they linger in a sensitive spot, and my voice catches in my throat.

"I'm very OK," I rasp out, watching the girl in the mirror nod, her pupils large and dark, while those of the man beside her blaze with promise. In that moment, seeing beyond his raw desire, the concern for me written in his tender expression, I hand over my trust to him, letting him lead the way.

"Good." He hums the word against my neck.

He pulls me in a little closer with the one hand splayed across my breast, while the other continues to explore dangerously close to where my body has become nothing but molten desire. "You relax back here, and I'm gonna make you more than OK, sweetheart."

He trails a fingertip along the line of my panties, from one hip to the other, teasing with a featherlight touch that provokes a low ache of wanting deep in my belly. Then his hand slides back to palm my thigh. One finger explores beneath the lace edge, then another, gliding down to the heat between my legs, and I whimper with anticipation as he lingers at my entrance. Heat flares and my body trembles with need.

"God," he groans out. "You are so wet. So fucking wet."

He slips a finger inside. My muscles reflexively clench around it, and I moan. He begins to move, slipping in and out, and I move with him, riding each thrust, urging him on with whimpers that spring unbidden from deep inside my throat.

Reading my expression of pure pleasure in the mirror, he whispers against my cheek. "You want one more?"

I can barely huff out the word, but a ragged "Yes" spills out in between my panting, and he thrusts a second finger into me. I can't help but lower my hips onto his fingers, driving them deeper. Seeking the pressure and release, the rough friction of his fingers curved inside of me, my body instinctively moves with his hand, the exquisite rise and fall causing waves of pleasure to pulse through my centre.

One thumb swoops in to find that sensitive bundle of nerves, circling slowly, the two rhythms in counterpoint, the strokes of his hand and the swirling of his thumb causing me to writhe in bliss. I arch my back, thrusting my hips forward, meeting every movement of his hand, hungry for that feeling of fullness. My head lolls back against his chest, eyes closed, as I ride the waves of colour exploding behind them.

"Open your eyes, sweetheart; look in the mirror," he breathes against my ear. "Watch what I'm doing to you. Watch me make you fall apart."

My eyes flutter open. "Good girl," he murmurs, his gaze meeting my pleasure-dazed reflection. "See how I know what you need?"

And he does. In the precise movements of his hand, while the other works its way under the lace of my bra, taunting a nipple, provoking ripples of intermingled pleasure and pain. He sucks at my neck, his teeth nipping and tasting, and I know I'll need a high neck top under my scrubs tomorrow. I'm marked as his and I don't care.

All the while, I watch as he coaxes me higher and higher with the perfect movements of his hands and murmured words of encouragement against my ear. My cheeks are a blaze of heat. He's playing me like a familiar instrument, as if he knows this melody by heart, and can evoke it effortlessly.

He talks to me almost constantly, checking in with how I'm feeling, and I huff out answers, monosyllables, barely recognisable as words. I've never had a lover so attentive to my needs. Finally, he senses I'm about to tip over the edge, reading the crescendo rising in my body, knowing I'm about to hit the high note, and he urges me on.

"Come for me baby, you're so close. I can feel it. Reach for it, sweetheart."

And I do, my whole body stretching towards a dizzying new peak. My voice becomes an exclamation as I arch my back and shatter into a million pieces. Only then do I allow my eyes to close, soaking in the blissful warmth engulfing my body, my toes curled in one shuddering sigh.

When I open them, Christian still watches me in the mirror with a satisfied smile.

"I don't think I've ever seen anything more beautiful." His low husk sends another shudder through me.

"I don't think I've ever come like that before," I whisper. And I know it's more than the skill in his hands. There's an invisible rope tying me to Christian, this feeling of some deep connection between us, as if he instinctively not only understands the needs of my body, but of my heart.

"I'm glad you enjoyed it because, baby, I'm only just getting started with you." His breath against my ear is a promise I'm happy to hold him to.

I free myself from his arms and scoot around to face him, raising my legs to sit astride his lap. I slide one finger down his lips, following the curve of his chin, and trailing down, down, to rest at his waistband.

"I think I'd like to get started with you," I say, curling my hand over the bulging denim between us. I unwrap my legs and stand, tugging him up by the waist of his jeans. Without taking my eyes from his, I unbuckle his belt and tear open the zipper. I grip at the boxer briefs, feeling the length of him hard against my hand.

"I think someone's ready to come out to play." I pull at his underwear, freeing his erection. "Sit down."

He does as I say, first kicking off his jeans and boxers, his eyes locked on mine. He sits on the bed, and I kneel between his legs, then sit back on my haunches, one hand gripping him firmly.

"Now it's your turn. To watch."

He smiles down at me, but I wipe that smile from his face, as the first sweep of my hand from root to tip triggers a moan, his mouth fallen open. I lean forward and take the tip of him in my mouth, tasting and teasing, lapping the small bead of salty-sweet liquid away, before taking the whole length of him deep into my throat. His hands fist my hair as he arches into me.

I work at him, one hand steadying the hard length of his cock as I lick and suck, my other hand slipping beneath his balls, stroking a small soft spot behind that provokes groans. His thighs tremble and tense, his hands gripping my shoulders, fingers curled, urging me forward. He bucks his hips into me with guttural moans, his head thrown back. "Oh, fuck Haley. That feels so fucking good." I feel so powerful, here in control of his building orgasm, and I pick up my pace.

"Stop, stop," he gasps out. I draw my head back, wondering what I've done wrong. But his eyes are closed and his face is slack with pleasure. "Too good," he mumbles, patting at my head. "You have to stop Haley, or I'm going to lose it."

"I thought that was the objective."

He reaches for me, sweeping his arms beneath my armpits, and scoops me up off the floor, turning me to sit beside him. He brushes a hand over my cheek.

"Believe me, it is, sweetheart. But I don't want to hurry this. I've waited a long time for you. And there's so much I want to give you. Let me."

He slides from the bed, kneeling before me, eyes dark and know-ing, and places a palm on each thigh, spreading them wide. With one fluid movement, he whisks my panties down to lie in a tiny damp puddle of red lace around my feet. I kick them aside.

I lean back, my body totally exposed, open to whatever he wants to do with it. He leans in to me, capturing me in a kiss. The sweet saltiness of having his cock in my mouth merges with the lingering taste of spice in his.

He trails delicate kisses along my neck, pausing to worship each breast in turn with firm lips that tug and tantalise. He tastes his way down my stomach, each press of his mouth triggering an explosion of small sparks as anticipation of where he's heading rises inside me. My hips cupped in large hands, he pulls me forward as his dark head dips low and I moan when his warm, wet mouth finds my centre. My knees tighten reflexively around his ears and he pushes them apart again, insistent. And all the time I'm watching myself in the mirror, my body arching as I ride wave after wave of sensation, powerless against the relentless tide sweeping me along with him, until I collapse back onto the bed with a searing, gasping shudder.

He smiles up at me, looking pleased with himself. He kisses his way up my thigh, my stomach, my breasts, and I whimper at the exquisite sensitivity of my body tingling beneath his touch. Still, I want more. I want all of him. Inside me, filling the emptiness of the past year, the deep yearning not only for the physical, but for someone to mend the gaping hole in my heart.

"Please," I plead with him. "Please. I want you inside me. To come with you inside me."

"Again?" he chuckles. "My greedy girl." And then "Are you sure?" he mumbles against my breast. He raises his head, dark hair tangled, curling in sweat-soaked tendrils. Stormy blue eyes meeting mine, and I can see him lick at his lips, still wet with the taste of me on them.

"Oh god, yes. I'm so sure." My chest still heaves, my breaths ragged.

"Condom?" he rasps out. "I don't have one."

"No, yes, no. Don't need one."

"You're on the pill, right?"

"Yeah, and..." I feel a slight awkwardness admitting to my celibacy in the aftermath of last year's heartbreak. "There hasn't been anyone since..." I refuse to say his name. I won't let that bastard into the room with us. "Not for a year."

Not since I had to undergo the humiliation of getting tested because my boyfriend was sleeping with someone else as well as me.

"Me neither," he says. "Despite what the papers would have you believe. And I'm clean."

I've never done this before, never trusted someone from the very first time. But I trust Christian. I shuffle back on the bed and stretch out my hand to where he's still kneeling between my thighs, pulling him towards me in clear invitation.

Without hesitation he's on top of me, his heat and weight and power poised as he centres himself, before driving into me with a hard, deep thrust, causing my breath to catch. I'm so ready for him, I simply grip him to me even tighter.

We immediately find a rhythm, as if our bodies are perfectly tuned to the same note, like this is a song we know well, deliciously familiar.

As he feels my rising arousal, the exquisite friction of our over-heated bodies sending my senses spiralling out of control, he quickens his pace, the movement growing less controlled. I arch my hips, locking my thighs around him, desperate to give him greater access, to plunge into me more deeply. The new angle only serves to heighten my pleasure and light flashes as a waterfall of bliss crashes over me and my body clenches tightly around him, my vocalisations a howl of release. He follows, his own tumbling shuddering climax coming with my name on his lips.

Afterwards, we snuggle under the covers, the room a little chilled now the explosive heat of our love-making has trickled away. I turn on my side, and he brackets me with his body, a protective arm across me.

"I can't believe you're really here." He coils a strand of my hair around one finger. "You know I dream about you, right? I feel like I'm going to wake up and find this is just the same old dream I've had before."

"You won't," I whisper. "I'm here. And I'm not going anywhere. This is exactly where I want to be."

More than that, somehow I feel like this is where I *need* to be, for him, and for me. For so long I haven't been able to see any way forward, any future. I've tried to forget the painful past year, and focus on the small good things in each day, not daring to hope for more. But this—this feels like not only a beautiful, surprising today. It feels like tomorrow. I lie there, a contented happiness settling upon me like a warm blanket. Listening to his rhythmic breathing is a soft lullaby, soothing me into sleep.

He murmurs the words into my hair, the faintest of whispers, as if it's a secret he's sharing only with the darkness. "I love you, Haley."

I pretend to be asleep, but I lie there, turning the words over in my mind. I've heard them before, and they were a lie. This time, with this man, I know he means them. And that is both wonderful and terrifying.

Day Ten

I SQUINT AT THE slant of moonlight forcing its way around a gap in the curtains. It illuminates the relaxed face of the woman sleeping beside me. Her hair is a mess, tangled across the pillow. My fault, but I'm not sorry, remembering the feel of those dark shiny strands twisted in my hands while she knelt in front of me, her beautiful mouth working me into a frenzy. My dick gives a sudden, immediate lurch. That part of me is never satisfied, especially not when the source of so much pleasure is pressed against me, that curvy wee arse, so ripe and peachy. I am so fucking gone for this woman. And not only because she let me use my body—my hands, my mouth and my eager cock all for her—to try and blot out all memory of the douchebag who didn't deserve her.

I want it all with Haley. Not just the sex, although I'd happily take that again right now if she wakes up with the need. But what I want with Haley are big things—a life, a home, a future—things I'm not sure *I* deserve with her, but I want them more than anything, ever. And I'm going to work my arse off to show her why she should want them with me, too.

Shifting my weight carefully, trying not to disturb her, I reach behind me for my phone. Fuck, it's almost seven. I feel guilty knowing she'll soon need to be up for work. I hate the thought of having to wake her, knowing I'm responsible for the fact she's facing Monday morning with barely four hours sleep. But, remembering how we spent those hours between stumbling in from the gardens and eventually falling into exhausted sleep, I don't regret it and I don't think she will either.

I've still got the smile of a satisfied man on my face. It's as if on the stroke of midnight, sweet little Haley's naughty twin came out to play and fuck if she isn't fun to be with. Making her come, shatter into little pieces in my arms while I watched her face in the mirror, was the most beautiful thing I've ever seen. I told her so and then got her to do it all over again twice more just to prove it.

She stirs with a small kitten-like mewl and stretches her arms.

"God, I wish I didn't have go to work." She twists to press her body against me and buries her head into my neck. "Not when I'm in bed with such a good snuggler."

"A good snuggler? Is that all?" Her breasts crushed against my chest feel so damn good, the peaks of her nipples erect and tempting.

"Nope. I think you've proved you are rather good at a lot of things." Her giggle tickles my shoulder. "But a snuggle is all I've got time for."

"Are you sure? I can be very quick as well as good."

"Hmm." She hums against my skin. "I definitely need a shower. Can't go to work reeking of you."

"We could save time by taking a shower together?"

Laughter bursts from her. "Nice try, but no." She shimmies up the bed and places pliant lips against mine, offering a kiss as her final word on the subject. "You stay here."

The sounds of her getting ready for work—the hum of the shower, the buzz of her hairdryer, the hiss of the coffee machine, her chatter to the dogs—are like a piece of music I could listen to on repeat forever. And it's within my reach to capture it. I know it is.

Before she leaves, she slips back into the room, perching beside me on the bed. Her newly-washed hair caught up in a ponytail, that green-apple shampoo in a cloud, her face fresh and shiny, and the smell of her floral perfume as she leans in to kiss me—it's like a waking dream.

"See you around five-thirty, yeah?"

"I'll be waiting right here."

"Oh, could you put the bin out? It's our collection day."

"Sure. Anything else you need me to do?"

"Cook me up another one of those dinners."

"Yeah, I thought I'd do tacos."

The conversation is mundane, like we're an old married couple with our daily routines. This is what it would be like to be with her. There's a simple beauty in it, the hint of a life that could be ours.

"Mmm, now you're talking my language. I'll be thinking about them all day."

"And I'll be thinking about you all day."

She gives me one last peck on my hungry lips, and slowly pulls her hand away from where it's wrapped in mine, stretching out her leaving that moment longer, as if she regrets she can't stay. I regret it too.

The moment I step out of the bathroom, an hour after Haley's gone, I have a sense someone is in the house. There's a presence in the otherwise silent rooms. The dogs are still out back on squirrel patrol. I gave up trying to trick the little shits into coming inside before I jumped in the shower. They're too obsessed with staking out the tree to worry about the cold. If they're not concerned about sitting out there without their cutesy Christmas jackets, then neither am I. So it's not them filling the empty space.

I refasten the towel around my hips and edge towards the kitchen. My bare feet are cold and silent as I pad down the wooden floor of the passageway. I'm almost at the kitchen door, when there's the scrape of a chair and muted footsteps headed my way.

I startle as a tiny figure appears in the doorway, silhouetted against the glare.

"Samantha?" My hands reflexively drop to protect my crotch, while my balls shrink at the sight of her, desperate to hide. I wouldn't put it past Sam to knee me in the groin just because I looked at her the wrong fucking way. Rachel might appear scary, but this is the one to watch out for.

"You know you shouldn't sneak up on people like that, Christian? Lucky I knew it was you or…"

"Don't tell me—or you'd have slammed me onto the ground and broken my arm again."

"I didn't break your arm," she protests. The barely suppressed curve of her mouth suggests she's not the least bit sorry.

"Might have fucking well broken it. It hurt for two days."

"I'm sorry," she says, but her grin argues otherwise. "But if it *was* broken, it would hurt for more than two days. Anyway, now I know who you are, I won't do it again. Promise. Besides, I don't think Haley would like it if I damaged her new toy."

I narrow my eyes, and a flush rises up my neck. Seems like girl-code demands you spill all the details.

"She told us things had got—"

"I let her climb all over me like ivy. Just like I heard someone else say they might like to do." I fire her words of last week right back at her with an arch of my brow. Now it's Sam's turn to blush all the way to the roots of her ponytail. Trust her to be still groomed to military grade neat even after an all-night shift. I'm pleased to have ruffled her cool exterior. "Do you have a problem with that?"

To her credit, she gathers herself to all of her five-foot-nothing and shoots me a glare.

"If you hurt her, I do have a problem. She might have only confessed to losing her clothes and joining you in the no pants dance, but I know Haley—she doesn't do casual sex. There are feelings involved here."

"I'm well aware of that."

While I wasn't expecting to be interrogated by Haley's friends so soon after we'd crossed into this territory, Sam's warning makes me want to fist pump the air. Whatever Haley told them this morning, confirms last night *was* more than an impulsive hookup for her, more than just sex. But her protective friends—and I'm pleased she's got them looking out for her—need to know it was more than that for me, too.

I saunter past her into the kitchen, dragging a coffee mug towards me. Sam settles herself on a high stool and glares at me across the counter. I take a deep breath. It's confession time for me as well.

"I've got some pretty big feelings for her, too. Did she tell you that?"

"She didn't need to. Haley never jumps into bed with guys unless she thinks the feeling's mutual. Even that creep of an ex, Jack, cared about her at the start. Just not enough to keep his dick to himself. You know about him and Paige, right?"

My blood seethes at the mention of their names. "Yeah. Maybe you should show me some of your Krav Maga moves in case I run into the guy."

She snorts out a laugh. "Jack would take one look at you..." She scans me from head to toe, daring to admire my bulky arms and chest with her gaze. "And he'd run a mile." Her smile slips away. "He hurt Haley so badly, I thought he'd broken her for good. Taken away her ability to trust anyone, to even consider a relationship. But, for some reason, she trusts you."

"And she can." I want to say more. Fuck it. I wish I could just lay it out there for everyone to know—tell the world I am in love with Haley Templeton, and that is why I *can* be trusted not to destroy her beautiful heart. However, I need her to hear those words from me first. I can't spill them now simply to ward off a Sam-attack.

"And can she trust you to protect her? From all the crap?" she says, mouth full of cookie. "Like the stuff that happened to Ollie?" Of course Sam would know about Ollie. He's her brother from another mother.

I hesitate. What the fuck can I say? I'll do my best. Put her first. But the truth is there's no guarantee, and Haley knows it as well as I do. Probably Sam does too.

"She can trust me to do everything in my power. But I'm not going to lie to you—that might not be enough." Dark eyes flash a warning. "But Haley and I have talked about this, Sam. While I might not be able to prevent it, we can be ready for it. Together. And *that* could be enough."

Sam gives a disgruntled huff, snatching at the cookie jar on the counter and helping herself to another one. She munches away thoughtfully while I wrangle the coffee machine.

"It better be, Christian. Haley gets hurt like Ollie did, and I swear I'll kill you."

"You'll have to beat Rachel to it. That's pretty much what she said." I shake my head. "I can't understand how someone as sweet as Haley has such vicious friends."

"It's because she is so sweet she needs us to look out for her."

"Fair enough." I can't really argue with that. "Want a coffee?"

"Nah, thanks, but caffeine's not the best idea right now." She stifles a yawn. "Need to get home to bed."

"Well, this has been nice," I say. "Sweet dreams."

With Sam's departure, it's back to just me and the two dogs. Despite my bravado with the ninja nurse, her visit unsettles me. I've never considered myself worthy of Haley, and it's as if Sam and Rachel can see it. No matter how much I argue otherwise, they talk as if it's inevitable I fuck this up. The pair of them waiting in the wings, poised to pick up the pieces when it all goes wrong. Can they see some flaw in me? I try and push my gnawing doubt aside and settle back into my Haley-recommended reading.

After an hour, I toss down the book, feeling my inadequacy compared to these fictional guys who seem to have all the right words, with their fancy declarations of love. Meanwhile, I struggle to think how I can tell Haley how much she means to me without scaring her off. After all, we've come a long way in a week and I don't want to push it too far, but I don't want to lose her.

The house is lonely without Haley in it. She takes her Christmas playlist with her, and much as I tease her about it, I miss it. Miss her. I pick up my guitar and go back to the song I worked on the other day. Is this a song for Haley? Yes. Is this a Christmas song? Maybe. Am I sorry about that? Not at all.

CHAPTER 31

Day Ten

Haley

MONDAY IS BUSY WITH a stream of clients through our Camden Town clinic doors. Word has spread through the local area and beyond; this clinic is more affordable than most. Despite our modest charges, these community clients are the lifeblood of the dog rescue, providing an income stream that allows us to subsidise our care of the homeless and abandoned, the battered and broken, who also arrive in sad regularity.

"Haley." Alice's voice is unusually sharp as she jerks her head towards the woman in the waiting room with a squirming puppy in her arms, and a smiling black lab by her side. I can't blame our receptionist for her impatience with me. I've been distracted all morning, going through the motions of my job, my mind consumed with the events of the weekend.

Separated from the warmth of Christian's bed, in the harsh light of a grey London day, I look back at what happened between us with no regrets. Rachel and Sam both made reassuring noises at the news. I came clean with my friends, firing off a message to our chat group while on the tube. I figured they'd work it out anyway the moment they see us together. They know me too well to try to hide it.

Here in the present, I'm still basking in the afterglow of last night. Yeah, the present is pretty good. It's what the future holds for me and Christian that causes an unsettling churning in my stomach. In three days' time, he'll leave. I want so badly to believe his assurance this *isn't* just a quick fling; over the moment we both go back to our real lives outside this odd bubble. Although I can't help but worry. Now he's satisfied his curiosity, sated his unrequited longing for me, will his fascination with me wane?

And then there's the dangerous whirlpool of anger and despair that threatens to capture me whenever I think of the *Wild For The Win* situation. We managed to put Rachel's crushing news aside yesterday. The enjoyment of our trip to the gardens, and our enjoyment of each other's bodies, pushed it into the background for a while. But here, in the reality of the clinic, it all comes charging back. With my hopes for both Christian and the rescue dashed, the disappointment threatens to drag me down.

"Sorry." I offer Alice an apologetic smile and hustle towards the woman. It's Lilian, one of my favourite clients and a long term foster parent, one of the people who are the backbone of rescue. She beams at me and I scoop her into a one-armed hug while the puppy between us nuzzles at my neck. I breathe his sweet puppy smell mingled with Lilian's spicy perfume.

"Good to see you, Lilian," I murmur. "And you too, Kona, you little troublemaker." The pup's mouth falls wide, laughing, as I tickle his chin. "How're you coping Jensen?"

The black lab swivels his head and I swear he rolls his eyes at me as if to say, "What do *you* think?" He's such a trooper, tolerating the regular interlopers his mama invites into their home. I take them through to the exam room, and Lilian places Kona on the table where he rolls on his back, eyes sparkling with mischief.

"He's looking good, Lilian." He bats at my hand with a playful paw.

"Isn't he?"

She beams with pride at the magic she's worked on him; her and Dana, our vet, whose surgical skill intervened when euthanasia was the only other option.

"You'd never know what a rough start you had, little man." We're having a game of tag, my fingers patting his playful paw and him trying to catch my hand in return. Kona is one of the 'Coffee Litter', all named for varieties of coffee beans and brews, each a different shade of brown, with dashes of creamy white. Kona's coat is a velvety caramel latte, and his eyes a strong espresso, their dark liquid depths glinting with mischief. This little guy is one of the lucky ones, rescued from an abusive home by one of our incredible animal warriors, people who bravely go into situations most would shy away from. As I stroke his tummy, as soft and pink as a peony petal, I wonder if there is a woman and children in that household who need rescuing, too. It's one thing Loreena shared that I can't get off my mind.

"You and Jensen have done such a good job, as always."

I pat the head of the labrador sitting patiently beside us. Hearing his name, he smiles up at me. Jensen is amazing the way he mothers these wee scraps who invade his home, teaching them how to be a good boy like him.

"You should see this little monster run," Lilian says. "So damn quick, even on three legs. Especially when he doesn't want to come in from the yard. Catch me if you can, and sometimes I can't," she laughs.

Kona has been a tripod for much of his short life. Even as a vet nurse, I knew, looking at the x-rays of his shattered leg, there was no saving it. Crushed, bashed—who knows how it happened—there was no way even a capable surgeon like Dana could fix multiple breaks or deal with the tiny shards of bone drifting inside.

As if to emphasise how quick he is, Kona leaps to his feet and does a little three-legged dance in front of me. My delight at his happiness is still tinged with sadness at what he had to go through. Pain and distress are gone now, but still there are the memories; and a lifetime compromised by the damage done. Like Christian's dog, Jet.

As I watch him twirling on his three legs, stumbling a little, his clumsiness not just a puppy's lack of coordination, an idea comes to mind. What if those bastards at *Wild For The Win* could see the sort of damage a snare does? Would they be so blasé about it, then?

"Lilian," I say, "would you mind if I took Kona for a few hours? There's someone I'd like to meet him."

"Sure," she says, her smile bright. I feel bad, hearing the hope in her voice. All foster parents want their charges to meet potential adopters. I doubt this meet and greet will result in a home for sweet little Kona. However, it could still do some good in the world. "Even if it doesn't get him adopted, being out and about is so good for his socialisation."

She's right. Hearing her words, I don't feel quite so bad. "OK, I'll give you a call," I say, wondering how I can beg for a few hours off.

"Today would work," she suggests. "If it suits you. I could leave him with you now? Pick him up later on?"

"Really?" Perhaps this is a sign from the universe my sudden crazy plan isn't so crazy at all. "Let me see what I can do."

I step back out into the waiting room. Dana is still talking over a prescription for her previous patient, a frosty-faced senior Staffie with back legs buckled by arthritis. I slip past, sharing a smile with her owner, an elderly man with similarly bowed legs who leans on a stick, bright eyes framed in a crinkled leathery face, intent on Dana's instructions. Behind the reception desk, I bail up Alice.

"How's the afternoon looking?"

She taps at her screen.

"A break in the traffic, thank goodness." She hums to herself, sliding a finger down the list of appointment slots. "Nothing much now until three-thirty, then solid till five."

It's twelve-thirty. I get my thirty-minute lunch break after we finish with Kona.

"Could Dana manage without me?" I venture. "Just for a couple of hours? It's something important."

"Is it something that will give me back the real Haley? Not the imposter who turned up in her place this morning?"

"Yes," I nod.

Her veiled criticism is fair enough, but Alice's furrowed brow and thin lips mask genuine concern. She's such a softie, mothering everyone who walks in the door, including the staff. She knows there's a reason for my unusual vagueness, and she's worried.

"Good, then do it," she huffs.

"I'm sorry, Alice," I sigh. "There's a lot going on for me at the moment."

"I can see that." Her softening eyes invite me to share more, although I don't. I can't. Realising I'm not seeking a confidante today, she places a hand on my arm, giving it a squeeze. "It's fine," she says. "Is two hours enough?"

"Yes," I say. "I think so."

I'll make sure it's enough. I jump on my phone and Google the production company. As I thought, it's over in Clerkenwell, not far from here. I'm already calculating how long a cab ride there and back will take. And now I also have a name—Peter Holt is the man in charge. The one who holds the power.

"After you finish with Lilian and Kona, you go. I can manage the couple of patients booked in. Routine checks, nothing fancy." Alice has worked as a vet receptionist for so long, she capably steps in where needed.

"Thank you," I whisper.

On the way back to the exam room, I dive into the store cupboard and grab a pet carrier, soft bedding and a small chew toy.

"You and I are off on a little adventure," I say, chucking the puppy under the chin as Dana arrives to check him over. Lilian smiles across at me and my inner traitor cringes. But my deception is for a good cause, an important one. I swallow hard and smile back as I try to summon brave thoughts about my uncertain mission.

Day Ten

I CRANE MY NECK, scanning the imposing columns of arched brickwork, like curved brows, with banks of windows rising five storeys beneath each of them. The building is impressive and far more attractive than one would expect. Even industrial architecture was beautiful back in the old days. Inside the walls of this intimidating former warehouse building, and the sprawl of old factory sheds behind, lie the offices and studios of Unscripted, the production company filming *Wild For The Win*—and which a couple of years back created *Star Power*.

I've been here before, three years ago. In fact, I came here many times, summoned for studio interviews, some with only Mum, Dad, and me sharing our reactions to the emotional rollercoaster ride my brother was on. Others included Ollie; him clasped between us, our family supporting him while he shared his hopes and dreams. Dreams that came true—not in the way he imagined back then, discarded before the finals—but with the show giving him a shot at something even better than a solo career. Ollie can hold his own on stage, his mellow voice enchanting the crowd, and his playful banter and shining personality endearing him to them. But when he steps out there with the band behind him, magic happens.

Christian was there for those interviews, too, with his family. My memories of them from that time are vague, but not of him. Like Ollie, he's mesmerising on stage on his own. But his power over an audience is different, a quiet intensity, the emotion pouring from him through music that makes you feel like he's baring his soul. It's still there when he's with the others, but you have to look harder for it, as if he's happy to hide some of his vulnerability, his bandmates a cloak for emotions he's still not comfortable sharing.

Not like when he sang for me the other night. There was nowhere to hide. I don't think he wanted to. He's done hiding what he feels for me. And, while that's frightening, there's something thrilling that this deeply private man, this thoroughly good man, cares for me. It's ignited a need to do everything in my power to help with the shitty situation he's in.

Which is why I'm here, about to demand this guy sees me. Peter Holt is Managing Director of Veritas Media Group, and so answerable for the actions of their subsidiary, Unscripted Productions, the company responsible for this mess.

I feel the weight of the pet carrier in my hand shift as Kona wakes up. He's been such a good boy, sleeping through the entire ride, the cabbie impressed with his tiny passenger. I place the carrier on the footpath and peer in. The puppy yawns up at me, showing neat white teeth, an adorable baby land-shark giving me his friendliest smile. However, it's not his sweet face I intend to use to get what I want today.

"Good boy, Kona," I coo and he wags his pointy tail, its small thwacks vibrating through the carrier. "Right buddy, let's go. Time for you to turn on the charm."

I scoop up the carrier and head up the steps. The double doors are almost twice my height, old school, not automated, with gleaming brass handles. I shoulder one open.

Inside, I'm immediately confronted by a reception desk. The woman behind it is straight out of a punk rock band, with lipstick the colour of dried blood, skin as pale as Morticia Addams, and black hair teased into a spiky halo.

"Good afternoon," she says. "How can I help you?"

My jaw drops open. The refined accent, and her polite words issuing from lips curving in a sweet cupid's bow, are so at odds with the rest of her appearance. I slam my mouth shut and shuffle uncomfortably under her gaze. Although there's a friendly expression in her freakish eyes—they're a bizarre shade of purple that can only be from coloured contacts—my bravado at marching in here, insisting Peter Holt see me and Kona, trickles away.

"I've come to see Peter Holt."

I try to sound confident, as if I'm meant to be here. But in my bulky puffer jacket, scrubs visible beneath, and a bobble hat pulled low, I definitely do *not* look like I should be here. Not in this room, where the aesthetic is urban cool. With some in ripped jeans and designer tees, others in chic athleisure wear, the staff look like they've tumbled off the pages of a street style magazine. They're dotted across a vast open plan office, most working at desks behind banks of screens, while a few relax on couches with slim laptops balanced on their knees.

"Peter," she says slowly, with a broadening smile. It causes her eyes to crinkle and I see she's not as young as her avant-garde outfit and makeup suggests. She may even be old enough to have actually been in a punk band. "Is he expecting you?" Her dark brows knot as she scans her own gigantic computer screens. "I can't see…"

"No," I say. "But it's important."

"I'm sorry," she says, like she means it, "but Peter has a full afternoon of meetings today. Can I make an appointment for another day?"

"Please." I'm not above begging. Despite her formidable appearance, she's got kind eyes, and I hope she might see the desperation in mine. "I need literally five minutes."

It's only now she notices the dog carrier sitting by my feet. Her eyes widen and her brows fly upwards when, as if on cue, Kona lets out a small yelp.

"Is that a puppy?" she says, her mouth tipping up at the corners.

I nod.

"You brought Peter a puppy?" Her expression is bemused, and there's confusion in her eyes.

"Well, yes—no—not exactly…"

"Oooh, can I see her? Him?"

"Him," I say. "OK." Maybe Kona will charm her into letting me see the elusive Peter.

I bend down, open the mesh door, and he tumbles into my waiting arms. I stand, cradling him against my chest, and he nips at the loose strands of my hair that have escaped my ponytail, oblivious to the crowd of people making a beeline for us.

It's like Stellar Riot has dropped into the middle of a busy street at midday. The staff materialise from their workstations, clustering around Kona and me, with chuckles of laughter, and shining eyes, as he works his puppy magic on the room. He wiggles in my arms, paws extended towards them, as if he's hoping to crowd surf across the group.

"Awww, he's only got three legs," someone whispers. There's a rippled murmur of sympathy.

"You first, Bethany," another voice calls. "Just don't hog him too long."

The receptionist unwinds herself, slides from behind the desk, standing tall and lean, arms spread like black wings. With gentle hands, she takes Kona and lays him across her shoulder, his tongue lapping at her long pale neck. Her eyes fall shut in dreamy bliss, as her nose ruffles the puppy's mochaccino fur, drinking in the smell of him.

"Guess I know what you want for Christmas." A voice, thick with humour, drifts from the back of the space.

The crowd parts and a man in black jeans and a white band t-shirt of The Cure, under an open plaid shirt, strolls between them. A smirk splits his face beneath a pair of velvet brown eyes. Although he's the most casually dressed person in the room, the deference of the staff and his unruffled demeanour leave no doubt—he's the boss. Peter Holt. Probably in his forties, he looks vaguely familiar, with his swarthy complexion, and a shock of black curls tumbling untidily to his shoulders. I'm reminded of a pirate—a friendly enough one with his beaming smile. The heavy silver ring in each ear completes the picture.

"Oh darling, yes," the woman, Bethany, breathes, "if only we didn't live in a glass box ten storeys up." Her mouth curves into a rueful smile.

I watch his hand reach towards her, smoothing the puppy's head with ring-bedecked fingers. Ornate heavy silver gleams on every finger of the other too, as he gently tousles the woman's wild hair.

"So, what brings Haley Templeton in here on a Monday afternoon, stopping my staff from work?"

My head snaps away from his hands and my disbelieving eyes jerk upward to meet his teasing expression.

"I never forget a name or a face," he says.

"Or every handbag or pair of shoes I buy," the woman drawls, her painted mouth twitching in amusement. "Husbands," she shrugs.

"*Star Power*, three years ago." He points a finger my way. "Your brother, Ollie, made it to the semis. Could have gone further," he says. "But the people seemed to have a soft spot for all the freaks that season."

"Yes," I croak out, in shock. "That's right."

"Peter Holt," he says, extending a hand to me. Mine shakes a little as he squeezes it, the gesture warm against the hard metal of his grip.

"Haley was hoping to see you," the woman says, words a little muffled with her mouth buried in Kona's fur. "But haven't you got Hugh Partridge due any minute?"

"Oh fuck, yes," he sighs. "Sorry Haley. Beth will make you a time—how's tomorrow morning?"

Panic leaps in my chest. Time is running out; if I'm going to make any difference, I need to talk to this guy now, with Kona here to press my point.

"Please." My voice comes out a desperate plea. "It really needs to be today. Just a few minutes. It's about *Wild For The Win*."

Peter Holt's eyes narrow. "Is it now?" His dark brows angle down in a fierce knot, like the captain of the pirate ship contemplating drawing his cutlass. "Well then, as that bellend Hugh just so happens to be the producer of *Wild For The Win*, you'd better come into my office."

"Beth, honey," he says, turning to his wife. "How about you let her bring the puppy?" He's already mesmerised by Kona; a good sign. "Maybe make her a coffee, too? She looks frozen to death. And when Mr Partridge arrives, don't let him make himself comfortable."

A minute later, I'm seated inside the sleek glass walls of Peter's office, the only one inside the vast otherwise open-plan space. Kona's sliding around on his desktop, lunging at Peter's hands as they play a game of puppy tag.

Beth delivers me a mug of milky coffee. I warm my hands on it, but the sweet liquid does nothing to soothe the agitated lump in my throat. Peter pauses a moment in the game and I meet his gaze with nervous blinks when he looks my way.

"So, what's up, Haley?" he asks.

All my resolve to berate this man for what his company has done fades away in the face of his friendly tone and obvious delight in Kona's antics. Peter's likeable, and I didn't want to like him. I swallow hard, trying to summon my indignation.

"You need to do something about *Wild For The Win*," I blurt out. "Do you *know* what happened up there?"

He looks at me a little shamefaced.

"Honestly? No," he says. "To be frank, I can't stand the damn show. I'd drop it tomorrow if I could. But you know how it is—got to pay all these people somehow." He waves a hand at the staff outside who've given up on a chance with Kona and have drifted back to their work. "My accountants said no. That we need it to prop up the bottom line. Cheap to produce. Draws the audience. Boosts the ratings. Keeps the bean counters happy. So, no, to my embarrassment, I haven't paid it any attention at all."

"Well, perhaps you should have," I bite back, my fire rekindled. The sight of him enjoying the antics of a puppy, while animals and people have been hurt by something he is ultimately responsible for, seems so wrong.

His eyes snap to mine, dark brows creased. "Perhaps you need to tell me why."

I scoop Kona off the desk and back onto my lap, his warm weight reassuring, and begin. Peter's full attention is on me. Elbows on the desk, fingers steepled, he listens without interruption as I detail the whole sorry mess—the snares, the unfair portrayal of Christian, the duplicity over Loreena's departure—before circling back to the reason I brought Kona. I rouse the puppy from his snooze and lift him back onto the desk. The puppy wobbles a little, trying to take control of his three legs, the stance a bit more difficult without a fourth to anchor him.

"Christian had a dog like Kona once. A tripod. He lost his leg in a snare. It was a long time ago, which makes it even more sad that still, today, we haven't totally banned them. And that shows like *Wild For The Win* support using them."

"That's why he was upset."

"Yes." I meet his eyes, pleading my case. "And that's why I'm here. Look, I know you can't undo what's happened. But there's still time to change what happens next."

"I see," he says quietly, chin in hand, eyes raised in thought to the high white ceiling. After a long moment, he turns his gaze back to me, reaching to scoop Kona in a hug against his chest. "OK, I'll see what I can do." I let out a breath. He's going to help. "As it seems you already know—" He pauses to suck at his lip. "The legal team has this sort of thing sewn up pretty tight. There are contracts and agreements in place. It's not always possible to undo them. But even if I can't, you have my word—there will never be snares used on any programme this company makes. In fact, I'm going to take on the oversight of animal welfare myself. It seems we can do better. A lot better."

"Thank you, Peter," I say, as he stands and passes Kona to my waiting arms.

"Do you *have* to go?" He holds the puppy a moment longer, as if reluctant to release him.

I nod. "Yes. Got to get back to work—and get this little guy back to his foster mama."

"Damn," he says. "Looks like I have no excuse to avoid that prick Hugh Partridge anymore," he grins.

He jerks his head towards a rangy man squeezed into a tiny tub chair in a small alcove beside the entrance, his long legs angled out in front of him, crossed at the ankles. Bethany obviously took Peter's comment literally. Hugh looks like he wishes he was anywhere but here. There's a scowl on his arrogant face and his fingers drum impatiently on the side of the chair. I'm hoping his day is about to get a lot worse, but just how much Peter can or will do to fix the situation is still unclear.

He turns, offering Kona one more affectionate pat on the head.

"Besides, if you don't get that puppy out of here, Bethany will have our house on the market and insist we buy something dog friendly."

"Maybe you should," I smile.

"Maybe we should," he agrees.

Day Eleven

I WISH I COULD stop time. Or at least slow it down. Tuesday is all but over, day eleven complete. We're hurtling towards the end of my twelve-day sentence and my vision of what comes next is blurry. The day after tomorrow I'm allowed to leave, go home to my apartment, and go back to my old life. A life I don't want anymore because she wasn't in it.

While the days are quiet here, with Haley at work—honestly, if it wasn't for the dogs, they'd be boring as shit—I have to admit I'm enjoying lazing around. Coming off the back of the insane schedule of our North American tour straight into *Wild For The Win*, I arrived in Scotland exhausted, although prepared to tough it out to win the money. But I can't say I'm not pleased with the unexpected consequences of the Scottish disaster. This chance to step off the treadmill that is life in the band was a gift I didn't know I needed.

And then, there's the best gift of all, the thing I've needed all my life: her. Beside me in bed each morning, sleepy limbs draped across me. Kisses that flutter like feathered wings following the lines of my tattoos, pausing to tease at my neck, provoking a shiver of arousal.

Bustling through the doorway every evening, her face rosy with the cold, buzzing like an excited kid with stories of her day, the people she's met, the animals she's helped. And the sad stories too, told with compassion in her green eyes, sorrow when the vet team has failed to summon a miracle.

Fussing over her dogs like a mother hen, putting their needs ahead of her own, showing the pure, undiluted goodness that is Haley Templeton. I love watching their joyful worship of her.

Dinners together, seeing her delight in the food I've prepared for her, like the chow mein she's tucking into now, are one of the best parts of my day. Caring for her isn't entirely unselfish. It brings me pleasure to offer whatever I can to make her day better. And I want to do that every day. But we only have one more.

"So, what happens after tomorrow?" It's as if Haley can read my mind. She tosses the question at me casually, seeming more intent on pursuing a piece of carrot round and round her plate, stabbing at it with an unruly pair of chopsticks.

"Nothing. Unless you plan to kick me out."

She snorts a laugh. "Why would I do that? And go back to cooking my own dinners?"

"Good to know my plan to make myself indispensable has worked. The way to a woman's heart is through her stomach."

"Well, this woman anyway." She pops a chunk of chicken into her mouth, casting me a sheepish look from beneath dark lashes. "Although I'm rather attached to some of your other practical skills."

Her mouth slants in a sly smile, although she blushes at her innuendo. Haley is so damn cute when she slips into sexy banter, a good girl venturing across the line on a dare and then scurrying back as if unsure whether it's safe to let me glimpse the temptation to be wicked she normally holds in check behind her sweet, innocent face.

"Seriously, Christian," she says, while not looking at all serious, lips curling up at the edges. "Stay. At least till the last of this mess is over."

"And then?" I'm struggling to hold back the neediness in my voice.

"And then we figure it out together. I mean, it's kind of back to front. People generally don't move in together first and then start dating."

"You want to go on dates? Damn, I thought I was off the hook." I love teasing her.

"Of course I do. Why wouldn't I?" Her brows raise and she tilts her head in a quizzical look, just like one of her dogs.

"You might change your mind when you see what dates with me are like."

"Believe me, I have very low expectations. Let me tell you about some of my dates." She leans forward, propping her chin on one curled hand, mouth tipped up in a bemused smile.

"Is this going to make me feel inadequate?"

"Unlikely. I did say low expectations."

"OK. Tell me what I'm up against."

"First there was Jared. Got it into his head we should go up the London Eye, as I'd never been. Forgot to mention he had a fear of heights. Ended up on the floor of the pod, curled like a limp pretzel, while I sat there pretending it's totally normal to be having a conversation with a guy lying at my feet."

"First *and* last date?" I grin at her.

She nods and rolls her eyes. "Absolutely. How the hell did I get tangled up with a dickhead like that?"

I'm as mystified as she is.

"Then there was Josh." She huffs out a sigh. "We went to a French restaurant in Soho. Very nice. Except he insisted on hogging the menu and ordering for us both, even though he had terrible French. Oddest meal I've ever eaten. Then to top it off, he'd forgotten his credit card, so I ended up with the whole bill."

"You're safe with me. Don't really like French food."

"As for the last one, Julian—invited me over for dinner, then fed me frozen pizza while expecting I'd find it absolutely riveting to watch him playing online games against a twelve-year-old in Atlanta."

"Haley, stick with me and you'll be fine," I tease. "I think I have exactly what you need to break the bad date curse."

"What?" Her eyes crinkle at the edges.

"A name that doesn't start with J."

"Of course! How come I never worked that out for myself? Just think of all the shitty dates I could have avoided."

She laughs, and I join in, although I immediately feel regret at pointing it out, considering the 'J' man she hasn't mentioned: Jack, who did a lot worse than take her on a shitty date. I decide it might be better to get it out in the open. Ask her about him—and then bury all mention of the bastard once and for all.

"And Jack too,"

"Jack too," she repeats, her voice quiet. "If only I'd known what I know now—don't trust a dentist."

"A dentist?" More evidence of what a prick he is. Surely there's some code of ethics—like a doctor—that says a dentist shouldn't hit on their patients?

"Yeah. Not mine." She's read the distaste in my expression. "Jack was Ollie's dentist."

"Really?" My brows raise again in disbelief. How is it I never knew this? But then, Ollie always plays family stuff close to his chest. Especially where Haley's concerned.

"Yeah, really. A pretty good one, actually. That's why he's so loaded. You know how dentists charge." That also explains why the bastard's got that toothy movie star smile I'd like to mess up with my fist. "We were at the pub one night—me, Ollie, Sam, a few others. Anyway, Jack was there. He came up to talk to Ollie, joined us in the booth. At the end of the night, he asked me if I'd like to go out for dinner sometime. He seemed nice." She blinks and swallows. "He was nice. Until he wasn't."

At the hurt in her voice, I change the subject. There's another tricky one we need to address. Might as well deal with that, too.

"Haley, there is a problem with dating me." I have to remind her. It's not fair to let her stumble into this blind. "Those dates might have been awful, but I bet none of them resulted in your picture plastered all over the tabloids captioned with bitchy remarks about your hair and clothes. You know it could get ugly?"

She nods. "I know."

And she really does. Haley's not only had a front-row seat to the ugliness, watching the girls who've gone down this road before her—Waverley and Kendra, Garrett's wife Liv, Teddy's stream of girlfriends—all paying the price for attaching themselves to a guy in a famous rock band. She's also had a backstage pass, seeing firsthand through Ollie's distress the damage it does to the man as well.

She inhales a deep breath, as if already steeling herself, and sighs. "Guess it's time to put aside any insecurities I have about myself."

"Yeah, it is." I lace my hand through hers. "But that's not the worst of it. You're going to have to trust me. Promise me you won't doubt me when you're bombarded with lurid and untrue details about every other woman your boyfriend's so much as stood beside in a queue at the checkout, whether it was last week or years ago."

"Yeah." A swallow ripples down her slender throat. "You might need to help me with that one. Up till now, I haven't exactly had the best outcome from trusting people."

I offer a reassuring squeeze of my hand. "I get it. But I promise you, Haley, this boyfriend is not like him, OK?"

"Boyfriend." It comes out softly, as if she's trying out the sound of the word. In her tone, and those wide mossy eyes, I can't read whether the title of boyfriend, and all the expectation that comes with it, holds attraction or triggers reluctance. I blunder on.

"Well, I assume, since you've told people you're my girlfriend, that makes me your boyfriend, right?" Her slight nod is encouraging, and I take her free hand, so small in mine. With one finger, I circle her tiny palm in nervous spirals. My voice comes out low, hesitant, wary. "And I want to be, Haley. Exclusive. No one else. Are you OK with that?"

There's a brick in my throat I can't swallow down waiting for her answer. There's no one else for me. Hasn't been anyone for so long, as if I created this space for Haley, knowing the time would come for her to fill it.

For her, this thing's so new. I don't really have any right to ask the same of her in return, but I need to know—badly. If she says no, and she wants to see other people, I think I'll lose my mind. The thought of her smiling that smile for some other guy, treating him to the music of her laughter, letting him put his hands on her, his mouth...

"There's no one else. I don't want there to be anyone else." Green eyes meet mine, soft and true. "Let's do this. Boyfriend. Girlfriend." She points a finger between us. "You and me."

Perfect answer. I slide from my seat and make my way to wrap my arms around my girlfriend. I inhale the sweet smell of her as I nuzzle into her neck.

"Sounds like I better get busy planning our first date. First impressions and all that."

"No time for that now," she says, whisking away my empty plate and stacking her own on top. "We've got a different sort of date tonight, remember?"

I groan, regretting my earlier moment of weakness. How could I have said anything but yes, when she called this afternoon, for the first time phoning me rather than sending a text? The sound of her words coming down the line was like a banquet laid out in front of a starving man, and I fell upon it gratefully, agreeing to her request without a thought. I can't refuse this girl anything, although tonight part of me wishes I could.

CHAPTER 34

Day Eleven

"PERFECT." HALEY STRAIGHTENS MY beard, a ridiculous white curly thing that resembles a small dog, looped behind my ears. She yanks down the hat so it covers the elastic twined around them, preserving the illusion that I'm no longer Christian Steele, musician, but the big fella himself, round and red and jolly. I'm still working on the last bit, given I'm only lately getting over my aversion to Christmas. How can a reforming Scrooge like me be cheerful at playing the number one role in the whole drama?

"Don't tell Ollie," she says, her mouth turning up in those two cute curves I love, "but I think you look more the part than he did last year." She runs her hands across my shoulders and I almost purr at the firm squeeze. "Broader, more like Santa should be."

"Aren't you a little worried? That you haven't heard from him?" I ask at the mention of her brother.

He's certainly been on my mind since yesterday's text. Part of me says I should have told her, but guilt made me put off bringing him into the middle of what we've got going on here. However, if Haley's concerned about him, I'll be forced to share the proof of life text. I'm hoping to avoid that.

"No," she says with a shake of her head. "You know Ollie. He loves all that travel stuff so much he probably signed on for some extra side trip, or maybe booked a few days by a hotel pool somewhere to recover after the tour."

She's right, Ollie is spontaneous, bouncing from one thing to the next like an unruly golden retriever with that sunshine grin lighting up his face. I'm still not sure it will be there when he finds out about Haley and me.

"Besides, you know Megan and friends will probably have a tracker on him. The record company would be all over it if one of their assets disappeared off the radar."

She's right about that too, and I huff out a sigh of agreement, my breath making the white beard flutter, despondent at the reminder this is my life too. Never free to go anywhere without someone knowing.

It's another reason this illicit jaunt to the dog rescue's kennel facility brings a strange satisfaction. The few people who are in on the secret of my whereabouts will think I'm stuck inside a house in Kensington tonight, when here I am about to climb into a cab with the girl I love, heading to spread some joy to deserving people and animals. And even though it means I'm dressed in this ridiculous suit, I'm happier than I've been for most days of my life.

She steps away and I stare at myself in the mirror, the real me buried deep underneath this costume. At least it fits, even though it wasn't made for me. There's heaps of room in the jacket to accommodate the fake paunch tied around my waist that pushes against the buttoned front, the velcro beneath straining at the sudden fifty pounds I've gained.

The trousers tailored to Ollie's lanky frame pool a little over my feet, but not so much they'll trip me. Just as well—we don't want Santa going down. The leather toes of my boots peeking out beneath the scarlet fabric actually look quite good, almost what the real Santa might choose for leaping in and out of a sleigh and clomping across rooftops.

I'm not sure the cabbie is so impressed when, after opening the door and ushering Haley into one side, I heave my bulky body into the other. He surveys me in the rear-view mirror with a shake of his head, a dramatic eye roll, his mouth twisted in a wry grin. Must be new to the job—surely any seasoned London cabbie has ferried a few Santas in his time.

"I feel like I'm missing something important here." I spread my empty hands wide. Haley arches a brow from beneath her pointy green elf hat that exaggerates the colour of her eyes. "Presents?" I say.

"Oh, don't worry about that. All organised. They'll be there."

"So we're going to the place where you work?" To my shame, I haven't asked nearly enough questions about the job she loves, or the rescue I hoped to help.

She shakes her head. "No. The rescue has four sites in London. The Trust works out of what we call HQ, over in Marylebone. Offices for the Trustees, the manager and her admin assistant, and the main vet clinic too."

"Mine is one of two satellite clinics, a little further out in residential areas. All the clinics treat our own rescue dogs, and offer small animal services for the public at affordable prices. They found locations where they thought it might be appreciated. Even though our charges are reasonable, the clinics are their biggest income apart from donations and fundraisers. It's part of what I love about the job, that I'm making a difference in more ways than one."

I feel a stab of guilt knowing the prize I was supposed to win for them, an amount that would also make a difference, is heading someone else's way.

"Then there's the kennel facility where we're going tonight. The adult dogs usually live there till they're adopted. A few with high needs and all the puppies go to our foster families out in the community. The little ones need more socialisation than they can get in kennels. We've got the foster party on Saturday." She hesitates a moment. "Would you be Santa again for that one, too?"

Saturday seems a lifetime away with the show's recorded final tomorrow night—I suppose we'll watch—and the live 'reunion' show the day after. Both stand between me and the end of the nightmare.

I have no choice about the live show. Like an ex-prisoner reporting to my parole officer, I must endure a seat on that studio stage with the world watching. If I survive what will probably be an emotional bloodbath, by Saturday I can be back with Haley, doing good in the world, even if it means dressing up in a silly Santa suit.

"Sure," I agree, resolving to keep my mind fixed firmly on what happens beyond the next two days.

The cab glides into a park outside a large warehouse style building. An older woman stands on the steps, dressed in a conservative suit, two large red sacks balanced beside her feet. Her face lights up as Haley hops out, while I pay the driver.

The sight of my girl, in her Santa's helper outfit, the short green skirt edged in white fur swirling around her thighs, the jaunty hat on top of shiny dark hair falling loose down her shoulders, her face glowing, grabs at my chest, my heart clenching at how beautiful she is, like a Christmas dream come true. I take my place by her side, as the woman stretches out elegant manicured fingers towards me.

"I'm Eloise," she says and I take her hand. "Thank you so much for coming..."

"Alistair," I say, giving my brother's name. This whole thing is risky enough without chancing my real name. Even hiding behind the convenient disguise, that might be enough for someone to connect the dots between Haley, Ollie, and me.

"These are for you, Alistair, or I should say, Santa." She points at the sacks. I hoist the larger one over my shoulder, and Haley snatches up the other. "Come on in," Eloise says, swinging open one of the tall double doors.

She ushers us into a wide reception area. At the counter, people are gathered around plates of food, drinks in hand. A buzz of conversation drifts between them but lowers to silence as they notice our arrival. All eyes are upon us.

"It's that time," Eloise sing-songs, and everyone breaks into enthusiastic applause. "That sack first, please, Haley. For the volunteers."

The group seems to know what's expected and falls into a line, facing me expectantly like kids at a department store waiting to see Santa. At least I'm not expected to offer them a seat on my knee. There's only one person here who I'd like to do that—the woman handing me the sack in her hand, eyes twinkling with anticipation. But I wouldn't dare do that in company. The sight of Santa with a tent in his red trousers wouldn't be a good look.

Inside the sack I find identical-sized boxes, all beautifully wrapped in Christmas paper and shiny bows. We move along the line, and I press a gift into each pair of waiting hands, offering a gruff 'Merry Christmas'.

Eloise follows behind me, murmuring personal messages of thanks. To her credit, she knows them all by name. Haley follows, a basket in hand, distributing giant candy canes, each with a small envelope attached.

Once we're done, we stand aside as they unwrap their gifts—boxes of Christmas chocolates—and peek inside the envelopes, grateful smiles creasing their faces.

"Gift cards," Eloise explains. "Somehow even that doesn't seem enough to thank these people properly for the hours they put in here, picking up poo, and hosing out kennels, walking unruly dogs who've never had the experience before. It's hard work and they do it without complaint."

"They're amazing," Haley agrees.

"Couldn't do it without them." Eloise smiles. "Right. Shall we head down to see the dogs? You'll need the other sack."

As I pick up the second red fabric bag, bursting with soft lumpy shapes, one of the volunteers peels off from the group with a smile.

"This way, Santa," she says.

We enter a long corridor and I can't help but get the feeling of a prison, except these inmates sound very pleased to see us. With so many dog voices in unison, there's no hope of conversation.

We stop at the first pen. The lower half of the gate is solid with wire mesh above. A tiny dog appears in mid-air, leaping higher than the barrier, giving a joyful bark at the top of the arc while suspended in mid-flight, then disappearing from sight below. Seconds later, it appears again, like a bouncing ball. Laughter spills out from the four of us, but it can't compete with the raucous barking echoing all around.

The volunteer opens the door, and the dog springs out into her arms. She waves me over, and I reach into the sack for one from the heap of dog toys all tumbled together inside.

"No," Haley mouths at me. She takes the sack, spreading the opening wide and crouching down in front of the dog. The little guy buries his pointed nose, burrowing in the toys, flicking some aside, until finally he emerges with a triumphant grin, a large turkey stuffie almost as big as him gripped between his teeth. He struts back into the pen, settles himself into the comfy-looking bed and shakes the turkey furiously, as if going in for the kill.

We carry on in this way down the length of the corridor and then back along another. Some dogs greet us with explosions of joy. Others are shy in the presence of humans. One or two are fearful and need gentle coaxing. However, each gets to choose their own Christmas gift and all will go to sleep tonight with an extra bit of comfort, the remainder in the sack set aside for any new arrivals over the coming days. Haley sadly assures me there will be many.

With the Santa run done, we're invited to join the party. However, the temptation of a cup of spicy eggnog and a chunk of Christmas cake is not enough to risk taking this beard off even though it itches like hell. I'm not taking any chances. Haley, however, needs no encouragement to dispatch my piece of the cake as well as her own, while in animated conversation with the group of volunteers. In this setting, she glitters like the tinsel Christmas garland strung behind the reception desk. She's so good with people, especially this big-hearted dog-loving group. I trail along behind her, nodding and smiling behind my beard, a silent Santa.

Eventually the crowd begins to thin, the women wrapping us in hugs; the men extending handshakes as they leave, and Eloise calls us a cab. This driver doesn't bat an eyelid as his costumed passengers climb into the back seat.

"That was so much fun." Haley's still buzzing as she stretches an arm around my shoulder. "Thank you for doing it. Ollie missed out on a good time."

Ollie's name stirs up a familiar niggle of worry, and after churning it over while we're paused at a traffic light, the question that's been lurking in the back of my mind for days finally slips from my mouth.

"What do you think he'll say?"

"About you taking over Santa?" Her brows wrinkle in a frown. "Don't be silly. He'll be fine."

"No, what do you think he'll say about us?"

She hesitates a moment, just a small missed beat, and then goes on. "He's going to be fine, Christian. His sister and his friend. Of course he'll be happy that we're happy."

I try to ignore the slight waver in her voice, as if she's not as confident as she wants to appear. I try to hold on to the thought that she's known him her whole life, so she should know him better than me. I hope Haley's right, but I'm terrified she isn't.

CHAPTER 35

Day Twelve

Christian

On Wednesday, I wake well before her alarm, listening to the even, peaceful breaths of the woman curled around me. With its canine sixth sense, one dog knows I'm awake. There's a lick on my elbow, a warm tongue. From the whiffy breath, I suspect it's Tully, but I keep my eyes firmly shut, not lured to confirm my suspicions. I have learned well: do not make eye contact. Sometimes it's merely boredom and if you don't interact, they'll flop back down with a sigh. If they persevere, it's a more urgent need.

It works, as I hear dog footsteps moving away from me, only to find their way to the other side of the bed, and Haley.

"Hey there, sweetie." Her voice is raspy with that sexy just-woken-up huskiness. I wish the words were for me, but the beating paws in response tell me they're for Tully, doing her happy dance. Haley rolls away from me, stretching out a hand, and I groan as a rush of cool air finds its way under the covers.

"These guys want out?" I ask.

"Yeah, probably."

"I love these dogs, but couldn't they just once allow us extra time in bed?" I grumble, moving to get up.

"I'll go," she offers, already sliding her legs around and pulling herself to sit up. She turns and adjusts the covers so I'm tucked in snugly. "You stay right there. I'll be back. I've got plans for you." She shoots me a provocative smile as she trails one finger across my lips and chin.

At first, she scrabbles around on the floor where our clothes are strewn, evidence of how frantically we removed them last night. Then, with a frustrated huff, she plucks the huge red Oodie from the chair and pulls it on. I stifle a laugh. It swims on her, but she loves that damn thing even more than her Christmas pyjamas. God, this woman is beautiful, even wearing a technicolour sack that masks all her best attributes in a layer of fleece.

The dogs need no invitation, bouncing off Haley's bare ankles with small yips of joy. I hear them charge through the door.

Within minutes, she's back, stripping back the covers, and the combination of the cool air and her proximity causes my cock to stand at attention.

"Well hello there," she says, settling beside me on the bed.

She stretches one hand across, grips me tight, and starts a rhythm of long, powerful strokes. I groan with the pleasure of it, my body willing to surrender all to whatever she desires. Without missing a beat, she swings a leg across to straddle me, my erection rearing up between us. She shrugs up the Oodie, revealing those honey-gold thighs.

Leaning forward, she laps at me with her tongue, circling and sucking, driving me insane with her devotion to the sensitive tip. Just when I feel like I'm about to explode, she pauses, releasing me, before raising her hips high and lowering herself onto me with a determined thrust. She sits there grinning at me.

"Looks like you have me at a disadvantage, Miss Templeton. If you really intend to use my body so shamelessly, the least you could do is get rid of that thing, so I can enjoy the view."

She sweeps the Oodie off over her head, arms raised while I allow my hungry eyes to wander over her full breasts with nipples standing at attention in the cold air, and I want nothing more than to take one in my mouth and give it some warmth. I pull the blankets back over her, right up over our heads, creating our own safe cocoon, where the world outside doesn't exist. Our eyes meet, her pupils huge, advertising her arousal.

"Happy with that, Mr Steele."

"Very," I say as she begins to move and from that point on, I have no coherent words, until I cry out her name, as she arches backwards, both of us convulsing in an explosive climax.

Afterwards she's lying slumped across my chest, limp like one of the soft toys the dogs have de-stuffed, my half-mast cock still inside her, twitching as if it could be roused back into action with a little encouragement.

"It's not too late to call in sick," I murmur into her hair as she slides off me.

"I wish," she groans.

I let her go without further protest, knowing her work is important. She'll be home tonight and we can do this all over again; for as long as she wants. With the connection between us growing stronger by the day, to the point where it seems almost tangible, I'm hopeful that's going to be a very long time, maybe a lifetime.

But I'm aware of the spectre of real life waiting for us beyond this house. It's a sinister figure, poised in the shadows with scythe in hand, ready to leap out and slash this bright thread of connection as viciously as it cut Waverley loose from me. It was bad enough facing the loss of Waverley in my life, but losing Haley is something I'm not sure I could come back from.

Fucking squirrels. It's their fault my feet are lumps of ice and my lips are blue. Even Haley's thick Oodie isn't enough to ward off the chill of the outdoors. Not when it barely covers my arse. I admit defeat and close the door on the dogs. The little bastards can spend all day outside on their futile surveillance mission for all I care.

My annoyance only ratchets up another notch when I hear footsteps in the kitchen, heading my way. I'm getting used to people wandering into the house unannounced. Doesn't mean I like it.

"Fuck it, Sam. You're really going to come around and check up on me every day while Haley's at work? Or are you secretly craving the pleasure of my company?"

"So, you've met the famous Samantha?" Ollie appears in the hallway, face lit by his famous mega-watt grin. "And lived to tell the story?"

Now that's a face I don't mind seeing. Even though we spent months together on the road, I've missed this guy. And much as I hate fucking reality shows after this latest disaster, I'll be forever grateful one gifted me the best friend I've ever had, a better man than I'd ever hoped would want me as a friend.

I had other friends, but none of them were like me. None of them were people I could be myself with. All the guys I grew up with in our rural backwater were mostly happy with the life marked out for them, going from school to a job. Most chose farming, of course; a few picked up trades; one or two went to university, but all doing sensible, useful things.

Unlike me. I worked crap jobs, played in bars, wrote songs and angsty lyrics—yeah, move over Taylor, I'm the original tortured poet—and pretended to be doing something with my life, when I was simply waiting for a chance to do what I was meant to do.

Ollie's road to success was different to mine. He had the flash education, years at the academy, formal training, a performing arts degree. In the end, though, it all came down to the same thing—a chance. Beyond *Star Power*, we both saw that chance and we took it. And, while we might be opposites, at the same time, we took a chance on each other, too. I fucking love this guy.

I grin up at my friend. It's so good to see him and I'm relieved he didn't get lost in the wilds of Africa, never to return. He in turn looks pleased I'm not dead by the hand of the ninja nurse.

"Fucking oath I've met Samantha. Sometimes I wish I hadn't. First time she slammed me into the floor and damn near broke my arm." I wouldn't confess that to just anyone—I do have a little pride—but there's no pretence between Ollie and I.

He gives a howl of delight. "That's our Sam." There's a fondness in his smile, and I'm reminded that Sam and the Templetons go way back.

"Good to see you, man. Although you look fucking terrible." I note dark circles under Ollie's eyes suggesting a lack of sleep. He looks like he could do with a decent meal, too.

He catches my raised palm in his, going in for our usual hand-shake, his grip a bit weaker than normal, before folding me into one of his Ollie hugs. He's a notoriously big hugger, and I've grown used to it, although this one feels a little bony.

"Yeah, picked up some gastro thing the last few days of the trip. Shitting liquid and puking my guts out. Had to hole up in a hotel in Johannesburg for a couple of extra nights. Wasn't about to climb on a plane in that state."

"OK, so apart from that, otherwise it was good?"

"Yeah, bloody incredible. My god, the wildlife."

He pauses, his eyes crinkling and then falling as they sweep the length of me, and his face contorts, confusion clouding his grin.

"Is that my sister's...?"

"Oh yeah, man. Bloody warm. A bit on the snug side, though."

The cloud darkens. "Why are you wearing my sister's clothes? Am I missing something here?"

There's an edge to his words, a sharpness in the set of his mouth, as narrowed hazel eyes laser in on me. No point lying.

"About that. Yeah. Well." I'm silently cursing my lack of prepa-ration for this moment. Haley and I should have talked about this. What to tell Ollie. When to tell Ollie. But we didn't discuss the first. And there's no choice about the second. I suck in a breath and swallow hard. "Haley and I have some news. We...we..."

Ollie doesn't explode, but the ice in his glare is somehow worse.

"You slept with my sister." The words come out flat. There's the same lethal undercurrent as when Rachel told me she'd kill me. Ollie doesn't have to say it. I think he wants to kill me, too. Take a number, buddy.

"It's more than that Ollie."

"So I take it, that's a yes. You slept with my fucking sister, Christian." His voice rises. "I let you stay here, give you a place to hole up so the bastards don't tear you apart—yeah, I caught up on the whole disaster sitting in the airport in Dubai—and this is what you do? Sleep with my sister?"

"You're missing what I said. Yes, I slept with Haley. But we're together, Ollie."

He huffs out a bitter laugh. "Yeah, so I'm supposed to be thrilled about that. It's meant to make it all OK. You take advantage of her, when she's at the low point of the year, when the last guy who did a number on her has just made her bitchy little friend his wife, when she's vulnerable, and now what? You and her are a thing? Come on Christian. I bet Haley's so screwed up she hasn't got a clue what she wants right now. But rather than let her figure it out, you leap in there and convince her what she wants is you."

He shakes his head, and there's a look of disgust on his face that I've rarely seen before. Ollie sails through life thinking the best of everyone. He's forgiving of things that would annoy the hell out of me.

The only time I've ever seen him look even remotely like this was when he confronted a jerk of a reporter who'd written shit about him and Kendra. It's an expression I'd never have expected to be levelled at me. I'm going to change that. He has to understand.

"What she wants *is* me, Ollie."

"Are you sure about that?" He shoves past me, his shoulder colliding with mine, and storms up the stairs. He stops part way up and glares down at me. "I thought we were friends."

"We *are* friends, Ollie. What's between Haley and me doesn't change that."

"And what about when there isn't a Haley and you? What then? Won't that change everything?"

I think I preferred the angry Ollie of moments ago, to the resigned one telling me Haley and I can't possibly last. Warning me when it falls apart, I'll not only lose her, I'll lose Ollie too. If I haven't lost him already.

"Maybe I should go."

His back is to me, and he's climbing the stairs again. "Best fucking idea I've heard today."

I pack my stuff quickly, thankful there isn't much. I wrap the photo of Jet in a sweater and place it carefully on top of the rest of my things in the duffle bag. My mouth can't help but edge up in a smile at the thought of her bringing it over for me.

This is what Ollie doesn't see. Haley and I are different, but at the heart of things, where it really matters, we are the same. We care about the same things, love doing the same things. Not the big things; the ordinary little ones we could build a life on. Like we've already started to do. There's a deep pit in my stomach, an empty void of the unknown, as I prepare to leave this place and time where I've been happy, unsure when—or worse still if—I'll get to recapture it. However, for now, while Ollie is so volatile, leaving is the best plan.

I bet he's slamming Haley with What-The-Fuck texts right this moment. It might be an idea to send one of my own. Let her know I'm out of here and I'm sorry for once again making a mess, and for dragging her into the centre of it.

I grab my phone and string a few words together. There's so much I need to say, but I'll leave that for when I can actually talk to her. For a guy who can pour his heart out in lyrics, I unexpectedly struggle with the mundane.

I stack the series of books Haley nudged me to read on her bedside table. There's a bookmark tucked inside the top one in the pile, the smallest but her favourite of the five, the one she calls the Christmas book, and it does have that feel about it. It's placed in the page where I took a pencil and gently underlined a sentence. I don't think she'll mind me marking the page. The books are full of her little scribbles in the margins, circles and hearts, smiley faces and highlights. I hope the words I've drawn attention to—the ones that echo how I feel about her, how my heart knew she was mine long before I realised it—help steady her through this rough patch with Ollie. Damn, those fairy guys know how to woo a woman. I don't feel bad about stealing their lines.

On top of the book, I place a small box wrapped in red tartan paper, tied with a bow nearly as big as the container. It's a gift I had ready to give her tonight as the final episode of the show rolled across the screen. I ordered it a few days ago—I've become the master of online shopping—my small thanks for how she's backed me through the whole *Wild For The Win* disaster. I won't get to see her unwrap it now, but I know she'll love it.

I lay the incriminating red Oodie on her bed. Why the fuck did I persist in wearing it, the evidence of my crime? Two pairs of eyes, one deep brown, one ice blue, stare up at me from the pet donuts on the floor. Even the dogs seem to judge me.

"Sorry girls, I fucked up."

They don't even offer a consoling tail wag as if they know there's nothing they can do to fix this.

Bag over one shoulder, guitar on the other, I leave like I arrived twelve days ago. Hat pulled down low, sunglasses on, and uncertain what the next few days will bring.

CHAPTER 36

Day Twelve

DIFFICULT AS IT WAS to leave him all sleepy and sex-sated in my bed, it's lucky I didn't succumb to the temptation of Christian and call in sick. Work is crazy and not to sound arrogant, but no temp would have kept up with all that needed to be done this morning. It's almost noon, and I haven't had a single break. I'm finishing up changing a drip for a ponderous Basset hound, still groggy from anaesthesia, when Alice pokes her head through the door.

"Someone here to see you, Haley."

"Sure. Give me a sec." I'm too engrossed in the task to even think about who it might be, but even if I wasn't, I'd never have expected to find Bethany Holt waiting for me when I step into reception. She's talking away to an elderly lady who has a curly white bundle of Bichon in her arms. Bethany coos at the dog, oblivious to the uncertain look I see in the owner's eyes when she looks my way. The woman's wariness isn't surprising. Bethany may be harmless, but her outrageous hair and makeup, and intimidating clothing, say otherwise. At first impression, Bethany looks downright scary.

She's once again dressed in dramatic black from head to toe, except for a pair of floral patterned combat boots. Over slim leggings, her baggy coat with angular collar pulled up against the cold, makes her look like a bat about to take flight.

"There you are." She pulls away from the dog and fixes me with those violet eyes. Her mouth, today coated in lipstick the colour of an espresso shot, curves in a smile. "I told Peter I'd find you here."

"Bethany, hi, how are you?" I splutter out, as a whisper of possibility stirs inside me. After two days, I'd almost given up hope my pleading with Peter Holt had made any difference.

"I'm great. Now I've found you. I can't believe we let you go the other day without so much as taking your phone number. I think we were all so entranced by little Kona. Well, never mind. I've got news." Her eyes dance and my stomach leaps in anticipation.

"Good news?" I suck in a hopeful breath, while still fearing disappointment.

"Very good news. So, Peter has made some decisions. But we need your help. You and Tommy Bunt."

I nod, agreeing even though I'm unsure of what's about to be asked of me.

"Don't worry. It's not much. All we need, my darling, is for you both to come along to the live show tomorrow evening. Wear something nice. You know how the girls get all glammed up for them? Here, give me your address." She shoves her phone at me. "Phone number, too. A car will call for you at six. One of the crew will fill you in on everything when you get there."

I have so many questions spinning through my brain, but it seems I'm not going to get answers because Dana interrupts, leaning through the door from the emergency suite.

"Haley, we've got incoming, I'm afraid. Cops have raided a dog fighting ring." Her mouth is set in a grim line. It's going to be a rough afternoon.

"Bethany, I have to go."

"Of course, darling." She pats at my arm with long, black-tipped fingernails. "Don't let me take up any more of your time. I can see you're needed."

"I'll see you there tomorrow?"

"You will." Her smug smile suggests maybe everything is going to be alright.

She flounces out the door with a swish of her jet black coat. I head for the ambulance bay, realising she never bothered to wait for me to say yes.

It's probably just as well the tube is packed. The press of commuters helps keep my exhausted body upright as the train sways and jolts along the Northern Line. Squeezed like a sardine, I manage to wiggle my phone from my handbag. It's the first time today I've had a moment to look at it and I'm eager to catch up on Christian's messages.

There's a pang of guilt at neglecting him. I look forward to his selfies with the dogs, the nerdy jokes, and the flirty suggestions. They brighten my day. And today I could have done with some of them to restore my faith in the goodness of people. Of the three dogs brought in from the dog fighting ring, we only managed to save one. Days like today are the worst.

My brows knit in a frown when I find only two messages. I open the first to see a selfie of him and Mularkey. He's still wearing my Oodie, like he was when I left him this morning. He's adorably ridiculous in it. What is oversized on me, swamping my body, with the hemline reaching my calves, is a figure hugging mini dress on Christian. I shake with laughter, a loud snort escapes, and the woman pressed against my back huffs her disapproval as if she's the fun police.

When I open the second message, my world upends.

CHRISTIAN: Maybe this was a mistake. I'm going home to the apartment. I'm so sorry.

I gasp in horror. It can't be right. This must be some kind of silly joke. I'm frantically trying to think of the punch line. He sent this hours ago, this morning, and I haven't replied. What will he think of my silence? With shaking fingers, I tap out a reply.

HALEY: What's happened? Tell me. Talk to me. Call me.

I stare at the screen, begging for those three little dots to appear, and when they do, my legs sag in relief. The dots hover for a moment as I wait, holding my breath. Then evaporate. I'm left with blank white emptiness. I sway, distress swamping me, each breath like a knife in my chest. The train jerks as it brakes for the next station and I stumble.

"You OK, love?" A woman opposite me, with kind eyes, places her palm against my shoulder, steadying me before I lose my footing.

"Yeah, thanks," I nod, but she sees the lie in my eyes.

When the train pulls into Leicester Square station, I'm first off, ducking and diving through the crowds of evening commuters frantic to get to the next platform. I'm in luck, finding a Piccadilly Line train waiting. I leap through the narrowing gap and the doors glide shut millimetres behind me. I slump in the doorway, panting.

Opposite me, a woman with dangling Christmas earrings smiles up at the man with his arm wrapped around her waist. He rolls his eyes and gives one of the tiny green trees a playful bump. Their banter, so like Christian's gentle teasing, is in stark contrast to the despair nudging at me. There should be a guy like this one waiting for me at home. What if he's not?

At South Kensington I fall out onto the platform and tumble up the escalators jostling my way past those who don't make way. I'm pushy and rude and I don't care.

Outside, my footsteps are precarious on a pavement slick with early evening rain; a hint of sleet, that faint metallic smell drifts in the air. I elbow my way through the streams of people hovering outside the shops and restaurants. It's a relief to turn into the side-streets where the dark hush swallows me up. I keep running.

There are lights on in the house, little golden beacons of hope shining down on me. If the house is lit, he must still be there. I fling open the door to find silence. The usual smells of dinner cooking are absent. There's no smoky crackle from the fire, only the hum of the heating system. I race into Christian's room and it's empty. His things are gone. In the lounge, there's no guitar case propped up in the corner.

I check my room even though I sense I won't find him there. He's made the bed and my neatly folded Oodie sits at the foot. My eyes are drawn to the bedside cabinet. There's a little present, Christmas wrapped, but I don't pounce on it like I normally would. It feels final, like a parting gift, and I don't want to open it and confirm my fears. Dread that what was between us is over spirals, a tornado in my stomach.

The books I loaned him sit beneath the tartan wrapped box, one with a bookmark tucked into the last page he read.

Above my head, I hear the flush of a toilet and the sound of footsteps and a door closing. Ollie's room is up there. He must be home. My heart lifts a little at the thought. It will be good to see him. A small optimistic part of me suggests maybe Christian's upstairs with him, catching up, as friends do.

"Ollie?" I call out and the footsteps start again, heading my way. Moments later, my brother appears on the stairs.

"Hey," I say, a smile breaking on my face. At least something good has happened today. I haven't seen my brother for three months. I've missed him. He's thinner than last time he was home, maybe a little too lean. Beneath the healthy glow of bleach blonde hair and sun-bronzed skin he looks tired, his normally dimpled cheeks angular, little crescents of purple below his eyes suggesting jet lag.

"You're home." I fling my arms around him, but his return hug is uncharacteristically half-hearted. I pull back to scan his face, worried he's not well.

"Yeah," he says. But he doesn't return my smile.

"Ollie, what's wrong?" His eyes lower. "Is it Christian? I thought he'd be here, but then he sent this weird message saying he was going back to the apartment." The words pour from me, my agitation notching up.

"He has."

"But why?" I've searched my mind for a reason and I can't find one. We'd separated this morning like every other this week. His lips on mine, a reluctant parting kiss and a murmured regretful farewell.

"He left because of me."

This is why Ollie won't meet my eyes. I retreat from him, crossing my arms across my chest, clutching myself protectively against what I suspect is coming, while still holding on to a tiny shred of disbelief. As the knowledge dawns in my brain, the warm joy of seeing my brother seeps away, replaced by a rush of ice cold anger.

"What the fuck have you done, Ollie?" My voice is shrill.

I step towards him and shove at his shoulder, willing him to look at me. His face blanches. It might be because of the f-bomb, which isn't my usual style, but if my brother has done what I think he has, then it's totally appropriate. In fact, if he's done what I think he has, there's going to be a blitz of them raining down on his sorry head.

"We had a few words," he sighs, shrugging his shoulders. How dare he shrug it off like that, like it isn't important? "It got a bit heated."

"A few words, right? And, let me guess, those few words were about me?"

When will my brother learn to butt out of my business? That I don't need him standing between me and anything or anyone that has the slightest chance of impacting negatively on me? He nods, not looking the least bit remorseful. I want to scream at the arrogance of him, thinking he knows best.

"Look Haley, I came home, and like, I knew he was here. I just didn't expect him to come strolling out of your bedroom, wearing your freaking clothes. I mean, it's pretty obvious what's been going on."

"Yeah, and what's been going on is between two consenting adults and is none of *your* freaking business." I spit the words at him.

This is so typical of Ollie. When is he going to realise I'm not eight years old anymore? He backs away from me, and I stalk towards him. He's not going to run away from what he's done. I am so fucking angry with my brother.

"Haley," he stutters. "I don't want to see you get hurt. After Jack..."

"Don't you get it?" I stab my finger into his chest. Sure, he feels responsible for Jack Maplethorpe coming into my life, but that doesn't give him the right. "This is nothing like Jack. Nothing at all. How could you even think that? Christian is your friend. You know him. You know he wouldn't..."

A sob strangles in my throat. There's the prickle of hot tears, and I swipe at them with the back of my hand.

"Haley, I didn't mean to..."

"I don't care what you *meant* to do. I don't care *why* you did this. Christian was here. And we were happy, Ollie. So very happy." I choke on the words, flailing at the tears that won't stop squeezing their way out of my bleary eyes, tumbling hot and painful, searing my cheeks. "And now, because of you, he's not."

At last I see the belligerent expression in his eyes soften, and there might even be a glimmer of shame there. Good. He should be ashamed of wrecking the first decent chance at a relationship I've had in over a year.

"Haley, I'm sorry." He fumbles the words. "I was just thinking of you."

"Are you sure?" I spit, not ready to let go of my outrage. "Because it sounds an awful lot like you're thinking about you. Making this all about you."

"Haley, I'm sorry. Really." He opens his arms. "Come here."

I waver for a beat, and then collapse into the familiar soothing space. I hate my brother right now. But I need him right now, too. He strokes at my hair as I sob on his shoulder.

"Hey, hey. It will be OK. You've bounced back from worse break ups than this."

I recoil in horror. "You think this is a breakup? You really think we've broken up? Because of you?"

"Well, yeah. But maybe not just because of me. Christian obviously realises this was a mistake. Otherwise he'd still be here, right?"

The words of Christian's text pound in my head, over and over.

Maybe this was a mistake.

Maybe this was a mistake.

Maybe this was a mistake.

I tear myself from Ollie's arms and storm into my room, hot tears lashing at my cheeks, blurring my vision, but I can still see that text, those words in cold harsh black on white:

Maybe this was a mistake.

I fling myself onto the bed, bunching up the covers in my fists, crying into them until they are a soggy mess. When I finally exhaust my tears, I sit in the gloom, brooding. The strands of blue stars twinkling in my window blink in their usual cheerful cycle, oblivious to all that has changed.

Moving aside the Christmas wrapped box, I reach for the book on top of the pile by my bed, the one where words about stars that listen and dreams being answered have always given me hope and comfort. Christian's bookmark is still tucked inside. Curious, I flick open to the page, and my eyes are drawn to an underlined sentence. In the half-light, the words seem to tremble, or maybe it's my unsteady hands. I understand the message.

His heart knew. It knew I was his.

It knew when he met me backstage at *Star Power*. It knew when he underlined these words. It knew when he slid the bookmark inside this page. Did it still know when he left the house this morning? Does it still know now? I want to text him and tell him that yes; I am his. But the taunt comes back at me:

Maybe this was a mistake.

I return to the little parcel. Perhaps I'll find a clue inside. My shaky fingers untwine the ribbon and pick open the tape. Inside there's a hinged box, green leather with a brass clasp. I flip it open and pluck out a snow globe. It's exquisite, possibly an antique.

In its centre, against the backdrop of a forest, there's a winter village. The vibrant painted houses glow as if they're lit up, window boxes and doors decked out for Christmas with minute garlands, and tiny decorations, wreaths and fairy lights. And tucked in the trees to one side, there's a wolf. It stares at me with golden eyes, without a hint of menace. Instead, those eyes seem to signal quiet resignation, as if it's pausing to take one last look at the village, alight and radiant with joy, before slipping back into the shadowy place it belongs.

CHAPTER 37

Day Twelve

THERE ARE SEVEN STEPS from the pavement to the door of Ollie's house. Seven steps for me to muster my courage before I go in there and fight for the woman I love. I never expected I'd have to make a choice between Haley and the best friend I've ever had. But if it comes down to it, I'll choose her every time.

I know I should have stood my ground with Ollie earlier. At the time, it blindsided me. It fucking hurts when a person who's always had your back comes at you like that. The sickening disappointment sits, an uncomfortable shifting weight, in my gut.

I take one last look at Haley's frantic text from two hours ago. The one I never replied to, scrambling for the words to comfort her, but abandoning the idea when they wouldn't come. Now I'm second guessing that decision to wait to talk with her until I've sorted things with Ollie.

"Fancy seeing you here."

I whirl to face the voice. Sam's sarcastic tone is at odds with the dancing brown eyes that peer up at me from beneath a stripy hat topped with twin bright pink pom-poms. A few stray dark curls frame a face rosy with the cold. In her bulky white jacket, she looks round and squat like a friendly snow person. Looks can be deceiving.

"Come to check up on me, Sam?"

"Yeah, Rachel too. Strength in numbers." She shoots a look further down the street where a silver AMG Mercedes edges into a park.

"Wonderful." I match her sarcasm with my own.

Just what I didn't need, these two siding with Ollie against me. I watch Rachel stride towards us, confident in glossy black heels and an elegant camel coloured wool coat.

"Don't look so worried, Christian." Her smirk suggests she enjoys the unsettling effect she has on me. "We're here to watch the final. Haley invited us yesterday." She scans my face, eyes narrowing. "What the hell are you doing out here, anyway?"

"Did she kick you out?" Sam chips in.

"You fucked something up, right?" Rachel's tone is accusing.

"No. And no." These two are so damn predictable, presuming it's me who's caused a problem. "Ollie came home."

"Ahhh." Sam looks at Rachel and something passes silently between them. "Don't tell me—he's being a dick about you and Haley."

"You could say that."

"Fucking Ollie," Rachel mutters.

I might be imagining it, but I get a strange feeling these two could be taking my side here. But even if they are, the last thing I want is the pair of them going in there, guns blazing. Dealing with Ollie is my responsibility. Although it's kind of nice to think they'd want to.

"Look, would you mind..." It's a big ask because it's freezing out here and what was a glimmer of rain has thickened to sleety splats on the pavement. "Would you give me a few minutes?"

"Sure," Sam shrugs, surprisingly compliant.

"Two. No more." Rachel holds up elegant gloved fingers. "In case you hadn't noticed, it's fucking snowing."

"Thank you." At the top of the steps, the huge wreath on the front door reminds me of the girl who placed it there, my sweet crazy Christmas loving girl. The one I'm about to go into battle for.

I bang the door knocker with three sharp taps. It swings open immediately, and there she is. There's my little Santa Baby, wearing the set of Christmas pyjamas that have become my favourite—both to see her in and take off. She stands in the hallway, mouth dropped open. The sight of her red-rimmed eyes and wild hair stabs at me.

"Oh my god, you came back." Her lips tip up in a delighted smile and small arms wrap around me, tiny fingers lacing across my neck, pressing me to her.

"Of course I did," I murmur, guilt washing over me, knowing things I've done today have caused her doubt. "No dogs?" I ask, noticing the absence of feet pawing at me.

I expected at least they'd be pleased to see me. I've missed the pair of them sitting alone in my too-quiet apartment this afternoon. Being dogless is not a happy state, one I'd like to do something about.

"Outside. Squirrels." She hums against my ear, her breath tantalising.

"Who is it?" Ollie's voice carries over the sound of the television.

"Tell him it's carol singers." I smile into her hair, inhaling the fresh smell.

She pulls back from me, emerald eyes glittering with mischief. "It's carol singers," she calls, giggling softly as Ollie's lack of reply signals he's bought the lie—and never watched *Love Actually*.

"I'm so sorry, Haley," I begin, smoothing back her untidy hair, tucking one of those wayward strands behind the dainty shell of her ear. "I suppose I knew all along he wouldn't be happy. But, coward that I am, I just put it out of my mind, and hoped that by the time he came home, we'd have planned how to break the news to him." I regret ignoring the prospect of Ollie's arrival while hidden away in our little bubble. "And he was always a bit vague about when he'd be back. Damn, I wish I'd asked the question."

"Me too." She sighs. "I should have guessed he'd react this way. He feels responsible because he's the one who brought us together. And scared because that's exactly what happened with Jack."

This reminder only makes my anger flare brighter. Knowing Ollie has lumped me in with the douchebag dentist, making assumptions I'll treat Haley the same as that piece of shit fires me up again.

"I'm going to sort this out with him, Haley. Fight for us."

"Good luck. That's what I've been doing on and off for the past couple of hours. Fighting with him. But he's still being a stubborn pain in the arse. Maybe when he sees us together."

There's an uncomfortable niggle of shame, knowing I left her to face Ollie on her own, to defend the two of us in a way we'd never expected would be needed. Although pride and gratitude also surge.

Haley has put us first, put me first, not flinching away from the hard stuff. Underneath, she's just as gutsy as her two bolshy friends, who right this moment announce their arrival with a clatter of heels on the steps. Rachel and Sam bustle in, pushing past us.

"Time's up." Rachel says.

They strip off coats and gloves and make a beeline for the lounge. I feel sorry for Ollie. I've got unexpected backup. He's outgunned this time.

We follow them through. Ollie's seated on the sofa, eyes widening at the sudden invasion of people. Sam slides in on one side of him and Rachel on the other. He shuffles uncomfortably under their twin death stares.

"What's this, an intervention?" He's looking a little intimidated. Can't say I blame him.

"Hmmm, maybe more of an interrogation," Rachel says, with that low voice that harbours a touch of menace.

"How about an inquisition?" Sam suggests brightly.

"Maybe not," Rachel argues. "Wouldn't that involve torture?"

"Probably." Sam presses a finger to her lips, eyes to the ceiling, as if mulling over exactly how she's going to torture Ollie. "Maybe not," she agrees after a beat. "Could get messy. Why don't we settle for a nice cross-examination since we have a kick-arse lawyer in the room?"

"Perfect. Cross-examination it is."

Rachel angles her body towards Ollie, blue eyes lit with a threatening gleam. It seems she's overruled my plan to deal with the situation myself. I decide to let her have her bit of fun while I gather my thoughts. I've been rehearsing what I want to say to Ollie for the last couple of hours, but I didn't expect an audience. It's thrown me that we've got company—especially these two who assume they have the right to wade right into the thick of the problem.

I move from where I've been watching from the doorway, and take a seat in one of the wide armchairs, vacant due to the absence of the dogs. Haley follows me and I pull her onto my lap. She shuffles back into me, and I try not to be distracted by the ripe curve of her bum, or the weight of her breasts beneath my arm, as we settle in to watch the entertainment. While the banter's all been a bit tongue in cheek, I get the feeling Ollie's about to be roasted alive.

"So, Mr Templeton—Ollie—I can call you Ollie?" Rachel's all courtroom serious as she fixes him with a smile that's borderline cruel, as if he's a mouse and she's a feral cat toying with him before she rips him apart. He nods, playing along with her, but I can see the disquiet in his eyes.

"I gather you've chosen to represent yourself?"

He nods again.

"Just as well, I think." She pauses, scanning the room. "Since I'm not sure there's anyone else here prepared to defend you." I can see she's right on that count. Everyone here is on Team Haley and Christian.

"OK, first question." She folds her arms, tipping her head to one side, mouth set in a terse line. "Would you agree that Christian Steele is a good man?"

Ollie nods again. Like one of those bobbleheads people have on their dashboards, it seems to be his only form of communication, dumbstruck under her questioning glare.

"I gather that's a yes, but would you state that for the record, please?"

When he finally speaks, he's answering Rachel, but looking at me. His hazel eyes meet mine, this morning's cold anger still there, but maybe also a flicker of shame.

"Yes, Christian's a good man." His voice is low, tinged with reluctance.

"Thank you. And would you also agree that Haley Templeton is an intelligent and capable woman able to make good decisions?"

"Absolutely," he says. He gives his sister a soft smile, and in his expression I see the love and respect he has for her, even though he hasn't exactly shown it today. "Probably better ones than me."

Rachel pounces. "Repeat that last thing you said for me, please."

"I said Haley can probably make better decisions than me." Ollie speaks confidently, loudly, as if he is indeed delivering his words to a packed courtroom.

"I rest my case." Rachel's smile is smug. "So—"

"Enough." I lift Haley off my knee, rising to my feet before settling her back into the chair. Rachel's had her fun, but this is not a game. This is my life and Haley's, not an episode of *Judge Judy*. It's up to me to take the stand in my defence.

"But—"

"I said enough, Rachel." I ignore the way her lips thin into a terse line of displeasure. I'm going to say what needs to be said. Even though I know there's a risk Haley may walk away from me once I do. "This is between Ollie and me."

I swallow, my throat thick with apprehension. I'm about to drag up stuff I thought Ollie and I had put behind us. But his reaction this morning suggests it's far from buried. Now there's no choice but to have it out with him.

"Ollie, I know why you're being such a prick about this. You don't think I should be with Haley. That, because she's your sister, she's off limits." I pause, inhaling a jagged breath. Once I say the words, there's no going back. "Just like Kendra was."

Three pairs of female eyes bore into me, the question they both want and fear to ask written all over their faces. I study Haley. She licks at her lips, skin pale, and I think I read a flash of hurt in her questioning expression.

I've worked so hard to get her to think well of me, to trust I'm a better man than everyone says. And mostly I am. Except for one lapse of judgement at a party over two years ago. I wish I could wind back time, because if I could, it's a night of my life I'd do over again very differently.

However, if we're going to have any chance at a future, Haley needs to know all of me. Secrets will eat away at you. And if she ever found out—it would only take a slip of the tongue from someone who was there, or from Ollie—it wouldn't be the knowledge that would end us, but the fact I kept it from her. So I'm telling her now, and she can decide what to do with it.

"One night at a party over at Teddy's, when Ollie was away—that trip to Peru just before Kendra and him got together—something happened between her and me." I close my eyes and take another deep breath, gathering courage. "She was drunk. We all were. And while that's the reason it happened, I'm not using it as an excuse. Even drunk, I knew I should have pushed her away, but I didn't."

The moment Kendra Cole cornered me against the worktop in Teddy's kitchen, pressing her shapely body hard against mine and kissing me like she meant it, will be forever etched in my brain. And that, under the fog of alcohol, I allowed my own instinctive response to overrule both my usual caution with women, and my loyalty to a friend, will always be one of my biggest regrets.

I knew Ollie was smitten with her, yet still I let it happen. Guilt drove me to tell him. He laughed it off, and we made a deal to put it behind us. Ollie made it seem like forgiving me for the drunken make out with the girl he'd been attracted to for months was the easiest thing in the world. Now I know different.

I swallow again, hard. I search Haley's eyes. They're calm; eerily so. Is there a storm behind them and it's coming my way?

"It was a mistake. It meant nothing to either of us. But that's not the point. It shouldn't have happened at all. Not when I knew how he felt about her."

"And you promised me." Ollie's voice is heavy with bitter disappointment. It tears at me, a painful reminder of my vow. "You promised, Christian. We agreed we'd never let a woman come between us. That we'd be straight with each other." He shakes his head, eyes closed, a ragged exhale filling the silence.

I turn back to him. "Ollie, I've been upfront with you about this since the moment you walked in the door this morning. And I was right. You think this is the same as what happened with Kendra. But it's not." He looks up at me, and I can see he's planning to argue back. "This isn't about you and me, Ollie. It's about Haley. Neither of us gets to make the rules. She does."

Haley's face is pale with tension, hands clasped over her mouth as with wide eyes, she scans between the brother she loves, and the man who loves her. Me. And while I am fighting for myself right now, I'm mostly fighting for her.

"Ollie, just because Haley's your sister, it doesn't give you the right to make rules around her. Whoever she chooses to be with—or has ever chosen—that's not on you, that's on her. When you act like you did today, it's disrespectful to the person she is. She's smart and capable—"

I can't help but flash a smile at this amazing woman, offering her my belief, knowing she doesn't always believe in herself.

"Haley knows what she wants. And if I'm what she wants..." My voice cracks, and I can hardly breathe for fear of what the next minutes will bring. "She may not. Not after what she's just heard." Her eyes are a deep unfathomable green, locked on mine. I don't flinch away. "But if I am, that's her decision to make, not yours to decide for her."

And then she's on her feet. Her arm loops through mine, and my heart pounds against my ribs, as without words, she signals her choice by taking her place at my side. We face him together.

Ollie's eyes dart between us. Thoughts ripple through them, as they flicker green and brown like autumn leaves whipped by the wind. He leans forward, elbows on knees, chin propped on his hands, as if deliberating. After a few beats of silence, he moves to stand, then hesitates a moment, but Sam elbows him forward. He's on his feet, reaching for Haley first, pulling her into a hug.

"I'm so sorry," he whispers. "I've been a jerk. A jerk who loves you, but still a jerk."

"It's OK, Ollie," she murmurs. "As long as you're a jerk who can apologise, it's OK."

He releases her and steps towards me. I take his outstretched hand. His grip is firm, as his eyes fix on mine, his expression more serious than I think I've ever seen in my normally upbeat friend.

"I'm sorry mate. I should never have said those things..."

"It's OK, man. I get it. I mean, I love that you want to look after her. But I do too. And I will."

"I know." Ollie pulls me into a bone-crushing hug and I realise that with a little time, a little forgiveness, everything's going to be alright between us.

Much as that's a relief, when he releases me, it's not the state of our friendship I'm most concerned about. I'm immediately searching for confirmation from her. As if sensing my desperation to be clear about where we stand, Haley inserts herself into the space between Ollie and me. She sends two small hands around my neck, slender arms pulling me tight. The tension gripping my chest eases at the whisper of her words against my ear.

"I want you Christian Steele. All of you. The good bits and the not so good. I don't need the perfect man. I just need you."

The rest of the world falls away as we breathe in each other, but it's only a precious moment before we're pulled back into reality, interrupted by Sam's brisk voice.

"Now, we've got all that nonsense behind us," Sam says, grabbing the remote, "time to place your bets on who's going to win Wild For The Win."

The TV flares into life, and we all settle back into our seats, turning our eyes towards it. As the opening music sounds, Ollie snatches the remote from Sam, bumping up the volume before flopping onto the couch beside her.

"So, what do you think, Christian?" he asks. "You should know better than anyone. Who's going to take the prize?"

"My money's on Gavin Markham." I'm sticking with my original prediction.

I'm glad it's Gavin who has a shot at winning this thing, not me. I'm glad it's not me there on that screen tonight, because if I was, the woman in Christmas pyjamas, curled against my chest, the green apple scent of her hair filling my nose, the downy skin of her cheek pressed against mine, wouldn't be my girlfriend. I wouldn't trade that for anything. I've waited a long time, and it's me who's the biggest winner.

"How does it feel?" Haley asks. "Knowing it's over?"

She's wrong. It's not over. This pre-recorded final isn't the end. I have to endure tomorrow night's live 'reunion' episode before I can put this whole nightmare in the past. One last hurdle; me there, live on camera with the critical eyes of the world upon me. It's a sickening prospect, but I'm bound by that contract. There's no escape.

"It's not done yet," I say gloomily. "There's still tomorrow. And I'm dreading it. They're going to rip me to shreds."

"They're not," she says, tilting her head towards me. There's an excited twinkle in her eyes, and her mouth curves up in a secretive smile. "Trust me. They're not."

CHAPTER 38

The Next Day

"No fucking way," Tommy mutters through gritted teeth as a gigantic brush hovers over his face.

Neither of us anticipated they'd swoop us off to hair and make-up. I'm observing from a swivel chair next to him. The make-up artist, Luka, declared my own attempts at painting my face passable, needing only the slightest touch of extra colour to suit the harsh stage lights. He's focused on Tommy, now.

"Got good bone structure there, Tommy." Luka smiles, blissfully unaware of—or pointedly ignoring—the bristling man in the chair. "A bit of product on that hair, yeah?"

He reaches for a large pot of clear gloop. I see Tommy's body cringe further into the seat as Luka's fingers dive in, coming out with a glistening blob of jelly. He massages it between his palms, then plunges his hands into Tommy's thick hair, taming its broom-like bristles into hip-looking spikes.

Luka turns back to me. "And Haley darling, I've got a little extra idea for you."

He grabs at a curling brush. With a few deft twirls, he transforms my normally straight dark hair. Elegant spirals frame my face. The soft waves make me feel pretty and feminine, so different from my usual practical hairstyle.

That little boost of confidence damps down the sour taste in my mouth from the nausea that rises every time I think of what I'm about to face. The eyes of the world will see me revealed for the first time as no longer simply a nobody. Now, I'm a somebody because a person who cares for me happens to be famous; and some are going to judge me harshly because of that.

I'm opening myself up to criticism, even hatred, simply because Christian says he loves me. But I'm up for it. Not to say I'm not afraid. I've seen from the inside how bad this could get. Ollie's unhappiness at the media attacks on Kendra reverberated through our family. The memory now whispers a warning. I've seen the sadness and anger in Christian when he talks about how they crucified him and Waverley. The echoes of the past pain still linger.

Although he's ready for it this time. We both know what to expect; no outpouring of vitriol by some heartless journalist will crush us. We will get through this together.

Christian is fiercely protective of me; and I recognise that, even two weeks ago, when he first stood at my doorway, something about this man stirred my own protective instincts.

We've made a pact: we're going to trust each other on this. Nothing can penetrate the shield built of his love for me and my feelings for him.

It's too soon for me to find the words; I'm not brave enough yet, too scarred by the last time I let myself label an emotion as love—but I am falling for him. I have the courage to say I'm falling in love. Such a crazy term, like it's a helpless plunge—and maybe it is. Or perhaps there was never any other option but Christian for me.

I stand, smoothing down the deep ruby velvet of my dress, the fabric luxurious under my fingertips. I took Bethany's suggestion to choose something glamorous, a kind gesture on her part, ensuring I didn't arrive here unprepared. Although, I've seen these post-final episodes before, and I knew the women would be in their finest outfits, with not a hair out of place, as if to remind the world this is the real them, not the wild unkempt creatures they became during the competition.

I don't think I'm particularly vain, but it felt important the world sees me at my best. Many are going to question Christian's judgement. I don't want to give them any extra ammunition.

This is the dress I bought for The Brits, back in February. With the band nominated for Best Group, it was the biggest event I'd ever been to. Still reeling from Jack and Paige's betrayal, seeing myself in the mirror that night, my bare shoulders framed with the soft ruffle of velvet, I'd had this sense of opportunity, as if this dress was a first step in reinventing myself. Little did I know back then that behind Christian's appreciative glances, there was so much more. Wearing it tonight, I feel like his High Lady, the swirl of soft fabric rippling behind me as I walk towards the studio door, although nervousness still flutters in my stomach.

Tommy grabs my hand. "Ready?"

He grins at me, cocky and confident. I accept the squeeze gratefully, needing his reassurance, because although Peter Holt called me to explain what should happen when we go in there, nothing is certain. Tommy shoves open one of the double doors, ignoring the light above that flashes 'Do Not Enter - Filming In Progress'.

We pause hand in hand at the top of the aisle, where steps flow down towards the stage. Heads in the audience turn, and we're met with a mixture of puzzled frowns and wide-eyed curiosity. On cue, a production assistant races up the stairs towards us, hand raised, blocking our way. He knows the script.

"You can't come in here. Who the hell are you?"

"I'm Tommy Bunt, Loreena's husband, and no little twerp is going to stop me from having my say about all of this."

Tommy waves a hand at the group on the stage. Loreena sticks to the script too, eyebrows flying towards her forehead, then creasing in as much of a frown as the Botox allows. The audience gasps, fascinated by the scene. It's time for my lines.

"And I'm Christian Steele's girlfriend, Haley Templeton."

My words are met with even bigger gasps. Some of the women look distraught. I hear a few hisses of disbelief and disgruntled murmurings. Several shoot me evil glares. I expected that reaction as jealous fans realise Christian is taken. There's genuine sympathy in the eyes of a few; everyone knows what's supposed to have gone down between Loreena and Christian in their little tent.

One guy has a camera trained on us, but other cameras are capturing him. He looks towards the floor manager, theatrically swiping a finger across his throat, as if questioning whether he should cut away. The floor manager looks between us and the group on the stage, gives a shake of his head, pausing dramatically before delivering the lines with a deep, convincing sigh.

"Let them in."

The tension in the room is palpable. Almost everyone expects this is about to get ugly and their anticipation wafts around us.

Loreena lets out a small gasp, raising her hand to her mouth. Beside her, Christian refuses to play the game. His eyes meet mine, soft and trusting, the blue like a friendly sea, a tranquil shade which he seems to summon only for me. His lazy smile says it all, and he no longer cares what the world sees.

There is no doubt the audience wonders how he can smile, given the four players in this scenario, about to meet for the first time following the insinuations of infidelity. They presume I'm about to rip that expression away from his cheating face as an awkward scene unfolds for their pleasure.

They watch in fascinated horror as Tommy links his arm in mine and leads me down the aisle, head held high, like a proud father walking his daughter to the altar. Both of us *are* proud of what we're doing here, part of bringing the truth to light and, in the process, hopefully getting a truckload of cash for others whose troubles are far greater than some bad publicity.

No one seems to question the convenient extra empty couch on one side of the stage, set there waiting for us. Tommy and I take a seat, Loreena giving us a sneaky wink. Christian's eyes flicker towards me, brows raised in query, as if checking I'm OK. I give a slight nod and a smile. I can't pretend to be angry at him like they want.

"Well, this is awkward." Behind one hand, Bernard Bennett directs the little aside to the audience, accompanied by a knowing grin.

But he doesn't know anything. That smarmy little shit is in for a shock. He turns back to Loreena and Christian.

"So, Loreena, Christian, given all the rumours swirling around the two of you and what went on in that tent." His voice is thick with innuendo. "Maybe it's time to spill the beans, let the cat out of the bag, dish the dirt—"

"Bernard!" His exasperated co-host Lisa Mayberry, fixes him with a disparaging glare.

Loreena leaps in. "Look, I'll make no secret of the fact I adore this man." She smooshes Christian's face, pinching his cheeks like an adoring mother with a baby, and he flicks her hands away playfully.

"But I'm sorry, people. Much as you might be in love with the idea of us." She points a finger back and forth between them. "Much as it might be disappointing, I haven't gone all Anne Hathaway on you."

There's a ripple of laughter as the audience realises they're *not* witnessing the real life re-enactment of that popular movie about a romance between an older woman and a singer in a boy band.

"There *is* something going on between us—but not that."

Her strident voice hushes to almost a whisper. "Christian, you know you're like a son to me." He squeezes her hand, and she wipes at one eye. But Loreena's not one to show too much sentimentality on TV. She turns to face the audience, leaning forward, one scarlet nail pointing at her face, as she attempts to pull her high brows into a frown. "And I mean, really people? I know my surgeon is good, but I'm old enough to be his mother."

There's a whicker of laughter, as the audience is taken in by her self-deprecating tone. Loreena's face is still stunning, even if propped up by artificial means, but she's made her point.

In the next beat, she rises from her seat, grabbing my hand, pulling me up onto my feet beside her. With a flourish, she raises her arm and twirls me beneath it like a dancer, posing me for a moment.

"Anyway. Look at her? Isn't she beautiful?"

There's a patter of applause, although some don't join in, fixing me with hard, envious stares. I think I catch a faint booing sound, but I brush it off. Christian is mine, no matter what they think. Loreena guides me to sit beside my boyfriend, who's smiling up at me in soft reassurance. She releases my hand to find his, then flings herself into the space next to Tommy.

"And *this* is the man I love and who loves me."

She pats Tommy's knee, and he scoops her into a hug before planting his mouth on hers in a kiss so passionate I can hear the mutual slurping as they devour each other on national television. There are whoops and catcalls and a round of exuberant applause from the audience.

Christian's arm slides round my shoulder, and he places a delicate kiss on my cheek, pulling me into him. No one seems to notice us. All eyes are riveted on Loreena and Tommy's enthusiastic public make out—until the slam of the double doors at the studio entrance draws everyone's attention.

Bethany Holt stands at the top of the stairs, dramatic in a high-necked black dress, cut away to reveal her pale angular shoulders. Beside her, Peter is in a variation of the jeans, band t-shirt (this one Led Zeppelin) and the loose shirt he wore last time I saw him.

Bernard and Lisa wear twin slack-jawed expressions of shock as their boss strolls towards them, his wife a dark exotic creature beside him. Stagehands scramble to produce two tub chairs. Peter and

Bethany slide into them. Glasses of champagne materialise in front of them, as well as one for me and what looks like whisky for Tommy.

The other contestants sit stunned, uncertain mutters between them. Lisa Mayberry hurriedly schools her features into a pleasant expression, her voice calm.

"Everybody, such a pleasure to introduce you to the people who make all of this happen—Mr Peter Holt, Managing Director, and his wife Bethany. This is such a surprise. To what do we owe the honour, Peter?"

Peter pauses to sip at the champagne and clears his throat. "Well, first, I'd like to congratulate our winner, Gavin Markham. Such a great cause too, Gavin."

Gavin beams beneath his thick dark beard, and the audience applauds wildly. He was obviously a popular winner. The only truly nice person amongst them. I'm glad he made it through.

"Beth and I are very proud our show is able to help out groups like Gavin's 'Football For All'. There's so much need out there." The audience nod and murmur in approval. "But..." He glances around the group seated on the couches, eyeing each one meaningfully. "There are other things about this show that we're not proud of. In fact, I'm downright ashamed of some things that have happened on our watch. And that's why we're here."

Lisa and Bernard shuffle uncomfortably in their seats, eyes darting towards the floor manager, hoping for a cue. He simply shrugs, spreading his hands wide, his expression of bewilderment mirroring that of almost everyone in the studio.

"We're here to apologise. We're also here to assure you *Wild For The Win*—and every other show under the Veritas banner—is going to operate a little differently going forward. You see Veritas, means truth, and I'm undertaking that from hereon in, that's what people are going to get. We're going to put the real back in reality."

He points at the audience. "Now, you know how it goes on these live shows. You get to hear all the stuff that happened behind the scenes. That's what you want to know, isn't it? What really happened?"

There's a ripple of applause.

"*I* can tell you what really happened. And what didn't."

Peter Holt spends the next ten minutes charming the audience with a blend of casual charisma and disarming sincerity. A few in the audience dab at their eyes when he offers Loreena and Christian an unreserved apology. There's a cheer from the crowd when he announces he's sacked producer Hugh Partridge and more heads may still roll. Lisa and Bernard shrink under the force of his pointed stare.

The audience applauds wildly when he announces the animal welfare stance he's insisting on for all their future productions. There are warm cheers for Bethany as she presents both Christian and Loreena with one of those oversized cheques—one hundred thousand pounds each for their chosen charities—not from *Wild For The Win,* but out of her and Peter's own charitable fund, The Holt Foundation. I didn't know this bit was coming, and my heart leaps in my throat when I realise they've not only saved the dog rescue—my job is safe.

"One more thing. One more thing." Bethany bounces in her seat like an overexcited child, interrupting Lisa Mayberry, who is trying to wrap things up. "A last, very important thing." She turns to me with an enigmatic smile and then casts her gaze across the audience.

"Do you believe in fate?" Her voice is hushed, mysterious. She's greeted with enthusiastic nodding.

"Me too," she says. "And a few days ago, fate delivered an incredible young woman to our doorstep." She stretches out her arm, palm raised. "Haley Templeton, people." There's an answering patter of applause as I shuffle in my seat, uncomfortable under the questioning stares of strangers. Bethany fixes her eyes back on the audience.

"You know there's a belief." Her voice rises, her tone emphatic. "One I hold very dear. I believe whatever you put out into the universe comes back at you threefold." She pauses for dramatic effect. "Haley, you've put so much good out into the universe. Now it's your turn for it to come back to you."

One of the assistants appears from the wings clutching another giant cardboard cheque, and even from here I can read my name on it in large looping writing. And the amount, all those zeroes. So many zeroes.

"Stand up, babe," Christian whispers against my ear. "This moment's all for you." I gulp in air, summon a smile although I feel like I want to throw up, and wobble over on my heels, to where Bethany stands, with Loreena now also on her feet beside her.

"This is just from us darling, Loreena and I." Bethany's eyes, today a disconcerting shade of yellow like a predatory big cat, meet mine and now they glow golden. "You're already doing such a great job working hard in the vet clinic, but we also know you want to do more. This is for you, sweetheart, to become the best you can be."

The two women move to flank me, each laying an arm across my shoulder, and I feel their affection. Two people who were strangers a week ago, who believe in me. It's humbling, and I mumble out words of thanks, but they're awkward as swirling emotions take hold. I don't even hear the hosts' closing words, too overcome by the gesture, as the realisation hits me: I can go to vet school.

"You knew," I say. "Why didn't you warn me?"

The after-show party was a whirl of champagne and laughter, congratulations and good wishes, even from a few unexpected people like Lisa Mayberry. But now, here, in the silence of the limo, I have time to reflect. I'm not ungrateful for Bethany and Loreena's generosity, but damn it, if the need to be independent isn't whispering those same old snide suggestions inside my brain.

I'm a failure; I can't stand on my own feet, always indebted to someone else; I live in my brother's house; I'm in a job I worry I'd never have got on my own merits, sure one of my mother's friends put in a good word for me before the interview.

"I didn't know," Christian says, and I believe him. I can trust him to be truthful. "I knew the two of them were up to something—Loreena was on her phone all afternoon, and shooting me smug looks."

"Surely you must have been the reason for it? How else would they know?"

I lean against Christian's shoulder, breathing in the spicy smell of cologne mingled with the fresh leather scent of the seat. Outside the black limousine, Christmas lights dazzle overhead, making little rainbows in the droplets on the window. Christian told the driver to take us the long route home. The central streets, Oxford and Regent,

Carnaby and Bond, look like movie stars on the red carpet, each trying to outdo each other with the most ostentatious dress.

"You must have told them something."

"Only Loreena," he sighs. "But I swear, Haley, I didn't even tell her you wanted to go to vet school. And certainly not that you couldn't because of the money. I wouldn't do that to you. That's no one else's business but yours. Yes, I *did* tell Loreena in conversation I thought you'd make a great vet. You've seen what she's like, a first class meddler whose brain shoots off in all directions without warning."

I can't help but laugh at the very accurate summing up of our friend.

"And the moment she and Bethany laid eyes on each other in the green room, they hit it off straight away. Insisted they both go to hair and make-up at the same time and spent the entire time chattering away. Look out world now those two have found each other."

"Poor Tommy and Peter."

"Are you going to do it?" he asks.

"Vet school? Wow, the fact I could hasn't even sunk in yet. I don't know. It's so weird when something you always wanted so badly but thought you'd never have, just drops into your lap."

"Don't I know it," he says, voice low, his blue eyes tender. "Happened to me twelve days ago, and my advice is, go for it. You won't regret it."

He presses his lips to mine and in that perfect moment, the passing lights rippling across us in colourful strands as if dancing in celebration, I know he's right.

CHAPTER 39

Nine Days Later

Haley

TULLY TUMBLES FROM THE backseat of the wagon, a whirling orange tornado of excited dog. I head for the other side of the car, where Mularkey's blue eyes plead with me for freedom.

"Easy girl, I can't get you out of here while you're wiggling so much." Mularkey tugs at the seat restraint while I fumble with the clip. The pressure of her struggles puts tension on the belt, making the task more difficult. The clip finally pops open and she's off, a streak of silver and white. They both stop for a pee—they like to synchronise—then begin laps around the front garden of Ollie's country house, before coming to a halt beneath one large tree, planting bottoms to the ground, heads raised and keen eyes scanning the branches.

"Oh, please, not squirrels. We'll never get them in," I sigh.

"Don't worry, I'll round them up." Ollie strolls down the front steps towards us. "Remember, I'm their favourite uncle." He's right. The girls worship Ollie, probably because whenever he's home, he ignores my instructions and feeds them treats from his plate.

"Good luck with that when squirrels are involved," Sam laughs as she pops the rear hatch of her mother's car, and starts to unload our cases. "Even their favourite aunt can't convince them away from those tree-rats."

Sam's not a big fan of wildlife since a day in the park when, like most eight-year-olds, we ignored the 'don't feed the squirrels' sign, and an overenthusiastic one climbed her leg and bit her hand.

"Yeah, if there's a squirrel in that tree, I don't like your chances, Ollie," I call from where I'm head down in the centre of the back seat, unloosing the belt that's kept Kona's travel crate secure on the journey from London to Somerset.

"And so, this is the little guy." Ollie smiles and steps forward to help me lift the carrier out. "Hey, there little man." He peers through the mesh, then flips the latch and Kona prances out, pausing to lick at Ollie's outstretched hand before racing across the driveway and diving onto the nearest piece of grass to squat. "Still peeing like a girl, I see. At what age do they stop that?" He grins at the caramel-coloured pup.

"Think about it Ollie." I roll my eyes at my brother. Kona is *never* going to be able to cock his back leg on lampposts like other male dogs, not when he only has one.

"Oh, yeah," he says. "I forgot, three legs. You don't notice it with the way he runs around so fast."

"Yeah. Even with three legs, he's going to have the best life." I know that for sure. "You haven't said anything, right?"

"Not a word," he promises, with a smile. "He's going to be so surprised."

Malcolm, one half of the lovely semi-retired couple who look after Ollie's house for him, bustles down the steps towards us, hands extended towards suitcases, ready to help.

"Ello there, Haley! You're 'ere at last, me lovely!" he calls out, his voice, with its Devon drawl rising and falling like a gentle countryside melody. "We've bin waitin' for ye all mornin', we 'ave!"

The wrinkles on his walnut-brown face deepen in a broad smile as I intercept him with a hug. I suspect he and his wife, Audrey, find the big house too quiet when it's only the two of them. They fuss over us like family whenever we're here, and we've come to feel like they're family, too.

"I didn't expect to see you," I say, unwinding myself from him. "You're off to your family for Christmas, aren't you?"

"Aye, this afternoon, me dear. Just need to load up all the li'l uns' presents, we do, an' then we'll hit the road, sure enough. We wanted to make sure all was sorted 'ere afore we left. An' to see ye too, of course."

"Well, now you have, you should get going. You'll want to be there before dark." Malcolm and Audrey's two daughters live down near Torquay. It's only a couple of hours, but when it's Saturday, two days out from Christmas, the traffic will be hell. "I'm sure everything will be fine here."

Malcolm's bushy brows knit in a frown. "I don't rightly know, me dear. Not with all that film crew muckin' about in there, actin' like they owns the place. Right bothersome lot, if you asks me. Struttin' 'round like lords o' the manor."

He casts a sour look at the three huge black vans lined up on one side of the driveway, with a small catering trailer parked on the other. I can imagine Malcolm is not at all pleased with bossy production staff, camera operators and sound techs invading the house. It's only going to get worse when the band's roadies arrive.

"They'll be gone before we know it," Ollie assures him. "They're on a deadline."

He grabs a suitcase, whistles for the dogs, who much to my surprise come running, Mularkey smiling in the lead, Tully laughing at her shoulder and Kona racing behind with small barks as if saying, "Hey, wait for me."

Stepping into Ollie's house this Christmas is like falling into the pages of a magazine. The last two years, I've brought along some decorations, he's made sure of a tree, we've decked out one lounge and the dining room and it's been nice. But it's hard to make an impact on a house of this size without considerable amounts of time and money. Ollie might not have the first, but with the second, this year he's created something breathtaking. Well, an interior designer with a generous budget has.

"You like it?" he asks.

"Of course I do. I love it." I don't know where to look. It's all so overwhelming. And this is only the entranceway. "Did you get lots of visitors through?"

"Hundreds apparently. Made a good amount of money for the village hall society."

The nearby village of Nether Wickham, struggling with a leaking roof on their community hall, came up with a plan: ask the owners of stately homes in the area to decorate and open their doors to the public for a couple of weeks before Christmas. A fundraiser for them, and a bonus for us, as our family will spend Christmas surrounded by these amazing decorations.

I stare, mesmerised by the sight. It's Christmas on steroids, everything supersized. I feel like Alice in Wonderland, shrunk to a tiny speck next to the towering tree, laden with baubles as big as my head. Luckily, it has sturdy branches, enough to support their weight and that of the garlands. Glittering tinsel snakes, they twine around the foliage like an exotic species of full-bodied python in a Christmas-themed jungle.

"We surely did. Visitors pouring in," a beaming Audrey announces as she joins us in the enormous hallway. Her brown eyes, framed with wrinkles etched by more than sixty years of her cheery personality, sparkle with pride. "My word, so many people there were."

"Couldn't have done it without you and Malcolm." Ollie's always generous with praise, particularly for these two.

"Oh, it was nothin' really," Audrey shrugs. "Even though it meant a bit of extra work, we 'ad a lovely time, we did. I 'ope they do it again next year. Are you nearly ready, my dear?" She looks across at Malcolm.

"I'll just see our Sam to 'er room, quick as a flash, an' then we can be off, my love. Won't take but a moment, it won't."

Malcolm reaches for Sam's suitcase, swinging it with the strength of a much younger man, as he heads for the grand staircase to the second floor.

"You and Christian are down here." Ollie grabs at my suitcase, heading off to the left. "I've given you the one that opens out to the side garden. For the dogs."

That simple no fuss assumption, Christian and I will share a room, is a relief to my ears after last week's upset. Ollie really has accepted we're together. I know he and Christian have talked a lot since, patching up the rift in their friendship that neither ever expected would happen, least of all over me.

"That's great Ollie. Thank you. It's perfect."

Giving the dogs direct access through French doors to the little walled garden will make life so much easier. Especially when one of them is a puppy. Lilian assures me Kona's toilet-trained, but he's young, so not reliable at holding on for too long yet.

I spend the next hour unpacking, then grab lunch—Audrey's left us a hearty beef and barley soup simmering in the kitchen, paired with home-baked bread—before retreating to the safety of the bedroom. It's busy in the house as the TV crew hustle back and forth, preparing the small ballroom—it's still crazy that my brother's house has an actual ballroom—for filming the live segment for a Christmas variety special.

Lying back on the bed, a new book in my hand, I retreat into a fictional world. However, I'm so tired, I eventually put my reading aside, and close my eyes, savouring the peace. Apart from the occasional muffled sound of conversation, and the odd bump and thump from the film crew at work drifting across from the other wing of the house, everything is hushed here in the country.

Exhaustion weighs heavily on me. It's been a long week. Loreena's words about the festive season putting pressure on already struggling households have played out in the clinic these past few days. So many dogs surrendered or abandoned, it's been a scramble to patch them up and get as many as possible into safe foster homes before the holiday break.

We collected Kona this morning, and already another unfortunate wee soul has taken his place at Lilian's. The Trust's kennel facilities are full to bursting and the worst is yet to come. I feel almost guilty here enjoying my break. At least the injection of cash from the Holt Foundation has pushed back the spectre of closure for now. And I'll have my job for as long as I need it, until, without even leaving Camden, I join the Royal Veterinary College intake next autumn.

There's no dog noise to disturb me. After a brief flurry of activity, sniffing every corner of the bedroom, the girls demanded out once more and are back in the garden, staking out a potential squirrel-bearing tree in the far corner. Kona, flipping from exuberant to exhausted again, in the way puppies do, sought the sanctuary of his crate. I draped it with a blanket, cocooning him in darkness. Now he's sleeping soundly, with only the faintest whisper of his breathing.

Joining him in a nap seems like a good option. After drawing the heavy brocade curtains on a sickly winter sun, I dive into my suitcase, seeking my new set of pyjamas. I saw them in a shop window on my way from the tube the other night and, unable to resist the wide-eyed dog in a Christmas hat on the front that looked so like Tully (or Christian when he's trying to tug at my heartstrings), I had to have them.

Christian will give me a hard time about them, I'm sure. He comments almost daily on my extensive pyjama wardrobe, usually when he's busy removing them from me. With a smile at the thought of him, knowing he's on his way right this moment, on the road somewhere between here and Cheshire where he's spent the last couple of days with his family, I slip between the covers.

Ear buds in place, I'm floating on the sound of Christian's voice, the strum of his guitar and the words of 'Untouchable', as he draws me into sleep.

My eyes flutter open at the brush of lips on my forehead, as cool fingers nudge their way along my collarbone.

"God, I've missed you," Christian mumbles against my mouth and my willing lips part in welcome.

"Missed you more," I say, in between his hungry kisses. "Even if your hands are freezing."

"Sorry," he says, dragging himself away with one last reluctant kiss. He sits on the side of the bed, unzipping his boots and tossing them aside with a thud.

"Fuck, it's mayhem out there," he says as his fingers work quickly at the buttons of his shirt.

"Really? I thought they'd be done by now. What time is it?"

"Almost three," he says with a glance at the chunky watch on his wrist. "No, apparently they've decided the ballroom is too big. Not enough 'ambience' and so we're going to be in the library. Ewan's running around like a headless chicken, and the crew are stomping around all pissed off. Believe me, in here is the best place to be for the next couple of hours. Especially given the plans I've got for you, sweetheart."

He tosses me a panty-melting wink, and stands, unzipping his jeans. I allow my eyes to rove over the strong thighs, the solid lines of those muscular arms and the trails of ink blooming there in all their wild beauty. I could look at him all day. The jeans fall to the floor with the clatter of a belt buckle.

"So, you think I'm going to let you hide out in bed with me? Just so you can avoid Ewan?" I prop myself up on one elbow, watching him strip off his underwear as he grins across at me.

"That's the plan. Plus, there are some new pyjamas that need removing, I see?" One dark brow quirks up, and he tosses me a sexy half-smirk

"Remove away," I say, sitting up, raising my hands towards the ceiling. He needs no further invitation. He whisks the top over my head, tossing it aside with a flourish. His look is molten as his eyes rove appreciatively across my naked breasts.

"You have the most stunning tits," he says. "Really, you're fucking exquisite, Haley."

I don't need the words to know he thinks I'm beautiful; there's no doubting the message in his smouldering eyes, but it still sends an electric thrill through me hearing him say it, how desirable I am to him, how much he wants me, hearing the neediness in his voice. After the hurt of rejection, the betrayal that shredded my self-confidence, Christian has built me up again, restored my belief that I am desirable, I am loveable. He's given me so much, and I want to give all of myself to him.

He sinks onto the bed, folding me in his arms, skin to skin.

"I've missed you, missed this."

His voice is gravel, low and raspy with possibility. I'm wrapped so tightly, my breasts crushed against his broad chest; I can feel the thud of his heart. I always feel so small and precious inside the safety of his arms.

"I missed you too. Two days felt like forever."

I wonder how I'll survive when it's two weeks. Or when the band goes on tour and it's two months. I push the thought aside. That's one of many things we still have to work out, as we weave his life and mine into one. But I've vowed to deal with them as we need to, not let anxiety over future challenges tarnish the wonder of the present.

For a moment we pause, float in this moment, breathing in each other's presence. Then, he leans me back a little, dropping his head reverently to each erect nipple in turn, swirling one, then the other in his mouth, his tongue flickering, teeth grazing, lighting me up with the sensation.

I cradle my head on his shoulder, inhaling his woodsy scent, so familiar and inviting, tasting his skin as I whimper against him, the heat in my centre rising with each insistent tug of his mouth.

After even this small separation, my need for him is urgent, as is his for me. I shuffle across, arranging myself on his lap, legs wrapped around his hips, grinding shamelessly against him, eager for the contact; the friction, even through the fabric of my pyjama bottoms, feeds my growing arousal.

He shoves me back gently, large hands firmly grasping the waistband, shimmying the pants down, his mouth trailing over each new piece of exposed skin, dotting small nips along my stomach, my hips, thighs, and then his deft tongue lapping at the wet heat at my core. I inhale sharply, encouraging him with the feral sounds that spill unbidden from deep in my throat, and my hands laced in his hair.

"God, the sound of you," he whispers from between my legs, his breath heavy against my thigh. "I love that sound."

"Come inside me," I invite, "if you really want to make me scream." I'm suddenly desperate for the weight of him upon me, the hard length of him driving deep.

"Oh, I promise I will, sweetheart," he says, sliding up my body, the eager thrust of his erection making me gasp. We come together greedily, each hungry to find the perfect rhythm that's already become like a familiar song, needing no thought, only feeling to take us where we want to go.

"Dog," he mumbles from deep in that languid post-coital state, not quite asleep, but barely awake. "I hear a dog."

"Hmmm, outside," I reply dozily. "Squirrel patrol. They can stay out there." I have no desire to leave the warmth of this bed, with Christian's limbs still draped comfortably over me, to let the girls in. They turned down my earlier offer, so they don't get to demand instant attention now.

"You sure about that?" he mutters.

I hear it too. A small yip from the crate in the far corner of the room. I'm instantly upright. Kona.

"Wait there," I say. "Keep your eyes shut."

I find my pyjamas scattered on the floor and pull them on. When I reach the crate, Kona paws at the mesh door. I swing it open and scoop him up, a wiggling, licking bundle in my arms.

"What's going on?" Christian calls.

"No peeking, you. Eyes shut." I command, making my way to the bed. "It's a surprise."

I place Kona on Christian's chest, and his eyes fly open. He takes in the laughing puppy mouth, inches away from him, that's aiming a quick tongue at his nose, and his face creases in delight.

"What the fuck? A puppy? You got a puppy?" His hands immediately set to stroking Kona's floppy ears, dodging playful teeth, while Kona bats at him with his paws.

"No, *you* got a puppy. Meet Kona. He's yours." He doesn't take in what I've said at first, too enthralled with the creature doing a tap dance on his chest. "That's if you want him."

Christian's face splits into the biggest grin.

"Really?"

"Really. And I know your place isn't ideal for a dog, and I know you're away lots. He can stay with me whenever you need. The girls have already given their approval. They're keen to have a baby brother."

"God, he's just so perfect. Thank you." He pulls me in, pressing a kiss on my forehead, which is the cue for Kona to make an opportunistic lunge for my hair.

"No," I say firmly, laying one finger on his wet nose while tucking the strand back out of his reach.

"Guess we'll be saying that word a lot for a while," Christian laughs. He stops mid-chuckle, lifting Kona up above his head and twirling him around, checking him out from all angles. "A tripod." He smiles up at the helpless puppy, who squirms in his grasp and gives a frustrated bark. "Even more perfect."

CHAPTER 40

Later That Night

Haley

IF YOU ASKED SOMEONE to imagine the most idyllic English Christmas scene, it would look like the library of Ollie's house tonight. Except for the two large cameras, the web of cables crisscrossing the floor, and the crew clothed in black gathered around for final instructions from the floor manager; and the drum kit to one side and three guitars propped on stands in front of a leather couch and two chairs. But otherwise, the room oozes festive cheer.

Not one, but two trees twice the size of mine, decorated in a traditional style, frame the couch. They glisten with trails of gold tinsel and winking fairy lights. Dotted in between are giant baubles of deepest emerald, and rich ruby red bows the colour of the velvet dress I'm wearing.

It's the same dress I wore to the *Wild For The Win* finale. So what, I'll have been seen on national television twice in the same outfit within a fortnight. No matter that the Princess of Wales seems to get away with recycling her dresses just fine, I'm fully prepared for someone to criticise my choice, and I don't care—I feel strong and beautiful in this dress and that's all that matters. That and the fact Christian told me it's his favourite of all my outfits. Although he did mention in the next breath, it made a refreshing change from Christmas pyjamas.

Every surface in the room is decked out with tastefully placed ornaments, luscious garlands and wavering candles wafting scents of sandalwood and cinnamon. There's the smoky overlay of burning pine, from a fire crackling in the enormous hearth.

The room has a homely feel, despite its oversized proportions. I can see why they chose it over the ballroom. It's the whole vibe they want for this variety show—performers in their own home, enjoying Christmas with friends and family. That's why we're here. Mum and neatly sidestepped the invitation, pleading a school benefactor's Christmas party they absolutely must attend. But, uncomfortable as it is facing live cameras, I won't shy away from doing this for Ollie and Christian.

Sam and I take a seat on our allotted sofa. It's wide and comfortable, and the forest green and red tartan upholstery fabric fits the Christmas decor perfectly.

"Hi, I'm Tabitha, Teddy's girlfriend." The bubbly blonde woman already seated at one end, who looks barely old enough to be out of school (although Ollie says she's twenty-two), blinks at us nervously.

"Hi, I'm Haley, Ollie's sister. And Christian's girlfriend."

I offer her a welcoming smile and try not to let the sympathy I feel for her show in my eyes. Girlfriend, in Teddy's case, doesn't have the same meaning as what the title means to other guys. Unfortunately, sweet, quiet, unassuming Teddy is the only one of the band still susceptible to the temptation of groupies. One day he'll grow up, but until then, girls like this will rotate in and out of his life as if it's the revolving door of a busy hotel. So this week, it's Tabitha. Next week, who knows?

"Samantha, sort of Ollie's sister, too." Sam leans across me, smiling at Tabitha, before settling back into the seat as we exchange a discreet, knowing look. I've warned Sam off Teddy. The last thing I need is one of my friends succumbing to his boyish charm.

Garrett's wife, Liv, pale and serene, arrives to take the final space beside us. She offers a slender hand and a shy smile. I'm surprised to see her. Garrett, the bass player, a few years older than his bandmates, draws a very firm line between his career and his personal life. He's protective of his gentle wife, rarely subjecting her to the limelight.

I wonder if Christian and I will get to that point, or if we'll even want to. Maybe it's because Ollie's in the band too, but I kind of like the idea of being part of it all, sharing in this thing Christian loves. In surviving the publicity around *Wild For The Win*, I've found unexpected strength, tucking away my fears of what fame will bring until the day comes when I actually have to face them. And, when it does, Christian and I will stand together, each trusting in the other.

Right on time, at five forty-five, the guys amble in. Teddy seats himself at the drums, his flying hands settling into small flurries of rhythm, random snippets, many of which I recognise.

Ollie takes his place in one of the oversized armchairs, Garrett in another. Christian heads for the couch. His eyes meet mine as he picks up his guitar. His mouth tips up in a smile, soft and sultry, as if it's just a moment between us and there aren't twenty others in the room.

The guys all strum away, tuning up their instruments one final time. It's an acoustic set tonight, Stellar Riot unplugged, perfect for the intimate nature of the segment. Familiar riffs drift towards us, teasing what's to come on the playlist.

Marky Lomas, one of the more likeable television hosts, strolls in wearing neat pale grey chinos, a white button down and a navy sports jacket. He takes a seat next to Christian and gives us a wink.

Right on the dot of six o'clock, a hush falls across the room, as we're counted in to the livestream. After a bit of reasonably painless banter between Marky and the band, cameras swivel towards us. I resist the urge to cringe under their gaze, try not to think of how many people will be watching out there, or worry about making an idiot of myself on live TV.

Ollie does the introductions, his casual ease in the situation damping down my anxiety a little. I manage to summon a co-herent response to Marky's unexpected spontaneous question about my job, and stick to the script when he mentions Christian and I being in a relationship and wishes us the best. As Marky moves aside to a chair, and the cameras turn back to the band, I exhale in relief, grateful that for the rest of the next ten minutes, my role is simply to be part of a supportive audience.

The band launches into 'Angel Mine', a fan favourite, and within moments of the well-known song washing over me, I can almost forget this is anything but the guys having a jam session at Ollie's house.

They follow it up with one of their latest songs, 'Captured', which has been well-received and is currently hanging in around number ten on the charts. It's got this compelling bass line and a killer chorus courtesy of Ollie and Christian's combined brilliance. I'd bet money on it going higher after tonight.

Two great choices, and the Stellar Riot fans will be happy. One more song, and this will all be over and we can be ourselves again, without worrying about the lurking second camera, swivelling between the band and us.

I'm taken by surprise when Christian opens his mouth to introduce the final song. It's so unusual for him to step in as frontman. Usually, he's happy for Ollie to take that role. He scrubs one hand at his neck, bites at his lip, and begins.

"As most of you know, my life's been in a bit of upheaval the last few weeks. I'd use other words to describe it, but hey, this is a family show, right?"

A burst of laughter ripples across the room. Christian's not quite as bad as Rachel, but he's had a few famous stumbles with unfiltered language in public. He strokes at his beard, casting a grin at Ollie.

"Some of that upheaval has been pretty tough. But there's one thing that's upended my life in the best way possible. One person, in fact. And that's Haley Templeton."

I see him begin to stand and realise what's happening here. Inside I'm screaming "No, no, no," while outwardly I smile and rise to my feet, a reluctant robot. Guitar in one hand, he extends the other to me and guides me to the space next to him on the sofa. Anxious nausea rises in my stomach, and I tighten my grip on his hand as if he's the only thing stopping me from crumbling under the weight of all those unseen eyes watching me.

"Sorry, I didn't warn you," he whispers. "This is my surprise."

"Just promise me you're not about to go all Billy Mack on us," I splutter out, leaning in close, quietly teasing him as I try to steady myself. "Promise you'll keep your clothes on?"

"I promise," he says, with a low chuckle. "You OK?"

"Yeah, I'm OK," I whisper back, even as I realise the tiny microphone on the lapel of his shirt captures my every word, and his too, and offers them to the world.

When he speaks again, he doesn't turn to the camera. Instead, his eyes fix on me, the blue deep and intense.

"We planned to do 'Untouchable' to finish tonight. But as it's my song, I got to tell them no. We've got a new song to share. One I wrote in the last couple of weeks. It's similar, because I wrote it for Haley, just like I wrote 'Untouchable' for her three years ago. Would you believe up until about a week ago, she didn't know that?" He laughs, a soft seductive chuckle. "It's been my little secret. So, now you know too. With this one, right from the start, I'm making no secret of the fact it's for her. It's called 'December Promise'. And it goes like this."

Teddy counts them in; the guitars find their way forward in a crash of chords, and Christian's voice rises to meet them.

It's a love song. I know it from the eyes of this man, fixed on mine, his heart laid out raw and vulnerable. It's there in the lyrics too, his declaration of love for me. And, as I promised, back when I had no idea of Christian's feelings or what he'd come to mean to me, I take his words with gentle hands knowing how much this costs him, understanding the risk he takes in offering it to me. And knowing that later, in the quiet time, when it's just us without the world watching, I'm ready to take that risk too.

I wonder if there's a camera capturing him from this angle. I hope so, because I want to replay this moment again, over and over and over, reliving it often across the years stretching ahead of us. When my memory becomes hazy, I want to be able to summon this image of him, the beautiful clarity of his voice, his face, his words, his love, and bask in the knowledge it's all for me.

While part of me protests allowing so many eyes to observe this intimacy between us, I'm prepared to share our love so the world can see the truth of Christian Steele, how good, and true and loyal he is. No one who sees this man tonight, singing this song for me, could ever doubt otherwise.

As he finishes, the last vibration of guitar strings quivering in the air like a sigh, the final shimmering flutter of the cymbals fading into nothing, the room pauses for a moment in silence, and then everyone breaks into applause. Christian lets his guitar fall to the floor and scoops me into his arms, and our mouths meet in a deep, lingering kiss.

"Surprised?" he murmurs against my lips.

"Very surprised," I say. "You wrote me a Christmas song."

"I did." His mouth tilts into the lopsided grin I love. "How did that happen?"

If you loved this book, I'd really appreciate you leaving a rating or review on your favourite retailer, review site or social media.

Want more of Christian and Haley?
Find an extended bonus epilogue
on my website
www.carolinecorvin.com

And turn over here to find them
in the first chapter of
Book 2 in the Stellar Riot Christmas series:

Not My Little Drummer Boy

Not My Little Drummer Boy

Chapter 1

THERE'S A RUMBLE OF footsteps in the hallway and the imposing wooden door bursts open. Haley tumbles towards me, arms as wide as her smile, three large dogs bouncing at her heels.

"Rachel, at last! I was starting to worry."

She pulls me inside, folding me into her like I'm one of her precious Christmas ornaments and she's the protective tissue. The dogs arrive in a flurry of fur, dancing canine feet performing their own welcome celebration as they circle us with wiggling bodies.

The chunky orange dog, Tully, butts at my calves, the cold damp of her nose penetrating my tights. Mularkey, more athletic, leaps up at me, managing a decent pirouette for a dog of her advanced age. Her pale blue husky eyes, almost level with mine, sparkle with mischief, although she's careful to maintain a space between us. Just as well. I don't want her hooked claws snagging my beautiful cashmere suit.

The third dog, Kona, ducks and dives in the background, still puppy-like, despite his huge size, but with better manners than his two doggy aunties. Now at just over a year old, he's finally grown into those big feet, no longer clumsy even though he's only got three legs. His caramel latte coat shines with little gold sparks under the light of the massive chandelier suspended high above our heads.

I can't help my free hand from dabbing affectionate pats at their soft heads. I love dogs, and the sight of these three in particular drags me up a little from the pit of exhaustion I sank into on my two-hour drive. But not as much as seeing my friend glowing with happiness at my arrival, as we gather to prepare for her wedding.

Haley releases me from her hug, hands falling to my elbows, and pinning me with a frown.

"You know it's after six. I really was starting to worry."

"I know. I know. Sorry I'm so late. The traffic was shit."

Escaping the city on a winter Friday night was never going to be easy, even though this sprawling country estate near the village of Sarratt is technically still in the Greater London area.

"And my boss threw a new case file on my desk after lunch," I grumble. "Wanted my opinion before I left for my 'holiday', even though she knew damn well I planned to leave at three. So it ended up being four o'clock by the time I got out of the office."

"Well, now you can relax and forget about all of that for a whole week."

I don't want to draw her attention to the laptop bag hooked over the handle of my suitcase. For the next week, I need to pretend

Haley and her wedding are my only focus. She deserves that from me. However, in my job, a week without work isn't a luxury I have available right now.

There's a partner's seat in the law firm with my name on it and damned if I'm going to let that fall from my grasp. I've lost too much lately—namely the fiancé who somehow slipped through my fingers without me realising it was happening until the night he came home two months ago and said he was moving out.

My personal life is a disaster, but I can still make a success of my career. That's all I have left, apart from my friends, who've surrounded me with love when my world fell apart.

"Let me show you your room. Get yourself into something comfy and join us downstairs. Loreena's making cocktails."

"I see in your case, comfy means pyjamas." Haley's pair of choice, Christmas-themed of course, have a pattern of wispy snowflakes on a green background that intensifies the colour of her eyes.

"What else?" She strikes a pose, one hand on hip, the other extended upwards in a 'ta-daa' gesture. I roll my eyes, but can't prevent a grin escaping. I adore this girl, including her crazy pyjama obsession.

"How many sets of Christmas pyjamas do you own?"

"Hmmm." She pops a finger to her lip, eyes raised to the ceiling in thought, giving little nods of her head as she counts. "Maybe ten? Twelve?"

I shake my head, exhaling a laugh. "Well, I'm sorry, but I'm not going to drink cocktails wearing pyjamas."

"You could. It's just us. You know everyone." By everyone she means the other two bridesmaids, and our host Loreena, the owner of this vast manor house.

"Nope, not happening. Besides, I don't want to risk upstaging the bride with *my* pyjamas. I packed my extra pretty ones," I tease.

Her mouth tips up in a knowing smile. Haley's been my accomplice in several bouts of retail therapy lately, designed to fill my sad, lonely Saturdays. And there may have been a little self-indulgence in the form of expensive lingerie.

The sets of pyjamas in my suitcase are stunning; delicate webs of silk and lace, and honestly way too sexy for lounging around in with your girlfriends. Sure, no guy is going to see how fucking amazing I look in them, and that's fine. I bought them just for me. To put them on and study my reflection in the mirror, while I think about that bastard Pierre. To imagine how if he could see me, the lustrous fabric hugging my curves, his handsome face would warp in regret at the sight of what he's walked away from.

"Nothing trumps Christmas PJs. You know that." She laughs and makes a grab for my enormous suitcase.

I sling my laptop bag over one shoulder, tucking it out of sight behind my elbow. Haley and I steer the unruly case between us, bumping up the wide staircase to the second floor.

A chorus of female laughter drifts upwards from the lounge room below, against the backdrop of muted rock music coming from somewhere deeper in the belly of this huge house. A throbbing bass line, clashing drums, a weeping guitar carrying the melody, and two voices weaving together. I'd recognise Stellar Riot's music anywhere from the sound of those two men alone: Haley's older brother Ollie, and the guy she's going to marry next Saturday, Christian, belting out vocals supported by the rest of their band.

"They're still going?"

"Yeah," she scrubs at her cheek, giving a little frustrated sigh. "I've hardly seen them all day. But if agreeing to them using this week as some sort of band camp was the only way I could carve out a space for the wedding, then I suppose the odd day like this is the price to be paid."

"One time, at band camp..." The words spill out of us in unison, evidence of evenings spent watching old movies.

"Well, it's only all the married people—or almost married, like you and Christian—who'll be getting up to mischief at this band camp," I choke out between giggles.

"Oh, I dunno. There are a few nice eligible single men coming to the wedding. You never know..."

"Yeah, maybe a quick shag in a back room during the reception. Might be good for my ego." I toss it out there as a joke, but in reality, maybe it's a worthwhile ambition.

Haley pauses part way along the wood-panelled upstairs hallway, twists an elaborate brass knob and swings open a door to reveal a vast bedroom. There's a fire burning in the hearth; it's gas but the dancing flames are so realistic I swear I can smell pine smoke. Along the mantle, a garland of greenery decorated with ruby ribbons and silver-frosted pine cones adds a touch of Christmas cheer.

A small Christmas tree sits on a side table, in front of heavy golden brocade drapes drawn against the drizzly winter night. The tree glistens with baubles of cream and gold, bows of green satin ribbon dotted in between.

"I see you've been busy. I suppose it's no surprise with you here. Christmas taking over the whole house."

"A team effort—me and Loreena. It's been fun. Took my mind off the wedding."

She smiles, but it doesn't reach her eyes, a slight divot of a frown lurking between them, a hint of tension. That's normal for a week out from your wedding. Although this is no normal wedding when the groom is a rockstar and they've agreed to let the world peek inside their perfect bubble. And that's why we're all here in advance. To give our special girl her people to lean on while she navigates the very public airing of the most important day of her life. I draw the conversation away from the source of her anxiety.

"You've done well with the decorations. But I expect nothing less from the queen of Christmas. And wow, this room. It's amazing."

The gorgeous four-poster bed and elegant decor are worthy of a luxury hotel, and the little touch of Christmas adds a homely, welcoming feel.

I dump the laptop and my favourite Prada handbag on the bed, and flop on my back next to them. Above me, intricate plasterwork sprawls across the ceiling, gilded flowers and vines winding around the cornices and a huge central rose around a delicate chandelier, the light bouncing off the walls casting patterns and shadows.

"Pretty nice, eh." Haley abandons the suitcase and joins me on the bed, lying beside me. She swivels her dark head towards mine, fixing me with mossy eyes, soft with empathy. "Thank you for doing this. You know, the whole bridesmaid thing. I know this must be hard."

I flail around for a reason to escape the pity that lurks behind her grateful eyes before she can see the storm in mine. Sitting up, I fixate on prising the shiny black patent Louboutin heels off my tired feet. Must have walked a bloody mile in these things between meetings today. Swallowing down the jagged lump in my throat, I find the words I must say, even though there's also a necessary lie within them.

"It's perfectly OK, Haley. Why wouldn't it be? Your happiness is absolutely the best antidote for this past couple of months."

She sits up, resting one gentle hand on my shoulder, mouth curving up in a sad smile. "You're the best Rache."

I press my point. "Haley, seeing you and Christian shows me what is possible. My life might be fucked up now, but there's hope. It won't always be this way." Will saying it out loud, manifesting what I want, make it come true? I'm not normally a believer in that woo-woo shit, but desperate times and all that. "You've been where I am, hun. And look at you now."

It's true. The only difference is that Haley had time on her side. She was twenty-five when her ex, Jack, did the dirty on her, leaving her brokenhearted, but still young, and beautiful, and with years ahead of her to find 'the one'. Me—I'm a whole ten years older.

My reassuring words to Haley aren't total fiction; I really do hold on to a tiny ember of hope. Although it's dimming by the day, as the clock ticks, counting the beats of a life passing me by in heavy sombre strokes.

I think that's what I resent most; giving Pierre some of my best years before he walked away. Fucking bastard. I'm determined not to let him win. Distancing myself from my friend and her wedding because it hurts to see her get what he promised me would only be an admission of his power over me even now. I won't allow it.

She wraps me in another hug, leaning her dewy cheek against mine. This girl is the sweetest person I know, so kind and unselfish. Christian is a lucky guy to have Haley, a fact I remind him of at every opportunity. I wasn't sure about him at first, but it's obvious he loves her, and I trust him not to hurt her. Besides, I told him if he ever did, I'd hunt him down, and he knows it's not an idle threat.

"I'll see you downstairs soon. Just follow the sound of drunken laughter. We started without you."

She pads out the door, her footsteps soft, muted by a ridiculous pair of reindeer slippers on her tiny feet. I can't help but smile. Time spent with Haley is always going to make life seem a little brighter.

"There we are, ladies. Next round." It might be the first Friday in December, bleak winter outside, but looking at the tray set in front of us, laden with a rainbow of cocktails, complete with little parasols and cheerful garnishes on toothpicks, anyone would think we've just landed in the Caribbean—not a house in the country near Watford.

"I'm just so excited to have you all here." Our hostess, Loreena Bunt, offers up an exuberant throaty chuckle. Blue eyes framed in enormous false lashes twinkle with delight.

"Cheers," she says and the five of us raise our glasses in unison, clinking them together companionably. "I'm so looking forward to getting to know you girls better. Haley's told me so much about you."

I'm looking forward to getting to know Loreena better too; reality TV queen from *The Real Wives of Watford*, and a woman keen to be surrogate mother to both bride and groom for the wedding taking place a week from now, here in her luxurious mansion. I've met her briefly once or twice, and I can see the qualities that endeared her to Haley and Christian; the Loreena Bunt TV viewers don't see.

But I'm not so sure about what her getting to know me better will reveal. I'm not confident in this version of me. Not when my life has become the script for a Bridget Jones movie; a sick joke.

What would I tell Loreena?

That I'm a successful thirty-five-year-old lawyer, although most people wouldn't pick me as being over thirty. Always wearing sunscreen and religiously slathering expensive serums on my face every night has paid off.

That I'm told I'm fun to be with once you get to know me and can see past my potty mouth. Capable. Responsible. Own a nice apartment in Notting Hill; financially independent—and for some reason, doomed to be serially single.

That two months ago, my fiance dumped me for his twenty-three-year-old PA. He claims he had the decency not to fuck her until he'd broken the bad news to me. As if I should be pleased about that.

That I've gone from the front of the queue for a happily ever after to languishing at the back with no prospects in sight, while I watch the people I love leapfrog past me.

My childhood best friend, Jenna, has found the love of her life in the form of my brother. Thankfully, it happened back in my Scottish home town, out of sight, although unfortunately not out of mind, with her texts alluding to sordid details of things I'd rather *not* imagine my baby brother doing with her. But he makes her deliriously happy. There's no trace of the sad jilted bride of a few years ago, and I love my brother more for that.

Samantha, seated next to me, with her tumble of dark curls and mellow brown eyes, oozes the contentment the care of a steady man brings. Her current boyfriend has passed the nice-guy test and six months in looks a solid bet for a long-term relationship. I'm so pleased for her.

Relaxing back in a huge armchair opposite is Liv, married to Garrett, the bass player in the band. Lithe and blonde with the face of an angel that lights up even more the moment he walks into a room, she's the smiling poster child for young love between high school sweethearts blossoming into a mature and enduring relationship.

And then there's Haley, the reason we're all here in one of the five lounges—yes, five—in this sprawling mansion that looks like it could have been the set for Downton Abbey. One week from today she's going to dash the hopes of his fans and marry Christian Steele, guitarist for Stellar Riot, and her brother's best friend and bandmate. This usually introverted, brusque man loves her so fiercely, and openly it makes even my tightly bound heart flutter at the sight.

And I'd tell Loreena I'm the sort of girl who can be happy for all of them. Really, I am. They deserve every bit of their fairytale romances. I'd just like one of my own, like I thought I had until it unexpectedly evaporated overnight.

Fortunately, right this moment there's a distraction away from all these gloomy thoughts: the beautiful man leaning in the doorframe, while the rest of his bandmates are in a huddle in the hallway.

My eyes are drawn to the source of a voice smooth as milk chocolate, a man with a boyish laugh who joins in their conversation, while fixing a pair of velvet-brown eyes on me. His mouth tips up in a slow smile, and I melt inside.

"Rachel MacDonald, are you staring at who I *think* you're staring at?" Haley, sitting opposite in the perfect spot to observe my wandering gaze, flashes me an accusing look.

"Hmmm, what?" I jerk my eyes away from him, slurping enthusiastically at my cocktail and giving my head a nonchalant shake, as if I don't know what the hell she's referring to.

"Teddy," she hisses, leaning forward with concerned dark brows, and her Cupid-bow lips thinned in disapproval.

"*No*," I say, forcing my mouth into a scowl of disgust. "No way. Just generally looking in that direction."

"Good," she says. "Because he's the last thing you need right now."

I love Haley and I'm not going to argue with the bride-to-be on the first day of this week-long gathering of the wedding party. Although maybe a quick no-strings attached fling might be *exactly* what I need.

And if Teddy 'Heartbreaker' Hargrove keeps looking at me like he is right this moment, by the end of the week, I could well be powerless to resist putting the final touch to the cliché that is my life and become the bridesmaid who has sex with one of the groomsmen.

I drag my eyes away, but I know they'll find their way back to him soon. He's like a bright street lamp on a dark night and I'm a moth stunned into stupidity by the light, ready to fling myself against him, even though it may well be my undoing.

Oh, I've been warned about Teddy. Not just by the tabloids and social media screaming reports about the way women rotate in and out of his life faster than the bench in a basketball game. Haley's cautions come directly from the source.

Her brother, Ollie Templeton, frontman for the band, and her soon to be husband, Christian, their lead guitarist, make no secret of drummer Teddy's indiscretions. But the way they laugh them off is kind of intriguing, as if he has some hidden redeeming quality, a get out of jail card, that allows him to be the stereotypical rockstar man-whore and get away with it.

I can see why you'd want to be indiscreet with Teddy. It's not just my Scottish blood that stirs heat inside when I see those deep red curls. His hair is the colour of maple syrup, shiny and thick, with a sexy dishevelled look that begs a girl to run her fingers through it. It's longish, turning up in unruly tendrils at his collar.

He's clean shaven, skin like milky coffee, youthful. No surprise, since he's the youngest of the group. Certainly much younger than I am, but hey, if reverse age-gap is doing it for Jenna, why not for me?

The long-lashed brown eyes, like a well-aged single malt whisky, project a puppy-dog innocence. Maybe those dreamy eyes are the reason all the girls he's hooked up with can somehow forgive him when he inevitably moves on. In a strange irony, he's the only blatant womaniser in the band, yet none of his exes have a bad word to say about him. The tabloids must hate that, never having real dirt to dish.

My eyes are drawn back to that sensual mouth. Which right this moment is twisting into a seductive smirk as he heads my way.

"Fuck," I say under my breath, trying to keep focused on Haley, but in my peripheral vision marking every step of lean legs in skinny black denim, large feet encased in worn Vans, strolling casually towards me.

Haley tosses me an "I told you so look", as Teddy arranges himself on the broad arm of the sofa, grinning down at me. He crosses one ankle over his knee, cocky as fuck, angling his body towards me.

"Rachel, right?" He leans back, relaxing one arm along the back of the sofa, an inch away from my shoulders. "You and I are going to be spending a lot of time together, I hear."

Yep, Teddy is my partner in the wedding party, and I'm wondering just how I'm going to conceal the landslide of lustful thoughts from spilling onto my face, or ignore the flush of heat between my legs triggered by his proximity, while carrying out the role of demure bridesmaid.

"Yeah," I choke out as I accidentally inhale a mouthful of my mojito instead of swallowing. My face flares and I hack out a cough.

"You OK?" Teddy looks genuinely concerned as I continue to splutter like one of Haley's dogs puking up a piece of bone, while tears stream down my face.

"Yes, OK," I wheeze. "Went...down...wrong way."

His large hand massages my back, rubbing up and down, his worried gaze fixed on my face, mere inches away while I clasp a hand over my mouth, trying to gulp some air while not spraying him with saliva. My other hand reflexively clutches at his knee in panic as I struggle for breath.

Teddy grabs the glass of water Loreena's thrusting at me, and like a caring parent, steadies it against my lips. I take small sips, the cool liquid offering welcome relief.

"Thank you," I rasp out.

His free arm slides up to curl across my shoulder, his thumb tracing soothing circles. I close my eyes and relax into it, stifling a moan of relief as slowly my breathing stabilises.

"Better now?"

I jerk myself back into watchfulness, and my gaze flicks to his. I nod without a word, as embarrassment and hyper-awareness of the contact between his fingers and the bare skin of my neck render me mute. I whip my hand away from his knee, awkwardly conscious that I've been gripping him so tight I probably left fingermarks on the taut thigh beneath those jeans.

"So, I see I've already taken your breath away." Even still unbalanced from my brush with death, I'm not immune to his playful wink. "Just wait until it's you and me arm-in-arm walking down that aisle. It'll be everyone else who'll need to catch their breath." Dark eyes rove my body, and the heated intention in his gaze provokes an echoing flush in my cheeks.

"Oh, Teddy, please." Haley shakes her head. "Do you ever *not* flirt?" The tone is admonishing, but she's smiling across at him, anyway. Yeah, that's the Teddy effect right there.

"Nope. If you've got it, why not?"

He sits up, mercifully releasing me from contact with his muscular arm. His knee jiggles rhythmically as he grins across at her with not an ounce of shame. The vibration only sends my brain in new dangerous directions as it conjures up lurid possibilities of a hookup with a drummer, a man with rhythm in his very soul. Matching my rhythm with his could be fun. I close my eyes and swallow hard, pushing away the images, not entirely unwelcome but definitely disorienting.

"Teddy, get your arse over here." Ollie's bellow echoes from the hallway. "Unless you don't want any say in the schedule for tomorrow."

"Coming." Teddy's reply is accompanied with a frustrated huff as he turns back to me. "So...are *we* on the schedule for tomorrow?" He's all boyish eagerness. "You know, wedding stuff?"

"No. Monday," Haley interrupts. "Fittings at eleven."

"Good. So the weekend's free for other things." His mouth tips up in a smug smile. "See you at dinner later, then, yeah?" He rises to his feet. "Save me a seat? Maybe we can make some plans."

"Sure." I smile and offer a friendly nod of agreement, my face a mask of polite calm while my insides perform an acrobatic routine worthy of an Olympic gymnast. On the exterior I'm sensible Rachel, heeding all the warnings, but underneath I'm teetering on a precarious ledge, unexpectedly susceptible to the reckless whispered suggestions flooding my brain. *Fuck it, why not? Just go for it Rachel. What have you got to lose?*

Logical me agrees with Haley: Teddy is a very bad idea. But when has a very bad idea ever looked so damn good?

ACKNOWLEDGMENTS

THIS CHRISTMAS OBSESSED GIRL was always going to write a Christmas book!

My love of Christmas grew from childhood memories and for those, I have to thank my mum and dad. What a wonderful gift of magic they gave us. Our family didn't have a lot, but we didn't know it.

There was always a tree, often a wildling pine, spotted on the roadside during a drive in the country on a summer weekend. Other times we'd visit our relatives' farm and find one there. Then there was the year Dad arrived home with a monster tree, source unknown, that wouldn't fit through the door. He was so proud of it and couldn't understand why Mum wasn't pleased.

There were decorations of fragile glass, and although every year a few ended up crushed by eager but clumsy kids, Mum never told us we couldn't help. My parents always made Christmas special and writing this series is a way to recapture that feeling.

As always, my editor, Jackie Cangro, helped me take this book from ideas twinkling at me like a string of Christmas lights to something I can hold in my hand. It was so much fun discovering Jackie and I share a mutual love of dogs and experience with dog rescue, both important to the shape of this story.

My writer friends once again came through with support and encouragement, most of all Loren Sorensen, who also inspired me with her own fun Christmas book. I must also thank the amazing Ollie (@Ollie_Creates) who brought my characters to life, not only in the cover but the amazing character art for this book. I'm in awe of her talent.

To my husband, David, who supports me to do this writing thing, and as a self-confessed Grinch, still allows my love of Christmas to take over the house; I am so grateful for you. When a man who is allergic still wrangles live trees into place, despite the sneezing, watering eyes and angry red tram tracks on his arms, he has to be a keeper.

And to you, readers, who keep the magic of Christmas alive through your love of Christmas books, thank you! It's for you I wrote this book, and promise the three still to come.

Merry Christmas!

Caroline

MORE FROM CAROLINE

Caroline's Tangled In Time series is time slip romance—but not as you might know it.

What if this life wasn't the only life?
What if parallel lives, the metaverse, and travel across time might really exist?

Follow the women of Tangled in Time as they find not only the love of this life, but the love of their other life. Stand beside them as the truth of a parallel time they never knew existed, and a man they never knew they'd loved, come crashing into the here and now.

This four-book series also has a fifth prequel novel. Each can be read as a standalone, and Caroline even suggests reading them in reverse order! After all, there's weird timey-wimey stuff going on here! Go to Caroline's website www.carolinecorvin.com to find out more.

Tangled Threads

**What if her future lies
in a time tangled past?**

Now the last of those who loved her are gone, there's nothing left for young teacher Kate Moreton in New Zealand. It's time for her to forge a new life. Pinning her hopes of finding friends, family—and maybe even love—elsewhere, she heads for the bright lights of London. What Kate doesn't know is this journey will lead her to two men, two loves, and two lives. And offer a future lifeline when her world falls apart.

Tangled Paths

**"In a world full of limitless lives,
of endless possibilities, I will always find you."**

Sarah Mitchell always put family first. Now, freed from self-imposed exile in her hometown, she's ready to jump back on the academic path she sacrificed for others three years ago. It's her time to choose a path. Or is time going to choose for her? When Sarah's future seems destined to be defined by loss, will time's tangled paths deliver her a second chance at happiness?

Tangled Hearts

**Two loves, two lives. One heart shattered.
Can a love from another time heal the pain of the present?**

Young emergency room doctor, Layla Angell, is living the dream: in the perfect job, surrounded by friends who are like family—including the man she's always wanted to be more than a friend. Life is full of potential. But the future is never promised. Caught in a time-twisted love triangle, Layla's connection to two men, across two parallel lives, offers a second chance at happiness beyond tragedy—if she can learn to accept the impossible.

Tangled Past

**When the past holds you in its power,
is love enough to set you free?**

Cassiopeia Tremayne isn't looking back at her sleepy hometown. Facing the future, all she can see is her dream of being a writer, just there on the other side of her final high school year. But Cassie's future also includes navigating the turbulent waters of two parallel but intertwined lives, forcing her to confront truths about herself, her family and the men she loves in two separate worlds. And when those worlds collide, will love give her strength enough to rewrite the past and become the hero of her own story?

About the Author

When not writing, you can usually find Caroline with her nose in a book from any one of an eclectic mix of favourite genres. While officially a resident of Auckland, New Zealand's stunning City of Sails, she has become adept at juggling her love of writing alongside her other magnificent obsession of travelling the world. Caroline didn't set out to write romance, but her characters took control the moment she let them loose on the page, reminding her that finding happily ever afters are the reason she's one of those people who sometimes reads the last page first, just to be safe.

Follow Caroline Corvin on all your favourite
social media or review sites!

Visit her website: www.carolinecorvin.com